Altars of Tomorrow

Altars of Tomorrow

by
KEN R. ABELL

RESOURCE *Publications* · Eugene, Oregon

ALTARS OF TOMORROW

Resource Publications
An Imprint of Wipf and Stock Publishers
199 W. 8th Ave., Suite 3
Eugene, OR 97401

www.wipfandstock.com

PAPERBACK ISBN: 978-1-5326-0921-3
HARDCOVER ISBN: 978-1-5326-0923-7
EBOOK ISBN: 978-1-5326-0922-0

Manufactured in the U.S.A.   FEBRUARY 21, 2017

Scripture taken from the HOLY BIBLE, KING JAMES VERSION, Public Domain.

For my friend, Rick Sider, who has always supported and encouraged me. In a long ago time and place he taught me truths about grace by embodying it—my prayer is that he would be immersed in the transcendent, marvelous, amazing, scandalous, awesome grace of God.

&

For Anita Irene, simply because her tenderness and toughness never ceases to spur me onward to continue marking up good clean paper regardless of the fact that commercial success remains an elusive mist on some far horizon. When black dogs of discouragement howl, her love and faith gives me a swift kick to remind me how to persevere and dream big dreams.

&

For our sons and grandchildren. May they learn, sooner rather than later, to treasure the special spark, gift, talent or inclination planted deep within by their Maker—may comprehension cause them to nurture those seeds and keep pressing on because life is short and eternity beckons.

&

For Computer Programmer Joe a.k.a. Coffee Roaster Joe. Many years before it was ever written I told him an idea for an opening sentence of a western. He expressed an interest to read that story, which challenged me in ways that are only understandable in the context of an abiding friendship. Seasons came and went, then I put pen to paper, and here endeth the saga.

Contents

ALSO BY KEN R. ABELL

Nonfiction

An Ordinary Story of Extraordinary Hope

Fiction

Days of Purgatory
Shadows of Revenge
Echoes of Evil
Nightmares of Terror
Pieces of Justice

Websites

www.wantedman.org
www.danceswithcorn.com

Acknowledgements

THE COMPLETION OF A six-book series is a crossroads. As I take a moment to look around and reflect on where I am, how I got here, and where I go from this point forward, I stand in awe of the steadfast faithfulness of God to me. I truly am a blessed man.

Many thanks and much appreciation to two people: First, Kathi Ellicott for her copyediting expertise willingly applied to my work. She catches errors and poor word choices to make me a more vigilant writer. Second, William D. Hastings, whose insights into characters keeps me alert and on the lookout. Also, his lexicon of jailhouse phrases has on occasion been raided and adapted for the sake of good storytelling.

chapter one

Crooked Roads

"Also when I cry and shout, he shutteth out my prayer. He hath inclosed my ways with hewn stone, he hath made my paths crooked. He was unto me as a bear lying in wait, and as a lion in secret places."

~JEREMIAH~

WHEN THE MAN FROM Conoy Creek rode into Creede he knew he was coming to the end of the trail. He intended to put his wandering ways behind him and settle in to help his daughter and grandson for however much time the good Lord granted him. His eyes were sore and tired, his body achy and cramped with kinks because, except for a brief stopover at *WT Ranch*, he had been in the saddle for the better portion of eight months.

The town was at the height of a silver boom. When Nicholas Creede discovered an abundant vein along East Willow Creek in 1889, the excitement couldn't be contained within the narrow canyons of the San Juan Mountains. The news flashed out of the Rio Grande Valley, which resulted in a rush of fortune hunters. In a few short years a cluster of mining camps swelled to a population of fifteen thousand, and became known as Creede.

The broad-shouldered rider was a consummate seeker, but not for the bounty of precious minerals or the worldly pleasures of wealth and power; the riches which he pursued and desired to possess had to do with being emotionally and spiritually centered. His perspective on the friction between the temporary and the eternal had been honed in the fires of adversity.

The silver-dappled buckskin snorted. He stopped to survey the area, hooking a leg over the saddle horn. "Alright, Gilgal. We're almost home," he said in a whispery rasp. He petted its mane, then reached forward to gingerly touch the stones sewn into the horizontal straps of the bridle. Faith and hope prickled his senses. He grinned and stretched, content and at peace. He removed his hat and absentmindedly finger-combed his gray-streaked hair.

Born and raised amongst the River Brethren in Pennsylvania, Deacon Coburn had become a man of the west. The appreciation of the outdoors nurtured in his childhood found full expression on the wide-open vastness of the plains and in the awesome wonder ever-present on the snow-capped peaks and in the luxuriant valleys of the mountains.

Each vista of natural beauty was a new miracle to behold. His adventurous spirit had done much to assuage the latent restlessness in his bones. In the midst of the years and miles, he had settled here or there for a time now and again, but mostly his residence was on horseback where he could explore uninhabited territory before civilization encroached to spoil it. He knew the beaten tracks and watering holes from Texas to Kansas to New Mexico and Colorado.

Now, as he sat easy and relaxed, he took in the seemingly endless chaos on the main thoroughfare that had the appearance of anarchy. It was midday so there was a cornucopia of commerce being dispensed at retail establishments housed in frame buildings or large canvas tents, all of which were jammed against each other on both sides of the avenue.

People were running to and fro, while darting past ore wagons, mules and sundry other horse and buggy traffic. A loose-knit pack of mongrel dogs scavenged for scraps at storefronts, or ran about with dirty-faced children scampering alongside them. In behind the central access road were overcrowded networks of laneways that gave approach to ramshackle cabins and households wedged into almost every available piece of real estate.

He heaved out a weary sigh for he understood that he was looking at a cross-section of the human condition—an intermingled mix of good and bad endeavoring to rise above the rabble to achieve respect or notoriety; where hard-working men digging and striving for a dream were ofttimes unwitting sheep to be preyed upon by cutthroat scoundrels and their ne'er-do-well associates involved in every kind of criminal enterprise imaginable.

Shylock moneylenders enforced by blackmail and strong-arm tactics. Sleazy saloons and gambling dens where the cards and dice were rigged and operated by sleight of hand veterans of shell games; whorehouses that catered to base instincts and treated women as vessels to be used and discarded. Coburn cringed, knowing that in a community where the weaknesses of the flesh were so explicitly indulged, the needs of the heart and soul would be neglected.

Just then, an explosion north of the business and residential borough spewed powdery earth heavenward. The detonation came from what had been tagged the King Solomon district, and the ground shook mightily for a stunning instant. A buzz vibrated in the springtime air while the sky was blackened by billows of gritty dust jettisoned by the discharge of dynamite.

As the haze of dirt dissipated over the settlement, Coburn pondered the opening chapter of Ecclesiastes, measuring each phrase against the beehive of industry and progress, and decided that the ancient writer had an excess of wisdom. "*Vanity of vanities, saith the Preacher, vanity of vanities; all is vanity. What profit hath a man of all his labor which he taketh under the sun? One generation passeth away, and another generation cometh: but the earth abideth forever.*"

The King Solomon sites in Willow Creek Canyon were a teeming hotbed of drilling and excavating; the ever-expanding underground complexity of shafts and channels necessitated a hardy round the clock workforce that were consistent producers of ore. The Holy Moses tunnels occupied the eastern perimeter of what was nothing more than an oversized gulch, and the Amethyst Mine and Last Chance Mine were on the western border.

Coburn stood in the stirrups, smiling grimly. The crow's feet around his eyes tightened as he studied the location of the blast, then articulated more Scripture. "*I have seen all the works that are done under the sun; and, behold, all is vanity and vexation of spirit. That which is crooked cannot be made straight: and that which is wanting cannot be numbered.*"

He tucked his longish locks beneath the cowboy hat and sat scratching at his bewhiskered cheeks. He yawned, arched his back and had a peek at clouds drifting aimlessly. His expression brightened. The gelding whinnied as he gave the reins a flick. He recalled the precise directions received from his sister, then Deacon Coburn proceeded onward to his destination.

At *WT Ranch*, Naomi Axler was in a reflective mood after spending several days visiting with her brother. The siblings had made the most of their time together by chatting about matters of the heart—family, memories, plans for the future, and nuggets of truth gleaned from the Good Book. She was concerned because he had ridden himself ragged and was exhausted. She prayed that he could continue to catch up on his sleep once he came to his journey's end.

Bread was baking. Its pleasant odor filled the kitchen. She sat at the table retrieving a treasure from a wooden box her husband had crafted for her. The cedar slats had a carved pattern of running horses on either side. Inside, filed in an order understandable only to her, was all the correspondence she had received since putting the east and the past behind her.

She pulled out the most recent letter from her vagabond gypsy niece. It had arrived just over a year ago, three months after it was dated and posted. She shook it out of the envelope and her lips pursed sorrowfully. As with all missives from Abbey Langton, this one was well-written, informative and full of detailed happenings. Regrets swelled in her as she read it.

January 14, 1891

Pine Ridge, South Dakota

Dear Aunt Naomi: I am aghast. I cannot even find the words to describe my outrage. It has now been two weeks since the 7th Cavalry slaughtered innocents in such a barbaric display of outlandish violence that I remain somewhat numb and in shock. My brain cannot process the unwarranted aggression or the images of women and children pleading for their lives.

I saw a mother with an infant in her arms almost cut in half by bullets from the revolving barrel of a Hotchkiss gun as she reached for the flag of truce not more than ten yards away from where I stood screaming at the soldiers to stop. I saw Langton running for his life; I saw his brother Yaz, whom I have unofficially adopted, stricken by a sword that put a six inch gash on the left side of his face. He was sliced to the bone, and I was helpless.

The madness of the U.S. Army began because of its overstressed and ridiculously paranoid response to a deeply spiritual religious movement, which in the white world would be referred to as a series of revival meetings. During the autumn of 1890 the Ghost Dance spread throughout the Dakotas, and the Sioux peoples were revitalized by its energy and call to reject the ways of the white man and re-embrace traditional customs.

I was privileged to sit in a large circle around an open field and witness a Ghost Dance up close. There was nothing dangerous or frightening about it—on the contrary; it was exquisite and uplifting. The drums beat in unison and the dancers, in specially sewn colorful shirts, moved in side-shuffle steps that stirred my soul and made me want to cry out in joy and wonder.

Standing Wolf, my friend and guardian, explained that the dancing prayers drew ideas and threads from ancient rituals and were nothing more than appeals to the Creator for him to renew the earth and wash away all evil—to restore to the Sioux nations a sense of pride which had been systematically stripped away by the destructive policies of Manifest Destiny.

Indian Agents, full of fear and loathing birthed in ignorance, wired hysterical reports to faceless, soulless bureaucrats in Washington, calling for protection and for the advocates of the Ghost Dance to be immediately arrested and confined. An order was sent to seize Sitting Bull, a great leader of dignity and charisma revered by his people. On December 15th, Chief Sitting Bull was killed at Standing Rock Reservation when soldiers attempted to arrest him.

When the news of Sitting Bull's death reached him, Spotted Elk determined that he would be the next target of the captains and kings. He led his followers southward hoping to find refuge at Pine Ridge. The U.S. Army intercepted the band and herded them like cattle to a camp on the banks of Wounded Knee Creek, where the Sioux were forced to surrender their weapons.

On December 29th Chief Spotted Elk, who was sick with pneumonia and dying, led his warriors to powwow with the army officers in an effort to defuse the tensions. While those talks were in progress, a scuffle took place between a Sioux and a bluecoat— a shot was fired which shattered the early morning gloom, and then, the roaring inferno of hell broke loose.

In seconds, volley after volley of gunshots were directed into the Sioux camp. Disorder and bedlam erupted. Disarmed warriors scurried to grab their discarded rifles, but were riddled by bullets from the Hotchkiss guns positioned on the heights. Those brutally efficient firearms bombarded the tepees with grapeshot. The stench of gun smoke was dense in the air.

Men, women and children scrambled to find sanctuary in a ravine, but were trapped by a withering torrent of gunfire. Langton and I made it to a gully against the creek, then turned to see that Yaz had fallen and Boxy was fighting to rescue him. The bluetick heeler got skewered by the same sabre that almost decapitated Yaz. I shrieked, and in what was nearly an out of body experience, I raced over and hoisted Yaz up in my arms and got him to relative safety.

I did not realize, until I crashed onto the ground with him, that Langton had also run back into the bloody fray to assist me. The three of us huddled at the water's edge with other terrified or injured survivors and waited in sheer horror for the butchery to come to an end. Yaz was bleeding profusely, but he kept his teeth clamped and not a whimper escaped his lips. I tore apart my petticoat and used it as a dressing to staunch the flow of blood as best I could.

When a semblance of calm was restored, I ventured forth to investigate the carnage, clutching Yaz to my bosom while Langton clung to my side. The killing field was littered with bodies. Spotted Elk was dead, as was Standing Wolf; along with three hundred other Sioux, and over half of the unarmed and defenseless victims were women and children.

I scavenged a needle and sinew, and got busy with the task of cleaning and suturing Yaz's gruesome laceration. Langton knelt beside him and I tacked his skin together in firm knots. As I write this, the boys are asleep and I have an oil lamp burning. Sometime tomorrow, I will examine the wound and decide if it has been long enough for me to remove the stitches.

In the aftermath of the murderous attack, troopers were dispatched to begin gathering the dead. There was no respect or deference offered. The deceased were roughly piled on carts and in wagons, but then, a blistery cold windstorm from the north delivered a blizzard that interrupted the grisly burial. A few days later, the soldiers returned to complete the job.

In an extreme act of triumphant savagery, a pit was dug atop the hillock where the Hotchkiss guns had been situated. It was an unbelievably callous choice—a fact that I vigorously expressed to every civilian and army authority figure present, but despite my spirited vitality and red-faced ranting and raving, my protests fell on deaf ears. The dead were unceremoniously dumped into a mass grave at the locale from whence the hellfire barrage originated.

I have important work to do as an eyewitness to this atrocity, but as soon as possible, I will be traveling to WT Ranch. Look for Langton, Yaz and me to come riding into the valley before the heat of summer. The news of the silver strike in your vicinity has whetted my appetite to once more reside in a boomtown and be at the hub of commotion. Though after the trauma of the Wounded Knee Massacre, the wildness of a frontier town will likely seem tame.

Pray for us. Please. Thank you.

Much love,

Abbey

Naomi Axler was crying as she refolded the letter. Her heart was heavy. She beseeched heaven anew for her niece and her two sons. She also boldly brought Deacon before the throne of grace, asking that her brother, a man intimately acquainted with the grief of bloodshed, would have a soothing balm of wisdom to heal the unseen slashes on Abbey, Langton and Yaz.

The curtains at the upstairs bedroom windows were drawn open and afternoon sunshine streamed through to reflect off a dresser mirror that had been angled for that purpose. A corner window sash was raised an inch or so to allow a small influx of freshness. The woman on the four-poster bed was sweated and ruddy-cheeked. Her hair was tangled and anxiety marred her face, but there was a gleam sparkling in her eyes as she rested from the last contraction.

Doc Fralick had his tools arranged on a round table, and though the tension was thick, he was calm and talkative. "You're doing fine. Have you taken a gander outside? Your baby is going to be born on a picturesque blue skies day. Couldn't ask for a prettier one. Maybe when all is said and done here, Malcom and I can get some fly fishing in before nightfall."

Dolly Wyant gave him an unbelieving look; scathing, even. "You won't be taking my husband anywhere. He best be downstairs pacing and gritting his teeth on my behalf."

"He was doing exactly that the last time I saw him."

"I'd expect nothing less," she said, shifting on the pillows. "And you can be sure, I'll be giving your wife an earful about your bedside manner. Implying that you'll coax my husband into abandoning me and his newborn child in favor of trout. I'm agitated by the suggestion."

"It was a lighthearted attempt at humor."

"A terrible joke, Doc," she replied, hands roaming over her distended belly as a wince creased her brow. She sighed a clipped chuckle. "This isn't a Sunday morning meeting or a summer picnic along the Animas River. I'm having a baby and it hurts like the dickens."

"You didn't really think it'd be easy-peasy, did you, Dolly?" he asked, dipping his hands in a basin of tepid water. He dabbed them on a towel while focusing on her private parts. "We talked about the pain factor, especially in consideration of your medical history and age."

She guffawed, a snarky lilt in her tone. "I don't need you to tell me that forty is a mite old to be going through this, but after several miscarriages and an unknown number of false alarms, Malcom and I had pretty much given up on the whole idea of having a child of our own."

Fralick tensed his lips to stifle a smirk, but could not keep it under wraps. "Evidently the two of you had not forgotten the romantic overtures or the how-to of making a baby."

"Not at all funny, Doc."

"Here we are and all signs are super and on schedule," he said, taking a knee at the edge of the bed. "Except for my concerns for your recovery, I'm anticipating a textbook delivery."

"Is there nothing you can do to hasten this, Doc?"

"The apple will fall off the tree when it's ripe and ready."

"I'm no tree and this is no apple. A watermelon maybe."

"Nature will take its course in the fullness of time."

"Which is when, Doc? When?"

"That's not my call, Dolly."

"Sometimes you can be infuriating, you know that?"

Fralick gave her a wry smile. "I've heard that from others."

"Do you ever take the counsel to heart?"

"Not often."

"Perhaps you ought to, Doc."

He shrugged casually, then twined his fingers together and flexed his arms downward. "Did I ever regale you and Malcom with tales from my days serving at an army outpost?"

Her midsection clenched involuntarily. She hitched in a rapid breath and cried out. "Oh, sweet Jesus, this better be it." She was sideward on the mattress her legs bent up with a flimsy sheet draped over her knees. "Oh, sweet Jesus! My guts are going to gush out."

"No. Everything is as it should be," the doctor told her, crouched low and at the ready. "Deep breaths, hands fisted, and wait . . . wait." He placed his right palm on the protrusion of her tummy. "Breathe. The next contraction will be here in a moment. When it comes, I want you to bear down and push as hard as you can, Dolly. Wait . . . wait. Now! One, two, three. Push."

She unleashed a shrill screech of a shout as she complied with his instructions. Her voice cracked and her shoulders crunched forward as her eyes bulged and rolled back in her head, lids fluttering like hummingbird wings. The intensity of her effort lasted all of thirty seconds. She gasped and shuddered, then collapsed and twitched spasmodically.

A robust wail filled the space vacated by Dolly Wyant's stress-induced outcry. Fralick busily took care of all that needed to be done with the umbilical cord and afterbirth, then secured a smallish blanket to swaddle the slick and wiggling infant. "Ten fingers, ten toes, rosy cheeks, a full head of dark curls, and eyes open and lit up. Does this lovely lady have a name?"

"A girl?" she panted, beaming through a blur of tears.

Fralick placed the bundle in her arms. "A *beautiful* girl, Dolly."

The mother was weeping happily. "Katey Rae."

He nodded approvingly. "I'll leave you ladies for a few minutes to go get Katey's father and bring him in for introductions." He was wiping his hands on a towel, which he carried with him as he went out the door. Satisfaction was stamped on the rusty-haired man's face; in times like these Doc Fralick realized that the study of medicine had chosen him, not vice versa.

At the Orleans Club in Creede, Lucinda Enochelli put the cards down and pushed her chair away from the blackjack table. As she sashayed toward the bar, she dug her fixings from a side pocket of her skirt. She had been dealing to three foul-mouthed miners. After repeatedly going bust, the men made threatening remarks about her ancestry, which earned them a vulgar fare-thee-well from her and the bum's rush from the joint by a ham-handed bouncer.

It was midday so business was thin—prospects for marks were few. She had a cursory look-see to be sure she wasn't missing out on any action, then tossed a smile at the friendly barber engaged with a customer at his station in an out of the way alcove corner of the saloon. She settled on a barstool beside the owner and operator of the establishment.

Jefferson Randolph Smith a.k.a. Soapy Smith had darkened eyes, a neatly-trimmed beard, and a reputation that preceded him; he organized rascals and rogues. "Still early, Lucinda. If I were you, I'd have a cigarette and a whiskey because sooner rather than later the nincompoops will be flocking in here and lining up to be ever so gently relieved of their earnings."

"A fine plan."

The self-proclaimed and largely undisputed boss of the camp stood and patted her bare shoulders. "I'll even go behind the bar and pour you a shooter so as to have a better view."

"All these young trollops you imported from Denver and you get your jollies by taking a snoop down the front of *my* dress?" she asked, putting a match to a newly-rolled ciggy.

"I never forego an opportunity to admire a fetching upper deck."

"I'm an old lady and saggy without the corset."

"Maybe so, but titties are always enticing," Soapy said, pouring two drinks. "Which is a good thing because scantily-clad prostitutes are the primary marketing tool to bring in clientele with jingly bits in their pockets and little hombres in their pants that snap to attention."

"To a lucrative fleecing." She held up her shot glass.

"Amen, sister." He did the same and clinked them together. They flipped them back and he refilled the short glasses. "Bouncy titties are a foolproof hook for all sorts of ventures."

Lucinda giggled girlishly. "The valley of promise between my bubbies has bankrolled much for me, and gotten me into or out of trouble more times than can be remembered."

"I have no doubt about that, Lucinda." The thirty-one year old lit a cigar and picked a fleck of tobacco off his tongue as he scanned the bar-room. The Orleans Club was the latest base of operations for all his far-reaching illegal activities. He was the proprietor of an underworld syndicate of flimflam extortion rackets that had seen success across the frontier. He even dabbled in political fixing where, for favors, he used intimidation to influence the outcome of votes.

"You exploit all the angles, but there's something I don't get."

"What's that, Lucinda?"

"Willy told me some three-card Monte escapades from Fort Worth."

"Ah-huh. Street hustles were a hot commodity."

"I heard it was a floating bait and switch circus."

Smith furled his eyebrows. "We kept the law and politicians hopping."

"You turned small-time swindling into a big-time empire."

"Are you any closer to what it is you don't get?"

"Right on top of it," she answered, stubbing her weed into a tin ashtray. "As far as I can determine your tried and true methods have no loopholes. Plus it's obvious that your notoriety as a bad man to be feared is as real as it gets, but that nickname doesn't quite fit."

"Soapy," he replied, laughing heartily. "Never figured it'd stick this long, but it'll likely follow me to my grave." He rolled the cigar between his thumb and forefinger, a wistful shadow passing over his face. "My path first crossed with Slick Willy in Fort Worth. I was a wise-ass kid bilking and using every ploy and short con imaginable to separate yokels from their coins."

"Willy tells me you were a natural."

"It came easy, sure enough. Never underestimate stupidity or greed. Win a prize in soap? How foolish can the bumpkins be?" he inquired, draw-ing a lengthy puff. "The treasure in a bar of package soap was a surprisingly profitable scam. A low investment that milked the get rich quick aspirations in people. *Everyone* wants a jackpot pay-off for next to nothing."

"And you provide the trickery and incentive?"

"Yup. It's a helluva gift I got, Lucinda."

"Glad to be on your team, living and learning."

Smith huffed a grunt and dismissed the flattery with a nonchalant backhand. "Now that we've stripped my bones clean there's something about you that has me buffaloed."

"Not surprising."

"Why's that?"

"I'm a walking, talking mystery woman, Soapy."

"Slick Willy clams up whenever the topic of you arises."

"That's good," she said, beginning to build another cigarette. "There are two reasons for his silence. First off, if he wants to enjoy my pleasures, he realizes that he cannot deviate from my nonnegotiable terms. Secondly, Mr. Phips knows next to doodly-squat about me."

"Why so secretive, Lucinda?"

"Why not is just as fitting a question, don'tcha think?" She batted her eyes and placed the unlit quirley behind an ear before slipping off the stool. A thrill touched her when she spotted a potbellied man near the craps table. Moistening her lips and swaying toward him, Lucinda Enochelli had confidence that her provocative charms would put the moves on him.

The afternoon was wisps of white brushstrokes on a blue canvas sky. Avis Lahay had no responsibilities until dusk. She stood at the edge of the breezeway taking in the day's beauty. Her heart overflowed because of the attractive artwork of her surroundings. She lowered her eyes to admire the groves of aspens at the base of the San Juan Mountains encircling *WT Ranch*.

The roofed veranda, along with two spacious bedrooms and a snug sitting nook, had been built onto Hans and Eliza Weitzel's ponderosa pine home to accommodate Avis and Stace Hawkins. It was Hans who designed the addition and insisted on the arrangements, which kept her filled with gratitude because both he and Eliza had great guidance for her son.

She moved to where a tripod table and a pair of rustic chairs formed a semi-circle. The roughhewn furniture had been cut from tree stumps. A leather journal and fountain pen waited for her on the tabletop. The reddish daybook had a butterfly engraved on its front cover. She adjusted the cushion on the seat and sat, then opened to a blank page and began writing.

May 9, 1892

> *Dear Diary: I have been unable to get Deacon out of my thoughts and prayers. I spent a couple hours with him each day he was here, which was wonderful, but there was something going on that has*

me troubled. Age is obviously creeping up on him, and he had lots of cricks and stiffness from the trail, but there was another issue, and I cannot put my finger on it.

No one else seemed to notice it, so maybe I'm going bonkers, or making a mountain out of a molehill. I just don't know—what I do know is this: When he greeted me with a hug, I sensed a weirdness that is unexplainable. It came and went in the briefest of instants, but a yucky feeling definitely rose up in me that was disturbing. I have never experienced anything like it.

I was so rattled that I arranged for a telegram to be sent to Mom. Not quite sure why, or what my expectations are, but it felt like the right thing to do. Deacon told me that he spent several weeks with her in Santa Fe last summer, which Mom surely appreciated. Their tenderhearted kinship is an unbreakable bond that goes back twenty-odd years.

As I ponder these thoughts, I am reminded once more that I have a tendency to borrow difficulties from tomorrow even though more often than not whatever problems I presume never materialize, or if my unpleasant imaginings do come to pass, time and again the Lord proves himself strong in sustaining me while providing all that I require.

Faith is a perpetual sojourn in which I am supposed to make strides forward, but sometimes I think I take backward steps because instead of simply trusting God one day at a time I run on ahead of him, then see or create potential complications. I have had ups and downs, but keep pressing on because the grace of the Lord never wavers. Yet, despite all the experiential evidence of his faithfulness, I still continue to take my life into my hands.

We are to pray for our daily bread, and for me that means to receive from God's bounty whatever I stand in need of for today. It is my sincere desire to consistently apply that truth until it becomes my default reaction. I am twenty-eight years old and at my snail's pace rate of spiritual growth, I may need to live to the century mark to achieve my goal.

Tonight after supper and chores, Eliza and I will certainly initiate what has become a favorite pastime; we invest an hour or so in the glow of lamplight to chat about the occurrences of the day and subjects of importance. I will open up to her regarding all of this stuff and can guarantee that she will have advice to steer my thinking in a positive direction.

I am so thankful for her mentoring. Her practical approach to life and faith encourages and challenges me more than she can possibly know. She never has a discouraging attitude or word, but instead, can always find a helpful or optimistic perspective in every situation. Her counsel and support in my role as a mother has provided me much reassurance.

Early on she took up the task of seeing to Stace's book-learning education. He resisted at first, but then, as she skillfully applied patience and incentive based disciplines, the lessons came alive for him. Now he reads constantly, asking questions of everyone about any and all curriculum. He has a deep-seated curiosity that keeps his mind alert and active.

We have been here for almost four years. There is no doubt that relocating to WT Ranch truly was a blessed God-thing. I've become Aunt Avis to all the youngsters, which gives me a great sense of satisfaction and purpose. The ranch work can be hard and dirty at times, but I have no complaints. There are seven mares due to foal before the end of summer, and because Pete and Caleb were generous in their teaching, I am an expert midwife of sorts.

Stace has flourished. He is a reliable and trustworthy workman who takes responsibility above and beyond his station. He will be fourteen in October and is already almost six feet tall with muscles beginning to bulge. His relationship with Hans is incredibly precious. The two are peas from the same pod, and are happiest when they're felling a tree, cutting firewood or fixing one thing or another. A job well done gives them tremendous pleasure.

Hans has taken Whitey's offhand term of endearment for Stace and now uses it as a proper name. I'm not sure how I feel about Stace being called Boss, but have not said anything against it and likely won't because the tone makes it clear that Hans is extending affection. The two of them are currently on a fact-finding business trip to Denver. They've been away for a couple weeks and are not expected back for almost a month.

I need to bring this to a close because I want to visit with Amanda for a spell before checking on the feed and water for the horses in the corral. She is going through an awkward phase as she tries to figure out who she is and where she fits. It doesn't seem so long ago that I was there, so it is easy for me to relate to her. I think we have a real solid connection.

She is talented and artistic. I recently commissioned her to knit a bulky sweater for me. It's multicolored with triangle designs that she devised without any pattern. When it is finished I am sure it will become one of the dress-up garments in my closet. I must shut my thinker down or else I'll jump to another idea. Time to hightail it and scoot.

She closed the book and hastily returned it to its shelf in her bedroom. When she came back outside she had a straw skimmer in hand. Her auburn hair was tied in a loose and floppy ponytail. She put the hat on as she began walking down the grade to the Axler homestead. Any worries or disquiets were washed away by a wave of contentment that refused to crest.

"Kind of closed in, ain't it?"

The log cabin was squeezed into a hemmed in alley that had so many similar box-like structures that it appeared as though the houses were stacked like a row of dominos; except the space between the dominos would've probably been wider. Deacon Coburn, hatless and flinty, sat on the porch in a hardwood rocker beside his daughter, who was in a matching chair.

"Kind of, indeed," she replied, laughing softly.

"I might get claustrophoby."

"Claustrophobia."

"Whatever one calls it, Abbey, I'm not wanting any part of it." He crossed his right leg over his left, ankle resting on the knee. His eyes crinkled and he raised a finger to her. "I surely ain't complaining because being here with you is finer than fine. Where's Langton?"

"He and Yaz are exploring."

"Running loose, are they?"

"Running loose and being boys," Abbey answered dryly. "If I know them they're figuring new and interesting ways to have fun and make some mischief without ever crossing the line."

"Lines can get crossed awful easy at their age."

"They are growing up good, Deacon."

"I'm anxious to see them," he said, scowling faintly. He momentarily pressured the heel of his right hand on his forehead, then hoed his fingers through his hair and sat back. "As for their upbringing, I'd expect nothing less than excellence, Abbey." His hands came together at his beltline as he got the chair moving at a moderate clip. "You have always had an inner strength. The spitfire ways of your childhood developed into character that has a backbone of steel."

"Thank you, Deacon." Her eyes sparkled gladly. She wore a buckskin skirt with a wide belt, along with a rust-colored blouse. Ringlets of golden-brown hair spilled from beneath the red kerchief that covered her crown. "You made a significant contribution to who I am today."

"Kind of you to say. Now that's enough mush."

"Agreed."

"How goes your writing?"

"I have a couple projects on hold," she replied flatly. "Since the debacle at Wounded Knee Creek all my writing energies have been concentrated on a campaign of correspondence to newspaper editors and know-nothing officials in our government, hoping to see truth prevail."

"A laudable effort, Abbey."

"Laudable, perhaps. Successful, not so much."

"Time and truth are hand holding companions."

"Maybe, maybe not, Deacon. I'm skeptical just now."

"Tell me about Yaz."

"His uncle was Standing Wolf, a Lakota wiseman who welcomed Langton and me into his heart and hearth, no questions asked," Abbey said straightforwardly. "He opened doors for me and schooled us in Sioux folklore. Langton and Yaz struck up a friendship from the moment we first arrived at the Sioux village in '86. We journeyed with that band until last spring."

"Langton will be immensely rich for the experience."

"He also has to deal with the ugliness."

"The massacre?"

"Yes," she replied, lips puckering angrily. "There was a Ghost Dance two weeks before the army lost its mind and went on a berserk killing spree. Everything about the innovative dance was inspirational. Afterwards, Standing Wolf performed a ritual ceremony with Yaz and Langton in which their blood was blended together—it was solemn and spiritual. They were brothers before that, but since then, they truly share a connection that is singularly unique."

"Having a brother is important."

"Langton and Yaz are tighter than twins."

"So I have two grandsons," he stated, easygoing and succinct.

"I knew you'd see it that way."

"What other way would be acceptable?"

"None."

"Family is much deeper than blood, Abbey."

She reached over to rest a hand on his forearm as she regarded him and began to take note of his demeanor. A pasty pale complexion accentuated the drowsy weariness in him. His eyelids were droopy and flickered in sporadic spurts. "You're worn to a frazzle, Deacon."

"Yeah, I am."

"You were never one to take care of yourself."

"True enough, I suppose."

"Looking to the needs of others."

He offered a lame shrug. "I'll live and die with my choices, but evidently some age has caught up with me and the trails are not as charitable as they were in my younger years."

"You need a shave and a haircut. You're looking like a dirty ragamuffin."

A flare of remembrance zipped across his face. "I ain't heard that since I can't recollect when. It takes me back. 'Twas your mother's phrase. She'd not feed a dirty ragamuffin."

"She had high standards."

"You've referred to me as a dirty ragamuffin more than once."

"Well, I am my mother's daughter."

"That you are, Abbey. Strong-willed and beautiful."

"Speaking of strong-willed." She shifted her bottom and turned her upper body to him, eyes narrowed and tense. "Shortly after I arrived in Creede last year, a Lucinda Enochelli looked me up. Claims to have known you in what she referred to as the olden days."

"Lucinda Enochelli? Not again?" he queried in a cantankerous tone. His eyes blinked and his jaw twitched. "The monkey shines of that woman are starting to get my dander up."

"What? She's got you riled?"

"I declare with an oath that I never heard the name until Delores told me of her at the Suncurl Café last summer," he said strongly. "Then Naomi mentioned her to me a couple days ago. The woman had stopped in at *WT Ranch* to speak to my sister. Lucinda Enochelli, whoever she may be, has her sights set on me and I cannot even conjure up a memory of her."

"She's quite insistent."

"Mayhap she be, but I ain't interested." He glanced around, rigid and squinty. "A shave and a haircut ain't no top priority, but where's Whitey? I expected to find him in Creede."

"He's here," she replied glibly. "He has a shack with a cot, but he's seldom there because all he does is work. He's usually at his chair from before noontime until long into the night."

"Seeing him will have to wait. I've got hefty resting to do," he announced, slouching back. He tilted a wink at her, then closed his eyes. He took a few deep breaths, and she watched in amazement as relaxation visibly came over him. The tautness in his torso and countenance vanished. A mere handful of seconds later, Deacon Coburn was peacefully catnapping.

~∾~

The man was cursed by a strain of insanity; of that, there could be no dispute or doubt. He paced through the beerhall tent spewing condemnation. Whoever the theatrical sermonizer had been in boyhood was long forgotten. He came from pious stock—he had grown up chasing through the hollows of eastern Kentucky in an era when snake-handlers and excitable revival preachers entertained hardscrabble farmers and unrepentant moonshiners.

The black and white of sin and redemption were strands woven into the foundational fabric of his underpinnings. As a young adult he joined a traveling troupe of salvation shouters and became a charismatic sensation on the circuit as he vehemently exhibited the showmanship of a first-rate Bible thumper who could fill the altars and the offering plates.

He was gaining celebrity status when the Confederates fired upon Fort Sumter. Driven by passions and a sense of destiny, he enthusiastically joined the fray. His rabid anti-slavery views clashed in family circles and communities of his home state, but he was a righteous man for whom compromise was despicable because it foreshadowed lily-livered principles.

He was a foot-soldier in the War Between the States. Faithful and undaunted, he obeyed superior officers with an unwavering trust in the virtue of the cause. He waded into the frontlines at Antietam and Fredericksburg, killing and maiming gray-clad soldiers. He demonstrated a vicious ferocity that had his garments bloody, but he escaped physically unscathed.

His psyche, however, had gross wounds inflicted on it—unseen injuries and damage done by the inhuman barbarities of close quarters combat accumulated inside him like pustules. Then, at Chancellorsville, as he jabbed his bayonet into the flesh of a wide-eyed rebel who bore an uncanny resemblance to him, those inner carbuncles released gushers of poison.

He screamed and screamed. His voice roared untethered shrieks that were unheard above the turbulent mayhem and gore of the battlefield. A cannonball smashed into the ground close enough to knock him out and send him airborne. He collapsed helplessly on a heap of mutilated corpses. When he regained consciousness his mind was irrevocably broken by the bloodletting savagery; the former was gone and he was resurrected as the Prophet Eliezer.

Now, carrying a long shepherd's staff that had a gnarly hook a foot above his head, the imposing redhead stalked around the smoky saloon while patrons kept at their doings and treated him as a sideshow freak. The frayed hem of the poncho-like quilt of animal skins he wore dragged in the dirt. His handmade vestment had a braided rag-belt knotted at his waist.

He targeted an audience for his latest homily and stopped, towering over a crowded table where a high stakes poker game was in full swing. "I am the Prophet Eliezer," he proclaimed in a full-throated voice that was akin to the croaking of a choir of bullfrogs. "God spoke a vision to me for I am his holy one. I have been called and am blessed by the breath of God."

He pawed at the whiskers that straggled to the middle of his chest—the full beard shaded close to orange and was highlighted by whitish patches. "I have been established by strength and might, and anointed to be the servant of the Most High. The wickedness of my enemies cannot afflict me or distract me from cleansing the plague of iniquity. My foes are idolaters and fornicators, and those who pander to revelry and drunkenness.

"A day of reckoning cometh. Sinners of all stripes will be beaten down before the face of God." His lips flattened and his frenzied eyes went loopy. "Mercy and grace will be swept away by the winnowing scythe of God's wrath. There will be no place to hide. Drinkers of demon spirits and liars and gossipers will cry out for rocks to fall upon them, but no peace or comfort awaits the faithless. Deviants and reprobates will sizzle in the scorching flames of hell."

"Piss off, you idiot!" a crater-faced man shouted angrily. The interjection set-off a burst of hooted catcalls and derision. Laughter merged with blasphemies. A blonde soiled dove, thick at the hips and busty, did a flouncing dance toward the pop-eyed cleric. She was attired in flimsy undergarments. She bared her breasts, which elicited salvos of whistles and jeers.

The Prophet Eliezer gawked. His shoulders shook in holier-than-thou fervor. "God will arise and all evildoers will be scattered. Those that hate devotion and saintliness will flee on the great and terrible day of the Lord. Like smoke is gobbled up by the wind, prodigals will be driven away. Let whores and gamblers and jesters perish at the presence of God.

"Hear the word of the Prophet Eliezer." He pounded the staff on the plank floorboards, swaying and slobbering excitedly. "You will plead unto God for deliverance and salvation, but all feckless lovers of debauchery will burn. The seed of lowlifes and Jezebels will be expunged from the earth because the judgment of God is a covenant of blood and sacrifice

"I am the Prophet Eliezer. I have spoken it, so shall it be." He paused dramatically and tramped toward the half-naked harlot, who was prancing backwards and shaking her melons at him. He halted and lifted the shepherd's staff above his head, then sudden-like froze in that position. His eyes zeroed in on a pair of youngsters. "Hellions! Away, you hellions!"

LC Beadle and Yaz Lightfoot were on their bellies under the canvas watching the spectacle in the beerhall tent. There were a dozen intriguing deeds

of interest, but their attention had gravitated to and became riveted on the wild-eyed orator, then in unexpected swiftness, that changed and their curiosity spiked to a previously unknown level.

They were snickering and slinking closer in an attempt to glimpse a frontal view of the cavorting woman, but all their strenuous efforts to do so were in vain. She never once twirled in their direction, but even if she had unawares accommodated them, their sight lines were being blocked by an ever-moving picket fence of legs and outstretched arms.

"Hellions! Away from here, you scallywag hellions!" the Prophet Eliezer yelped and glowered at them. "Or else I will strike you blind." He hopped and skipped with a momentum that shocked the boys and defied his colossal dimensions. He slammed his staff down on the edge of the uplifted canvas, effectively trapping them. "Where will you troublemakers go?"

"Let us loose, mister," LC said, squirming in futile fierceness.

"I am no mister, boyo," he replied hotly. "I am the Prophet Eliezer. Thou shalt not be free from the snare of sacred zeal. Hearken unto me and be chastised by the abomination of woes that will redden your eyes with sorrows and contentions. Woe unto those mockers who call evil good, and good evil; who rise up early in the morning to follow the babbles of tomfoolery. Woe unto those pitiful souls who walk in darkness and get lost because they have shunned the light.

"The darkness will consume them for the Lord God Almighty will turn his face away from all who choose wickedness over righteousness." He glared stormily, bending low to eyeball his twisting and turning captives. "You boyos are feasting on bitter fruits. Your stomachs will sour and your blood run cold. Maggots will crawl around your skulls and eat your brains. You will have no peace all the days of your miserable lives. Thus saith the Prophet Eliezer."

All through the vitriolic soliloquy LC and Yaz never stopped wiggling to escape, and just then, fate or chance intervened to rescue them. A massive explosion of dynamite from one of the nearby diggings sent repercussions through the ground that distracted the man who had them pinned down. His weight came off the shepherd's staff and released them.

The brothers bolted, but again, in unforeseen nimbleness, the Prophet Eliezer dropped to a knee and wielded the giant cane like a horsewhip, snapping it under the fringe of the tent and using the hook to trip LC. He tumbled face-first in the dirt. He heard bellows behind him and saw Yaz, who was already ten yards ahead, pivot and come running back to him.

LC accepted his helping hand. "We gotta be gone, Yaz."

"Yeah-huh." The nine-year-olds took off and raced down the principal artery side by side past a mule-team train of carts and wagons loaded with ore and driven by no-nonsense teamsters. A coarse vapor of dust wafted aimlessly, falling over the town like grainy raindrops. The avenue was congested with pedestrians who were oblivious to the plight of two boys skedaddling.

They stutter-stepped in unison, then careened around a corner and scampered down a backstreet. A mangy mutt protested being roused from slumber and yapped at them. LC started laughing and soon Yaz joined the merriment. They decelerated on cue, dove and rolled into a secret hidey-hole—a dugout under a stoop. They were both smirking ear to ear.

"Too close."

"You got that right, Yaz."

"Yeah-huh."

'Did you see that woman?"

"Not her jigglies, LC."

"Me, neither."

Yaz tapped his forehead. "That man ain't right up here."

"No matter. We better go."

"Mom will be looking for us?"

"We're responsible for supper, Yaz."

"Yeah-huh."

"For what are we waiting?" LC asked, eyes lively and challenging. He gave Yaz a mighty enough shove to knock him on his backside, then took off in a ballyhoo. He sprinted as fast as he could and had a decent head-start, but it was only seconds before Yaz Lightfoot dashed into the lead, then slowed and set the tempo equal to the speediest pace LC Beadle could manage.

The cornflower blue of the Colorado sky went on forever. It was an exquisitely perfect afternoon for a leisurely stroll, and though an urgent woodworking project awaited in his shop, Doc Fralick had no intention of hurrying home. He cherished the scenery surrounding Durango, the whistle-stop where, ten years ago, he chose to hang his shingle mostly because of the beauty of the Animas River Valley snuggled in so intimately by the San Juan Mountains.

Main Avenue had a few other pedestrians—and he knew them all. Genial nods and waved greetings were the constant in the small town that was as friendly as friendly could be. Wherever he went he carried the leather satchel that contained an assortment of the basics necessary for the practice of medicine, and was known as Doc to everyone.

The Animas River—*Rio de Las Animas*, the River of Souls—snaked its way through the interior of the community. His smile was large as he sniffed the freshness rising from the water, but knew that he had to resist the temptation. He wanted to swap the medical bag for his tackle box and meander to a favorite spot to get in some fly fishing before the sun set, but that was not to be for there was a promise to keep; a bassinet that had to be finished pronto.

He had migrated westward from the Old States in the mid-seventies. He picked up odd jobs while pursuing medical studies with a civilian surgeon on an army post. The heavy duty book learning and practical hands-on experience were exhausting and exhilarating. He never once vacillated in his resolve to buckle down and complete the intensive training. His arduous toils were rewarded in an improvised graduation parade put together by soldiers.

Then, in moves to scratch the itchy feet of wanderlust, he did itinerant doctoring for a couple years before settling in to build a practice and serve the hamlet of Durango. He had carved out a storybook life, and now, a block from the house, Doc Fralick sped up and decided he needed to put time to use on the special task in his woodshop at the back of the property.

Meanwhile in Creede, Whitey Fitzgerald relaxed in the barber chair, captivated and amused by the business in the Orleans Club. His eyes were tightened by a smile that climbed up his cheeks. The joint was crowded and as animated as a barnyard of squabbling chickens. Sluggish tendrils of bluish smoke clung to the ceiling in stagnant pools.

He got to his feet when a ruddy-faced regular in a Panama hat folded his cards at a poker table and sauntered over. "Why, Mr. Slick Willy Phips, welcome to my little corner of the world," he said flamboyantly. "Have a seat and I shall proceed to make you pretty."

Phips hung his headgear on a hatrack against the wall, then plopped his block-bodied girth down. "You, my good man, can get to work on a shave and a haircut *tout de suite.*"

"I can't do a talkfest in a foreign lingo," Whitey said, click-clicking testily. His eccentric habit of peppering conversations with a suction noise between cheek and gum had become more incessant as age accumulated in him. Smallish in stature, he possessed charm and a king-sized personality. "I don't know any toot or sweet so you be euchred and out of luck."

"*Tout de suite*. It's French, Whitey," Willy replied, sing-songy and pretentious. "I ain't no smooth talking fancy-pants, but I like the way *tout de suite* tingles on my tongue. It kind of slides off all slippery and is just another way of saying immediately or right away."

Fitzgerald rolled his eyes. "Are you making a remark?"

"By no means, my good man."

"I was once a slave in Alabama and I knows a remark when I hears one," Whitey said grumpily. "You be going around the backdoor with your toot and sweet to tells me that I be getting slow and crotchety, but when it comes to barbering I gots the proper speed."

"No intention to say otherwise."

"You want to be dapper and distinguished?"

"As always, Whitey."

"Well, let me fill your ears with some pieces of truth." Whitey draped a sheet around his customer's neck and fastidiously tucked it under the collar of his shirt. His quick wit and easy laugh disarmed others and provided inroads where he never kowtowed. "If I has to be tooting and sweeting, you gonna be nicked and hacked, not dapper and distinguished."

"I submit to your expertise."

"As you should." Whitey nodded, somewhat smugly. "When it comes to barbering and teeth doctoring I still be the best there is 'cause I ain't no fly by night here today gone tomorrow man. I gots staying power." His complexion was high-yellow; time had added a spiderweb of wrinkly laugh lines on his face, but his nappy hair remained as snow-white as when it first sprouted that color whilst he was a peewee scamp. "You gots any good gossip for me?"

"You know my ears are always open."

Fitzgerald had scissors and comb in hand, but hadn't started cutting yet; he was simply clacking them together like a kind of maestro. "I has to inspect this scalp of yours before I can gets all the different directions of hair to behave. You best start yakking up a storm."

"The hottest hearsay circling the camp just now is that Bob Ford is looking for a lot to purchase," Willy said, voice rising and falling in its characteristic inflection. "He has plans to open a dancehall and weasel his way in to get a piece of the action. Soapy is still cheesed off at him for getting liquored up and shooting out windows and streetlamps at Eastertime."

"He and that gunman Joe Palmer had themselves a hog-killin time."

"A couple of big talking braggarts who ought to have been tossed in the hoosegow, but both have some value to Soapy and his partners, so no harm no foul," Willy opined, puckering his lips. "Ford has got more stink on him than a dead skunk, but like a frigging cat he keeps landing on his feet. He's been exploiting the fame of killing Jesse James for ten years."

"Shot him in the back, no less." Whitey was on task; the comb in harmony with the scissors, which never stopped snip-snipping. "A boaster and a coward is all he be."

"He cheats at cards too, Whitey."

"So do you."

"Sure enough," the gambler said, "but as the name implies, I ain't *never* been caught because I am slick and silver-tongued." He tented his eyebrows as a smarmy grin crimped his lips. "At this fine establishment I render a percentage of my winnings to the house and I ain't nowhere near stupid enough to ever shortchange Soapy Smith. He can be ruthless."

"He gots hisself a decent heart."

"You think?"

"I knows. When he sits in my chair we talks plenty," Whitey answered pointblank. He put the scissors and comb on the shelf beneath an ornately framed oval mirror, then picked up the brush and soap-cup. He began whipping up lather. "Mr. Jefferson Randolph Smith be a perplex stumper. He gots some jagged edges, but underneath all that crust he's okey dokey."

"Odds are he doesn't show that side to many."

"If'in he did, he'd be done as a rackets kingpin."

"Seems about right."

"I ain't wrong, I can tells you that much. I be as right as rain," Whitey said, beginning to daintily dab frothy soapsuds on the gadabout's stubby whiskers. "Let me ask you something."

"I think not."

"What you say?"

Phips flexed his hands under the linen covering. "I'm of a mind that you want me to be a chatterbox about Lucinda, which as we have discussed before, will not happen because that is a probe that's restricted. I cannot help you, my good man, even if I had some information."

"I just be jabbering."

"Maybe so, but I ain't flipping on Lucinda."

Fitzgerald took a step back to regard him suspiciously. "So you does have truth about her that you be hiding. I gets where you be coming from." He returned the brush and cup to the shelf, then procured a straight razor. "I knows that Lucinda Enochelli has an undisclosed interest in Deacon Coburn, which seems a bit unnatural so I just be trying to get to the bottom of it."

"A bit unnatural? What's that supposed to mean?"

"Deacon be the best man and friend I've ever known," Whitey replied peevishly. He was sliding the straight-razor against the black leather strop attached to the side of the chair. "I ain't no naïve greenhorn. I been up and down and around. And I has a soft spot for Lucinda, but there be something wrong in this here happenstance. What's her story? What secret is she hiding?"

"I can't say."

"You canst say or you won't say?"

"Can't, Whitey. I swear I have zero knowledge."

Fitzgerald increased the briskness of the flogging motion of stropping the blade. "You means to tell me you make whoopee with that woman and she be a riddle to you?"

"Exactly."

"I ain't no gullible rube, Mr. Phips."

"Hand to God," Willy said, raising his right hand and lifting the sheet. "I ain't spinning any lies. She's tightlipped about anything to do with her past. She put a kibosh on me trying to crack her, but I do no complaining because she's still the feistiest woman I've ever had."

"I be afraid she intends harm to Deacon."

"Of that I am entirely uncertain, Whitey."

"That don't calm me none."

"Ain't that reassuring?" Willy quipped smart-alecky. "Perhaps it'd be best if I go and seek absolution from the Prophet Eliezer before you put that straight razor to my throat."

Fitzgerald click-clicked, peppy and gleeful. "You'd not find any forgiveness from the Prophet Eliezer. I tried gabbing with that crank once. He railed at me for being a jungle-bunny nigger and told me I was going to burn to a crisp in hell. I gave him a big smile, tipped my hat and assured him that I'd open the door for him when he arrived at the brimstone palace."

"How'd he take it?"

"*I am the Prophet Eliezer,*" Whitey mimicked, and punctuated it with a rapid-fire series of clicks. "That poor soul is bent and I gets scared trouble be brewing because of him."

"Not to worry, Whitey. Trouble ain't nothing new."

"Shut that trap so as I can shave you shiny."

"As ordered, my good man."

Fitzgerald got busy using the razor with a theatrical flourish. When he was bending low to remove bristles under his chin a blasting mixture of nitroglycerin detonated with such closeby gusto that it jarred the Orleans Club and the building vibrated. He stagger-stepped backwards and exclaimed, "Whew doggies! I done be hogtied! I could've gutted your jugular."

"Naw, not with your steady hands."

"Steady hands ain't gonna matter if'in my feet gets knocked out from under me," Whitey groused, eyeballs protruding. "Jumping jiminy cricket, I ain't no trapeze man. I be a barber who has made his scissors purr in boom-towns on occasion. Abilene at its peak. Dodge City, too. The stench and clamor of a cowtown is preferable to breakneck explosions night and day."

"We are at the core of a silver *boom*, my good man."

"Really?" Whitey jested, flashing a broad grin. "I must've missed that news, but I best take it into consideration for future reference." His eyes were twinkling as he nimbly handled the blade to finish the job, then rubbed in a ration of bayberry-scented lotion. After some genial bantering over payment was negotiated, Whitey Fitzgerald went outside for a short stroll.

The grays and scarlets of eventide were coalescing across the sky. Abbey Langton, responding to the latest eruption of dirt into the airstream, closed the front door carefully so as to not disturb her father's naptime, but then smiled knowingly when she saw that he was fully awake. She smoothed her skirt as she took a seat in the hardwood rocker beside him.

"Kind of ear-splitting, ain't it?"

"Closed in and ear-splitting, that's Creede," she replied, emitting a slightly apologetic chuckle. "Sorry you didn't get much sleep, but am quite pleased to have the visiting time."

"I'll tie on a lengthy snooze soon enough," Deacon said, squinty-eyed. "I've been doing lots of looking over my shoulder thinking lately. Reminiscing is fine, but has its ups and downs because just like life itself, the good and bad compete and get all tangled up together."

She timidly touched a spindly gold chain visible at her neckline. "That never changes, does it? Every good and perfect gift comes with its own measure of distress or heartache."

"That's the price we pay for living and loving, Abbey."

She kept fingering the necklace. "And living and loving is worth sorting through all the quandaries and quagmires that can be dished out because life is a magnificent adventure."

"That's the only honest and healthy perspective."

"So what memory lane have you been traveling down and why?"

"Old Blue. Abilene," he answered, hunching his shoulders. "The why of it is because I have this talented daughter who writes exciting tales under the heading, *Bandit, Champion of the Western Trails*. I have read every installment and am always stirred by pride and pleasure."

"I hope the facts get fictionalized just right."

"No worries on that front, Abbey."

"I'm glad for the affirmation. Thank you."

"The narratives ought to be gathered together."

"That's one of the projects on hold," she said sunnily. "A bigwig editor in New York is waiting for the final edits of the whole collection of stories to be published in book form."

"Get to editing, young lady. Chop, chop."

She blushed brightly. "First thing in the morning."

"Alright. That's resolved."

"You are such an encourager."

"I do what I can, Abbey. It ain't much."

"And self-effacing to a fault."

Coburn exhaled a resigned, almost helpless sigh. "I pray so. It's a day-in day-out battle to be true to conviction. Two verses keep me diligent. A Proverb of Solomon: *When pride cometh, then cometh shame: but with the lowly is wisdom.* If I forget to remember that one, a beatitude of Jesus reminds me about the assurance of genuine humility: *Blessed are the poor in spirit: for theirs is the kingdom of heaven.* I ain't where I once was, but I ain't where I want to be."

"You're much farther along than me."

"I'm older and trekked more miles, is all."

"The inner struggle never ends, does it, Deacon?"

"Not this side of glory," he replied, head shaking in a slow rhythm. "We each have a slew of weaknesses of the flesh which the Enemy seeks to exploit so as to steal optimism and hope, or to kill relationships and dreams, or to destroy perspective and all that is dear in our hearts. Satan is a merciless adversary, so vigilance must be more than a spiritualized watchword."

"That can be a hard truth to learn."

"It's the hardness that teaches us, and when we are not attentive students we default to aimlessness and become unwitting targets to be deceived," he said, even and earnest. "Truth is not easy to apply, nor should it be. It is circular, having no beginning or ending, and there are no loopholes for it never changes. Every generation must put it into action for themselves."

"You should've been a preacher, Deacon."

"Nope," he answered severely. "I've heard that from my childhood upward, but I have been blessed to be a pilgrim on the path the Maker of heaven and earth ordained for me."

"You are an inspiration to me, and many others."

"To God be the glory."

"So be it." She leaned back and rocked effortlessly. "In an unrelated concern, a while back I received a longish telegram from Hamilton Bell in Dodge City informing me that Butch Mackenzie passed in his sleep. The powers that be on the town council sponsored the funeral for such a prominent citizen, which according to Hamilton, assembled an overflow crowd."

"Butch was grouchy, but truly a tenderhearted man."

"Yes, and generous," she said pensively. "A lawyer contacted me. Butch bequeathed a sizeable sum to Langton, which is payable to me due to his age. When the bank-draft arrives I'll divide it equally between Langton and Yaz, and open separate savings accounts, though neither of them will know about those deposits until they're ready to go off on their own."

"My inclination is that Butch would approve."

"He had a high regard for me."

"And rightly so." He altered his upright posture by slouching forward to rest elbows on knees. "Some years ago I had the same news about Big Bull. I was in Wichita when a Western Union runner chased me down. The telegram was three weeks old, so I didn't get to Texas for the interment, but made a point of going to the grave to pay respects and say my piece."

"Must've been a superb tribute."

"Big Bull likely deserved better. He was a helluva man." He clinched his fingers together and nodded reflectively. He stared at a far horizon. "That was the autumn of '90, then I rode on a roundabout route to Santa Fe. Left the Suncurl Café last September, and since I had never been to Arizona, took a detour in that direction before making nomadic tracks to Colorado."

"You've been in the saddle since September?"

"Mostly, I reckon."

"No wonder you're frazzled."

"I was born for it, Abbey. What else would you have me do?" he asked rhetorically. He gave her a thumbs up. "To Butch Mackenzie and Big Bull Wallace, gone but not forgotten."

"Men larger than life," she said, toying with the spindly chain. She lifted the circular gold locket from beneath the rust-colored blouse. She caressed the intricate floral design around its edges, then thumbed the clasp. The top popped up to reveal a photograph of her deceased husband. "Come September it'll be ten years since Sam was killed. I still miss him."

"You'll do so until the day eternity comes knocking for you."

She shuddered a breath, misty-eyed. "Sam Beadle was a *helluva* man."

"And a great friend. Did he ever tell you that I threatened him?"

She giggled musically as the waterworks streamed down her cheeks. "Yes. After our wedding, in the wagon on the way to Willows Rest, he said that you went all curly wolf on him. Vowed to make him a capon if he ever made me cry anything other than happy tears."

"I heeded my responsibility to protect you, Abbey."

"For which I am ever appreciative," she said, taking hold of his hand. "Just so you know. Sam caused me to shed buckets of happy tears, but not a single angry teardrop." Her lips pursed and she heeled the moisture away from her eyes because she heard familiar laughs. She looked down the alley and saw her sons dashing homeward in a fast-paced crisscrossing pattern.

"Who do we have here?"

"Come on, Papa. It's me and Yaz."

"Me? Me and who?" Deacon asked, low and stony-faced.

"Langton Coburn Beadle and my brother Yaz Lightfoot."

"Can't be," Deacon countered gruffly. He raised a finger and jabbed it at them. The boys were dillydallying at the edge of the porch, noticeably surprised and standoffish. He gave them a thorough once-over while suppressing a grin to maintain a stern expression. "My grandsons are half-pint squirts, but you two are on the way to be strapping lumberjacks."

"Quit fooling, Papa. You know it's me Langton."

"I do. You favor your father."

"That's what Mom tells me."

Abbey smiled gently. "Actually I call you a spitting image."

"Are you too big in the britches to give an old-timer a hug?"

"Nope, Papa." Langton shuffled his feet as one eyebrow dipped while the other tilted lopsidedly. "I can squish the stuffing out of you." He then delivered a humongous hug.

"I have officially been squished," Deacon said, chuckling.

The lad slipped sideways. "Your turn, Yaz."

Coburn raked fingers through his gone-to-seed beard, recognizing the wary caution in the dark-eyed boy. He stood defiant and aloof; he carried a whitish scar that traced from the hairline at the left temple to the jawline below the earlobe. "My joy is great in finally meeting you."

"I am Yaz Lightfoot."

"You are my Lakota Sioux grandson."

"LC Beadle is my brother. Abbey Langton is my mother."

"And I am Papa. Why Lightfoot?"

Yaz frowned glumly, evidently puzzled. His mother spoke up and rescued him. "Standing Wolf dedicated the name to him during the ceremony that made these gentlemen brothers."

"When I run I am the wind," Yaz chimed in matter-of-factly.

"Me and Yaz are both quick, but he is the quickest ever."

Coburn's overgrown moustache twitched. "Hence the name."

"Yeah-huh."

"Yaz Lightfoot is a good name. It has integrity and strength. Bear down and shoulder it with pride and humility. You have the look of an honorable man growing inside you," Deacon said, focus fixed on him. "We are tied together, you and I. You are my daughter's son and my grandson's brother. I offer you the counsel of my years." He stretched forth his right hand.

Yaz immediately accepted it and inclined forward so that the handshake melded into a fleeting embrace. He sidled out of it. "Our mother has told me and LC stories about you."

"She might do some exaggerating."

"Not about you, I don't," she said pithily.

"Me and Yaz can tell when Mom exaggerates."

Abbey subdued a squeak of a giggle. "I suppose you can."

"So how goes it?" Deacon asked, eyeing the youths.

"Me and LC were poking around and looking for fun."

"Find any?"

"A little bit, Papa. Me and Yaz always do."

"That's a fact, of which I have no doubt," Deacon intoned, deep ruts furrowing his brow. "When I was your age and the chores were all put down I never had difficulty finding fun."

"Excuse me," Abbey interjected, blunt and insistent. "Speaking of chores. Am I mistaken or is it creeping up on mealtime? I'm wondering who has the task of preparing supper today."

"Me and Yaz, Mom."

"Me and LC will get to it now, Mom."

"Hang on a minute," Deacon said, raising a hand. "I need a special favor. First thing in the morning I want the two of you to run fetch Whitey and let him know I'm in town."

"Sure thing. Pap Whitey will be excited," LC replied, head bobbing. "He calls me and Yaz his pipsqueak partners in crime, even though we never get into any real trouble."

"Pap Whitey is the best. Me and LC trick him all the time."

Coburn put the rocker into motion. "I'd guess Whitey gives as good as he gets in the trickster department." He tugged heavily on his chin-whiskers. "If it is agreeable with your mother, I also have a job for you two. I need you to go to the livery and tend to exercise for Gilgal. Put the bridle on and take my faithful horse for a walkabout every day. Alright?"

LC and Yaz were smiling and nodding enthusiastically.

"I'll pay a dollar a day. That's fifty cents each."

"Wow, that's a big whoop!" LC yelped, giving Yaz a chummy nudge.

"The money will go to your mother for safekeeping until she decides what's best to do with it." He flinched a grin. "Have we got a deal?" he asked, hands outspread in a shrug.

"Yes, sir," they answered in unison.

She cleared her throat good-naturedly. "Just now, however, you work-men have meat and vegetables requiring your labors. Get to it." The admonition spurred them into action. She braced for the inevitable slamming door, which occurred on cue. She gave her father a significant and meaningful glance, then Abbey Langton went inside to surreptitiously supervise her sons.

Shortly after midnight, Lucinda Enochelli and Slick Willy Phips were sweaty and catching their breath, snuggling beneath a fluffy quilt because the air was chilly. The large brass bed, in a room on the second floor of a boarding house, squeaked and creaked up a storm, but that never impeded them from copulating whenever the mood struck.

"We rang the bell once again," she said, sighing merrily. She burrowed deeper and peered through the shadows at the austere accommodations. A pair of Queen Anne chairs were on either side of a tallboy dresser, which had oil lamps situated on it to provide yellowish hues against the darkness. The clatter of the twenty-four hour hurly-burly invaded their cocoon.

"A couple old coots still hard at it."

"Yepper."

He fixed his pillow, then cuddled closer. "I had an interesting exchange with Whitey this afternoon. He expressed the nutty notion that your intention is to harm Deacon Coburn."

"What did you tell him?"

"Absolutely nothing as per our arrangement."

She grabbed a fleshy love-handle and gave it a mellow squeeze. He put up an overacted protest, which she rejected with a throaty laugh. "Good to know that you faithfully keep your lips fettered, though in all reality, you have no true knowledge of my purposes, do you?"

"Nothing of consequence, to be sure."

"Whitey is a darling. I'll iron it out with him."

"He's a good man, Lucinda. As, I'd guess, is Deacon Coburn."

"I've never insinuated otherwise, have I?"

"Not in my hearing."

"So what's your problem?"

"Ain't got any as far as it goes."

"Have you made deductions about my interest in Coburn?"

"Are you laying a trap for me, my sweet Lucinda?"

"Why would you suspect such a thing?"

"The real question is, why wouldn't I be guarded?"

She tootled a chirp. "Are you suggesting that I'm devious?"

"Are you implying that you're not?"

"I'm as virtuous and innocent as you, Slick Willy."

"Not quite, dear lady. I'm barefaced about my chicanery."

"And I'm two-faced?"

"You have a conspiratorial agenda," he volleyed back coolly. "By defini-tion, anyone who keeps a lid on her intent and past as aggressively as you have, has a proclivity for conniving. You have no defense to offer, Lucinda. I submit your clandestine relationship with the Beadle kid and his Injun friend as the damning piece of evidence. You got those nippers spun up."

"Point taken."

"You're using them."

"Stick your self-righteousness in a sock, Mr. Phips."

"Please don't pretend you're not using them."

"Pretend I'm not using him? Why the dickens would I feign such a thing?" she retorted in heated sarcasm. "Please don't insult my intelligence. I've been used plenty and used others just as much. It's the way of the world, Slick Willy. Of course I'm using the two of them."

"To what end?"

"If at all possible, to gain an advantage."

"An advantage? How so?"

"I want no surprises when I connect with Coburn on my terms," she answered, open and forthright. "For that to be a possibility I need to gather every tidbit of information I can get."

"Is Whitey's intuition blarney?"

"Me desiring to hurt Deacon Coburn is ludicrous." She propped up on an elbow and arranged the blankets better. "We've been to San Francisco and despite the togetherness of traveling found no reason to part company. This has been a mutually beneficial relationship and obviously there's some-thing good between us, so on this occasion, I'll whet your curiosity: I have something that belongs to Coburn, the contents of which I know nothing."

"Could it be detrimental to him?"

"I doubt it, but I cannot say with certainty."

"Is there anymore news as to his whereabouts?"

"Are you digging deeper into my business, Slick Willy?"

"Sneaking steps to the secrets, I suppose."

"Are you daft, or taking liberties?"

"Taking liberties with your talkative mood."

She laid down and got comfortable. "There's been nothing since LC told me about the March telegram from Durango saying he'd be in Creede for the springtime flowers."

"Could be any day now, if he ain't already here."

"I suppose."

"Are you in the middle of something, or are you ready for him?"

"I was born in the middle of something, so I'm always ready," she replied, snickering. "Please snuff the lamps." She lifted the covers and he complied with her request. When he slid back into bed, she tucked him in and assertively held him tight. She soon heard his snores, but for Lucinda Enochelli, sleep was a peek-a-boo harlequin who frolicked out of reach.

Sally Twosongs awakened alone. The house was dark and quiet. She reached across the mattress for her husband, but he was gone and the bedsheets were cold. Her heart filled with empathy for she knew he was troubled, but true to his nature, he was being closemouthed and detached. She sank into the pillow and stared at the ceiling for an instant, then got up.

The floorboards were cold. She put on a pair of doeskin slippers as she stood and pulled the cumbersome comforter off the bed to drape it around her shoulders like a shawl. It dangled behind her as she stepped lightly toward the living room. She stopped in the doorframe and leaned against it to watch him. Love swelled in her bosom as mist welled into tears.

He was near the fireplace in the tall-backed oak rocker that had been handcrafted by his father as a wedding present. Their dog, a two-year-old redbone hound, had stretched out with its back against the hearthstone. Its ears perked in her direction, but she unsmilingly raised a finger to keep it in its place. She went to him and sat at his feet, using his shins as a backrest.

Logs were crackling. The flames, blues and oranges, whirled and frisked like tiny ballerinas. A smile pinched at her lips. She folded the eiderdown bedding over her lap. Not a word was spoken, but in the poignant silence much was communicated. The soundless conversation lasted for ten minutes, then he broke the stillness in a low voice.

"Shadrach is completely blind."

"I'm sorry, Caleb."

"Do you remember when Rainy was killed?"

"Like it was yesterday."

"That's how I feel. Helpless. Useless."

"What can I do for you, Caleb?"

"Be my little bright star."

"Always and forever."

"Some events are unforgettable and the memory revives all the same emotions," he said, dull and somber. "When Rainy died was the day I first loved you. While I dug a grave you sat off by yourself with your flute and played a mournful tune that was good for my soul."

"I remember it well," she replied, modifying her angle so as to gaze into his eyes. "I first loved you a wee-bit earlier. You sat in the dirt clinging to Rainy's lifeless body, blood on your hands and forearms. I hung over your back and hugged your shoulders, weeping furiously."

"And now here I am, helpless all over again."

"A frailty that comes from being human."

"I feel as weak as a child, *lucero*."

"You should. A dear friend is dying."

"Twenty-six years old," he said, hands coming to rest on her shoulders. "It doesn't seem all that long when measured against its steadfast faithfulness. The stallion has *never* failed me."

"Nor I."

"If it comes to putting Shadrach down, I can plainly say that I don't have the wherewithal to pull the trigger. I can scarcely provide proper grooming and nursing," he admitted, regrets and shame creeping into his voice. "I repudiate this feebleness in me, but still it weighs me down."

"That's entirely natural."

"My feelings are all out of alignment."

"Again, that's entirely natural, Caleb."

"And I should just concede that fact?"

"Yes."

He frowned. "No explanation as to why, Sally Twosongs?"

"You must be honest in your heart. Face the sadness straight on."

"I will heed that advice, though I'll not like it."

"What else is new?" she asked, laughing handily.

"I am aware of my stubbornness, Sally Twosongs."

"Glad to hear it."

He shifted his bottom. "Avis has been a godsend. She has picked up the slack from my hesitancy. By default she is Shadrach's caregiver. Her soothing touch is special."

"The Creator knew what we needed."

"Yes. Avis and Stace are a windfall for *WT Ranch*." He took hold of the single braid of her hair and fiddled with it. "Stace has given Pa a boost by taking on the woodcutting load. Now Pa just supervises. I've never seen anyone who enjoyed hard work as much as Stace."

"I have. His name is Caleb Weitzel."

He grinned sheepishly. The dog snuffled and stood. "Apparently Bobo is in agreement with you." The hound cocked its head, then padded to the front door and plopped down. "Bobo is a fine successor to Rainy and Hank, though its independent streak can be maddening."

"Bobo is receptive to every command from Bethsuelo."

"That's important," he replied, rolling her braid between his fingers. "I was in the barn sitting on a bale of hay yesterday staring at Shadrach and thinking about end of life stuff when I had a sober interaction with our daughter. I guess she had been watching me for some time. She came over, took hold of my hands and said, *Shadrach knows you are hurting inside.*"

"A correct intuition."

"I'm sure, but then her eyes got glassy. *Black clouds of sorrow are coming.*"

She scrunched around. "You heard her say that?"

"Loud and clear, Sally Twosongs."

"Did she tell you anything else?"

"*All is as it should be. Don't worry, Daddy.*"

"Her gift is getting stronger."

"True. I don't know if I should be excited or vexed."

"Every gift from the Creator is to be treasured and nurtured, Caleb."

"True again," he said, accidently bumping against her as he stood. He chuckled and wobbled awkwardly until he caught his balance. "I will always be a support and encouragement to Bethsuelo, but just now, there's a few hours before daybreak, so I'm going back to bed."

"Where I will embrace you and whisper prayers for us."

The longhouse was warm and cozy. A golden haze fluttered around the edges of the room like the fraying fringe of a tattered scarf. Everyone was asleep except for the patriarch who sat cross-legged at the fire. He wore buckskin leggings and a beaded pullover shirt. His black hair was thick and longish, cascading over his shoulders. He had a stone resting in his right palm which he periodically studied with an intensity that made his face shine.

His head was bowed in thankful supplication, but then he sensed a presence and felt eyes on him. He looked up and smiled broadly. "What are you doing here, my old friend?"

"Charley Jondreau? I didn't recognize you."

"The hair, eh," Charley said, pushing it off his forehead and behind his ears. "I shaved it in mourning and respect for Grandmere, but she is here and requested that I grow it, so I did."

"Where is here?"

"Here is here, preacher-man."

"What is this place?"

Jondreau scowled. "It is no mystery or secret, eh."

"I'm confused, Charley. Where am I?"

"We knew each other in a realm where evil had sway and power."

"And now?"

"Evil has no place in paradise."

"The afterlife? What am I doing here?"

"The Great Spirit has his reasons, eh."

"What am I doing here?" he asked again, scowly-faced.

"Sit with me and we shall talk of the past and future."

Deacon Coburn squatted across from him. He had a protracted look into the dim recesses, but despite aspirations to placate an inquisitive disposition, he could not discern anything beyond the haze of the golden barricade that closed around them. "I've ridden a thousand miles or more, so my brain may be a bit fuzzy, but jawboning with you will definitely revive me, Charley."

"Time is running away from us, preacher-man."

"It's always a fast-mover, ain't it?"

"We number our days by numbering our moments, eh."

"My ordeal with Smoky Crowe taught me that lesson."

"You learned it well?"

"I think so, yes," Deacon replied, flint-eyed serious. "There have likely been lapses, but since I was reborn in the high desert I've made every effort to be intentional in that area."

"That's the crux of life and death, eh."

"Help me understand, Charley."

"I lived, I died. We walked together for a spell," Charley said in a monotone. "It was a morally profitable journey, but the moments vanished into the vapor of the past. You are living, you will die, eh. Your deliberate steps are the moments you cherish as pearls, but the string will be broken and the gems scattered in foggy memory. Only eternity lives forever."

"Are you saying that life is pointless?"

"Not at all, my friend," Charley answered, eyes lively. "Though the foolish treat life as a headlong rush to the finish line of death, we know the truth, eh. Our flesh and blood adventure on earth is prelude for the eternal.

We are shaped by decisions, shined or scarred by how we choose to respond to the good and bad happenings that come in unequal measures."

"So the Apostle Paul was correct?" Deacon asked wryly. "*For our light affliction, which is but for a moment, worketh for us a far more exceeding and eternal weight of glory; while we look not at the things which are seen, but at the things which are not seen: for the things which are seen are temporal; but the things which are not seen are eternal.*"

"You got it, my old friend," Charley said, transferring the stone back and forth from one hand to another. "The race is not to the swiftest, nor the victory to the strongest. The haughty will be cast into thorn bushes, but a crown awaits those who in weakness are emptied as a sacred offering. Fight the worthy fight until you can fight no more, eh." The golden haze increasingly darkened and enclosed him. "Never stop kicking and punching, preacher-man."

Charley Jondreau disappeared. The unyielding directive came alive. Deacon Coburn woke up to the cadence of the words thumping vibrantly against his eardrums. *Never stop kicking and punching, preacher-man.* Lying on his back on a lumpy pad on the floor in his grandsons' bedroom, he kept his eyes closed as the inspiration hammered into his subconscious.

Naomi Axler was humming a hymn as she finished preparing breakfast for her husband. The tune came from her River Brethren rearing when it had been sung a cappella in German. She remembered pressing against her mother and harmonizing. She could still blend the notes, but from too many years of disuse the language had lost all meaning. Snippets lingered at the edges of her mind, but this morning, not a single lyric of the song was recallable.

The scent of bacon and coffee intermixed in the kitchen with the freshness of dawn. She had the window above the sink open several inches and was enjoying the morning. She had a peek outside and saw the slow-footed man she loved returning from the chores. The brim of his hat obscured his face, but she detected a tiny bend on his lips. She fixed him a plate of fried potatoes, eggs and bacon, then poured two mugs of robust black nectar.

"Naomi," he called, entering the house and stomping his feet. "Something just happened that I'm having difficulty deciphering." He moseyed into the kitchen and hung his headgear on the back of his chair. "What do you think Amanda volunteered to do? You'll never guess."

"She scuttled through here in pajamas to inform me that she would forego breakfast," Naomi said, dropping into a chair across from him. She sipped her coffee and watched as he readied himself to put the eating irons to work. "What did she offer to undertake?"

"Not just offer, Naomi. She's doing it."

"What, pray tell?"

"Hooking the team up to the buckboard."

She put the mug down. "Our daughter Amanda? Prissy Amanda?"

"Yep."

"What's gotten into her?"

"I asked her that and received an icy glare."

"Likely just a new phase."

"Or she's anxious to get on the road to South Fork," he suggested as a frown deepened the more or less permanent cast of his face. The lines lessened on occasion, but were never completely erased. "Maybe she expects to get some dress shopping in on the trip."

"That could be it, Pete."

"She's headstrong, I can tell you that much."

"You'll get no argument from me."

"She does come by it honest," he said, swallowing slowly. He took another forkful and spoke while he chewed. "She's like the pretty woman who cooked me this tasty meal."

"Did you just call me stubborn, Mr. Axler?"

He scratched at the perpetual two-day stubble on his cheeks. "Sort of, I suppose, but not at all unkindly. On you stubbornness is a fragrance as sweet and pure as honey, my dear."

"And you're a flattering charmer," she chided, gazing at him over the rim of the mug at her lips. "Temperament-wise Amanda has my strengths and also my weaknesses and faults."

"Mirror images is my input."

"I'd not argue much on that observation," she said, finishing off her coffee. She eased off her chair and got a refill, then returned to her seat. "What is bothersome and problematic is that I remember my own teenage years. When I was Amanda's age I was serious-minded and had an inclination to the practical, rather than her ofttimes ridiculous flights of fancy."

"Different time and place."

"I'll grant you that, however, her wild streak needs to be tempered," she insisted in a terse tone. "Fourteen years old and the only thing she gets excited about is wanting to move to Creede because, according to her worldly expertise, that's where all the fun and action is at. Plus it's beyond obvious that she's got a preoccupied inquisitiveness about boys and such affairs."

"Boys? The devil you say."

She nodded adamantly. "I cannot tell you the number of times I've noticed her staring doe-eyed at Stace. He doesn't seem to have discovered girls yet, but that'll soon change. When his interest is pricked, he'll read that look and her body language, then watch out, Pete."

"The inference ain't reassuring."

"You best get your head out of the sand."

"She's only fourteen, Naomi."

"Sparks will be flying quicker than you think."

"You must be mistaken." He put his knife and fork down on the empty plate as his head wagged in a hesitant motion. "She's only fourteen," he reiterated, eyes enlarged in disbelief.

"My mother was married at fourteen," she replied, offhandedly deadpan. Her eyebrows perked up as she gave him a no-nonsense shrug. "Deacon was born when she was fifteen."

"I'll have a heart to heart with her today."

"I will pray for you to have the proper tact and words."

"That'll be helpful, Naomi. Thank you."

"Be patient and understanding, but firm and resolved," she said, puddles of emotion forming in her big brown eyes. She sniffled a bit and smiled strongly. "I'm already restless for your return. I'm hoping for a letter from Jesse. We haven't had any in almost six months."

"That one was posted from Cuba." He stood and leaned toward the window. "Hard to believe that our son is a seafaring world traveler and now, his sister has taken up the tasks of a teamster." He gestured and she came alongside him. A chuckle passed between them. They marveled over the sight of their persnickety daughter operating the buckboard. Her attire was inappropriate for the job—a frilly Sunday-go-to-meeting dress and floppy sunbonnet.

"Land sakes. She should've worn a suitable outfit."

"She's almighty pretty though, ain't she?"

Naomi puckered her mouth. "Strikingly so."

"Like her mother."

"That's enough. You get now." She gave him a lip-smacking kiss, then shooed him with a swat on his backside. He was grinning as he retrieved his hat and sallied forth. She waited until she heard the departing clip-clop of the mules, then hurried to the front porch. As the wagon trolled onward, Naomi Axler murmured earnest prayers for the driver and his passenger.

$$\approx\approx\approx$$

The last thing Whitey Fitzgerald did before hitting the sack was to rig up an intricate series of cans across the roof of his shack. He did so in a sneaky and stealthy manner, but even so, it was a meddlesome endeavor that disturbed some of his neighbors in the alley. He blabbed amiably and alleviated their complaints with a continuous onslaught of wisecracks.

He had invested a considerable amount of thinking in the scheme. His handiwork was wired to several triggers buried at various approaches—any one of which would cause the cans to come crashing down in front of the dwelling and entirely entangle whoever activated the convoluted snare of a burglar alarm. The project came as a result of a jolt that had caught him off-guard and put him in a mood contrasting between jovial and crabby.

When satisfaction that the apparatus was functional seeped into his bones, he went to bed knowing that the contraption would forewarn him and frighten enterprising intruders. There was anticipatory exhilaration in him so he tossed and turned, punching and fluffing the feather pillow for an hour or more. A sly smile creased his lips as he finally succumbed to slumber.

Dreams populated his sleep. He was a snot-nosed tyke, barefoot and running past a cotton field where his fellow slaves labored beneath a blistery sun. He had a slingshot in hand and a jackrabbit in his sights. It zigged into the woods and he ducked beneath branches without breaking stride. The rabbit paused, hind legs flexing. He aligned the target in the Y-frame and drew the loaded pocket to his ear. The twang and swoosh of the release rang out.

Then, before the projectile hit or missed, he was carried away to a favorite fishing hole. The slingshot was replaced by a cane pole. He was sitting on a grassy knoll that had a steep slope to the waterline. Birds were chirping in a tree behind him. The sky was cloudless. Catfish were swishing around the bottom of the bog, which mucked up the currents. The stick bobber twitched and dove. He yanked back, but out of the blue, a clattering racket struck his eardrums.

He jumped awake, click-clicking laughter. "Gotcha, gotcha, gotcha!" he squealed, hippity hopping across the floor wearing one-piece red thermal long-johns and woolen socks. He threw open the door and erupted in merriment when he saw the culprits. "Gotcha good, didn't I? You bin outfoxed by the master. That be what's called a booby trap for catching pranksters."

LC Beadle, muttering and stamping his feet, was red-faced and gritting his teeth as he animatedly extricated himself from a snarl of netting created by tin cans and jumbled coils of binder twine. Yaz Lightfoot had gotten stuck in a similar predicament, but instead of being shamed and in emotional disarray, he was stoic and cold-eyed. He calmly and methodically slumped his shoulders to disengage and slough off the jangly paraphernalia.

"You gots me a few days ago and I put you on notice," Whitey said, still cackling so hard that he was wheezing. He came outside and sat on a tripod stool located on the stoop. "Snuck into my room at day peep whilst I be sawing logs like there be no tomorrow, and scare me awake so frightfully I almost filled my drawers, and wouldn't that'a bin a fine howdy-do?"

"Yeah, but . . . "

"Yeah, but nothing, Langton Beadle," Whitey cut in, grinning triumphantly. "I done got you and Yaz, and that better be the end of it, mister smarty-pants. I ain't no spring chicken. I done be the one who birthed you so you best treat me kindly." His eyes were twinkling and his jocularity was coming under control. "Besides, by now you gots to know that when it comes to hijinks and horseplay you ain't gonna get the upper hand on a crafty crackerjack like me."

"Yeah-huh."

"Me and Yaz ain't yielding."

"Figured so," Whitey said, clapping his hands. "I be in fine fettle, so we shall play on, but I gots to give you a fair warning. My eyeballs be peeled as sharp as a cat all over mice. I won't be getting got no more, but if'in it so happens, I be coming back with guns a-blazing."

"Sounds like a challenge, Pap Whitey."

"That it be, Langton."

LC exchanged a smarmy smile with his brother. "We accept."

"Yeah-huh."

"First off, clean up this mess of cans here."

"Yeah-huh, Pap Whitey."

While the boys were busy collecting and carting the mishmash to an ever-expanding pile of rubbish behind the shack, Whitey leaned against the knotty lumber of the exterior wall and yawned hugely. The dawning was spreading brightness and warmth into nooks and crannies. He click-clicked contentedly. "Another dandy day to be a go-getter at all the doings."

"Pap Whitey, we almost forgot."

"What, Langton?"

"Papa is here."

"What you say?"

"Yeah-huh. He rode in yesterday and I met him for the first time," Yaz said, poking his head around the corner of the building. "Me and LC was to come get you for him."

"Deacon be here in Creede? I gots to get myself together."

LC shrugged indifferently. "We're off to the livery to care for Gilgal."

"I'll sees yah when I sees yah," Whitey said, clambering to his feet. He went inside and speedily got dressed in a pair of trousers and a cream-colored shirt. He was looping his arms into a checkered vest when he exited. He had to make a stop to take care of his morning necessaries, then Whitey Fitzgerald would be on his way to a reunion with an esteemed companion.

At *WT Ranch*, Sally Twosongs and Bethsuelo were on an early morning outing to the storage shed nestled in an aspen grove far removed from other outbuildings. Dew, as heavy as a rainfall, dripped off branches and clung to the grassy undergrowth. The redbone hound was soaking wet, loping in and out of the woods on both sides of the gravelly pathway.

"Bobo's taking a bath."

"Being frisky, is all, Bethsuelo." Just then, the sun crested above the mountaintop, and in nothing flat, the streaky grays in the valley were dispersed by golden-white rays that glimmered off the wetness. She took hold of her daughter's hand and knelt in front of her. "The sunrise contains much more than light against darkness. The Creator's message of hope, grace, mercy and beauty are written in the colors. Our response to each sunup must be gratitude."

"I say thank you in my heart every time I see love, Mommy."

"I pray you see it often."

"Are you worried?"

"I don't think so, Bethsuelo. Why do you ask?"

"I *feel* it in you."

Sally Twosongs crouched closer. "Tell me about it."

"Shadrach is dying. Daddy hurts."

"So do I."

"I know, Mommy."

"Shadrach is family."

"Daddy needs to cry."

Sally Twosongs pursed her lips and nodded slowly. "Maybe so. He at least needs to not be upset for being sorrowful and grieving. He can be hard, and lots of times it's difficult for me to get past your father's defenses to help him. That, I suppose, is the worry you *feel* in me."

"What are defenses?"

"That isn't easy to explain, but I'll try." Sally Twosongs stood and they strolled hand in hand. "Daddy has a tender heart, but he thinks he has to keep that fact hidden from others. He doesn't even understand that he does it, but would likely claim that he does."

"Why?"

"He's a man, plain and simple," Sally Twosongs replied laughingly. "So he automatically uses quietness and withdraws to try and protect his heart. Those are his defenses, quietness and withdrawal. He doesn't like dealing with hurts and sad emotions. Does that make sense?"

"And hard work, Mommy."

Sally Twosongs paused in mid-step for a split-second. "Yes, that's a perceptive insight, Bethsuelo. Doing jobs from dark to dark is another defense that your father employs."

"Daddy's defenses are kind of funny."

"He can't fool you?"

"Nope. I *feel* his heart."

"Have you ever told him so, Bethsuelo?"

"Nope. Should I, Mommy?"

"Only when *your* heart tells you he needs to hear it," Sally Twosongs answered as they arrived at the shed. There was a plank bench built between a pair of aspens on which mother and daughter took a seat together. "Trust your heart, Bethsuelo. The Creator planted a special seed in it that is both a blessing and a burden for it puts much responsibility on your shoulders. You must learn to listen and respond to those unusual feelings that sprout in your heart."

"Like when I asked if you were worried?"

"You are a clever young lady who makes me proud every single day," Sally Twosongs professed staunchly. "We had a meaningful heart-to-heart because you spoke up."

Bethsuelo pondered that for several moments. "I understand, I think," she said, waving to the dog. Bobo trotted over, plunked on its haunches in front of her and offered its right paw. She didn't react quickly enough so it began whining. She leaned forward and gave it a thoroughgoing shake. The hound dropped and rolled over on its back. She giggled, then blinked. Her eyes, as dark as coal, got glassy and sparkly all at once. "We should go be with Aunt Abbey."

"Why? Are you missing LC?"

"Nope."

"Oh, is it Yaz you're sweet on?"

Bethsuelo crunched up her nose. "Nope. Mr. Deacon is going to heaven."

Sally Twosongs balked. "Pardon."

"Mr. Deacon is going to heaven," she restated candidly. Her expression had an intensely wistful innocence. "His dry bones will come alive and he'll be with your friend Mr. Charley."

Sally Twosongs bit down on the inside of her bottom lip and a hitch of breath caught in her craw. She shivered slightly. Torrents of denial and nostalgia mixed together and churned into a solidifying self-doubt. Her flesh weakened. She closed her eyes and thought about the man she had first known as Mr. Deke. Hot tears trickled down her cheeks and she swiped them away.

"I'm sorry, Mommy."

"Let's go home."

In Santa Fe at the Suncurl Café, Delores Solrizo sat in a bentwood rocker on the porch, fidgety and apprehensive. Storm clouds were gathering. She watched the thunderheads forming a fortress in the northern sky. *Wintertime clouds*, she thought as she rustled her skirt so she could cross her legs. A leather satchel was beside her and a large handbag in her lap.

Waiting, on this particular morning, had her in a worrisome mood. The day seemed to be getting away from her because she had someplace she had to be and wanted nothing more than to be on her way. Even though she realized that there was time to spare, her restlessness had her imagination running rampant. She kept alternating her attention from the nearly vacant San Francisco Street to the swells shape-shifting into colossal mushrooms.

Her heart was heavy. Try as she might, she could not divert the impulse to fret. She had made arrangements for a buggy and driver to take her to the train station, but rashly wished that she was already sitting on the platform. She wore a plain caped dress and a squarish sunhat with thick ribbons tied loosely under her chin—utilitarian traveling garments.

Her mind was racing with thoughts of a man she loved and trusted as a big brother. She flew backwards in time and came to rest on a scene from the streets of Abilene on a hot summer day in 1872. She was known as Flora then, and repercussions from an ugly incident in her past had just encroached on her resolve to put the whoring trade behind her.

In desperation she sought out Deacon Coburn because he projected genuine compassion and integrity—he had known her when she was the mistress of a whorehouse in East Texas, but never once did he pass judgment or snub her in any way. Instead he went above and beyond as a gentleman to treat her with much respect and dignity. She was drawn to his kindness.

What he told her in the shadow of a graveyard radically changed her perspective, and became ingrained in her for she memorized the phrases. She had a routine glance around to be sure no one was in earshot, then spoke aloud in a firm and whispery voice: *"Now you listen to me, ma'am. Be encouraged by God's grace and mercy. And don't you duck your head to anyone. Walk these streets with your head held high and your heart bowed low in humility."*

In the ensuing twenty years she had determinedly aspired to live out the true meaning of those words. There were inevitable fits and starts, but mostly she had stayed the course. Now, her thoughts and feelings were all akimbo and her vision was blurry. She dabbed at teardrops, then opened the jumbo-sized purse and withdrew the telegram from her daughter at *WT Ranch.*

Deacon was here. He went to Creede. Concerned about his health. Pray.

After reading it thrice, she returned the cable to the handbag and exhaled wearily. The weight inside her ribcage increased. She stood and stepped onto the street, wondering if she was overreacting by putting feet to her prayers. Her eyes went to the black-striated clouds threatening the horizon. An icy sliver slid down her spine, and suddenly, Delores Solrizo was afraid.

"When did you become a slacker?"

Deacon Coburn stirred beneath the blanket. His eyes fluttered open. He vigorously fisted them, then propped up on his elbows to stare blankly around the room. Confusion was evident in the set of his jaw. It took an exorbitant amount of time for him to orient to his surroundings. He focused on the man silhouetted in the doorframe. "Age done whacked me down, Whitey."

"Ain't no day for lollygagging," the barber shot back with a spry click-click. "If I gots to shake your bones outa the sack I'll done do it. I ain't seen you since forever and a day, so you best be up and at it 'cause there's goings-on that needs your clarifying and interpreting."

Coburn shucked off the cover and sat up. "Can I get some pants on?"

"You're a sorry sight in holey underwear."

"And you're a remedy for sore eyes, my old friend." He pushed up off the pad and took a tipsy sidestep that required him to lean on a dresser to maintain stability. He delayed for many moments before grabbing his denims and yanking them on over one-piece flannels. "Does this satisfy your fashion requirements or do I need a shirt?" he asked, buckling his belt.

"You needs a shave and a haircut, I can tells you that much," Whitey answered, backing into the hallway. "That woebegone mountain-man scruffiness ain't at all becoming."

"Becoming to who?"

"You be as shaggy as a sheepdog."

"I ain't barking, am I?" Deacon followed him into the kitchen and greeted his daughter with a genial nod. She had an apron on and was standing near a large cast-iron cookstove.

Fitzgerald grinned impishly. "Not yet you ain't, but who knows?"

"If I bite you, then you got a complaint."

"Speaking of biting," Abbey interrupted, eyes full of happiness. "I'll not put an end to your bickering, but to keep your strength up for another bout can I fix some breakfast?"

"I ain't hungry," Whitey replied, taking a seat at the table.

"Me, neither." Deacon said, dropping his backside into a chair across from him. "I'd take coffee and a shot of whiskey if you happen to have a bottle stashed anywhere around here."

"I do. Bought it special for you." She filled a mug of hot coffee from the pot on the stove and placed it at his left hand, then got the bottle out of a cabinet. She extracted the cork, poured a splash in a tumbler and set to his right. "You have the most eccentric taste buds ever seen."

"Many thanks, Abbey."

"He just be nit-picky."

"Me? Nit-picky?" Deacon blurted, chuckling thickly. "Ever hear about glass houses and throwing stones, Whitey? I ain't the one with hard and fast rules for how to brew tea."

"That be different."

"How so?"

"I ain't gonna give you the satisfaction by enumerating the differences," Whitey parried, eyes tapering into slits. He tapped a finger on the tabletop as if to accentuate his argument, then abruptly stopped and began poking it at him. "A man who washes coffee down with liquor ain't got a sophisticated enough palate to appreciate the pleasantries of properly prepared tea."

"We can't all be highfalutin, Whitey."

"I ain't no highfalutin man. I be down to earth."

"You two are precious," Abbey said, laughing musically. "You haven't been together in a number of years, yet start back into squabbling as easily as a pair of cooing mourning doves."

"We likes each other, that's all there be to it."

Coburn tipped her a wink. "I enjoy the grumbler's company."

"And I be fond of his gloomy-gus ways."

"Mercy sakes. A gloomy-gus? Me?"

"If'in I'm a grumbler you be a gloomy-gus."

Coburn swigged a mouthful of coffee. A tremor went through his fingers when he put the mug down. He clamped his hands together and gave them a dismissive shrug. "My muscles are still tired. Too many miles in the saddle, but had no time to fritter because Creede beckoned."

"You be here now and we gots to talk," Whitey said, click-clicking nervously. "There be a woman on the lookout for you. She be as brassy and vinegary as a salty old sailor."

"Lucinda Enochelli."

Fitzgerald was flustered. "You know her?"

"No," Deacon grunted, eyes pulling tight. "As far as I can tell I ain't ever met her, but in the last while I've heard the name plenty. The woman is as tenacious as a dog with a bone, but I know her not. Its seems as though I'm always winding up somewhere one step ahead or behind where she's at, and to be honest, I ain't got much interest in whatever it is she's selling."

"You wants me to tell her that, Deacon?"

Coburn mulled it over as he had another swallow of coffee. "No, I suppose not. I ought to respect her persistence enough to hear her say her piece. She's been beating the bushes to find me and since we're now here in the same town I guess I can have a sitdown with her."

"Is that what you wants me to tell her?"

"Tell her jack-squat, Whitey. Let it play out on its own."

"She knows where I live," Abbey said blandly. "I see no reason whatsoever to initiate contact with her. Forgive me, and I will stipulate that I could be wrong, but in the here and now, I implicitly do not trust the woman. She has a mysteriously dark aura that perturbs me."

Fitzgerald hissed a low whistle. "Miss Abbey be onto something important. I sees the woman every day and she treats me kindly, but it be clear that she's hiding some secrets."

"I ain't concerned about any of it," Deacon replied, scratching at his beard. "No reason to borrow trouble. I ain't ever claimed to be a saint, but I always tried to do my best. There ain't no apologies left in me for regrets and failures. If Lucinda Enochelli is holding a marker against me, I'll handle it and move on. It cannot possibly be worse than the places I've already been."

"That's certainly true, Deacon."

"I betcha she's got nothing."

"Even if that's so, Whitey, sometimes, like it or not, nothing can be an abundance of something." Deacon emptied the mug in a rush, then tossed back the whiskey and mashed it between his teeth before allowing it to trickle down his throat in measured squirts. "Can that be the end of discussions for now? I'd like to make acquaintances with the closest outhouse."

"I'll walks you to it, then I gots errands and work."

"Let me get a shirt and boots on."

An hour later, Abbey Langton was in a hardwood rocker on the porch, hands clenched in her lap as she scrutinized her father. He was lethargic and dozing in the other chair. She wanted to deny her observations, but the accumulation of evidence was becoming progressively difficult to renounce. Her heartbeat was rapid. She had detected diverse symptoms in him that were disquieting; connecting the dots prodded her to draw startling conclusions.

His eyes flickered open. He pressed a bleak smile at her. "I conked out."

"What's going on, Deacon?"

"Whitey never changes, does he?"

"Arthritis has him slowing up," she answered, releasing her hands as she rocked haltingly. "We spend Sundays together. The boys think he walks on water or some such thing. He wrestles and jokes around, and regales them with yarns and tall tales, of which he has an unlimited supply. You should know that he's told them a dozen or more involving you."

"He's a bigtime embellisher."

"Perchance, but he speaks of you in heroic terms."

"I ain't no hero, Abbey."

Her eyes narrowed and her voice took on the dour resonance of a schoolmarm when she spoke. "Your modesty is commendable, but please do not burst the bubble for Langton and Yaz. Whitey hasn't quite put you in the mythic category, but he has underscored strengths and traits I'd like to see emulated in my sons. I can and have used you as a positive object lesson."

"Don't build my pedestal too high."

"Be true to who you are, Deacon."

"I'll toe whatever line you need me to, Abbey."

She giggled softly. "That's handy information to have."

His eyelids started flapping like broken shutters. He groaned and became rigid. His breathing quickened into wheezy gulps and his hands trembled into fists. Then, as unexpectedly as it came upon him, the spasm passed. He bent forward and held the sides of his head in his hands. His complexion was mottled; red and white blotches discolored his cheeks.

"What's wrong with you?"

"Nothing, Abbey. Just need more sleep."

"Do you swear to that, Deacon?"

"It in no way rises to that level of importance," he rasped, dragging his fingers through his hair as he straightened in the chair. "Were you able to get a start on editing this morning?"

"Yes. I got the manuscript out . . . " She snappily terminated her response and glared at him in a mix of distress and anger. "No more diversions. What is going on with your health?"

"Merely tuckered out and raggedy around the edges."

"There's something you're not telling me, Deacon."

"I'm not sure of your inference."

"Being coy and reserved are generally acceptable, but now is not the time or place to practice your charm," she said, eyeing him with a demanding intensity that was palpable. "Your hands are palsied and you just had a convulsion of some kind. I'm pulling rank on you. No more hedging. I am your daughter, and I expect nothing less than honesty and full disclosure."

Coburn exhaled and his tree-branch shoulders slumped as his body seemed to sink and shrink into the rocker. His mouth constricted in such tautness that the wooly-worm covering his upper lip appeared to be a picketed gate plunging shut. He glowered at nothing in particular, detached and stony-faced. Watery mist glistened in his eyes, which were unfocused.

"Deacon, talk to me, please."

"I got some news awhile back, Abbey."

"What kind of news?"

Two months ago, snow was fluffing from a leaden sky when Deacon Coburn rode along Main Avenue in Durango. He was tensely scouting for a shingle. His eyesight was giving him fits. Clear and distinct one moment, then without warning he would experience blurriness and black spots. He could determine no redress to rectify the troublesome pattern.

A pedestrian he encountered had given him directions, and by his estimation, he figured he had to be close. Gilgal kept sniffing and snorting, acting skittish and excited. He patted its mane and muttered a command to behave. The gelding reluctantly acquiesced; he could feel eagerness coursing through its muscular frame, and he vaguely wondered why.

He came to a two-story brick house with a broad porch. Prominently displayed on a pole near the street was the sign he had been seeking. He pulled up, dismounted and flipped the reins into a knot over the hitching rail. A kink between his shoulder blades caused him to wince as he climbed the steps. He removed his hat and shook it, then opened the door and stepped inside.

After introductions followed by a half-hour of poking and prodding, which included having his ears probed and eyes almost turned inside out, Coburn alighted on a wingback chair in Doc Fralick's office to impatiently wait. A swirl of frustration percolated in his belly because the medical man demonstrated an audacious over familiarity that grated on his nerves. The doctor sat behind his desk preoccupied in turning pages and studying several textbooks.

Coburn's elbows and knees were tingly from having his reflexes repeatedly tested. He surveyed the room. The décor was masculine, the carpentry rich and ornate. There was a large picture on a shelf that garnered his attention—not the photograph itself because in his view the subjects were unrecognizable. The intricately designed frame fascinated him. It was carved and tooled reddish wood with stones embedded in it; three on each of the four sides.

He started to stand so as to appraise it more closely, but dizziness accompanied by a wave of nausea made him lightheaded. He massaged his temples and uttered a groan. The sour bile and vexing irritation commingled in him and took up residence as a solidified lump in his gullet. He crunched forward and clapped his hands. "Are we ever gonna get to it, Doc?"

"Yes, of course," the doctor said, tapping one of the books. "I am quite absorbed by all that I've been reading. The research is extensive, but by no means conclusive. We're talking about your brain and central nervous system. It would be disingenuous for me to foster false hope by telling you that medical knowledge in those areas provides categorical answers."

"Hope is always good," Deacon replied, smiling wryly. "Hope fixes us."

Curiosity sparked in Fralick's eyes. "Sounds like a poem."

"Long ago words from a friend."

"Wisdom, Deacon. Pure wisdom."

"I'd not disagree."

"You're a man of faith?"

Coburn slouched back. "From my earliest years."

"As am I," Doc stated evenly. "I had to do tons of book-learning along with practical training and dissections of cadavers. One cannot delve into the complexities of human anatomy without concluding that a Supreme Being is the catalyst at work in the masterpiece of life."

Coburn nodded in approval. "A logical and upright evaluation of an ordinary apple would compel the same deduction. Nature itself is an interwoven orchestration that proclaims the language of God. Humankind would do well to listen and heed its truth." He squinted inflexibly. "Hope fixing us has to do with authentic hope, which can only be found in the eternal."

"We'll have no debate, you and I."

"Can we get to the nitty-gritty?"

"The marrow of the matter?" Doc queried, chuckling.

"Yes, let's dig at the marrow."

Fralick swiveled in his chair. "How long have you had these headaches?"

"Ten years or more, I guess. Off and on."

"Have you ever had head trauma?"

Coburn tilted sideward and his face screwed into a quizzical grimace. He thrust an index finger against his temple and jiggled it around while his jaw flexed. His countenance became almost surly. "I was knocked unconscious with the butt-end of a rifle way back when."

"How long were you blacked out, Deacon?"

"No idea. Got revived by a horse licking my face."

"Any other trauma?"

"Does war count, Doc?"

"Likely, yes."

Coburn moved around in the chair as though the cushion had instantaneously converted into an entanglement of tacks and broken glass. His gaze darkened and dulled as the lines in his forehead deepened. "I was in the thick of the slaughter at Fredericksburg and Chancellorsville, then had a bellyful of hand-to-hand killing at Gettysburg and walked off the battlefield."

"Consciously made a choice to do so?"

"No. Completely disengaged."

"What happened next, Deacon?"

"I wandered aimlessly westward."

"Aimlessly?"

"Had amnesia for a time."

Fralick perked forward. "Short-term?"

"Almost a year."

"When the fugue passed were there memory gaps?"

"Not at all," Deacon answered, eyes hard and steely. "*Everything* surged to the forefront. My past was a spinning kaleidoscope that put the period of memory loss in context. I had total recall of relationships and experiences. I may be a mite slow on the uptake nowadays, but still have no difficulties remembering. So what's the prognosis, Doc? You got one or not?"

"I wish I had better news," the physician replied, compassion brimming in his eyes. "My best analysis of your symptoms and history combined with the information I compiled from my medical books leads me to believe that you have an inoperable brain tumor."

"I'm a private man, so mum's the word."

"Certainly, Deacon. It's confidential."

"It ain't new information, Doc."

"I beg your pardon?"

"Some time ago I saw a doctor in East Texas when I traveled there to say goodbye to a good friend," Deacon said, brandishing a cockeyed smile. "The sawbones had the foulest breath I ever smelled. He examined me, though not as thoroughly as you. Nor did he ask any questions about head trauma. He gave me some powders and told me I probably had a few years."

"It could be down to a few months now."

"If that's the way of it, so be it, Doc."

"That's a dignified perspective."

Coburn hardened and scoffed at the idea. "Ain't got nothing to do with dignity. The days written for me were done so by the Creator. All that's left for me is to run the race hard to the finish line. It's appointed unto man once to die. No one gets to cancel that appointment."

Fralick pursed his lips and waggled his fingers against the desktop. "I'm a tad confused. Why'd you stop to see me if you already knew the diagnosis? For old times' sake?"

"Old times' sake? What's that supposed to mean?"

"I'm not mistaken, Deacon. I assure you."

Coburn frowned frostily. "You got me befuddled, Doc. I came partially for confirmation, but mostly to find out if there's anything to be done to help with the lapses in my vision."

"Spectacles, perhaps."

"Tried 'em. More trouble than they're worth."

"I can prescribe laudanum for the pain."

"Not necessary. The pain ain't intolerable."

"That's difficult to imagine."

"It's my noggin, Doc."

Fralick stared at him. "You don't remember me, do you, Deacon?"

"Should I? Have our paths crossed?"

"Karl Fralick. Winter of '78."

Coburn sat up straight, eyes crimped. "Fort Union."

"I told you I'd never forget your horse."

"That you did."

"I recognized you when you rode up."

"Sorry for my forgetfulness," Deacon said, manifesting a contrite hunch of his shoulders. He laughed, dry and reticent. "To my credit, I warned you I was a mite slow on the uptake."

"My wife is elsewhere. I'd not like her to miss you."

Coburn stood. "I got miles to go."

Fralick spun the chair around to glance out the window. "Not to worry," he said, grinning broadly. His lips parted wide and wider as his eyebrows sloped up. He closed the textbooks and shuffled them aside. His naturally ruddy skin-tone blushed into bold crimson on his cheeks. He got up and held the door open. Coburn exited the office and Fralick trailed him.

Deacon Coburn ambled onto the porch and took note that it was no longer snowing. He slid his hat on and glanced upward. Contentment tugged at him and pleated the lines around his eyes. Patches of blue were rupturing through the grayness. The air was as fresh and sweet as the advent of springtime. He inhaled deeply, like a man savoring the taste of newness.

He noticed a woman petting the silver-dappled buckskin, a toddler at her side. The horse was not docile; its whinny had the features of a cheerful guffaw as it stomped its hoofs. Her back was to him and she was talking to the child. Coburn stepped down the stairs. His vision blurred and a haze floated above her like a halo. He approached and heard her telling the boy about the stones in the horse's bridle. She turned around. His heart clogged up his throat.

"Max? What on earth?"

"Actually, it's Maxine now," she said, hugging him. "Maxine Fralick." They clung to each other as though they were drowning in an ocean of emotions. The firmly emphatic embrace extended for several minutes and the plethora of silent tears shed were audible. Neither seemed capable or willing to let go, as if they required the mutual strength to remain on their feet.

Coburn had his hands on her shoulders. "I swear, I thought you were dead."

"Charley sacrificed his life for me."

Coburn broke free and eased backwards to regard her. Her cheeks were rosy, strawberry tresses framing her face and bouncy on her shoulder. The hard-edged cowgirl he had known as Max Dawson wore a fashionable dress and was becoming thicker in the middle. He coughed to clear his throat. "I ain't one to criticize or complain, but you should've contacted me."

"Apologies, Deacon."

"Accepted, but not needed."

"When Smoky Crowe was killed, everything came unglued," she explained bluntly. "I buried Charley and walked away from his grave fully intending to go to *WT Ranch*, but I was physically and emotionally exhausted. I rode in solitude and meditated on the whole shebang, and right or wrong, came to a rigid decision to put all the former things behind me."

"I understand that kind of difficult choice."

"I cut myself off from everyone, Deacon. I didn't even try to wire or write anyone," she said, averting her eyes as if she was disconcerted. "I was camped out by the river on the outskirts of Durango, resting and reflecting for a few days, when I met Karl while he was fly fishing. One thing led to another and my heart was spinning. We got married in April '89." She caressed her midsection. "Now I'm the momma of one and in about three months it'll be two."

"Well, glory be."

She hoisted the lad onto her hip. "Say hello to Cody Dawson Fralick."

"Nice to meet you, Cody."

He played shy. She ruffled his carrot-colored hair. "He's an urchin, Deacon."

"No doubt," he replied, distracted and bemused. His eyes lit up as he reached out and rubbed the gelding's neck. "Gilgal was frisky and enlivened when we bellied up to this spot. My trustworthy mount *knew* you were here." He turned around and took a long gander at the house. He brusquely wheeled about to peer incredulously into her eyes. "The picture frame."

"Yes. Our wedding picture."

"The stones?"

"Karl made the beautiful frame," she said, pride in her voice. "The stones are from where Charley Jondreau stood strong and watched Smoky Crowe die." A glint of reverence showed in her eyes. "Seems like a lifetime or more ago. I've changed, but I'm still the same, I think."

"The flesh never loses its instinctive defaults."

She chuckled demurely. "That'd be my assessment."

"I've got many miles ahead of me, Max."

"Maxine," she corrected as she sidestepped and her son clambered down. "Turn yourself around, Deacon, and go inside. I'll give you a good feed for supper and you'll stay the night so we can do some proper visiting, then I'll send you off with a stick to your ribs breakfast."

"I'd not want to intrude."

"It's no intrusion if I insist."

"Deacon," Doc said, chortling quite jauntily. He had taken a seat on the top step of the porch to observe the reunion as a bystander. "My wife

Maxine is a Sunday school teacher and a respected member of the community, but allow me to assure you that the contrary and mulish ways of Max can whipsaw out awfully quick. You'd be wise to capitulate to her wishes."

Coburn had another look at the sky, where there was now more blue than gray. He doffed his hat and held it at his waist as he bobbed his head in surrender, which stimulated a hearty gust of laughter from the doctor. The two-year-old teetered past him, and then, while he nibbled on his bottom lip to suppress the gleam of a smile, Deacon Coburn rambled to the front door.

When her father finished his recollections from March in Durango, he got up and went inside to acquire a few items from his saddlebags. Abbey Langton remained in her rocker, eyes moist and backbone stiffened. She had listened attentively and made no comments or raised any questions. Now, as she attempted to process the information, her senses were flooded.

The congested neighborhood seemed to be even more overcrowded than usual, swarming with men and women doing their business oblivious to her disjointed feelings. Her thoughts were helter-skelter and tripping backwards. There was distressing tension circling around her lungs like a barbed-wire tourniquet being twisted tighter with each shallow breath she took.

A deliberate exercise of inhaling deeply swelled her chest and she shivered as the rigidity lessened. Another slow and intentional intake of oxygen served to decrease the discomfort to a near normal level. She continued to be purposeful in managing her breathing until the turmoil released, and with her eyes closed, she found herself swathed in a sweet memory.

She was nine years old and secure in her cozy childhood home in Ohio. The kitchen table was set, and the tasty aroma from a tureen of chicken and dumplings filled the candlelit room. She sat across from the straight-shouldered handyman she knew as Mr. Lawrence. Her mother served them heaping helpings, then took her seat at the head of the table.

"I'm hungry and grateful, Angela. Thank you."

"You're most welcome, Lawrence."

"Jobs are getting done. The pole corral is functional," he said impassively. "The porch is repaired, too. I shored up the foundation and replaced floorboards, so it has lost its droop."

"Just in time for snow to fly. I can feel it in my bones."

"Can you really, Mom?"

"No, that's just an expression, Abbey."

"Mr. Lawrence, will you go someplace else when wintertime comes?"

He put his fork down. "Is there a problem, Miss Abbey?"

She gave him an ambiguous shrug. "Nope."

"Have I worn out my welcome?"

"Not at all, Lawrence," Angela answered as the briefest of smiles shimmered at him. She promptly switched attention to her daughter, eyes contracting. "Why do you ask, Abbey?"

"We're kind of getting to be a family, aren't we?"

Angela shrank back in her chair. "Do I understand your question?"

"This is nice, isn't it?"

"Of course," her mother replied warily. "What are you getting at, Abbey?"

"I was thinking, is all."

"Thinking what, Abbey? And be specific."

"Christmas, Mom."

"Yes?"

"If Mr. Lawrence is staying we have to make plans."

"That's a splendid idea, dear."

"I will be here for Christmas," he said, heartfelt and plainspoken. "I would not dare miss it. Unless, of course, you fine ladies grow tired of my company and give me the heave-ho."

"Not me."

"Nor I," Angela declared, stifling a giggle. She cast a tender look in his direction, then forestalled and hastily looked upon her daughter. "We will begin planning after supper."

It was then that the glimpses from yesteryear began to fade into sepia shades. The images were disappearing so fast that Abbey heard herself gasp as she mentally grappled to hang onto them. The last thing she saw before the vivid recall diffused into nothingness was her mother's beaming appearance melting like wax to be transformed into a wretched death-mask.

Abbey swallowed. Her eyelids opened, which was akin to a dam being breached; rivulets whooshed down her cheeks. "Mr. Lawrence is dying, Mom," she whispered shakily. "And I'm not ready to say goodbye." Her disclosure was punctuated by a detonation of dynamite that sent a copious geyser of dirt into the atmosphere. She viewed the soaring plume of filth and thumbed away her tears, then Abbey Langton decided to go for a walk to get her heart aligned.

chapter two

Secrets & Shenanigans

"He that hath ears to hear, let him hear. But whereunto shall I liken this generation? It is like unto children sitting in the markets, and calling unto their fellows, and saying, We have piped unto you, and ye have not danced; we have mourned unto you, and ye have not lamented."

~Jesus of Nazareth~

Around noontime that day, Deacon Coburn was sitting alone on the porch, with a gift wrapped in brown butcher paper on the floor beside him. The muscles at the hinges of his jaw were cinched into cramps that intermittently puffed out. He had a piercing headache that was akin to darning needles stabbing at the backside of his eyes.

The rocker was still as he kept his focus riveted on the Bible in his lap. He had been studying the same passage for almost an hour. Sometimes the words seemed to be on the move, but he kept a finger under each line while he ruminated on the ramifications of themes penned in a first-century lockup by an itinerant cleric. Three verses from the opening chapter of Paul's epistle to his co-laborers in the Macedonian city of Philippi had him enthralled.

He read them audibly. *"According to my earnest expectation and my hope, that in nothing I shall be ashamed, but that with all boldness, as always, so now also Christ shall be magnified in my body, whether it be by life, or by death. For to me to live is Christ, and to die is gain. But if I live in the flesh, this is the fruit of my labor: yet what I shall choose I wot not."*

To live or to die. Coburn's mouth puckered into a perceptive smile. Here was Paul, a scholarly apostle, contemplating the inexplicable divide between life and death. He had earthly reasons to be discouraged because he was sequestered in a jailhouse and awaiting trial in front of the Emperor Nero, but instead of bleakness, his response to the circumstances was an audacious declaration of faith; his *earnest expectation and hope* was that no matter what vagaries the future held, God's sovereign will would prevail and he would in no way be shamed.

Paul trusted God tremendously. Coburn was impressed and inspired. He speculated as to where the foresight to be persistent in faith originated even while approaching the threshold of eternity. He reviewed what decades of personally digging through and analyzing Scripture had communicated to him about the man whose perspective had been radically altered in an encounter with the risen Christ on the road to Damascus.

The missionary tentmaker from Tarsus had accomplished and suffered much on behalf of the Kingdom of God. In his migrations throughout the Mediterranean world dominated by the Romans, the Hebrew of Hebrews and former Pharisee badgered the establishment by boldly proclaiming Christ crucified and resurrected. He confronted darkness, and in doing so, he incurred the ire of potentates along with enduring a multitude of hardships.

By his own accounting, he had been whipped five times and beaten with rods on three occasions. He experienced shipwrecks three times, and on one of those debacles, floundered on the open sea for a night and a day. He constantly kept on the move, yet there was no refuge for him because danger plagued him; in the city, country or at sea Paul coped with peril from Jews, Gentiles and false believers. He had known hunger and thirst for the sake of the gospel.

Coburn marveled and wondered anew: How could a flesh and blood human being rise above pitiless misery and adversity to write exhortations and insightful certainties, which were in fact, living truths that spoke across the ages? The conclusion was that Paul of Tarsus obviously put into practice what he believed and taught to others; to him temporal misfortunes were brief and momentary afflictions because he remained fixated on the eternal reward.

That example forcefully cuffed Coburn in the chops. Dryness creepy-crawled up his throat. The principles of eternity were ingrained in him, but just now, those precepts coiled into a stranglehold that would not relent, and was at once, pleasurable and disconcerting. He exhaled in a rush as the exceedingly real challenge sank roots deeper into his heart.

He closed his eyes. "Our Father who art in heaven," he murmured keenly. "You are my light and my salvation, whom shall I fear? You are my strength in weakness, of whom shall I be afraid? As I walk through the valley of the shadow of death I will fear no evil for thou art at my side step by step. Truly my soul waiteth upon thee. May your grace shine through the darkness that seeks to encompass me. Hear my cry, O God; attend unto my prayer. Amen."

Slippery warmth tickled the downy fuzz at the nape of his neck as counsel from a dream took hold of his senses: *Never stop kicking and punching, preacher-man.* He sat up straight and stiffened his backbone. Determination stamped itself on his face and he purposed in his heart to be true and faithful until, in that mystifying transformation, he entered heaven's gates.

He stared at his Bible, then fluttered pages until he came to a treasured bookmark. It was a dog-eared letter that he kept at the center of the Good Book. The stationery was yellowed, the creases fragile and damaged. He took it out, but refrained from unfolding it. With tender care he simply held the keepsake against his bosom for several moments, then returned it to its slot.

A sheen of dampness shone on his cheeks. He blinked repetitiously, as if his eyelids were broken shutters being battered by a windstorm. The flapping frenzy quivered to a stop. He sat back and took a dozen relaxing breaths, then Deacon Coburn drowsed into a nap where memorable sketches from long ago happenings invigorated his courageous willpower.

"Whatcha doing, Papa?"

Coburn woozily joggled awake. His head went side to side in mechanical monotony as the sandman's fog cleared. He grinned when he saw his grandsons in front of him. "Resting up."

"For what?" LC asked chirpily.

"The big rest."

Yaz frowned hard. "Whatcha mean?"

"I got tough slugging ahead."

"We can help."

"Yeah-huh."

Coburn worked his jaw so that it thrust forward as he thoughtfully cupped a hand around his chin-whiskers. "I reckon that to be a factual assessment. You're youngsters, but not greener than grass pups, so let's set matters straight with no punches pulled or ducked." He bore in on them. "You can help by bucking up to be the men gaining traction inside your skin."

LC crinkled an eyebrow. "Inside our skin?"

"Men become the choices boys make," Deacon said, an ominous nuance in his husky voice. "That's why putting your brains to work is essential. Thinking situations through to take results into consideration can reduce blunders. Not eliminate errors or oversights, but at least lessen them. No one gets to live without their share of slipups or lapses in judgment."

"Did you make mistakes?"

"Of course, Yaz. None that I take pride in," Deacon replied frankly. "Some of my gaffes knocked me on my buttocks and put their mark on my outlook, but none defeated me and that's a lesson you gentlemen must learn." His hands came together atop his Bible, which was situated on his lap. "Everyone has to develop the savvy to rise above and soldier on past inevitable mistakes because that's where wisdom grows and character is developed."

"Papa, you sound like Mom."

"Yeah-huh."

Coburn chuckled. "Hearing positive instructions from different sources ought to give you boys an edge, so listen closely. Wallowing in false steps and feeling sorry for yourself ain't at all useful. Doing that beats you down and your life will be defined by the mistake, which can be tragic. New chances and new choices are *always* available to those who dare to seize them."

LC sat in the other rocker and was immediately joined by his brother. Their faces were matched expressions of curiosity, eyes widened and brows scrunched into furrows. LC puffed up his chest. "Me and Yaz have lots of daring in us. We know what it means to take chances."

"Yeah-huh."

"Daring will become recklessness if it's not moderated by wisdom," Deacon said as he reached down and picked up the butcher paper wrapped gift. "Our enthusiasms need to be tamed and channeled for purposes that are bigger than our minds can ever grasp, which is why the One who created us provided a guidebook that enriches our intelligence and perspective."

"The Bible," LC stated, shrugging.

"A wondrously complex riddle of revelations."

Yaz scowled. "A riddle?"

Coburn gave him a gentle smile. "I was a young boy and now I am an old man. The Bible has been an integral part of my life from my childhood onward. I have studied it, memorized it, applied it, and in frail and fallible efforts endeavored to live it. On all my trails, it has never failed to amaze me or engage my intellect to unravel bits and pieces of the mystery."

"Mom uses it to teach us morality."

"Yeah-huh."

"A lifelong learning," Deacon said quietly. He repositioned so as to get eye-level with his Lakota Sioux grandson. "Yaz, occurrences being what they were and are puts me in a thorny dilemma where I must express regret and gain a measure of forbearance from you. I have something for Langton, but nothing for you because I wasn't aware that you were here."

"Yeah-huh."

Coburn resumed, dead-eyed solemn. "Take to heart what I wrote for Langton, and know that I am now obligated to this promise, Yaz: I'm going to make arrangements to order a Bible exactly like this one. And just in case I move on before it arrives, I will write words special for you, which your mother can transcribe in your Bible. Truth from me to you."

Yaz nodded agreeably. "Yeah-huh."

"Yeah-huh," Deacon said, shooting him an affable grin. He then handed the package over to his other grandson. "Make this your go-to book on the roads that carry you through life."

LC unceremoniously tore the brown wrapping off and tossed it aside. He slowly turned the black cowhide Bible over in his hands, then sniffed it. "It's just like yours, Papa."

"Except it's new. Mine is over twenty years old," Deacon replied blandly. "Now stand up straight and tall, and read aloud the handwritten note opposite the presentation page."

"Ah, Papa. Do I have to?"

"As a matter of fact, yes you do."

LC scuffled his feet and momentarily bellyached. His cheeks flushed as he glanced awkwardly at his brother. His spine and shoulders became wooden. Then, he delivered the message clearly, pausing here and there to silently sound out unfamiliar pronunciations.

> Proverbs 4:23—"Keep thy heart with all diligence; for out of it are the issues of life."

> Langton—Always guard the wellspring of your heart. To do so means that you must be genuine in seeking to understand the Bible. Do not treat it as a symbol of anything because it is God's Word to us; it's an infinite revelation imparted by an infinite God, which means that it cannot be completely comprehended by the

finite minds of mankind. That fact should never hinder its study because not only does its pages provide opportunity to explore the Creator's intricacies, we also uncover the heart and soul of the human race struggling to achieve significance and meaning in the midst of the disorderly messes that are life in a fallen world. The Bible never sanitizes the human experience, but instead, we ascertain how to reconcile our personal battles because in the real-life context of God's Word, faith and doubt are involved in the fisticuffs of a rowdy barroom punch-out. While you guard your heart and reflect on your path know that God is not threatened by honest dissent or skepticism, but hypocrisy and compliance to religiosity is abhorrent to him.

Proverbs 4:26—"Ponder the path of thy feet, and let all thy ways be established."

Many prayers,

Papa

When he came to the end Langton Coburn Beadle had twinkles in his eyes and his kisser was wrinkled inquisitively. "Thank you, Papa, but there's some words I don't understand."

"Yeah-huh."

"You got a dictionary, don'tcha?"

"Yes, Papa," LC answered politely.

"The two of you get to it at the kitchen table. I'll expect a report later," he said, rising to his feet. "I'm taking a stroll and will return soon enough." He paused until they scrambled inside. His face tensed as he tottered off the porch. He had a cursory look around, then Deacon Coburn tucked his hands in the pockets of his pants and accelerated toward the nearest privy.

In Durango, Maxine Fralick draped a small blanket over her son on the chesterfield in the living room. He had spent much of the morning in the woodshop with his father and was now snoring in whispery snuffles. She brushed aside his unruly hair and bent low to buss his forehead. When she stood erect, her hands went to support the small of her back.

She sighed and took a backward step. A twinge went through her distended abdomen, then the baby gave an energetic kick or elbow. She smiled and rubbed her belly in a circular pattern as she walked directly to her husband's office. "Is that bassinet finished yet?"

He looked up from behind his desk, where he was coordinating a stack of files while munching on a ham sandwich. "As a matter of fact my part of the project was done as of an hour or so ago." He wiped his mouth with a linen napkin, grinning roguishly. "Cody helped with the final touches, but now, per your instructions, the woodwork needs some frills and such."

"You are an exasperating man, Karl."

"Why, whatever do you mean?"

"I have been anxiously awaiting the opportunity to get started sewing, and you know that full well, Mr. Fralick," she answered, eyes sporting sharpness at him. "I have lace and satin material at the ready, but need to see the baby's bed and make proper measurements before I can get started on the skirt. You have purposely kept me in the dark as to its look and design."

"I had my reasons."

"Were they worth getting me frustrated?"

"I wanted the craftsmanship to be a surprise, Maxine."

"When do I get to be surprised?"

"It would be good for you to hold your horses until Cody wakes up," he replied, taking a bite of the crusty bread. "He is so excited to be involved in these preparations for his little sister or brother. I'm not sure how much he actually understands, but he has surely picked up on our enjoyment and anticipation. When he's up and about we'll bring the bassinet in for you."

"I will hold my horses that long and no longer, Mr. Fralick."

"Message received, ma'am."

"So I'll not have to stomp my feet?"

"That'd not be a healthy choice."

"Perhaps not, but I'll do so if necessary."

"A completely avoidable demonstration," he said, finishing off his lunch. He dabbed his lips with the napery, then blithely winged it onto the plate. "You shall be appreciative. I am particularly pleased by the series of intricate details I managed to chisel into the spindles."

"Now I'm all the more eager to see it."

He held up both hands and urgently pressed them in her direction. "Just hang onto your horses because I have something to discuss with you as your doctor not as your husband."

"That's a hocus-pocus I'd like to see you pull off," she gibed as she slowly sat in a wingback chair. "Are we going to play a game of pretend and make-believe?"

"You know what I mean, Maxine. Don't be difficult."

"Me? Difficult? Never."

Their eyes met for an instant and a murmur of amusement passed between them. He put an elbow on the desktop and his lips flat-lined in a bottled-up smirk. "Be that as it may, I noted that you skipped breakfast this morning, and yesterday you only pecked at one meal."

"No appetite, Karl. I'm just not hungry."

"You have to keep your strength up, Maxine."

"I drink milk and nibble throughout the day."

"Heartburn? Indigestion?"

"Not so much, Doc Fralick," she answered casually. "On those infrequent times when I do experience an upset stomach I have that antacid you prescribed, plus peppermints. And, before you ask, I have nothing further to report in regards to pregnancy issues."

"You are an irascible and obstinate woman."

"I never heard that complaint during our courtship."

"I was lost in the promise hidden in your eyes."

"Nor on our wedding night."

He reddened as a smile veered across his face. "All too true, so I withdraw the comment with displeasure that it was ever raised. Your stubbornness has a delightful bend to it."

"You bear that in mind for future reference, Mr. Fralick."

"I will indeed."

"On another matter," she said, snappy and clipped. "I visited Dolly this morning and took over a basket of fresh-baked biscuits. It was gratifying to cuddle her bundle of blessing. Katey Rae is a sweetie-pie. Do you know what her father has planned for that baby girl?"

"Making a fisherwoman out of her?"

"I suspect that's a given, Karl," she replied briskly. "Malcolm has conceived a brainstorm about getting Katey betrothed to Cody. Dolly tells me that she truly supposes he's serious."

"What kind of dowry do you guess we could get?"

"Karl, don't encourage that nutty notion." She rose and sidled to the doorway. "I'm going to peek at our son, and perhaps, rouse him so as to finally lay eyes on the bassinet." The glow of happiness shadowed her expression, and despite her enlarging girth, her gait had a perky bounce as she departed. Her heart was exhilarated and overflowing, and on this day, Maxine Fralick couldn't foresee any scenario that had the potential to hinder or intrude on her serenity.

A half-mile from South Fork, the two-mule team plodded along in docile servitude. Pete Axler held the reins loosely as the buckboard rolled at a steady pace, while his daughter kept up a barrage of chatter. It was a balmy noontime. The high roof of the sky had been painted bluer than blue and decorated with brushstrokes of wispy clouds along the southern horizon.

A bald eagle was circling above the Rio Grande on their right. Amanda stopped talking and held her breath in awe. She pointed excitedly when it dipped its wings and was a mere ten yards or so above the waterline. Pete joined her in observing the magnificent bird of prey, which seemed to hover for a suspended moment before it plunged into the river. There was splashing and it caught a fish in its talons, then the eagle flapped mightily and carried its meal away.

The two continued to watch in silence. Axler took the opportunity to get a word in edgewise. "The eagle likely waited half the morning to grab that trout," he said, giving her a gentle nudge. "It got its reward of a meal by being patient and vigilant. I have been busy developing those attributes while driving and listening for an opening to speak."

"Oh, Daddy. You exaggerate."

"Nope, not at all."

"There were lulls."

"Not many, peanut."

"Have I been a blabbermouth?"

"I heard and paid attention to every word, Amanda Irene," he replied, giving her another little prod with his shoulder. "More importantly I discerned all the underneath emotions."

"Underneath emotions?"

"Words don't come from nothing, peanut."

She slouched back and toyed with the chinstrap ribbons of the wide-brimmed sunbonnet as she scanned his expression. "Words spring from feelings, is what you're telling me."

"Yep."

"And because of my talkative ways you understand my feelings?"

"For an old-school man of corrals and stables to understand a young girl's feelings would be a miracle out of the Bible," he answered, flinching a feeble shrug. "The best I can do is hear how your frame of mind is shaped by your feelings, then try to figure what all of that means."

"So what do you hear, Daddy?"

"That you want to live in Creede."

"Is that news to you?"

"Nope."

"Mom won't listen to me."

"We can discuss it." He turned sideways and eyeballed her. She carried her mother's winsome beauty and single-minded disposition, but had his chalky coloration—flaxen hair as blond as to be white, and alabaster skin that, unlike his lined and weathered features, was smooth and unblemished. He smiled, smallish and gaunt. "You can do anything you want, peanut."

"I can?"

"Yep."

"Really?" she squealed, slapping her hands together. "I can go live with Abbey and get a job and everything? You will let me move to Creede? I can go and do and have fun and be me?"

"You can do anything you want, peanut," he said again, shoulders slumping forward. He twiddled the reins and stared at her. "Just remember that every choice has a consequence."

"I know that, Daddy."

"Do you, Amanda Irene?" he enquired in a tone that had taken on a tenderized severity. "Life is all about the choices we make. We learn to adjust or flow with the stuff we have no control over, but our conscious choices are different. We become our choices. When all our choices get piled up on top of each other that's who we are, whether we like it or not."

"I don't need a lecture. I get those from Mom."

"I ain't lecturing you, peanut," he replied in unreserved sternness. "I was under the impression you wanted to have a discussion and that means an exchange of viewpoints and information." He modified his posture to look at her. "Am I right or wrong about that?"

She met his gaze with a flippant nod. "I'm taking note, Daddy."

"How often have you seen me whittling?"

"Too many times to be able to count."

"Think of whittling and choices," he suggested as the wagon passed the barn-board signpost welcoming them to South Fork. "Each hunk of wood I start with has artwork inside it. I have to be careful and cautious to be sure that my hand guides the blade to make the proper choices as to where to cut and where to refrain from cutting. I can fix some poor decisions and false cuts, but if I make a big foul-up at a crucial juncture, the project has to be scrapped."

"Me moving to Creede would be a big foul-up?"

"We can choose to do something in an instant that results in a heart-ache for life," he answered, shoving his hat up his forehead. He steered the buckboard into town and took a look at the Denver & Rio Grande Railroad water tower. "There's no ifs or ands, peanut. Ain't no way around the fact that we are responsible for every choice, no matter how we happen to feel."

"The gist is that choices have consequences."

"It's a law, Amanda Irene."

Early that afternoon, Deacon Coburn was back on the porch of his daughter's cabin. She had not yet returned and his grandsons were off on a carefree escapade of one kind or another. He was relaxed as he indulged in a long-time practice of playing people-watching games. The crammed and cooped up neighborhood provided a variety of opportunities.

Across the way a woman was quibbling with a man over the price of eggs and wilted vegetables he was peddling. The hagglers were hard-bitten and determined to gain the upper hand in the boisterous bartering. The dishwater-blonde had her fists firmly planted on ample hips while the chinless vendor balanced the basket of wares under an arm and turned on an oily charm. A smatter of dickering ensued, then a bargain was struck that appeared cordial.

With that entertaining transaction resolved, Coburn changed his incline in the rocker so as to monitor the pedestrian traffic on the rutted alleyway—miners, traders, buyers, sellers rushing about as if commitments had spellbinding power. He was drawn to a tall redheaded man in an animal skin robe walking with the authority of a towering shepherd's staff. Coburn gulped dryly. He felt tingling at the base of his skull and pounding between his ears. A distinct remembrance from a nightmare that had once inhabited his dreams took center-stage in his mind's eye.

The bedraggled man had wild-eyes and an unkempt orangish beard. He approached in swaggering peacock strides, then halted in front of him. "I'm looking for Abbey Langton," he said in a croaky bullfrog voice. "I have need to speak to her about secrets and delinquents."

"She's not here just now. Can I help you?"

"I am the Prophet Eliezer," he announced, stepping onto the porch. He swayed and rapped the prodigious walking stick on the floorboards before dropping his bottom in the vacant rocking chair. "I've asked around and am told that Abbey Langton is responsible for a son who runs with a scar-faced heathen Injun. I'm here to enlighten her about those hooligans."

"Mr. Eliezer . . . "

"The Prophet Eliezer."

Coburn squinted, hard-eyed and distrustful. He dismissed the correction with a flick of the wrist. "Well, Mr. Eliezer, I am the lady's father and I will be happy to chat with you about my grandsons, but I must put you on notice that I do not tolerate rudeness or unkindness."

"And who are you to tell me what is tolerable?"

"I might ask the same of you, Mr. Eliezer."

"*Who* are you, mister hoity-toity?"

"Deacon Coburn."

"I have heard that name," the Prophet Eliezer said, stroking the disheveled whiskers sprawling on his chest. "It was a barroom in Dodge City in '84. You were nowhere to be found, which according to an ill-tempered Western Union man, was good for me. He grumped and crabbed, and told me that you would put me in my place and hogtie my preaching."

Coburn smiled, drolly amused. "So you're a preacher."

"A prophet."

"An utmost high calling, Mr. Eliezer."

"I am the Prophet Eliezer and I will not be mocked."

"I dreamt of you once. It was straight-arrow true, my friend."

"We are friends?"

"I strive for friendship at all costs. Is that not gospel?"

"The gospel is a double-edged sword dividing sinners from the righteous," the Prophet Eliezer intoned, mouth twisting into an ugly sneer. "Thus saith the Lord God Almighty. There will be no mercy for those whose hearts have waxed and waned, whose ears have grown deaf and whose eyes are blinded by the trinkets and jewels of the world. The end of this iniquitous generation will be a firestorm of wrath as the reapers separate the wheat from the tares."

He stretched forth his arms, high and lifted up. "The devil sowed wicked seeds that have burgeoning roots, but depravity shall not prevail. Evil will be thrashed and torn from the earth in a glorious harvest. Angels will gather the tares and cast them into a fiery furnace. The day of the Lord cometh in splendor and magnificence, and there will be weeping and wailing and gnashing of teeth. On that triumphant day the righteous shall reign in victory and shine forth as the sun."

He inhaled audibly, and Coburn seized the moment to butt in a comeback. "Preaching at me ain't conducive to a conversation. Especially when it is a bigoted and poorly developed rant that errs on the side of judgment." He wiggled a poignant finger at him. "You ought to check out the Bible I read because it states in no uncertain terms that mercy triumphs over judgment."

"I am the Prophet Eliezer. I have spoken it, so shall it be."

"I am Deacon Coburn, and this I know: God ain't no hater," he said tenaciously. "We're created in his image, but we're cut from the crooked timber of humanity, so ain't none of us righteous. God gave his only begotten Son to redeem the soul of every man and woman."

"Evildoers will burn in everlasting hellfire."

"Why are you here, Mr. Eliezer?"

The red-haired man puzzled over the inquiry. He became detached and unresponsive. His eyeballs protruded and appeared to spin counterclockwise. Then in a single breath, a sickeningly real fragment of normalcy returned and launched a blast of vitriolic majesty that roared from his throat. "The son of Abbey Langton and the scar-faced heathen are hellions. I am here to warn you and the woman who is your daughter that they shall be cast to the outer darkness."

A chill of anger passed over Coburn. "You best leave, Mr. Eliezer."

"Heed me! Elsewise doom is coming."

"I've heard enough," Deacon said, pushing to his feet. Exhibiting a restrained ferocity, he escorted the fanatical zealot off the porch, tangling with the shepherd's staff in the fracas. He stood watchful until the Prophet Eliezer turned a corner at the end of the alley, then Deacon Coburn, intrigued and uneasy, sat and contemplated all that had transpired.

At the Oxford Hotel on 17th Street in Denver, Hans Weitzel and Stace Hawkins were preparing to have a meal in the men's only dining room. They had ordered, and were enjoying the stately ambience and each other's company. Though they had been in the big city for two weeks, on this their first visit, both remained inquisitive and curiously engrossed.

Denver, from the Arapaho *Niinéniiniiciihéhe'*, was now the third largest metropolis in the west, lagging behind Omaha and San Francisco. It was prosperous and expansive, the connecting nerve center for over a hundred different railroads that served as the gateway linking the hinterland interior to the richness of the Rocky Mountains and beyond.

Hans Weitzel, a sixty-seven year old man of seasoned experience, was beguiled by the social excesses and express industrialization of the Gilded Age. He never ceased being amazed by the mills, factories, escalating population and changes he had eye-witnessed. His forearms were on the table with his hands locked together. "It's a whole other world, Boss."

"That's what you keep telling me, Mr. Weitzel."

"I grew up on a hardscrabble farm in Germany," Hans said gingerly. "When I was your age all I knew was the cycle of sunrise and sunset. Worked from dark to dark most every day. Plowing, planting, harvesting, mucking out stalls, slopping hogs, feeding livestock, sheering sheep, fixing or building fences and pens, going to market. There was no leisure time. Now I look and see all these fancy gadgets and technology, and wonder, where does it all end?"

"New inventions likely have no limits."

"You really think so?"

"Sure. I've read Jules Verne."

"Those are just farfetched stories, Boss."

"Imagination is where newfangled ideas are born."

"Maybe you're right." Weitzel removed his tweed cap and twirled it in his hands before placing it on his lap. He rubbed a palm over his silvery scalp as he shook his head. "Look at this enormous five-story building that is truly a city within a city. It is steam heated by an on-site power plant, and has electric and gas lighting, plus water closets and vertical railways."

"Elevators."

"No matter what they're called, I'll keep taking the stairs," Hans said, lips squashing into a disdainful pucker. "You won't catch me stepping into a steel-box and trusting it."

"The future is coming at us, Mr. Weitzel."

"Not if I take my blacksmith tools to it."

Hawkins gave him an off-center grin. "That'd be a neat trick to see." He leaned back in his chair because a pallid-faced waiter in a black waistcoat and crisp white shirt arrived with their meals. The man performed his tasks, genial and efficient, then stepped back and asked if there was anything else he could get for them. Upon receiving a negative retort, he departed.

"Are we thankful, Boss?"

"Amen."

Weitzel put his knife and fork to work slicing the steak into bite-size hunks. The beef was smothered in caramelized onions and had a baked potato on the side. "We're feeding at a trough like a baron and a prince, which we ought not to take for granted. I got off that farm and was apprenticed to a wizened artisan from whom I learned the craft of forging iron objects. My brawn and brains opened doors to the future. What's going to do that for you, Boss?"

"Since the future's coming at us that's a fair question," Stace replied in a manner which could be mistaken for flippancy except for an innate coldness in his piercing blue eyes. His lips bowed upward as he masticated a mouthful of beef and onions. His hair was brown and curly, his face still babyish and fringed by peach fuzz. "I will always read and study everything possible about subjects that interest me, but lately I've been learning about law enforcement."

"That'd be a worthy field of opportunity to explore."

"Mom never told me much about my father before she passed," Stace said, continuing to eat as he talked. "And Aunt Avis gets a sourpuss if I raise a question about him. All I know is that he was a gambler and bounty hunter who got himself killed by a bad outlaw. I figure it would be an adventure walking the line between hoodlums and law-abiding society."

"A sometime dangerous adventure."

"There are dangers in breaking horses or chopping wood," Stace answered nonchalantly. "We minimize those hazards by taking precautions and doing the job right and proper. That's a lesson I heard and seen from you, Mr. Weitzel. You told me it applied to all areas of life."

"You got a firm grip on the future, Boss."

"Thank you, sir."

Weitzel flinched crabbily. "The name is Hans. Perhaps by the time we're done dealing with these bankers and lawyers you'll oblige my wishes by using it as the handle for me."

"Time tells all, Mr. Weitzel."

"We do have time to spare," Hans said shrewdly. "This filing paperwork and getting facts is turning into a waiting game, but since the expenses are being footed by the consortium seeking to purchase that hundred acre parcel *WT Ranch* owns outright we'll linger and live large."

"Should we send a telegram to Caleb?"

"No news to report, and Caleb will take no news as good news," Hans replied, cleaning his plate with a slab of bread. "So we'll take in the sights and sounds of Denver, then after all is said and done we'll return to *our* peaceful mountains." He stood, pausing to admire the frescoed walls. His face cracked in a wide smile as he headed off with his young friend beside him. Hans Weitzel planned to go to the in-house barbershop and treat Stace Hawkins to his first shave.

In Creede, Lucinda Enochelli sat on the top step of the boarding house's stoop, which was oriented on a backstreet and had a cave-like hideaway hollowed beneath it. Her eyes were strained on the main thoroughfare as she smoked a cigarette. She was engaged in a clandestine foray that did not occur daily but often enough to be referred to as commonplace.

The sun was sloping toward its nighttime destination and in a half-hour or so it would decline low enough to cast her in shadows. She had her elbows on her knees and was restless and squirmy, transferring weight from one butt-cheek to the other as if ants were building a colony in her bloomers. She dropped the spent weed and crushed it under the heel of a boot.

Her purse was at her side. She reached for it to get her fixings, but then saw the roguish duo with whom she had cultivated a covert relationship.

The boys were running and skidded to a halt in front of her. She bent forward and scowled at them. "What are you little shits doing?"

"Me and Yaz are looking for chores."

"What am I, your meal ticket?"

LC hooked his thumbs in the front belt-loops of his trousers. He bobbed side to side on the balls of his feet while making a funny face that had the effect of projecting one huge question mark. "We just wanted to earn a nickel or two for hard candy and maybe some licorice."

"Yeah-huh."

"Is that all I am to you little shits? An easy-touch chump to scam for nickels?" she asked, eyes hot. "You two bo-peep in and out of here like rabbits which makes me wonder if you are at all dependable. Is there any news to report, or do you just have deviltry up your sleeves?"

"Yeah-huh. Papa is here."

She sat bolt upright. "In Creede? Deacon Coburn?"

"Came yesterday."

"Are you two even reliable?" she queried scornfully. Her lips pinched and she discharged a gob of spittle. "That spicy snippet should have been delivered forthwith, LC." She yanked open her purse to get the drawstring pouch of tobacco and papers. Her fingers trembled as she built a ciggy in a fitful spurt. "Did you let the cat out of the bag, or is our secret still hidden?"

"Seems dumb to me, but it's under wraps."

"What about you, Yaz?"

"Yeah-huh. Me and LC are together in everything."

"Our friendship is our friendship," she said, firing up the coffin nail. "It's between us and I have reasons to keep a lid on it, which are neither here nor there." She drew a puff and exhaled it through her nostrils. "I pay you well for piddling jobs, but that'll end if you ever cross me."

"Me and Yaz are loyal."

"Yeah-huh."

"That'll prove itself out one way or the other, won't it?"

"Whatcha mean?" LC asked, frowning.

"Either you'll stay buttoned up or you'll flap your gums," she answered, moistening her lips as she took another long drag. "Silence proves loyalty, yakking proves you to be liars."

Yaz darkened, jaw clenched. "Me and LC ain't liars."

"I trust that to be so." She fluffed her shoulder-length raven hair. "I ain't going to lose any sleep because I always have bigger fish to fry than stewing over the toing and froing of a couple little shits." She snuffed out the cigarette and tossed it over their heads. "I can tell you that I ain't shuffling cards this evening. I'm going to see that sideshow freak Eliezer."

"Me and Yaz saw him yesterday afternoon."

"Finally minded my suggestion. Was it eventful?"

"He gave me and LC a scare."

"Did he?"

"Used his big stick to pin us down," LC replied edgily.

"I'd not allow that without payback."

Yaz sidestepped toward her. "Whatcha mean?"

"That lunatic needs a comeuppance."

"A comeuppance?" LC inched closer to her. "What's that?"

"Taken down a peg. Knocked off his high horse," she explained, eyes hardening. "You little shits need to prank him good. Give him a taste of what he done to you." She rummaged in her purse. "Are you up for making some mischief with me being your hush-hush helper?"

LC puzzled over the proposal. He glanced at his brother. "Whatcha think, Yaz?"

"Yeah-huh."

"This ain't no apple pie order," she said strictly. "It'll take bravery." She pulled her fisted hand from the purse and unfurled her fingers. A single firecracker and two matches were cradled in her palm. She passed them over to LC, who timidly took the offering as reluctance rumpled his brow. A shiny smile brightened her expression, and became persuasive and reassuring.

"What should we do with these?"

"You ain't stupid, LC," she answered, eyebrows tented to a high peak. "When that creepy carnival barker is at full steam, give him an old-fashioned hotfoot and make him jump. Wait until I'm there so I don't miss the fun. Afterwards maybe I'll get you little shits a whole string."

"That'd be something."

"Yeah-huh."

"Now scat and be gone."

The boys exchanged excited grins, then bolted. She never even bothered to view their hurried flight. Instead, as a naughty chuckle rumbled in her throat, she cavalierly rolled a smoke. Her heartrate quickened in expectation of what she had set in motion. She lit the weed. Grayness was seeping from the sky. Lucinda Enochelli, who on the day of her birth sixty-one years ago was given a different name, stayed on the stoop until the colors of twilight covered her.

∾∾∾

Daylight was fading on the roadway through Wagon Wheel Gap. Amanda Axler had a ramrod stiff posture on the seat beside her father while she took in the prettiness of the reddish hues flaring in the west. Her enjoyment of beauty was disrupted when the mules brayed loud complaints as the buckboard jounced through a potholed patch and pitched side to side.

"Egad, Daddy!"

"Ain't no way around that mess, peanut." He was hunched over and had a tense grip on the reins. "Especially when the driver was erratically woolgathering and got waylaid by it."

"I was daydreaming too," she said, removing the floppy sunbonnet. Her hair was tied up in a rubber-band, which she released. The golden-white tresses, straight and fine, spilled over her shoulders. "I've been thinking about choices and consequences, Daddy. Is it really a law?"

Axler scratched at the grizzly stubble on his chin. "Yep. Cause and effect, Amanda Irene. If I choose to throw a rock into still waters there'll be a splash followed by ripples. *Every* time. There's nothing anyone can do to prevent or change the effect caused by the thrown rock."

"That's not bad."

"Consequences don't necessarily have to be bad," he pointed out, relaxing his hold on the reins as the wagon cleared the gauntlet of chuckholes. He checked on the cargo to see that the crates and burlap bags of supplies were secure, then turned to her. "Many choices we make have good results, which is what we want, but weighing out decisions can be complicated."

"Because no one knows what tomorrow brings?"

"That's part of it, to be sure."

"Mom constantly nags that tomorrow has no guarantees."

"By the bye that's wise advice," he said, laidback and folksy. "Bad choices aren't always obvious, peanut. No one would reach into a roaring fire to grab hold of a red-hot rock because they'd burn their hand, but what if the danger could not be seen until it was too late?"

"The fire is hidden in some unknown tomorrow?"

His pale eyes narrowed into slits as a swell of pride swept over his face. He gave her knee a tap. "You got some wisdom there, young lady. The trick is to put it into practice, especially at the crossroads. In those places gather all the information possible and invite counsel from others because none of us have near enough brains to figure on all the chances beyond today."

"Is that how you've done it, Daddy?"

"Not always, Amanda Irene," he admitted drearily. "Should've and surely could've most times, but like you, I was once chomping on the bit to be off and on my own. I weren't no quick learner, even though my grandfather, the wisest man I've ever known, taught and modeled these principles we're hashing over. I didn't get smart and start applying the stuff he poured into me until after I hit a long stretch of rough roads, kind of like those potholes back there."

She contemplated the ebb and flow of the discourse. Her hands kept busy twirling the hair-loop around her fingers and snapping it at regular intervals. A mile passed and the only sounds to accompany the elastic twang was the revolving wheels, birdsong in the woods and the swishing tails of the mules. Then, she sighed wistfully and advanced the discussion. "Daddy, your ideas about whittling resonate with me because I can easily relate them to knitting."

"Makes sense, peanut."

"For example, take the sweater Aunt Avis commissioned me to knit," she said, sounding slightly grandiose. She repositioned her posterior to address him directly. "I had to have a pattern so I imagined it and blocked it out on paper. That was fun and it made me think through colors and schemes. Now as I work on it I cannot deviate from the plan, or else the triangle designs won't be exactly the same size. A wrong choice is a bungle costing me time unraveling."

"Life is as simple and complex as that, Amanda Irene." He touched her knee again, then raised a finger to her. "Which is all the more reason to put your imagination in gear to develop a pattern for where you want your life to go and what you expect from it. Unless you decide to be a moth fluttering mindlessly around lamplight with no particular direction or destination."

"That's interesting, I guess."

"One more thing and I'll put it to rest," he said, leaning closer to her. "A botched decision in whittling or knitting might be fixable, but repairing or unraveling a big foul-up in life may be impossible because tilling the acrimony of those consequences can follow us to our grave."

"I hear you, Daddy. Loud and clear."

"So we understand each other?"

"Choices have consequences," she replied prudently. She stared at the flickering blink of the first star for a spell, then graced him with a sly smile and added, "It's a law, Daddy." Giggles bubbled over her lips and she gave his cheek a soft peck. She slouched and crossed her arms. Her emotions were spinning, but as darkness eased across the sky, she had a plan. Home was twenty minutes away, and upon arrival, Amanda Axler intended to have a gabfest with Aunt Avis.

～～～

Meanwhile at *WT Ranch*, Avis Lahay had just completed her evening chores and was ready to extinguish the pillar-mounted oil lanterns when she heard barking. A side-door of the barn soon cracked open and Bobo scampered inside followed by Bethsuelo. The redbone hound yapped twice, did a spin move, then trotted over and she kept at its side, pigtails swinging.

"You're too late. Work's all done."

"I didn't want to shovel horse poop, Aunt Avis."

"Don'tcha think I know that, lazy-bones?" she teased, laughing in a familiar way. She sat on a bale of hay, pulled her knees up and wrapped her arms around her shins. "I've never known you to be acquainted with shovels or pitchforks." Her hair, longish and gingery, had a velvet ring holding it in a ponytail. "Pots and pans or singing songs and painting is where you shine."

"I cooked the venison stew for supper."

"It'll be a lip-smacking delight, I'm sure."

"Grandmom baked bread. Aunt Naomi made apple pies."

"Has everyone gathered at your house?"

"Waiting on the buckboard."

"Pete and Amanda will be along shortly," Avis said, removing the leather gloves. She chaffed her hands together. "We've got us a teeny piece of time here, and since I haven't seen you in a few days let's do us some visiting. Have you been hibernating or something?"

"That's just plain silly, Aunt Avis."

"What's been keeping you busy?"

"Quilting with Mommy and Grandmom."

"Sounds like fun," Avis said affably. "I wish I had talents in that area, but I'm all thumbs. I tried to learn needlepoint once, but I pricked my fingers into bruises." The dog jumped up and settled beside her, its head worming onto her lap. "Evidently poor ole Bobo has missed me."

"Daddy says Bobo has gone cuckoo."

"When did he say such a thing? And why?"

"At supper last night," Bethsuelo replied, perching edgewise on the hay bale. "Bobo has been skittish and needing lots of affection. Not behaving much." Her shoulders and eyebrows popped up. "All Bobo does now is whine or twirl in circles or mopes about like a sissy."

"What's wrong, Bobo?" Avis asked, stroking its head. The sad-eyed dog thumped its tail heavily and squirmed tighter against her. "What's troubling you, boy? Are you getting sick?"

"I know what's going on, Aunt Avis."

"Please tell me, Bethsuelo."

"Bobo is smart and sensitive."

"Of course. What is it, Bethsuelo?"

"Bobo feels what I *feel*."

Avis stiffened. "Tell me straight, muffin."

The nine-year-old pouted. "Mr. Deacon is going to heaven."

"Excuse me?"

"Mr. Deacon is going to heaven."

"How do you know?" Avis inquired, but in the same instant that the question was out she insistently waved it off. "That was dumb of me. Really dumb. I trust your intuitive insights."

"I told Mommy this morning."

"What'd she say?"

"Nothing, Aunt Avis."

"Nothing? She must've said something, Bethsuelo."

"Her heart had a big pain in it."

"Oh, dear Lord."

"I *felt* Mommy's hurt. Like I *feel* yours now."

Avis bit the inside of her bottom lip, which did not reduce its outward quiver. She gave the hound a nudge, then scrambled to her feet. "We have to get to Creede to be with Abbey."

"Mr. Deacon will need us too."

"We'll give him hugs. Lots of them."

"LC and Yaz are going to be in big trouble."

"Then we really have to scoot," Avis answered impulsively. She proceeded to douse the oil lamps—a task made difficult because Bobo tagged along underfoot. "It's too late now, but we'll go early tomorrow." Her thoughts were shimmying. "Let's be ready to unload the wagon, then we'll wash up for supper." She snuffed the final wick and shivered. Her eyes were quick to adjust to the darkness, but her vision was unclear, because Avis Lahay was crying.

The Orleans Club in Creede had a rollicking early evening crowd. A well-dressed hooker, whose good looks were obscured beneath layers of rouge and lipstick, tinkled the ivories of an out of tune piano, while revelers clustered around swaying and singing off-key. Games of faro and poker were happening, and highrollers were lined two-deep at the craps table.

Whitey Fitzgerald stood at his station watching the action through curtains of bluish smoke that parted sporadically as it wafted to the ceiling. He sipped black Darjeeling tea from a china cup and saucer, savoring its taste and floral aroma. His eyes glinted joyfully when the hard-shelled kingpin of the town meandered toward his alcove corner of the saloon.

"Whew doggies, Mr. Soapy Smith," he exclaimed with an emphatic click-click. "You got yourself a chipper and bushy-tailed bunch of customers putting money into play."

"Grist to the mill, Whitey," the rakish entrepreneur replied, loosening the knot in his cravat as he took a seat in the barber chair. "We're gonna make us a chunk of change tonight, and you'll know it because I'll be the one crying all the way to the bank." He released the top three buttons of his jacket. "Are you spry enough for a haircut and a trim of my beard?"

"I ain't fagged out," Whitey answered, taking a couple gulps of tea to finish it off. He placed the cup and saucer on the ledge that held the tools of his professions—barbering and dentistry. He shook out the linen cloth and swept it over him in a crackle-pop flourish.

"You got the panache of a magician, pal."

"I just be me. A little old nigger barber."

"Are you in a yakkity-yak mood?"

"You knows I always be up for chewing the fat."

"I just returned from a stroll to get some fresh air," Soapy said, smirking. "I could've sold tickets to what I saw on the street in front of the hardware store. A man and woman were fighting like Kilkenny cats. Spitting and cussing. I was readying to intervene on the dame's behalf when she coldcocked him with a roundhouse right and he went kerplunk like a felled tree."

"Was she marked or hurt?"

"Not that I could see," Soapy replied, chuckling glibly. "The sassy broad hiked her skirt up to give his crotch a thorough stomping before she trundled off like nobody's business. One helluva sight. That poor fella ain't going to be getting his jollies in the sack anytime soon. "

Fitzgerald had the comb and scissors poised to get started, but retreated a step to gather his laughter into a manageable snicker. "He might could become the next *petrified man*."

Smith guffawed. "He was laid out as stiff as a girder."

"That's what I be meaning." Whitey's hands began moving with speed and dexterity as he combed and clipped. "*McGinty, the petrified man* was shriveled up and as dead as a dodo. I stood in line and paid my dime to see him on display. Satisfied my curiosity, but got a sour stomach for my troubles. That exhibit was uglier than blackhearted sin at midnight."

Smith gave him a devil-may-care grin. "Quite lucrative though. I purchased the goon from some miners who unearthed him not far from here. Placed him on a slab and did a bit of razzle-dazzle promotion, then a horde of the unwashed paid to parade past *McGinty*."

"A dime a piece couldn't have filled the coffers."

"You were in line, Whitey, but you missed the real spectacle," Soapy said, rolling his eyes. "The profits didn't come from the ten cent entrance fee. It was the entertaining operators of shell games and three-card Monte that raked in a bonanza. *McGinty* was mere window dressing to provide a captive audience for my talented associates to fleece the flock of gawkers."

"You be a crafty ruffian, you know that, Mr. Soapy Smith?"

"I do indeed, Whitey," the flimflam man answered impertinently. "No regrets either. I learned I had an aptitude for it whilst a youngster in Coweta County, Georgia. My grandpop was a politician and my old man was an attorney so maybe there's larceny in my bloodstream."

"Don't get me wound up about politicians and lawyers."

"Flannel-mouthed liars, one and all."

"Too kind, Soapy."

"It's all business, Whitey. Life is business," he said, almost as a kneejerk reflex. "At the Tivoli Club, my joint in Denver, I figured I covered my butt and all the legal bases by posting a sign in bold capital letters at the entrance that stated a truthful warning; caveat emptor."

"What the heck be caveat emptor?"

"Caveat emptor is legalese Latin: *Let the buyer beware,*" Soapy replied haughtily. "I run shills and games of chance that are deftly slanted in favor of the house. I make no bones that my aim is to make money. Saps who come into my establishments to engage in cards or dice with my crew ought not to whine when their pockets get turned inside out. My enterprises are regarded as shady or untoward, but I'm purely a businessman looking out for my interests."

"You ain't got me fooled, Mr. Soapy Smith," Whitey told him, working on shaping his beard. "I see how you really be in the underneath. You be a scoundrel, but you gots a generous streak, and anyone in real need who puts the arm on you gets taken care of just fine."

Smith leaned one way then the other as his eyes, hooded and dark, surveyed the recesses and populace of the smoke-filled barroom—he evidently had to be sure that no one was within earshot. "Thanks for saying so, Whitey, but let's keep that tenderhearted crap between us."

"I done hobbled my lips already."

"Son of a slut!" Soapy uttered, abruptly sitting up to shed the sheet. "Sorry, Whitey, but I gotta get to it because Bob Ford and Joe Palmer just waltzed in like roosters on the prowl. I want to talk to them like I want a hole in the head, but I need to set some matters straight."

"You know Bob Ford has plans to open a dancehall?"

"Nothing happens in this town that I ain't aware of, Whitey," Soapy said as he gained his feet. He dipped into a pocket and came out with a hefty bankroll, then peeled off three ten dollar bills and handed them over in payment for services rendered. "Not a word about that being too much or I'll kick your ass. You ever need anything, Whitey, you call upon my friendship."

The onetime Exoduster from Alabama click-clicked as he tucked the money into a slot on the inside of his vest. The piano player was jangling a melody that sounded like it belonged in a church-house. He settled on the barber chair, closed his eyes and listened, and there, amongst charlatans and carousing, Whitey Fitzgerald cheerily hummed and murmured the tune.

Outside a beerhall tent down the street, shenanigans were afoot. LC Beadle and Yaz Lightfoot were on all fours at the back of the canvas pavilion searching for a breach to be exploited. An ever-moving choreography of frisky shadows were capering around them. Torch lights blazed from taverns and other nighttime businesses of the twenty-four hour camp and reflected off the steep walls of the canyon which housed the boomtown.

LC was in the lead. He slunk along at a slow, methodical pace. His breathing was shallow and thin. He felt a tap on his ankle, and craned his neck to see Yaz coolly pointing a finger to a feasible site where the coarse tarpaulin was rumpled and loose. It was at a different location from the one they had used yesterday. Unfaltering nods of agreement passed between them.

Yaz went under first, then LC squeezed head and shoulders in beside him. There was a clamorous cacophony—the voices from a contagion of chitchat buzzed into babel. Cusswords flew freely, and *every* expletive rose above the stridency. Their eyes were saucers, but all that could be seen were legs and feet because an overcrowded table was in front of them.

Once again looks were exchanged and an unspoken decision was made. There were no qualms or hesitations as together the brothers squirmed all the way under and crawled to an open space where, on their haunches and leaning against each other, a major range of carryings-on could be overseen. They shrank against the tarp-wall in an effort to make themselves small.

The noise was continuous, rising and falling like the undulating pulse of waves crashing on a rocky shoreline. A shrill blasphemy hit an ear-splitting peak, followed by a raucous uproar of derisive laughter. Even though they goggled and rubbernecked to do so, the boys could not see the source of the jarring swearword, nor the reason for the mockery.

As the siblings were stretching and straining they spied Lucinda Eno-chelli on a stool at the roughhewn plank-bar held aloft by several sawhorses. She was drinking beer and smoking whilst positioned in their direction with her gaze fixed on them. Three pairs of eyes linked for a long enough instant that the boys wriggled beneath the rigidity of her impish expectations.

A filthy insult was hurled at a woman, which provoked a response that started a chippy fistfight. The brawl ended in a jawbreaker blow that put a big-bellied man into a helpless sprawl ten feet away from the junior interlopers. A rangy whippet of a miner crouched over the fallen bloke and jabbed a finger in his chest. "She may be a whore, but she's still a lady, arsehole."

The altercation was over and done with when the resident moralizer flipped aside the entrance flaps and postured arrogantly in the doorway. "I am the Prophet Eliezer. You miscreants are degenerate sinners one and all," he bellowed in righteous rage as he heatedly shook the shepherd's staff. "The voracious fires of hell will consume your bones and entrails."

A prickly hush fell over the beerhall, which was plucked clean by Lucinda Enochelli. She began clapping scornfully. "The harebrained circus clown is in the house so let the frigging show begin," she said, contempt dripping off her tongue. Her sneering applause grew stronger and louder as more and more of the assembled merrymakers joined in. Soon the rhythmic reproach built into shrieks and foot-stomping glee until it struck a shattering crescendo of jeering.

"Thou shalt not ridicule God's anointed!" he railed in teeth-clenched fury as he lumbered inside and banged the staff on the floorboards. "There is none here that seeketh after God. Your throats are open graves. The putrid vomit of poison and cursing spews forth from your mouths. Destruction cometh from your lewd and evil deeds. The depravity of wickedness is as bloody menstrual rags rotting in the sun and rising as a stench in the nostrils of Almighty God."

He whirled and stormed toward the raven-haired woman at the bar. He loomed over her, eyes bulging and body shuddering. "You, an immoral woman of sorcery and abominations, dare to lampoon the Prophet Eliezer? Thou art a harlot, a witch, a liar. Iniquity is your bedfellow and falsehood your bosom buddy. The lake of fire and brimstone awaits your shameful soul."

Lucinda Enochelli had her head lowered, but even a cursory read of her body language made it transparent that she was not intimidated. She took an extra-long drag on the cigarette and inhaled, then met his glare straight-on as she blew a stream of smoke in his face. "I don't give a tinker's damn about any of the hogwash that pours from the floodgate of your buffoonery."

The Prophet Eliezer reeled in his footsteps and clawed at his shabby beard which was speckled with gobs of spittle. He tilted forward on the balls of his feet. "Woe unto you, idolater and evildoer! The day of the Lord shall descend upon you like a plague of locusts, then vultures will feast on your remains. I have spoken it on behalf of the Lord Almighty, so shall it be."

"Get out of my face, chucklehead. Your breath is fetid garbage."

His mouth wrenched open. "I am the Prophet Eliezer . . . "

"Go away and don't bother coming back."

It was then that the wayward tykes went into action. LC had the two matches ready. His fingers were sweaty and shaky, and because of that the first strike failed; he concentrated and bore down harder, but the second and third attempts were also unsuccessful. He paused and steadied his breathing, then scratched the heads together a fourth time and a flame flared.

Yaz didn't wait even a second. He had the tip of the two-inch long fuse sizzling and was sprinting with the firecracker held on the verge to be thrown. LC was tardy to react. The matches singed the tip of his index finger, which was the jolt that got his feet moving. He legs and arms were pumping fast. What he saw unfold clogged his throat in tension.

Yaz whipped in close as though he was invisible. He tossed the firecracker and it seemed to float and become suspended in midair. He slammed into a painted lady and took a tumble that had him somersaulting into his escape, so he missed seeing the placement of the banger. It was a once in a lifetime chance that could not be repeated if tried a thousand times.

The striped cardboard explosive landed on the floor and slid under the tattered hem of the Prophet Eliezer's animal skin robe. He was pop-eyed in disbelief and frozen on the spot—as if nothing that was happening had anything to do with him. That is, he was ignorant and detached and unmoving until the instant the firecracker detonated. When the burning fuse contacted the black powder the noise-maker went off with a blast between his grime-encrusted sandals.

A childlike squeal leapt off his tongue as he jumped high enough to go over the barstool if that had been his objective. There were shouts and hoots of hilarity from the startled onlookers, which increased into burbling exuberance as the Prophet Eliezer crash-landed in a bone-jarring, board-cracking thud. His face was contorted into a horrendous grimace of fear and loathing. He flopped onto his back, howling sobs as his appendages flailed like a floundering tortoise.

The culprits saw none of the afterclaps. They were fleet-footed and vacated the scene while the victim of their stunt was still, quite literally, up in the air. The crisp night embraced them, and a million twinkling stars witnessed their homeward bound getaway. They ran side by side in enthused jubilation. The sloppy grins of drunkards were plastered on their faces, and LC Beadle and Yaz Lightfoot were already plotting their next bang-bang antic.

Deacon Coburn was lost and forsaken. He had no inkling as to his where-abouts. His instinctive steps were carefully guarded for there was someone or something hidden nearby in the underbrush of the dense forest. The nighttime blackness was as bleak as a bottomless pit because the moon and stars were locked behind a solid crypt of clouds.

His eyes, squinty and angst-ridden, flittered back and forth as he crept along the narrow pathway through the haunted woodlands. Whoever or whatever was lurking in the tangled bushes disturbed his sensibilities—the stealthy footfalls paralleled his movements. A canopy of creaky branches above had his imagination alive with fantasies of bony fingers threatening to reach down and clutch him, and there were rustles whispering from every direction.

A foreboding in his gut screamed at him to run; put one foot in front of the other and vamoose at an extreme velocity. His temples throbbed and his throat tightened as his heartbeat thumped like the wings of a gigantic albatross thrashing to takeoff. The insistent urge to run thundered through him, but he forcefully resisted it and remained calm and coolheaded.

A growl came from the jungle of undergrowth to his right. He halted. Frosty gooseflesh slithered at the nape of his neck as an outrageous arctic wind hammered the corridors of his soul. He waited, though once again was tempted to run. He held fast, hands flexing uneasily. Another growl, louder and much closer, and sounding somehow sinister and aggressive.

Inside his head he saw a rabid creature with bits of flesh and blood from a recent kill glistening on its fangs. The beast had jaundiced eyes, mon-strous jaws, and steam rising from its nostrils. He blinked to make the awful ugliness disappear, but it refused to do so. The feral and ghoulish imagery had dug spurs deep into his consciousness. He was scared; physically and emotionally fearful for what was skulking just beyond the edge of the woods.

An unearthly glow materialized in the vicinity of the growls. The yel-lowish aura dispelled fear and ignited hope in him—it had a vibrancy that shimmied skyward and invaded the gloomy darkness as it moved at an angle toward the path ahead of him. He began walking hurriedly, then stopped in a suddenness that almost tripped him. The peculiar golden light emerged from the wilderness, and what was inside it made his mouth cottony.

A large gray wolf, noble and empathic, took stock of him from within the halo of living brightness. The animal was extraordinarily beautiful and demonstrated an infectious friendliness that engaged him. It pawed the ground, wagged its tail and barked a command to follow, then trotted onward and the shimmering radiance continuously bathed the wolf.

Coburn jogged briskly to keep up. When the wolf inside the golden bubble came to a clearing of grassy terrain, it gave a backward glance and yap-yapped as it sped up. He increased his efforts, lifting his knees and lengthening his strides. He arrived at the fringe of the meadow and stagger-stepped at what he saw—across the field was a slumbering village of longhouses, and the shining wolf sat like a sentinel at the entryway of a particular dwelling.

He walked to it. Halfway there he realized that the cheerless darkness had been softened by nightlights. The full moon, white and luminous, cast the landscape in enlightened hues, while stars blanketed the sky and glittered like new-cut diamonds on black velvet. He was awestruck as he knelt beside the animal and spoke in a dry rasp. "Thank you for finding me, my friend."

The wolf's soulful eyes gleamed affectionately, and the celestial aura around it pulsated. A breath of wonder shivered from his lungs. The canine whined and bobbed its head toward the door. Coburn rose and entered the lodge, which was warmly lit by firelight that flickered a footpath to the firepit, where Charley Jondreau sat comfortably cross-legged.

"My companion found you, preacher-man."

"I was lost. Where am I? What is this place?"

"You asked that previously, eh. Have you become dimwitted?" He chuckled happily. As before he wore a beaded pullover shirt and buckskin leggings. His thick black hair lay across his shoulders while he twiddled with a stone in his right palm. "It is known by many names. Canaan, Elysium, the happy hunting ground, life everlasting, the city of Zion. Call it what you like."

"What am I doing here?"

"You asked that too, eh."

"Tell me, Charley."

"Why not ask the Great Spirit?" the Iroquois man queried, joy dancing in his eyes. "You are free to do so, but I'd not extend much energy waiting for an answer. The Great Spirit has an endless capacity for lovingkindness, but do not test his grace and patience. He gave you a brain to solve puzzles and faith to accept those mysteries too wonderful for you to fathom."

"Have I been chastised?"

"Let's chit and chat, you and I."

"Never knew you to chit or chat, Charley."

"This is the exception that proves the rule, eh."

Coburn generated a half-baked grin as he sat on his heels across the campfire from him. He remained in that position for a moment, then settled on his buttocks with his right leg folded under his left knee. "I was frightened. Is that forest a barrier to dissuade trespassers?"

"How should I know, preacher-man?"

"It was miserably dark and scary."

"Your dream, your darkness."

"I don't understand."

Jondreau cupped his hand around the stone and deliberated on it as though it possessed answers to the conundrums of the universe. When he resolutely fixed his gaze on his guest there was hardness in his expression. "You claim willful ignorance, preacher-man. You have eyes but refuse to see; ears but cannot hear; a heart that has closed itself off to unwanted feelings."

Coburn flinched as if he had been pinched. His face puckered. He hung his head, then lifted it and stared at the flames licking at a log. "I have tried to do my best to repair relational bridges whenever doable, but we were five, and I am only in relationship with my youngest sister. I've had no contact with my other siblings since before the war tore me apart."

"Your memory cries out, eh?"

"It would seem so, yes."

"Search your soul."

"I do daily. Hourly sometimes," Deacon said morosely. "I evaluate all situations, and mostly I've come to terms with my shortcomings and deficiencies. As far as it has been possible for me I've kept the peace and made amends. Failed plenty, but stayed at it and never quit."

"The past is chasing you, eh."

"I'm not sure, Charley."

"Reconciliation must be realized, preacher-man."

"To whom? To what?"

"I cannot see that far into the past or future," Charley replied, smiling nebulously. "There is still kingdom work for you to do. Compassion to be poured out. Guidance to be given. Hope and redemption to be lived. Never stop kicking and punching, preacher-man." He held the stone between thumb and forefinger, then closed his fist around it. "A reward awaits you, eh."

Inky shades dropped from above until all was pitch-black. He stirred, arms and legs twitching. His lungs were aflame. When Deacon Coburn came awake he sucked in a colossal quaff of breath as though he had been encased underwater. He lay on his back staring at the ceiling while attempting to analytically piece together meaning from the visitation.

Their nakedness beneath the comforter was honest and innocent. Daniel Twosongs snuggled closer to her backside and held on tighter, a hand on the rise of her hip and the other cuddling her breasts. Her skin was smooth and dampened by perspiration, her scent sweeter and more potent than thriving blossoms of lilacs. The intoxicating fragrance filled his senses.

"You'll have me domesticated quick as a lick," he purred quietly.

"Partially domesticated perhaps."

"No. Completely. I'll never leave you."

"You lie, Daniel."

"Maybe a little." He had met her on the streets of Taos and was immediately smitten by her charms—a brilliant and easygoing smile that illuminated dusky-brown oval eyes combined with perfectly balanced top and bottom circles flat-out did him in. The capture of his heart was completed in white-flag surrender the moment she spoke his name in a honeyed voice.

The courtship, though conducted under the supervision of her family, had spontaneity and swiftness that disconcerted her father, a prominent businessman. He read the handwriting on the wall of their relationship and intervened to arrange for an early wedding at *Nuestra Señora de Guadalupe*, Our Lady of Gaudalupe. The liturgical ceremony celebrated the mystery and majesty, which resulted in them basking in the bliss of their first night together.

"You are a nomad, my dear. That'll not change."

"And when children come along, Consuelo?"

She rolled over and pressed against him chest to chest, then tilted her head enough to peer into his eyes. "I love you, dear husband. We've made love exactly once and I'm still all a-tingle. I had no clue that it'd be so much fun. Mother never broached the subject and the nuns severely said it was my duty to submit." She giggled earthily. "If our physical tenderness is submission, I'm positive we'll be busy bees and you'll have me in a family way in no time at all."

He kissed her salty brow. "Practice will make us even better."

"Tell me true, Daniel. You had previous experience, yes?"

"I had previous experience, no."

She cooed affection against his cheek, then smooched his lips. "You are such a splendid gentleman. I cannot imagine a better fit than us. You are my special gift from God."

His hands linked together against the small of her back. "In a broken world you are my perfect turquoise gem, Consuelo." His embrace increased in ardor and she responded in kind. It only took seconds for their desire to become a fever which was taking its natural course.

The passion was interrupted when she capriciously reared up and pushed him away, then threw off the covers and stood gawking at him on the mattress. "What are you doing loitering and puttering around?" she asked in a scolding tone. "Go to Deacon. Now! He needs you."

He catapulted from sleep and stepped lively. He scuttled halfway across the floor of the rock-walled grotto before reality took hold and he became cognizant of the fact that it had been a delightful dream; its origins were an abiding devotion which was fleshed out by memories. The shock ending was akin to being awakened by getting drenched by a bucket of ice water.

His stomach had knots twisting inside out. The declining campfire produced fading traces of light that danced off the walls and ceiling of the cave. His mind couldn't hold the huge swells of emotion breaking over him. He murmured her name aloud and searched the campsite as if he expected to see her. He purposed to breathe evenly and rubbed his eyes, which were moist.

It was coming up on ten years since his wife passed from time to eternity. Their decades together had fulfilled much of the promise expressed in the passionate affection of their wedding night with one glaring exception. There were no children from their union, but that wearisome sadness was rectified by the miraculous rescue and redemption of a dark-eyed girl named Sally, who became Sally Twosongs, a truly warmhearted daughter of stalwart faith and prayer.

He quivered in remembrance and wiped tears away again. He went and tipped his boots upside down to be sure no creepers had taken up residence. Satisfied, he hopped on one foot then the other to pull them on. A sixty-three year old Navajo man whose mother came from the white world, he went outside and faced the east to greet the gift of another day of wonder.

He was in southwestern Nebraska or northeastern Colorado, taking sanctuary in the natural cavern-like hollow of a bluff beside a tributary of the South Platte River, an exceptional shelter discovered a short while after he began riding with Deacon Coburn. The newfound companions had spent the winter of '67-'68 here investing hours talking theology.

Go to Deacon. Now! He needs you. The command echoed through him—its urgency had him in full-blown planning mode. He would not err.

The horizon was a sliver of pinkish-orange. Before the sun completed its rise, he'd have his minimal gear packed and be on horseback, seeking guidance from the Father of lights mile by mile as he rode steadily southward.

At *WT Ranch*, the valley was enveloped in swatches of gray because dawn had not yet spiked over the mountaintop. Naomi Axler, in housecoat and slippers, stood alone in her kitchen, sad-eyed and full of sorrow as she thoughtlessly stared out the window at the dreary colors. She was physically and emotionally exhausted for she hadn't slept more than a wink or two.

The brewing coffee saturated the room with its full-bodied bouquet. Her taste buds were whetted and her equilibrium in need of an energy boost. She had not even tasted the enchanting beverage until she was in her thirtieth year and widowed, and journeyed to the western lands of Kansas to find a fresh beginning. Her introduction was pleasurable and she was straightaway addicted; her hostess served it hot and as black as sin, which became her daily norm.

She heard shambling footsteps behind her, but did not bother turning around. "The coffee should be ready in a minute, Pete. If you can sit awhile before chores I'll get you a cup."

"That's not necessary, Naomi," he said, placing a hand on her shoulder. "Why don't you sit and I'll serve you?" He pushed aside her brunette locks and bussed the back of her neck. "It'd be good for us to talk some. I'll make time for it now. Did you get any sleep at all?"

"Not really."

"Why not unload on me?"

"I'm unsure what I'd say, Pete."

"No matter. You know I'm a good listener."

She gave a faint nod, then took a seat. A letter brought home from South Fork yesterday was propped against the centerpiece on the table. She had not yet unsealed it, nor did she even reach for it now. Her heart was in too much turmoil. She vaguely watched him get their coffee. "Am I wrong? Is my insistence wooden-headed? Selfish? I just don't know what to do."

"Wrong? Wooden-headed? Selfish? I think not, Naomi."

"Then what is it?"

"Honesty."

Creases tweaked her brow. "Honesty? That's interesting."

"It's true," he said flatly. He placed a steaming mug in front of her, then sat at the head of the table and had a sip from his own. "In painful grief, you are being true to your feelings."

"I was thinking different this morning."

"How so?"

"I should go to Creede."

"Last night you said that you'd not."

"Then I was in a flux of guilt that kept me awake."

"Guilt? *That's* wooden-headed, Naomi."

She stared unbelievingly at him. Murky doubt and unspoken questions swirled in the pools of her brown eyes. "When Deacon was here we had such a blessed visit. We shared many childhood memories, and talked about life and faith. It was apparent he was ragged and worn out, but I thought it was just from hard traveling. To hear the report from Sally Twosongs and Avis that Bethsuelo is convinced Mr. Deacon is going to heaven is quite disconcerting."

"As is it should be."

"Is it possible that she is wrong?"

"I'd not place a bet on it, Naomi."

"Me, neither. I guess."

"That little girl *knows* things, which cannot be explained."

"I'm not arguing that," she said, taking a swig of coffee. "If they aren't already gone, Avis and Eliza will soon be on the road with Bethsuelo. I was adamant last night, but am I shirking my responsibility by staying here instead of going to help Deacon and Abbey?"

"I respect your reasons."

"I haven't even told you the why of it."

"Naomi, whatever is in your heart is real."

"Oh, Pete!" A partially suffocated sob leapt forth. She pressed fingers over her lips and shook her head sadly. "I want the last memory of my big brother to be as it is now. A stopover off the trail when he was weary and fatigued, but still vital and full of wisdom and caring."

"You have my unconditional agreement and support."

She lifted her mug and took a small drink, then stared at him over the rim. "I assisted in nursing my father as he withered away and died. It was brutal and made a horrid impression on me. Then when Adam fell off the roof . . . " Her voice cracked and wavered. She gulped several quaking breaths. "I held my first husband in my arms and felt the warmth leave his body." She held his gaze. "Am I wrong and selfish to want to avoid watching my brother pass on?"

"Not at all. There is integrity in your decision."

"I'll pick up the slack and do ranch-work."

"Of which I have no doubt."

"Deacon will understand, won't he?"

"In a heartbeat," he replied, draining his mug.

She smiled bravely. "Last evening, in the unloading supplies followed by the communal meal and interaction about Deacon, we didn't talk of your trip to town. How was Amanda?"

"We had us a constructive go-around. I'm hopeful."

"Happy to hear it."

He stood and stretched. "She's deep waters, Naomi."

"I will gladly join you in being hopeful," she said candidly. "You get to it. I'm going to read the mail you brought home, then have a feast ready for when the chores are done."

Her lanky husband was on his way with a wink and a grin. She waited until she heard the front door shut before she got up and poured herself another helping of coffee. She held the cup under her nose and savored its aroma for several sniffs. When she returned to her seat she took a slow swallow and put it down, then opened the letter from her niece and sat back to read it.

March 28, 1892

Abilene, Kansas

Dear Aunt Naomi: It has been too long since I made the time to correspond. I have no excuses, which means the fault is mine alone. I so appreciated your Christmas letter. It warmed my heart and made me smile. Of course I intended to respond in a timely fashion, but one thing gave way to another, and now, in just a few short weeks it will be Eastertime.

It was a hard winter on the plains. Bitter cold and much snow, which so far has given way to a wet spring. It has been drizzling off and on for such a long succession of days that I've lost count of the number. The moisture in the soil will truly be a boon when planting time arrives, which will be wonderful, but as you know, farm work must be done regardless of the weather conditions, so my men have had a rough go of it of late, without complaint, mind you.

I have a legion of rich blessings. Sometimes I wonder how and why, but then I am reminded of the bottomless well of God's love and grace, and my soul sings praises that make me weep in joy and gratitude. I still grieve for my unborn babies, but glorious light from above came and shattered the chains of gut-slugging despair.

The oppressive demonic darkness that sought to entomb me in the past has not returned, and I pray that it is no more.

It was difficult, but Scripture promises that we "rejoice in hope of the glory of God. And not only so, but we glory in tribulations also: knowing that tribulation worketh patience; And patience, experience; and experience, hope: And hope maketh not ashamed; because the love of God is shed abroad in our hearts by the Holy Ghost which is given unto us."

I cannot comprehend the workings of our Lord and Savior except in the context of faith. He made a miracle in our lives. I believed and I received. After an extended bleakness, Abraham and I hashed out our feelings and fought for reconciliation, which was in no manner easy. It wasn't magic, nor did it happen without the mutual application of a truthful reckoning and coming into agreement with God regarding our spiritual condition.

Our hearts were broken and unkempt. The miscarriages plagued us, though until we genuinely allowed the brightness of Christ to shine into our lives, I thought I alone suffered. I never understood the weight of guilt and anguish the terrible losses put upon my husband. Our perspectives and emotions were stripped to the bone, and over the course of many months of baby-steps our relationship, by God's amazing and awesome grace, was restored.

On this side of the miracle, the marital tensions and disgraceful domineering seems like it occurred in another lifetime to another couple. We are as we were when we were newlyweds, tender and kind to each other while being encouraging helpmates. Abraham sat Eli and Seth down with me present, and spoke justly to them about his failings in his responsibility as a husband and the leader of the family. There were tears and healing, and much bonding.

It is getting late in the afternoon. I have a stoneware pot of chicken-corn soup on the stove. My hardworking men will be arriving one by one from their various tasks, then we will sit down at the table for supper, where Abraham will read a Bible passage and Eli or Seth will pray. After the meal and clean up, I suspect a Dutch Blitz tournament is in the offing.

I am blessed beyond all imaginings, Aunt Naomi. Thank you for your never-failing support, love and prayers. When you stood strong with me in the midst of my questioning gloom, I was strengthened. You have enriched my life in ways that cannot ever be enumerated. May our great God of all wonder and mercy put his boundless arms around you and hold you close.

In peace,

Anna

Sunbeams were slicing through the windowpanes to splash across the tabletop. She set the missive aside, teary-eyed and rosy-cheeked. She enunciated thanksgiving for the power of hope and redemption, which naturally led to prayers on behalf of her brother; she asked God to encircle him in an unfathomable peace. Then, Naomi Axler got busy cooking breakfast.

On the south side of the Raton Pass, the wind was yowling like a banshee from some underworld insane asylum. At an elevation over 7,500 feet above sea level, the northbound train was dead on the tracks, blocked by an epic blizzard dumping copious amounts of snow which had accumulated into a fortress-like barrier that plugged the tunnel.

Delores Solrizo sat in a backseat of the last passenger car—behind it was the caboose. She tried to determine the happenings outside, but flurries of white were all that could be seen in every direction, so she tightened the shawl around her shoulders as she calmly put her mind to work figuring a plan on how to make-do and overcome this battering by Mother Nature.

The walls and windows of the conveyance were creaking as the spring snowstorm repeatedly launched attack after attack. She mulled over the situation while assessing her fellow travelers. There were a dozen others sharing the safe haven of the Pullman coach, and most were panicky or in varying degrees of distress, but there was one notable exception.

A black girl was sitting sideward at midpoint, legs pulled up and upper body hunched over so she was almost a ball crunched beneath a blanket. She ignored the hubbub around her and kept focused on the ceiling, seemingly oblivious to the unnerved undercurrents of agitation. Her lips were pursed in a peculiar way as her head swayed ever so gently.

Delores watched her for a good long while, and in doing so, decided that there was some intangible about the young lady that was attractive, if not downright compelling. She felt a sense of confidence emanating from her, and Delores soon concluded that she was humming a melody which could not be heard above the rushing winds and clamoring fretfulness.

"We're going to die!" a pessimistic loudmouth bellowed, rising to his feet. "God only knows how long we'll be stranded here. No food, no water." He stomped into the aisle and paced erratically. He was jowly-faced and chunky around the equator, and possessed a foghorn voice with a twangy reverberation. "We'll starve or die of thirst, or more likely freeze to death."

"That be the all and end all," a squeaky woman agreed, head bobbing like a chicken pecking at its feed. "We're all done in and you can be sure that the railroad dicks know there's no hope. That's why a porter hasn't come given us a report from the engineer."

"You're exactly right, lady," the fleshy doomsayer remarked. "Ain't no way to run a railroad. Likely ain't even caring about us mutts. They ought to be providing for us."

"Mister," Delores said, standing. "I note that you're not a baby or crippled, so you have the capability to see to your own needs. If you cannot say something helpful, then with all due respect, please sit down and shut your big bazoo. Elsewise someone might put a cork in it."

"Who the hell are you to talk smart-alecky to me?"

"Someone interested in solutions, not stupidity," Delores answered straight-faced. She was five feet from him and inching closer. His cheeks flushed the color of blood as he retreated to his seat. She maintained composure and spoke authoritatively. "We haven't been immobile for all that long, so we need to get a grip and use our brains. Let's not give in to apprehension or despair because none of us are alone. We are in this uncertain dilemma together.

"My name is Delores Solrizo," she said, bold and persuasive. "I am not worried one iota and I'll tell you why. We have shelter and clothes. The dining car has a stocked pantry, and I'm sure the foodstuffs will be rationed out fairly. As far as thirst, snow melts, as any tadpole child knows. We'll scrounge whatever containers we can, and after the wind subsides, pack them with snow. We will stick together and do the best we can to see each other through this crisis."

A smattering of applause ensued along with a few mild grumbles. Delores dusted off an appealing smile from youthful days and used it to disarm the man she had backed down. He gave her a boyish grin that became a self-effacing shrug. She nodded, then turned and leaned over to speak quietly to the black girl. "Would you be kind enough to join me for a visit?"

"Will do, ma'am."

"Delores," she corrected, eyes brightening.

"Best I can do is Miss Delores, ma'am," she replied pleasantly.

When the two were settled side by side in the backseat, Delores inclined toward her and softly brushed her hand. "Miss Delores is fine as long as it isn't punctuated by a ma'am."

"What be your story, Miss Delores? Why you want to talk to me?"

"I enjoy friendships, so for starters, what shall I call you?"

"Emma Rafferty is my name."

"Well, Emma Rafferty, what's *your* story?"

"I'm from Memphis, Tennessee," she answered, lips parting in a grin that highlighted her high cheekbones. She was the wisp of a sapling willow, small-boned and skinny. Her kinky hair was clipped short and she had a cute pug nose. "I was born free to sharecroppers who had been slaves. I'm on my way to Denver where I've been promised a job singing in a nightclub."

"A nightclub? How old are you, Emma?"

"Old enough."

"And what age would that be?"

"Turned seventeen two days ago, Miss Delores."

"That's not old enough, dear child."

"I'm a singer and a musician."

"Does that make you wise to the ways of the world?"

"Just hungry for success," Emma said vivaciously. "Emotions come alive in my voice. I can sing any style of song. Piano is my signature instrument, but I'm proficient on guitar and banjo. I do a passable job on the fiddle if called upon. Music is in my heart and soul."

"There are pitfalls and dangers, Emma."

"You mean men and sex?" she asked, edgy and jaded. "Boys and men have been trying to get over on me since I was eleven. I don't abide any sweet-talk lies or pushy groping. My grandpappy taught me about respect and a special trick that makes men walk funny."

"Just the same a nightclub is not a proper place for a young lady," Delores said, forehead furrowed. "What did you mean when you said emotions come alive in your voice?"

"I can show, but can't tell you."

"Please do."

Emma Rafferty had no hesitation. The tall and gangly teenager who had the seeds of a pretty woman germinating in her, got up and waggled her arms and legs. Then, demonstrating a maturity far beyond her years, projected a sunny and unassailable poise. "Ladies and kind gentlemen, I invite you to a singalong. I promise if you join me it'll make you feel good."

There was derision from the captive audience, but that did not deter her. She began in a fragile voice, which proved to be deceptive. "*Michael row the boat ashore, hallelujah. Michael row the boat ashore, hallelujah.*" Her charisma was contagious; she rocked the riveted spectators in the cradle of each note. "*Sister help to trim the sail, hallelujah. Sister help to trim the sail, hallelujah. Michael row the boat ashore, hallelujah. Michael row the boat ashore, hallelujah. Jordan's river is chilly and cold, hallelujah. Chills the body but not the soul, hallelujah.*"

Delores Solrizo, along with everyone else, was struck by mesmerized silence. The girl, whose scrawny appearance suggested that a stiff wind would easily knock her on her backside, had the pitch-perfect pipes of an angelic choir. She made eye-contact and connections which were irresistible. At the beginning of the third verse, no one was a disengaged observer; *everyone* had caught the bug and were involved—clapping, tapping feet, or singing along.

"*Michael row the boat ashore, hallelujah. Michael row the boat ashore, hallelujah. The river is deep and the river is wide, hallelujah. Milk and honey on the other side, hallelujah. Michael row the boat ashore, hallelujah. Michael row the boat ashore, hallelujah.*" Emma soothed it to an end by allowing her voice to trail off into breathy whispers, then without more than a moment's pause, she varied her position and launched into *Jacob's Ladder*.

"*We are climbing Jacob's ladder. We are climbing Jacob's ladder. We are climbing Jacob's ladder. Soldiers of the cross. Every round goes higher, higher. Every round goes higher, higher. Every round goes higher, higher. Soldiers of the cross. Sinner, do you love my Jesus? Sinner, do you love my Jesus? Sinner, do you love my Jesus? Soldiers of the cross.*"

She closed her eyes as the evocative phrasings became even more captivating. "*If you love him, why not serve him? If you love him, why not serve him? If you love him, why not serve him? Soldiers of the cross.*" She reprised the final verse again and again; each time it soared to newer and more goosepimply heights. When she brought the song to a seamless conclusion, the last note faded into the ether. In contrast to the shrieking storm outside, stillness permeated the interior of the passenger car, which was promptly interrupted by sniffs and tears.

The rotund man who sounded like a foghorn jostled buoyantly out of his seat and stepped toward the front exit. "I'm going to see if I can get any news. And tell the engineer not to worry about this carriage because we've got everything under control." An ovation of huzzahs burst forth. He turned scarlet, and the ebullient cheers escorted him as he departed.

"The power of music," Delores marveled under her breath. She glanced at the rangy songbird, who seemed to have melted into the surroundings. The teen had resumed her scrunched posture under a blanket. An excessively prolonged squall pummeled the train. Delores Solrizo stared out the frosted window and devotedly prayed for God's peace and protection.

At midday in Creede, LC Beadle and Yaz Lightfoot were still jacked up on juice and adrenaline from the single firecracker, and now the mischief-makers had a whole string. Their hush-hush helper had provided the necessities. LC had the bangers secreted in the waistband of his trousers, while Yaz kept the matches hidden in his loosely clenched right fist.

The brothers were lying in wait on the main thoroughfare, which was a potpourri of hustle and bustle. The boardwalks were a teeming mass of people—men, women and children shopping, running errands or loitering and agitating the gossip pot. Wagon and horse traffic alternated between being a steady haul of commerce to occasional rushes. LC and Yaz had secured a reasonably effective perch in an alley across from the grocery store.

"How much longer?"

"Don't know, Yaz."

"Whatcha think he's buying?"

"Don't know that either."

"Yeah-huh."

"Are you ready?"

His answer was a subtle gesture with his chin. LC heeded the impromptu pointer and saw the Prophet Eliezer emerging from the grocery store with a bag of goods in the niche of his left arm and his shepherd's staff in his right hand. The overbearing merchant of doom strode into the street, which required a swarthy driver to forcefully halt his wagonload of ore, otherwise the unhinged evangelist would've been trampled beneath the hoofs of the mule-team.

"Watch your step, jackass!" the dark-complexioned man shouted in a fury.

"I am the Prophet Eliezer. I shan't be barked at on the avenue," he hollered, squaring off to confront the teamster and the long-eared mules. He shook his head. His grimy hair was matted into a shaggy crown that bounced. "You shall not pass! I will call down fire from heaven."

The boys went into action. Yaz lit a pair of matches on the first strike and protected the blaze by cupping a hand around it. LC eased the fuse to the flame and took off as though a pack of coyotes were yapping at his heels. A misstep off the raised boardwalk put him into a stammering nosedive that resulted in a nimble shoulder-roll onto his feet at full speed.

He neared the objective and stole a look at the sparkles fizzling close enough to the bundle of firecrackers to induce a charge of fear that triggered his adrenals. The energy surge burned through him and made his legs kick into a faster gear. He zeroed in on the target and hurled the ammunition. The loads of tightly packed black powder started pop-pop-popping in mid-air and landed at the feet of the cleric, between him and the fully loaded ore wagon.

The zip-zap explosions continued unabated for thirty seconds or so, but it seemed much longer because the pandemonium was excruciatingly frantic. Screeching hee-haws blistered the air as the mules bucked and thrashed in such wild hysteria that the wagon wobbled rowdily enough for the front wheels to loose contact with the hard-packed roadway. The teamster, blaspheming in thunderous howls, clung to the reins and fought to gain control, forearms engorged and eyes distended as he humped over and held on for all he was worth.

Terrified madness had taken hold of the Prophet Eliezer. He was lost and floundering inside of a tortured reality that was a living nightmare clawing at him. When the bursting barrage of bangs began he jumped and jittered a craze-eyed jig as untethered screams spouted forth like splashes of boiling liquid from some inner caldron. The bag of groceries went flying, as did his shepherd's staff, and he landed in a heap scant inches from stomping hoofbeats.

He flopped and twitched. The sounds gushing out of him were sickening. Whimpers and whines alternated at regular intervals with huge sobbing wails. In his herky-jerky horror, his arms flapped and punched while his legs flailed like pistons broken free of their moorings. The ragged hem of his garment hitched up to his hips, revealing ghost-white legs smeared by grayish layers of crud. He curled into the fetal position, shuddering and babbling nonsensically.

The sight was horrendous and shocking; painful to witness, but that did not prevent a whooping throng of passersby to encircle the dreadful scene. As the Prophet Eliezer suffered a chilling mental breakdown more and more watchers gathered into tightly clustered clumps of mockers. The crowd numbered more than fifty and was rapidly increasing as the bizarre entertainment garnered a life of its own, nourished by gibes and taunting hysterics.

LC Beadle and Yaz Lightfoot were side by side, crouched in petrified fear as they peeked through ever-moving gaps between and around legs. They had been fastened on the same spot since the first scream tore from the Prophet Eliezer's throat. There was no laughter in them; not even a budding hint of it, but rather, distressed embarrassment bloomed nasty petals, along with a desperate need to escape because getting caught meant punishment and dishonor.

Their faces were wrenched, hands fisted and lips cramped into bloodless lines. They had seen the entirety of what their hands had wrought, and now, seeing the towering redhead reduced to weeping like a frightened baby made them numb. Just then, a single word shouted in anger disrupted the mockery and went through the boys as sure as a lance cutting to the core. The brothers leapt and raced off as if snarling hellhounds were barreling down upon them.

～～～

"*Enough!*"

Deacon Coburn, steel-eyed and grim-faced, had been a distant on-looker from the beginning of the outlandish prank. A hankering for canned peaches had him out and about on his way to the grocery store. He jogged into the middle of the deranged mob and attempted to hush the mules. He jabbed a finger at the weather-beaten driver. "Get a crew from this rabble. Back the wagon up and move on. Everyone else, if you ain't gonna help be gone and out the way."

"We didn't mean nothing, mister. We was just funning."

Coburn seethed in enflamed indignation. He wheeled on the flat-nosed miner who had piped up, and got eyeball to eyeball with him. "This is a man who God loves and for whom Jesus died," he said in a barely restrained growl as he pointed to the cowering mountain of broken humanity. "You all have treated him egregiously. May God have mercy."

A bunch of men had the wagon reversed far enough that the teamster could steer it past the Prophet Eliezer, who remained a hulking lump shivering and crying. Coburn knelt beside him and placed a hand on his shoulder, which had disastrous results. The Prophet Eliezer recoiled and cringed inwardly, batting his arms in a frenzy while yelping thickly slurred words.

"Don't touch me! Don't touch me! Don't touch me!"

Coburn held his hands at half-mast surrender. His face was a jaw-compressed grimace and his fingers were inflicted by tremors. He slipped onto both knees and while in that position silently prayed. As he did the Prophet Eliezer shook like a leaf in a whirlwind. His eyes were wide and bulgy, his countenance warped and twisted, his breathing stressed and thin.

The loitering ridiculers had withdrawn in shiftless shuffling, and assembled two-deep on the boardwalk on both sides of the street. A spooked melancholy, akin to the kind that infiltrates the sickroom of a loved one suffering on their deathbed, dropped over the city block. Tension swelled and rippled as the lookers-on bunched soundlessly against each other.

A high-pitched and undulating caterwauling rocketed to the sky, which instigated a collective gasp that was a stupefied sucking noise. There was a stomach-turning feature in the torturous cries shrilling from the Prophet Eliezer's grossly distorted mouth; he was crumpled over and trapped inside a spastic convulsion, palms flattened against his ears as his upper body heaved and quaked, while his lungs responded to the bloody horrors ripping his brain apart.

Coburn heeled the brim of his hat up his forehead. With compassion in his eyes and tears on his cheeks he ever so carefully rested his hands on the man's quavering shoulders. There was no repeat of the previous debacle.

"Get it out, brother. Get it all out," he whispered in a shivery rasp. "Ain't no reason to cling to it, my friend. Hold onto me. We'll get through it together."

The Prophet Eliezer stared hollow-eyed at him. "Who are you?"

"A friend, a brother, a fellow battler of inner demons."

"Who am I? Where am I?" There was blank vacancy in his face, which was ashen and drawn in taut lines. His head swiveled hesitantly. "What strange battlefield is this place?"

"The frontline trenches."

"I cannot go on. I must die."

"Not today, brother," Deacon said tenderly. He extended his arms around him in a strong embrace, pulling him close as he rubbed circles in the area between his shoulder blades. "Rise up and be free. *The Lord upholdeth all that fall, and raiseth up all those that be bowed down.*"

"The Lord attends not to me. I have been shamed."

"You are wrong. There is no shame here."

"What strangeness has become me?"

"I know not, brother, but God does. Trust his mercies."

"God is deaf and blind to my travails."

"No, my friend," Deacon replied, hugging him even closer. "In the deepest, dreariest pit of our lives God is light. *If I say, surely the darkness shall cover me; even the night shall be light about me. Yea, the darkness hideth not from thee; but the night shineth as the day: the darkness and the light are both alike to thee.*" His calm manner was a pacifying balm. "Take hold of our Lord's hand in the darkness. Receive his grace and allow me to walk alongside you."

Together, in burdensome and stammering motions, the men pressed against each other and shakily pushed to their feet. The Prophet Eliezer's legs functioned like those of a newborn colt slip-sliding on a patch of ice. Deacon Coburn gave him his shoulder. The two shambled in lopsided steps, angling away from the center of the street. All gave them a wide berth.

Lucinda Enochelli shrank away and hid her face. She had been amongst the spectators since before the first firecracker exploded—she saw the Prophet Eliezer descend into emotional wreckage; she gloated in the contempt expressed, but then, waves of shock shattered her as she observed the broad-shouldered man she had known in a world that no longer existed.

His empathy and kindheartedness mortified her and made her blush in weak-kneed disgrace. Now, Deacon Coburn passed within ten feet of her, assisting and mostly carrying the man she had targeted for a gratuitous practical joke that turned into an unspeakable horror. Her heart climbed into her throat and was joined by a slime of nauseous bile. The vinegary sourness thickened her tongue. She coughed it into her mouth and spat crudely.

Without any conscious choice her feet were moving along the boardwalk in the opposite direction of Deacon Coburn and the Prophet Eliezer. She was not alone; many of those who had joined in the castigating scorn were demurely fleeing, eyes averted. No smiles or nods of acknowledgement were exchanged because heads were hanging low.

She hurried. She stepped off the boardwalk, lifted her head and glanced upward. The moon, bleached and ghostly, was visible in a crystalline blue sky. She stared oddly at such a rare daylight manifestation, while debating whether it was a charming anomaly or representative of a bad omen. She decided it was not good, and immediately wanted to hide.

Her mind was going backwards in time even faster than her legs could carry her. She had blundered—she had made hundreds of errors in judgment; no, her erroneous choices across the years ranged in the thousands. Tears, hot and feverish, singed her eyes. A singularly obsessive mistake haunted her; she should have never sought to find Deacon Coburn. She lengthened her strides for she aspired to disappear—Lucinda Enochelli intended to become a recluse.

"What the hell are you doing?"

The door closed. Lucinda Enochelli, glum and detached, cast a nebulous look at the block-bodied man in front of her. The curtains were drawn across the window as a bulwark against the afternoon sunlight so the smoke-hazed room was dull and gray. She had moved a Queen Anne chair beside the bed and was on it, in petticoats and a camisole. A cigarette smoldered between her fingers and the ceramic ashtray on the floor was overloaded.

"Soapy expected you an hour ago," Willy said, fanning the air.

"Who cares?"

"Soapy, for one. Me, too."

"I'm in no mood for gambling."

"Since when, Lucinda?"

"It's my business."

Phips widened his eyes. "No double-dealing?" He swung the other Queen Anne chair away from the side of a tallboy dresser and planted his rump on it. "What's wrong?"

"Leave me be, Slick Willy."

"Why would I do that, sweet lady?"

"I want peace and quiet, and to be left alone," she replied, leaning sideward to snuff out the cigarette. She dusted off her palms, then reached for her fixings on the mattress and busied her fingers rolling another weed. "Just turn around and go back to the Orleans Club."

"No, I'm going to stick here a bit."

"Why not leave me be?"

"Give me a reason as to why I should."

"Do whatever you want. Why the hell should I care?"

"What's going on, Lucinda?"

"Nothing that concerns you."

"Something happened."

"Nothing. Absolutely nothing."

"Then what's the problem?"

"My life, Slick Willy. *That's* the problem."

"You need to talk to me."

"No one has what I need."

"And what is that, Lucinda?"

She puffed crankily. "A do-over."

"For what?"

"A clean slate for my entire frigging life," she answered, blowing a stream of smoke downward. The olive-skinned brunette who had once been known as Coco, crossed her legs and shook her head as regrets lined her face. "A clear conscience would be nice to experience."

"You and me both, sweet lady."

"I've done rotten stuff."

"As have I. We're a pair of blackguards, so what?"

"My offenses trump yours. I guarantee it."

"Again, so what? We are what we are, Lucinda."

"You ever been in prison, Slick Willy?"

The query straightened his backbone and deepened scowly ruts on his brow. "No, I ain't enjoyed those crummy quarters. A local hoosegow a time or two, but never the big house."

She dropped the stump of a butt in its depository. "A man named Logan Treglor got himself incinerated carrying out an arson plan I participated in. I was arrested at the scene, and though the coppers had no evidence to convict me, my refusal to cooperate with the investigation got me a seven year stint. Logan was much more than a friend so I couldn't rat him out."

"Where? When?"

"Philadelphia. The early days of the war."

"Does this have anything to do with Deacon Coburn?"

She laughed, disparaging and bitter. "No. Sadly, he was gone by then. Maybe if I had stayed connected to Deacon my life would have turned out different, mayhap even better."

"How would that be possible?"

"He was an upright man."

"What the blue blazes does that prove, sweet lady?"

"He still is honorable, perhaps even more so. I saw him."

"Did you speak to him?"

"No. The circumstances were inappropriate."

"Since when did being appropriate influence you, Lucinda?"

"Fact is, I won't go see Deacon now."

"Why the frig not?"

"He's too good, too kind."

"Whatever your history with him, he's just a man."

"He's too holy, Willy."

"He ain't holy."

"No? He surely seems like a holy man."

Slick Willy Phips corkscrewed his face in disbelief. "Am I to understand that you've waited all these years and traveled countless miles, and after all of those trials, you're not going to make connections? I thought you had something significant that belonged to Coburn."

"I need time to think."

"I'll leave you to it," he said as he stood. He shoved the chair back to its spot beside the dresser, then was out the door, which he slammed hard. She rapidly put together another smoke. When she fired it up, she bent forward and rested elbows on knees. A buildup of griefs and guilt gutted her emotions and soon, Lucinda Enochelli came unglued and wept uncontrollably.

At the Fralick home on Main Avenue in Durango, Maxine sat behind the desk in her husband's office. Afternoon sunlight was stretching long shadows across the floor. The baby was active, and even though much strain and tension were in her body, her mood was contemplative. She held their wedding picture in her hands, which kept making slight adjustments as she thumbed each of the twelve stones implanted in the reddish wooden frame.

The front door opened and closed. Her lips curled in a wry grin because it was almost four o'clock, and he was on schedule. She heard padding footfalls go through the living room into the kitchen. There was hesitation, then a low hiss of a whistle and the hallway floorboards squeaked. A few seconds later, Doc Fralick entered his workplace with the black medical bag tucked under an arm. He was greeted by the sheer warmth of a twinkly-eyed smile.

"Here you are, Maxine."

"Here I be, Karl."

"Cody is snoozing and snuffling on the couch." He put the bag down on its shelf beside the door, then sat in a wingback chair in front of the desk. "What are you doing?"

"Thinking. Remembering. Looking ahead."

"Sounds like a lot of stuff happening."

"These stones are more meaningful than I could've ever imagined," she said, still holding the frame so as to caress the significant mementos. "When pressed, Deacon explained the stones in Gilgal's bridle, but prefaced it by recounting the Israelites crossing the Jordan River. I carried his telling of that Bible story around in my head for a decade, musing on it at frequent intervals. Then when Charley was killed I picked up these stones, after first resisting the idea. Now I see them as symbolic of my spiritual journey; past, present and future, I suppose."

"How so?"

"I had a tenuous view of God for most of my childhood," she replied mildly. "We weren't churchgoers, and my parents seldom talked about faith and God, but whenever the topic arose, it was obvious that they had their beliefs. For me, God was too remote, too unpredictable. Then when Smoky Crowe slaughtered my mother, I shutdown all chatter on those matters."

"A natural human response."

The strawberry-blonde shrugged as she moved around in the chair. "It was Deacon Coburn who gave me a different perspective. He planted seeds of hope and faith in my heart. He put Bible stuff in terms that caused me to think about them in ways I had never considered." She set the wedding picture down. "He was never preachy. Always genuine and practical. There was no disconnect between his talk and his walk. His faith expression was automatic."

"I heard some of that way back when at Fort Union."

"I don't doubt it, Karl," she said, hands absently rubbing her ballooned midsection. She shifted her bottom again "I'm not sure where I'd be or what condition my heart would be in if I'd not spent time on the trail with him. His viewpoint about the hardness of the world was filtered through the lens of Scripture, which evidently caused him to routinely choose to be amazed by the mysteries of God seen in the beauty of nature. My faith outlook owes much to him."

"He definitely has a handle on eternity."

"He lives what he believes, to be sure."

The doctor sat forward, aloof and tentative. "He's dying, Maxine."

"What?"

"He might already be dead."

Her eyes flashed hotly. "And you're telling me this now?"

"There was nothing anyone could do for him."

"That can't be."

"It is, Maxine. I'm sorry."

"You're sorry?"

"Sincerely sorry."

She fixed a glare on him. "You lied to me, Karl."

"No, I kept a confidence."

"You gave me a cock and bull tale about Deacon merely riding through Durango," she said, laboring to get on her feet. Her lips constricted into a full-blooded pucker. "According to your *crappola* version he saw your shingle, and recognizing the surname from Fort Union, he simply stopped in to say hello. That, Karl, was a bald-faced falsehood."

"I was being true to his wishes."

"You *lied* to me!"

"I kept a confidence, Maxine."

"We're going to *WT Ranch*."

"No. Your time to pop is too close."

"So what? You'll be with me."

"I can't, Maxine. What about my patients?"

"Let me tell you something, Doc," she said in a condescending tone. She stepped out from behind the desk and went to him, eyes narrowed and simmering with anger. "Deacon Coburn is your patient. You really want to get in a knock down drag out with me, Karl?"

"Maxine, please be reasonable."

"This is me being reasonable, Karl," she answered, hands on her hips as she stood over him. The air rippled with currents of stormy coldness. Their stares locked in an insistent glower that progressively congealed the frigidity soiling the space between them. Her bearing became even harder. "There's no leeway here, Karl. I am going to *WT Ranch*. Alone or with you."

A biting twinge whitened his lips. "Maxine, please."

"What's it going to be, Karl?"

That evening, at a log cabin in Creede, there were matters being adjudicated that had two boys standing as rigid and red-faced as a pair of painted toy soldiers. Their eyes were moist, their breathing shallow and restrained. They were sequestered in their bedroom with the door closed while Deacon Coburn and Whitey Fitzgerald sat side by side on one of the beds.

"You crossed a line," Deacon said sternly. "Why?"

"We meant no harm," LC replied, weak and shaky.

"Yeah-huh."

Fitzgerald click-clicked rapidly. "Meant no harm? I never thunk you did, but intentions and results be different. You has to use your brains. That poor Eliezer ain't right in the upstairs and you done scared a living bag of nails out of him. Where'd you get those firecrackers?"

"They got them and used them, that's the issue," Deacon sliced in, gruff and terse. "The how of it ain't my concern. What's most important to me is that my grandsons learn a bred in the bones lesson. We ain't vacating this room until I'm satisfied as to that outcome." He made a brusque motion. "Get your bottoms comfy on the floor, boys. We may be here a spell."

"Yes, sir."

"Yeah-huh."

"You be in a heap of trouble, but there ain't gonna be no whuppings," Whitey said, face crinkling into a generous grin. "Because whuppings don't teach what needs to be learned."

"Pap Whitey's onto wisdom, so pay heed."

"Yeah-huh."

Coburn hunkered his upper body forward. "No one can know anyone's hidden struggles and pains. For example, you gentlemen were at the Wounded Knee Massacre, were you not?"

They nodded in unison. "Yeah-huh."

"Was it enjoyable?"

"Nope," LC answered quickly.

"Any good memories?"

"Nope."

"Why not?" Deacon asked, smiling gently.

"Lots of people suffered and died," LC replied, eyes darkening. "It was awful, Papa. The bluecoats kept shooting and fighting. Yaz was badly wounded and it could've been worse. Boxy tried to rescue him but a cavalryman killed our dog with a sword. Me and Yaz were screaming scared and angry. So was Mom. She cried and squawked at the soldiers to stop."

Coburn squinted. "Do you ever have bloody thoughts about that day?"

"Yeah-huh."

LC hung his head. "I have bad dreams."

"Me, too."

"Who knows?" Deacon queried curtly.

"Just me and Yaz."

Yaz glanced at his brother. "And Mom."

"I be tracking this just fine," Whitey said, sliding off the mattress to sit on his haunches so as to be eye-level with them. "Let me ask you spuds something. Would you like to be terrified by memories of Wounded Knee because someone startled you by pulling a dirty trick?"

"No. That'd be mean."

"Yeah-huh."

"It be sinking in, Deacon."

Coburn's mouth twitched as he coughed to clear his throat. He switched his focus from one grandson to the other as he spoke firmly and sympathetically. "We all have hurts inside us. Pain wrapped around bad memories that have no end. We pray and press on to put cruel junk behind us, but the past, especially the hurtful wounds stick in our hearts like dust bunnies."

"Mr. Eliezer, he be carrying heavy burdens. His brain be broken."

"We cannot know the troubles or scars folks have inside them," Deacon said, eyes brimming with sorrow. "Which is a good reason to be respectful and put all efforts to bear as we endeavor to treat others exactly how we want to be treated regardless of their behavior to us."

"That be the Golden Rule," Whitey told them, click-clicking heartily. "Jesus hisself taught that when he gave a sermon on the mount: *Therefore all things whatsoever ye would that men should do to you, do ye even so to them: for this is the law and the prophets.*"

"Me and LC get it, Pap Whitey."

"Yes. Me and Yaz are sorry. Very sorry."

Coburn brushed aside the bushy outcropping of his moustache. "You'll need to do some confessing and talking to your mother in the morning." His flinty gaze bore in on them. "Then I'll take you to Mr. Eliezer. You'll make amends with him and offer to do any and all odd jobs he needs doing for as long as he needs them done. Do we understand each other?"

"Yes, Papa."

"Yeah-huh, Papa."

May 11, 1892

Dear Diary: It has been an exhausting day. We started a little later than I would have liked, and arrived in Creede by mid-afternoon. Eliza and Bethsuelo were quiet, so we largely traveled in the company of our own thoughts. We intended to quickly find a room in a boarding house, unload the few belongings we brought along, then see to storage of the buckboard and care for the mules and Cookie at the livery, but all of that took until past nightfall.

We made the rounds to almost a dozen establishments before we finally found these meager lodgings. It's not much more than a lean-to cobbled onto the backside of a clapboard building. The good news is that it has a private entrance, the bad news is that a communal privy is a few short paces from the door. There is one good-sized bed that Eliza and I will share, and a cot for Bethsuelo. A rickety table and a pair of hard-backed chairs are the other furnishings.

Oh, yes. There's also a battered metal oil lamp, left here no doubt, by some miner. It has a defective burner in which the wick slips or gets stuck so it goes from blazing bright to dim at will. It requires off and on tinkering to maintain steadiness, and that is not at all conducive to thinking and writing. All in all, these pricey accommodations are quite disagreeable.

Just now, Eliza has Bethsuelo tucked in for the night, and is reading her a Bible story. Such a precious sight to behold and experience from my perspective as a fly on the wall, though actually, my perch is wobbly furniture that'd better be used as firewood. I am not exaggerating. Every time I shift weight I have to be careful for fear of tipping over. The chair's legs are uneven and the joints have been distressed to the point of being loose. Oh, well. Such is life.

At first light we will make our way to Abbey's cabin. It will be so good to be with my sister, especially at this difficult time. She and I are blessed with a bond that is truly vital to my well-being. We were last together at Christmastime at WT Ranch, so after the initial greetings, we'll surely arrange significant face-time for the opportunity to catch up and share our lives.

I want to hug Deacon and never let go. I will try with all my might to stay strong, but I know my emotions will fail me again and again in the days ahead. He is the inspirational glue that holds a widespread bunch of us together, and though we will rally around him, he will insist that he has no troubles and likely serve to be a great encouragement to us. Which is a safe and proper place to draw this installment to an end, or else the waterworks may begin.

Avis Lahay perused what she had written, then closed the journal and absently fingered the intricate details of the butterfly engraved on its front cover. She clipped the top on the silver fountain pen and slipped it in the daybook's spine. She put her elbows on the ramshackle table and buried her face in her palms while nibbling the inside of her bottom lip.

"It's alright to cry, Avis. Healthy, even."

"I know, I guess," she said, straightening up as her hands dropped onto her lap. The seat creaked noisily beneath her fanny, which elicited a taut smile. "Be mindful, Eliza. The other chair may be a mite sturdier than this one, but I'd be unwilling to make that a promise."

"Not to worry," the long ago schoolteacher from Souderton said as she lowered her still slender frame onto the refugee from the kindling box. "Hans would stir up a fuss if he saw this rattrap, and it'd be especially loud when he heard how much the shysters were charging."

"We didn't and don't have much choice."

"I know," Eliza replied forthrightly. Her complexion was pale and there was tiredness evident in her eyes. Her hair, which used to be thick and straw-colored, was now at sixty-two, thinned out and blended to pretty shades of grayish-white. "I'm not complaining because it's just the economics of a boomtown, but I guarantee that my husband would be making a ruckus."

Avis chirped a giggle. "Yes, I can almost hear him."

"If you had my ears you'd hear him loud and clear," Eliza said, laughing effortlessly. "Tomorrow we need to send a wire to Hans and Stace at the Oxford Hotel in Denver to let them know what's happening. Hans has never had much use for telegrams, so unless there is a miracle or an unprecedented disaster I doubt we'll hear back, but at least they'll have the news."

"That's imperative." The flame sparked in a frenzy. She rapped the base of the oil lamp with a knuckle, then jiggled the wick until it burned calm and evenly. "How's Bethsuelo?"

"A beautiful soul, she is," Eliza answered, low and frank. "The muffin fell asleep halfway through me reading about Queen Esther, which tells me that her gift of foreknowledge isn't disturbing her imagination or making any impressions on her. In my prayers I habitually make requests for exactly that to be the norm rather than the exception, as it so often seems."

"She certainly has mysterious insights."

"As did and does her mother," Eliza said, staring thoughtfully at the lamplight. "Sally Twosongs was eleven years old when we became acquainted. She possessed an incredible inner strength and a spiritual awareness that was quite astonishing. I've watched the same traits grow and develop in my granddaughter. God has touched her with a special blessing."

"Bethsuelo has frequently amazed me."

Eliza slumped back, sighing wearily. "More and more I have become convinced that life goes around in circles. Some big ones, some little ones, but always circular and cyclical. What has been is that which will be again." Her voice had dour threads of sadness woven through each word. "When I first met Deacon, almost a quarter century ago, he was in a grim and dismal state. I prayed continuously and nursed him away from the brink of death. Now, here we are . . . "

The faulty burner flamboyantly malfunctioned. It hissed as sputters of fire and black smoke shot up the chimney shade, then the flare sizzled and extinguished. The sting of coal oil imbued the darkness. The ladies exchanged chuckles of resignation. A moment later, both decrepit chairs groaned as together they gained their feet and began preparing for bed.

The moon was full and yellowish, a pockmarked jewel shining above the mountaintops overshadowing Creede. Abbey Langton sat motionless in a rocker on the porch of her log home looking at the vastness of the star-speckled sky as she handled the locket on its spindly chain around her neck. She had her lips pursed because tears were on the verge of erupting.

She was not alone. Whitey Fitzgerald had carried a chair from the kitchen and spun it around to straddle it and rest his chin on its back. Her father was in the other rocker, a longhaired elder statesman who had his right leg folded over his left as he kept easing back and forth. His expression was sharpened to a determined hardness. "You can't beat yourself up, Abbey."

"I am really questioning my mothering skills."

"You ought not do that, Miss Abbey."

"Why not, Whitey? My sons are desperados."

"They just be boys, Miss Abbey."

"That's a true reckoning," Deacon said, tersely encouraging. "We had us a productive palaver. They comprehend the wrongdoing of their ways, and bright and early tomorrow will be about the business of making amends and restitution. This episode ain't gonna be anywhere near their last venture into misbehavior because the mischief in their blood is a rite of passage."

"Not their last venture into misbehavior?" Abbey questioned, stiffening her posture. She gaped at him as though vines or some such abnormality had sprouted from his ears. Her eyes widened to the popping point. "If that's the case, what am I supposed to do, Deacon?"

"Exactly what you've been doing."

"My tactics have failed, methinks."

"A hiccup is all that occurred today."

"Seems a tad more serious, Deacon."

"It'd be a mistake to give it credence it doesn't deserve."

"I knows them, Miss Abbey," Whitey said bluntly. "They gots lots of rowdiness and rough-housing churning inside, but ain't an ounce of meanness between the two of them."

Coburn nodded and scratched his chin. "I wholeheartedly agree with that assessment. They got a solid foundation of character that at this juncture requires extra supervision. There ain't no malice or nastiness in them. Full of spit and brine, yes. Desperados, no."

"If'in Langton and Yaz be desperados, then I be one too."

"That ain't high praise, Whitey," Deacon offered in a tone that, at least for a fleeting instant, lightened the mood on the porch. "I've had my concerns about you time to time."

"I ain't no hayseed. That be a remark."

"A josh, is all."

"I knows 'cause I be the one clucking."

"I appreciate you two attempting to cheer me up, but I'm afraid that my conscience and thoughts have plummeted into an abyss." She sighed a choked laugh. "I feel like a failure."

"Failure be stupid talk, Miss Abbey."

"I'll say it again: You can't beat yourself up, Abbey," Deacon urged, severe and uncompromising. "Keep bending the saplings in the direction you want them to grow. Be consistent in love and expectations." He slowed, then stopped rocking "Set the bar high without any coddling or allowing excuses, but grant them room and opportunity to fall or get knocked on their buttocks because it's only then that they can learn how to get up and keep going."

"I've tried to do all of that and more."

"No doubt, young lady. You're doing a great job."

"I do have doubts, Deacon." A dribble of teardrops had formed links of wetness on her cheeks. The fingers of her right hand were clasped around the gold locket and she was gently squeezing the treasured token. "I wonder what Sam would think of my mothering skills."

"Sam would be impressed and encouraging," Deacon said, swallowing an audible breath. "You cannot condemn yourself based on this incident. It's a blip." His insistence cut about as effectively as an expertly honed razor blade. "The worse thing we can do is to blow it up into a defining defeat in their young lives. Our task is to use it to forge the consequences into a positive life-lesson that will get trapped in the drainpipe at the bottom of their brains."

Fitzgerald abruptly stood and wagged a finger at both of them. "That be why we must operate together. We has got to put our wisdom in the same pot and dole it out equal."

"I just feel like I've let Sam down."

"I don't mean to be stepping outta line, Miss Abbey, but I knowed Samuel Beadle," the barber chimed in, eyes glimmering. "Samuel Beadle was a friend of mine before you come to be his sweetheart. The day you walked into Abilene was the finest day of his whole life. If'in he could be here now his chest would be swelled so big that buttons would be firing like bullets."

"Dear, sweet, wonderful, encourager Whitey."

"Langton would make Samuel prouder than proud."

Coburn uncrossed his legs and leaned forward, eyelids sagging. "True enough. LC and Yaz will rise above this gag gone wrong. No one ever makes it from infancy to manhood without a snag or two along the course. I'm heading way over yonder and I got no earnest concerns for my grandsons. Their mother is straight-arrow true and their hearts are fertile soil."

She sniffled and pressed her palm over the locket. Strength surfaced from a deep well of resilience; it slipped off her lips in a murmur. Calmness was in her heart as she rocked the chair. She pushed an unconquerable smile at the most important men in her life, then Abbey Langton sat back and gazed at the moon, which was being scraped by a thready web of clouds.

chapter three

Olden Days

*"I have seen the travail, which God hath given to the sons of men to
be exercised in it. He hath made everything beautiful in his time:
also he hath set the world in their heart, so that no man can find out
the work that God maketh from the beginning to the end."*

~SOLOMON~

THREE WEEKS LATER, THE morning dawned bright and beautiful. Blue
skies dominated from horizon to horizon. The air was pristine and in-
vigorating crispness. Outside of Creede, a pair of riders enjoyed the scin-
tillating dance of sunbeams glistening on a colorful array of wildflowers
decorating the grassy carpet of a dew-bathed meadow beside the Rio
Grande.

Deacon Coburn reined Gilgal to a halt. "A gift."

Avis Lahay followed his lead. "Yes. Beautiful."

"From sunrise to sunset, around and around it goes," he said, squinting. "Each day is a gift from the creator of the universe, and not a one of us
can ever be grateful enough."

"We must always try to do our best."

"That we must," he rasped dryly. "While we humbly put forth the best
we got we proceed in confidence, knowing that the amazing grace of God
fills in the gaps of our feeble failings."

"It's always that way, isn't it, Deacon?"

"Forever and always, as long as we're breathing."

"Life can be peculiar."

"In what way, Avis?"

"The uncertainty, the fickleness of it."

"Life has zero guarantees, except its uncertainty and fickleness," he replied, flexing back as his hands locked behind his head. He had gotten into the habit of not wearing his cowboy hat. He swiveled his shoulders slightly to get her in his sightline. "That's why it is essential for us to appreciate those seasons when God provides us remnants of sweetness. If we respond to his mercies with thanksgiving, a comprehension regarding the fragility of life is cultivated."

"And empathy for others encountering heartaches."

"Great point."

"Thanks, but I likely learned it from you," she said, smiling softly. "I figure the only way to nip self-pity in the bud and give it walking papers is to take a look around to see that no matter how tough or difficult we think our situation may be, there's always a sadder story nearby."

"The only healthy way to live, I expect."

"It's the perspective that keeps me centered."

"Same for me on most days."

She rubbed Cookie's neck. "And on other days?"

"King David's eloquence."

The strawberry roan whinnied impatiently. She drawled an appeasing whisper. "I've been camped out in Psalms for many months with an emphasis on being purposeful in personalizing the poetic prayers and appropriating the powerful truths. The Lord is *my* strength, *my* rock, *my* fortress, *my* deliverer, *my* provider, *my* shield, *my* salvation, *my* stronghold, *my* shepherd."

"Amen." He placed his hands on the saddle horn. "*The Lord is my light and my salvation; whom shall I fear? The Lord is the strength of my life; of whom shall I be afraid?*"

A warm breeze picked up. She quickly removed her skimmer to enjoy the wind riffling her gingery locks, which were unbound. "You really aren't afraid of dying, are you, Deacon?"

"I ain't afraid of being dead." He slid to the ground and took hold of his mount's mane to give it an affectionate tug. The horse nickered in response. "Dying, on the other hand, is a whole different proposition. I am troubled that I won't finish the race strong and die well."

"Die well?"

He gave her a hard-edged glance accompanied by an expansive shrug. "I want to be used up and empty when my time of dying comes, but of that date and time I have no say."

"It'll be too soon whenever it is, Deacon."

"You get no say either, Avis. It will be when it will be."

"I'm praying Mom will get here," she said, slipping the skimmer on. "I got a telegram from Raton. First the train was delayed for more than a week by a massive snowstorm, then when the digging out was done, there was a breakdown that required extensive repairs."

"I'm sure your mother is rolling with it all and making do." He dragged a hand through the tousled thicket of shoulder-length hair and chuckled. "Delores and I have had a remarkable friendship, but she never ceased to cheerfully complain about my disheveled appearance."

She smirked, eyes lively and gleaming. "I remember. Once I heard her ragging on you and she said something like: *How can a man whose best friend is a barber have sheepdog hair?*"

"Me and Whitey have had us a time." He rumbled an enlivened laugh. "When I consider a fraction of the variables involved, I am persuaded and indeed convinced, that my life has been marvelous. When I go home to glory, no sad tears, Avis. Only celebratory tears allowed because I will be free and fully know the eternity set inside me by God's design and purpose."

"I can't make any promises about tears, Deacon."

"We'll meet again, Avis." He took a couple hesitant steps and moved in front of the gelding. He locked his hands on the bridle's horizontal straps, then while thumbing each of the stones he forcefully pressed his brow against the horse's forehead. The silver-dappled buckskin swished its tail. He stretched and backed up. "Please ask Stace to take good care of Gilgal."

"He'll be proud to do so."

Coburn began strolling through a bank of daisies and daffodils. "The variety of flowers are a reminder that no matter how bitter a circumstance, our experiences can be redeemed and our life renewed. Every springtime, after being buried by frost and snow these delicate bits of loveliness thrive. In another time and place I picked wildflowers for my mother. She had a wealth of heartfelt wisdom about spiritual matters gleaned from the natural world."

"I've gathered much of that from you."

"Mostly her voice, would be my suspicion," he replied, taking a knee. "She never missed an opportunity to teach practical truths from observing the birds of the air, the mountain laurel, the currents of a river, the changing seasons, the setting sun, the rising moon. She had acquired an inexhaustible stockpile of insights by being in alignment with the rhythms of nature."

"You are most definitely your mother's son, Deacon."

He laughed modestly. Then, without warning, he demonstrated the innocent glee of a child by diving face-first into a patch of grass. He rotated onto his back, enthralled by the ceiling of blueness. He meshed his fingers together atop his belt buckle as a chuckle rattled around his gullet. "I'm sore and bone tired, but this rare pleasure of dewy freshness will revive me."

She dismounted. "While you nap, I'll collect some flowers."

His eyes drooped shut. Birds chirped and twittered in the stillness. He floated into a thin sleep, which ended when back-to-back explosions of dynamite from the King Solomon district north of town shattered the tranquility. In the echo, plumes of grime spouted its smudge to sully a section of what had been an immaculate sheet of blue. The companions swapped grins, then within moments, Deacon Coburn and Avis Lahay were on horseback returning homeward.

Meanwhile, at a shack on the ledge of an incline against the western wall of the community, LC Beadle and Yaz Lightfoot, without ever thinking of it as such, were paying penance. The one-room shanty built on a foundation of tree stumps sat off by itself, elevated twenty-odd feet above the neighboring residences, appearing to be a crow's nest lookout.

The boys were busy working for the owner, digging a drainage ditch of sorts. They had been hard at it for five days straight and were finally coming to the end of the line. A shovel and pickaxe kept being traded between them at regular intervals, and they only rested when they were satisfied with the progress, or when told to do so, which happened just now.

"Time to take a breather and feed the beast, boyos!" a tall redhead called from the doorway of the dwelling. "Are you scallywags hungry and ready for hardtack biscuits?"

"If you are, Mr. Eliezer," LC replied politely.

"I surely be."

"Yeah-huh."

"What are you waiting for, Christmas?"

The brothers scurried up the slope, placed their tools against an outside wall, and then stepped onto the overhang of a veranda. "We'll be finished before noontime, Mr. Eliezer."

"Maybe so, maybe not," he answered lightheartedly.

LC tilted a frown at him. "How come?"

"After grub I have an errand for you to run."

"Alright."

"Yeah-huh."

"Glad that we settled that pickle in a pig." The man formerly known as the Prophet Eliezer was hardly recognizable. The gone-to-rot animal-skin vestment had been discarded; he wore store-bought dungaree bib-coveralls over blue flannel long johns. The bedraggled hair and frazzled beard were sheared off in a military cut and there was a few days of reddish stubble sprouting on his chin and cheeks. A stylishly pruned moustache shadowed his upper lip.

"Mr. Eliezer?"

"Yepper, what is it, LC?"

"Me and Yaz are awful sorry for what we done."

"Yeah-huh."

"Do you boyos want to make me mad?"

"No, sir."

"Then stow the apologies," he said, handing over two biscuits a piece. "I heard you the first dozen times. Your antics were horsefeathers, but that's done and done, and all is well that ends well. I have forgiven you, so can we put that yesterday behind us and be friends?"

"Me and LC would like that, Mr. Eliezer."

"Then let's make it so."

"Whatcha got for us to do?" LC asked, nibbling on the crusty rations.

"Danged if I remember," Eliezer replied, dropping his big body onto a bench that had been hacked out of hefty logs. "Beats the heck outta me how my memory comes and goes like a mosquito buzzing between my ears. I tries to grab it and off it goes until whenever comes."

"We ain't in any hurry, Mr. Eliezer."

"Yeah-huh."

"I'm long in the tooth and I heard tell that you can't teach an old dog new tricks, but I ain't dumber than a coal bucket," Eliezer said regretfully. "I should be able to hold onto an idea so as to explain it. Sometimes I be jawing a mile a minute and my brain keeps pace with my mouth, but then, quicker than a lick I'm fumbling to connect dots inside my noggin."

"That's why we're sorry so much."

"Yeah-huh."

"Ain't your fault my thinker is broken." His face crumpled into a pain-racked contortion. "Chancellorsville was the hellfire kettle that catawamptiously chawed me up and spat me out like a ball of snot. You two boyos weren't shooting cannonballs at Chancellorsville, were you?"

"No, sir," they answered together, heads shaking.

"Then done be done."

"Papa says we are to respect your wishes," LC said, rather emphatically. "We still have a lot to learn about living the Golden Rule." He was sitting on the porch with his legs dangling over the edge, while Yaz stood leaning against the doorframe munching on his second biscuit.

"Your Papa is a real man, boyos."

Yaz squatted, eyes darkening. "He's sick."

"Yepper, he told me."

"Yeah-huh."

Eliezer clapped his hands together. "Not to worry, boyos. That's what he'd tell you. He knows about grace and mercy and second chances. He will saunter through the pearly gates no questions asked." He got dreamy-eyed, then chucked to his feet. He sniffed the air as his head tilted back. He took a step away from the bench and started chuckling perkily. "Apples."

LC crooked an eyebrow at him. "What about apples?"

"That's what I want. The errand I got for you," Eliezer replied, jubilant laughter in his voice. His cheeks flushed. "Apples. Go to the grocery store and see if they have any apples. If none are for sale, then ask the clerk when a supply will come in. If they do have a bushel of apples set out be sure to get the pricing information for me. My taste buds want apples."

"Alright."

"Yeah-huh."

"What you waiting for, Easter?"

The brothers smirked at each other, then LC Beadle and Yaz Lightfoot jumped and were running down the steep grade as if they were on fire. There was the obstacle of a split-rail fence extending partway across an alley at the bottom, but the hindrance didn't slow them for even an instant. They hurdled and cleared the barrier, and guffaws of jolliness trailed behind them.

By mid-morning at *WT Ranch*, Naomi Axler was way too anxious to wait. Her husband and daughter were taking an excessive amount of time at the corrals and barn. The sunlit kitchen smelled of fresh baked bread cooling on a rack. An unopened letter on the table had her interest aroused. Sally Twosongs delivered it from South Fork late last night, and now, Naomi arbitrarily decided to take a seat. She tore the envelope and shook the pages free, grinning impishly.

March 30, 1892

Caribbean Sea

Dear Mom and Dad: Good morning. As with every letter, I figure I'm more than safe greeting you in that way, since if I know you two at all, you're sitting at the kitchen table having coffee together while Mom reads this dispatch aloud. It is being written from just outside of Kingston, Jamaica on the deck of the Diamond Duster, a full-rigged iron hulled clipper that was built in 1875 to carry 500 ton of cargo, and remains sturdy and sea-worthy.

The day is cool and cloud covered. The air has a distinctly sweet aroma that is difficult to describe, but it tickles my nostrils. Just finished a four hour stretch of nonstop work, but my jobs are finished for the time being. I've got an hour or so before another round of responsibilities will need my attention. I am situated not far from the wheelhouse with my pad and pen.

The ship is in full sail and the greenish-blue water is rolling and choppy. A stiff wind is behind us and the going is good and pleasant. We are on course for Savannah with a cargo of molasses and rum. I've been to that port city in Georgia numerous times. It's quaint and agreeable, but like any place else, the waterfront docks are rough and rowdy.

There has been no official word, but the scuttlebutt says we will anchor long enough to unload, get provisions, and then acquire a consignment of cotton to be transported to Toronto, Canada. If that gossip is true, it will be my first time to Canada, which is exciting. I am always enthused by the idea of going where I've never been to see sites I've never seen.

Toronto is on the north shore of Lake Ontario, which is one of the Great Lakes. The idea of exploring that area has got my imagination lit up. A shipmate told me about Niagara Falls so that natural wonder is on my agenda. I have a goodly sum of money stashed away, and will likely take leave of this outfit and spend some weeks reconnoitering the city and countryside before travel-ing to see the rapids and falls on the Niagara River. All in all, a great adventure.

After that, I'll hire on with another merchant vessel, which will present no hardship or problem. I have done so many times, always departing on solid terms. My leather attaché case has a half-dozen letters of recommendations from previous captains I've served under. Not a one I solicited a reference from balked at do-ing so, which certainly has much to do with my work ethic and upbringing. I see a job that needs doing and do it, no big whoop.

Thank you for raising me the way you did. The more exposure I have to different points of view and attitudes, and the increas-ing distance from my childhood makes me truly appreciate the important stuff that was ingrained in me by your teaching and example. I cannot tolerate sloth or jerry-rigging tasks or repairs. I was paired up with a sluggish quipster a week ago to check and mark ropes that needed to be replaced. His haphazard and lacka-daisical approach infuriated me, but I kept my temper. I think Mr. Weitzel would have tossed him overboard.

Two nights ago there was a spectral display of peculiar lights in the northern sky. I was on nightwatch and alone on deck. I watched the phenomenon with an ever-expectant eagerness, and it took me all the way back to Bulldog Mountain and those ex-traordinary happenings with Sally Twosongs when Hank fought that bobcat, and in doing so, sacrificed life to protect me. It seemed to be faraway, but also, the memory was so vital it felt like yester-day. Strange.

Tell Uncle Deacon the next time you see him that I am ex-tremely grateful that I inherited wanderlust from him. As much as I miss home and family, and the mountains surrounding WT Ranch, I am spellbound by the seafaring life more than can be expressed. Seeing exotic ports of call, meeting and interacting with all kinds of different people and cultures thrills me. To learn from others and come to understand common ground connections en-riches me.

It's a breathtaking windswept world packed full of voyages and ventures that are available to me just now, and I hope and ex-pect to take full advantage of these opportunities. I cannot imag-ine putting down roots any time soon, though somewhere in my future a trip home will come to fruition. I'll keep you appraised of my travels via correspondence. When I am in a seaport for a length of time long enough to get a reply, I'll send a telegram.

Give my salutations to Amanda. I think of all the fun we had during our growing up years with much fondness. I hope she has the same feelings. We had us some special times that's for sure. A spat over silliness here or there, but nothing serious ever. You are all in my thoughts and prayers. Be not afraid for me. I am well, and because of past training and practice, have full confidence that I have the aptitude to adjust or adapt to whatever circum-stances evolve.

Take care until the tidal currents shift for me to see you again.

Warmest Regards,

Your son, Jesse

Naomi scanned the opening paragraph again—a smile broadened her lips and reached up to make her eyes shiny. She hurriedly got to her feet, rushed to the wood-box and chose a couple splintery chunks of fuel to stoke the fire in the cookstove, which was a bed of red coals. Satisfied that flames would develop, she prepared a pot of coffee and put it on the stove, then Naomi Axler stood at the window, tarrying expectantly for her husband and daughter.

"Miss Avis, you be prettier than the morning."

Avis Lahay and Deacon Coburn looked up to see Eliezer on the overhang of his porch waving happily at them. She acknowledged the welcome as Deacon loosely tied the reins of their horses to a post of the split-rail fence. Side by side they made their way up the elevation to the shack, and it was easily evident that Coburn was weak and struggling to maintain balance.

"A sight to warm the cockles of an old coot's heart, Miss Avis."

"You are an irascible gentleman, Mr. Eliezer."

"I can't remember nothing about who I was before Chancellorsville, but have decided that I weren't no mister," he replied, a deferential grin encompassing his face. "I'm going to start calling myself just plain old Eliezer Smith. I think that'll be a fitting moniker for me."

"Makes a fine impression," Deacon said, staggering drunkenly. He teetered, weaved and almost fell, but Avis latched onto his forearm solid enough for him to gain relative stability.

Eliezer Smith bolted into action. He scampered down the hillside and wrapped Coburn in a sideward bear hug. "Lean on me." He half-lifted half-dragged him to the porch and put him on the log bench. "You sit tight and get those lungs full of oxygen so we can talk some theology."

"Sounds like a plan."

"You got him, Miss Avis?"

"I do, Mr. Smith."

Eliezer hooted as he dashed inside. He returned momentarily with a Bible under an arm and a stool in hand, which he strategically placed near the bench. He settled on it. "Those little shavers were here again and I expect they'll be back later. Ain't been nothing but kind to me."

Coburn rested his right ankle on his left knee. "Glad to hear it."

Avis sat on the floor with her back against the wall. "Me, too."

"I am pleased by their friendship," Eliezer said, flipping open his Bible and fluttering its pages until he came to the passage he wanted. "You up for some brain stretching, brother?"

"Always ready to listen and learn, my friend."

"Chancellorsville done me in."

"Gettysburg for me."

"Both glimpses of hell."

Coburn winced. "Amen, brother."

"Which got me thinking about Paul's thorn in the flesh."

"The Civil War is a thorn in the flesh of this country."

"That it is, Deacon, but personalize it," Eliezer said urgently. He straightened his backbone and placed an index finger on the text. "II Corinthians 12:7–9 reads: *And lest I should be exalted above measure through the abundance of the revelations, there was given to me a thorn in the flesh, the messenger of Satan to buffet me, lest I should be exalted above measure. For this thing I besought the Lord thrice, that it might depart from me. And he said unto me, my grace is sufficient for thee: for my strength is made perfect in weakness. Most gladly therefore will I rather glory in my infirmities, that the power of Christ may rest upon me.*"

"*The messenger of Satan to buffet me,*" Deacon repeated, head shaking slowly. "The thief, the enemy of our souls, comes only to steal and kill and destroy, and those blood-soaked battlefields stole, killed and destroyed more than we will comprehend this side of glory."

"You picked the words right out of my mind," Eliezer said, laughing genially. "Paul's thorn in the flesh was the messenger of Satan, the robber baron who kills and destroys. Was the thorn physical? Bad eyesight? Hard of hearing? A crippled leg or some such thing?"

"We don't exactly know, do we?"

"No, but here's my theory of late," Eliezer answered, hunkering forward. "Given our similar experiences of horrors in our yesteryears, is it possible that what tormented Paul was emotional and spiritual? Wounds of shame and guilt because of his choice to reject Jesus of Nazareth, which resulted in him going to war against the followers of Jesus. Paul became a zealous participant in murder who tendered much violence in the name of his hatred of Christ."

"Then he met the risen Christ on the road to Damascus."

"Exactly!" Eliezer exclaimed, beaming excitedly. "When confronted by the blinding light of the One he had breathed constant threats against, his heart and perspective were changed, but I am suggesting that even in that radical transformation, the realization of his misguided fury was something he could never escape. Paul went on to be greatly used by God, a standard-bearer for the gospel, but it is my opinion that he never forgot from whence he came.

"He preached and taught and lived grace, but like the flesh and blood man he was, he could not shutdown the inner workings of his mind. The memory of his determination to destroy the Jesus movement was the cross he shouldered, the thorn pricking his flesh; a reminder of his desperate and almighty need for benevolence. In a brilliant letter written to Timothy when Paul was an old man, he referred to himself as the chief of sinners, the absolute worst of sinners."

"The thorn being the infamy of his bygone days?"

"Exactly!" Eliezer said, closing the Bible. "His regrets haunted him. He pleaded with God three times for the affliction to be removed, but the response he received from God was that in Paul's weakness God's strength would be made perfect because his grace was all-sufficient."

"Interesting," Deacon murmured, jaw clenching. "As I consider this tract of reasoning in the context of my life, in the reality of what I live with day by day, I lean toward full agreement. We cannot undo or change the hurts and harms of our past. We grab hold of all the grace we can scrounge, but still, the deep roots of toxic recollections produce unbidden nightmares.

"In those prickly moments, we must choose, with God being our provider of wisdom and fortitude, to no longer be influenced by the ache and baggage of our lives. The thorn is always present, but by God's miraculous grace we are made strong to press on to the higher calling the Lord puts upon our lives. And in all of this our faith is expanded and God is glorified."

"Is that what you believe?"

"It truly is, Eliezer."

Avis Lahay had remained silent, listening intently. She now cut in. "If you'll accept input from a layperson, all this makes practical sense to me. There are horrible memories in my past. I have no control over them making their presence known. The images can be upsetting, but I always have the choice to release and let them go, or dwell on them and be dragged down."

"Yes, yes, yes, Miss Avis!" Eliezer clapped gleefully. "As feeble and complex as we are, that's the thorn that snags us, and if we choose wisdom, keeps us seeking at the mercy seat of God. Just like Paul we are jabbed by the thorn, and must respond by firmly choosing to put all our yesterdays behind us as we reach onward to take hold of all that God has for us."

"An enlightening word, my friend," Deacon said, visibly wilting. He took a swift upward peek. The sun was still some degrees east of its apex. He drew a heavy breath and it was exhaled as an exhausted sigh. "I wonder, Eliezer. Could you please assist me down to that fence and get me seated in the saddle? I'm in dire need of rest, and Abbey will be waiting for me."

Eliezer Smith and Avis Lahay joined forces, and got on either side of him. The threesome wobble-shuffled at a measured gait that kept all vertical, though there was doddering instability. When he was comfortably mounted, Deacon Coburn held the reins nice and easy. Avis smiled tensely and doffed her hat to Eliezer, then rode down the alleyway alongside the dying man.

༄༅༅

The streets of Creede had become a maze-like diversion for Lucinda Eno-chelli. There was numbness in her and a stony expression on her face. Her heart and mind were engaged in a tug of war conflict. She knew where she wanted to go, but was avoiding the destination, so she had rounded the same block repeatedly; both clockwise and counter clockwise.

Her morning had begun with three shots of bourbon to take the edge off her nervousness, followed by chain smoking the same number of cigarettes. She had spent an inordinate amount of time mentally and emotionally preparing for this day, but now that it was here, a part of her wanted to find a place to hide. Sleep had become the rarest of commodities; for seven straight nights fitful slumber kept her in a constant state of tossing and turning.

She wore a conservative-cut dress that was the drab color of dirt and unadorned by any frills or lace. It was not at all pretty or flattering, but it equaled her discombobulated mood. To her, the unimaginative apparel was reminiscent of prison garb, but even so, two days ago she had decisively made the purchase specifically for this occasion. The high-collar, combined with binding undergarments, did much to obscure the prominence of her top-heavy curves.

She had been walking for more than an hour and was getting nowhere. The strap of a paisley handbag was looped around her fisted right hand as though she was afraid that some thug might attempt to snatch it. At each turn of a corner she would compulsively touch a side of the oversized purse as if checking to be sure that the contents were secure.

The document inside was an unopened envelope, which at this point in time, she thought of as a valuable treasure because she had invested a number of years on a cross-country trek to deliver it to its rightful owner. Along with a tidy sum of cold hard cash, it had been discovered in a safe-deposit box entrusted to a Philadelphia attorney who handled her father's estate.

Now, with the sun beginning its westward crossing, her heart told her there could be no more hesitations or delays. Her breathing was shallow, creating stitches of tension in her lungs. She mustered nerve and audacity as she pushed past an assembly of loitering pedestrians, then stepped off the boardwalk and sashayed deliberately along the dusty avenue.

She remembered the young man she had once known. From this distance that era seemed to be more than a lifetime ago. He had been straight-laced and so serious-minded as to be somber and downright gloomy. The fluid dynamics of their relationship, which for a fleeting briefness broached the subject of matrimony, were knotted together by parallel objectives.

A naughty smile bent her lips. She laughed aloud at a recollection of his puritanical ways. Her shameless flirting had always garnered an awkward reaction, and she had so enjoyed his embarrassed discomfort. The memory bucked up her resolve and courage, and then, Lucinda Enochelli increased her pace and set-off directly to have a sitdown with Deacon Coburn.

The golden haze in the longhouse was thicker than before, but Charley Jondreau was unchanged. He sat cross-legged in the cozy warmth and radiance of the smallish campfire. His buckskin leggings and beaded pullover shirt were the same, as was the long black hair resting on his shoulders. His head was bowed in humble supplication. His fingers were twined together in an old familiar way while he thoughtfully twiddled the stone around on his thumbs.

A rustle caused him to look up. "You are back again, eh."

"Not sure why, Charley."

"Time shortens, preacher-man."

"What am I doing here?"

"There's that question again."

"Wanting a straight answer, Charley."

"Sit with me. We shall talk, eh."

Coburn eased into a squat. He then made an adjustment and stretched out so that he was propped up on his elbows. He stared at the flames. "Confusion is a cloud within me."

"The past is at odds with the present."

"How so?"

Jondreau grinned. "That's for you to tell me."

"Regrets from the past are thorns in my flesh."

"Now you have your straight answer, eh."

"I ain't following, Charley."

"Your mind is troubled. Search it."

"I have. I do. My regrets are unfixable."

"Your future brings a different view, eh."

"Help me to see, Charley."

"The past is prelude to the present and future."

"Tell me something I don't know."

"There is a scab on your heart, eh."

"That ain't helpful."

"The unhealed wound of a son."

Coburn scowled, squinty-eyed. "My father? Amos was a hard and mostly fair man. The whys and wherefores of the conflict between us and his grind on me remain a mystery."

"His pathway was not yours?"

"No. We were both headstrong."

"The relationship was ruptured, eh?"

"We had contrasting viewpoints and opinions."

"That is the way of fathers and sons."

"My decision shamed him."

"Tell me more, preacher-man."

"Unsure of where to begin, Charley."

"At the pressure point of the breach, eh."

"Slavery. Abolitionists. The war."

"Evil begetting evil."

"Slavery was blasphemy."

"And the war wasn't blasphemy, preacher-man?"

"The foulest of blasphemies."

"Violence begets violence. Blasphemy begets blasphemy."

"Truer words were never spoken," Deacon replied, gloomy-voiced. "Right or wrong, the River Brethren community of Conoy Creek disciplined and disfellowshipped me. The shunning put an extreme burden and stain on the family, especially Father. I was off and doing. None of it mattered to me, but my suspicions are that it weighed heavy on him and crushed his spirit."

"Your choices are not responsible for his responses, eh."

"I reckon not, but there it is," Deacon said despairingly. "I wanted no dissension between us, but my conscience could not abide the blackhearted and unspeakable abominations visited upon those captives shackled by the chains of slavery. I came to believe that war against slavers and proponents of that vile institution was the only course of action available. My beliefs were contrary to the way of peace. When President Lincoln called for volunteers I enlisted."

"What then?"

"Father's condemnation put much remorse in me."

Jondreau stopped twiddling his thumbs and flipped the stone up and snatched it out of the air with his right hand. He squeezed it hard, smiling knowingly. "Yet you went to war, eh?"

"I betrayed myself."

"To experience what?"

"Bloodshed. Horrors."

"An endless supply, no?"

"Bodies broken and shattered, hearts utterly blackened," Deacon answered, struggling to sit up. He crossed one leg under the other. "I was lost and nearly destroyed. Just one lone man suffering through the grotesque slaughter amongst thousands and thousands of other fractured souls. I was fortunate to find myself and be found by the persistent compassion of God."

"In hindsight, what's been learned?"

"My idealism deceived me, Charley."

"You were blind, but now you see?"

"Yes, clearly."

Jondreau dug deeper. "Any other insights?"

"The consequences of my choices have no end."

"So your father was right, eh?"

"I cannot apologize for my life, can I?"

"Your guilt cries out."

"I made a tragic mistake. I was wrong," Deacon said, lips pinched. "The way of peace moves slowly and costs much in terms of sacrificial service to humankind, but looking back, wisdom tells me that more understanding and effort should have been extended. Though the price is high and the results appear unattainable the way of peace is the proper choice."

"Now you seek forgiveness, eh."

"I walk daily in God's forgiveness."

"What of the balm of *your* forgiveness?"

Coburn bristled. "My forgiveness?"

Jondreau shrugged it off. He pushed his thick hair back with his left hand, then casually opened his right to study the stone cupped in it. His eyes sparkled in the firelight as his mouth flexed and tightened into its bulldog guise. "You must forgive yourself, preacher-man."

"What's so important about that stone?"

"You are not ready, eh," Charley replied mildly. "Go. Be faithful. Press on."

Coburn stood, tall and statuesque. His face was furrowed into a puckered mask that was a mixture of desperate yearning and blunt bewilderment. His shoulders, distinctively broad and as sturdy as an oak plank, sank and inclined forward. He looked around at the gossamer wreath of golden vapor collapsing in on him, and tenaciously remained stationary in his footsteps.

"For what are you waiting, preacher-man?"

It was early in the afternoon. Abbey Langton had anxiety seeping from her eyes. She sat stiff and erect in the rocker on her porch watching her father sleeping restlessly in the other chair. Her concern darkened her countenance. Her auburn hair, highlighted by tints of gold that had become more prominent in recent years, was tied back beneath a blue-checkered bandana.

The joints of the chair began to squeak softly, so she quit rocking. A crawling rash of goosepimples on her forearms were itchy, but she ignored the annoyance. She felt cold and out of sorts, drawing in shivery snippets of air, which belied the warmth of the sunshine. Her gaze drifted onto the hemmed in alley, and in an instant, the heat of anger filled her belly.

She leapt to her feet and rushed off the porch so rapidly that she almost tripped down the two steps. She restored her balance and became a blockade, arms locked in a fierce fold below her bosom. Her expression, hardened into a stink-eyed glare retrieved from childhood, was fixed on a wide-hipped brunette in a long-sleeved dress as dull as dishwater. The woman carried a paisley handbag, and stopped ten feet away, determination and purpose in her posture.

"Now's not a good time," Abbey said tautly. She had her feet set apart and planted firmly to guard the entranceway to her home. "In fact, you are not at all welcome here, Lucinda."

"Please. This is not easy for me."

"Then turn around and leave."

"I can't, Abbey. Please."

"Who are you? What do you have to do with my father?"

"If his memory works, you'll find out soon enough. Please."

Abbey bit the inside of her lip hard enough to draw blood. The tension and anger in her spiked, but then, as she peered into her visitor's pleading eyes, which were as black and shiny as polished onyx, empathy and compassion clogged up her throat. She hesitantly eased backwards, then with suspicion and wariness on her face, she motioned for the woman to follow her.

Lucinda crept onto the porch and stared unbelievingly at the man she had invested years pursuing in a sometime irrational quest. His scruffy hair and wildman beard were streaked by dense strands of grayish-white, and the net of wrinkles around his eyes were deeply cut and drawn. "My God, we've gotten old, haven't we?" she whispered, dry and hoarse.

Abbey touched his shoulder. "Deacon, Lucinda Enochelli is here to see you."

≈≈≈

He came awake in a spasmodic jerk. His eyelids flapped and blinked, and his disorientation was obvious. His lungs clamped shut and he felt like he was drowning in a sea of madness. He clutched the arms of the rocker as though the chair itself was a life-preserver keeping him afloat. He eyeballed her, head shaking and jaw quivering. There was a blur of an aura around her. The past rushed into the present. "Alice? Alice Gallagher? Is that you?"

"By God, you remember."

"Is it really you? Alice?"

"I could ask the same of you, Deke."

"I ain't heard my name shortened since I can't recall when," he said, heaving to his feet. He took a short, stuttering step and reached for her, and though she demonstrated a conspicuous reluctance, he wrapped her up in an exuberant embrace. "I could have been asked a thousand times who Lucinda Enochelli was and I would've *never* came up with Alice Gallagher."

A staccato burst of throaty laughter escaped her lips. She pushed back and extricated herself from his arms. "Not sure if that is good or bad. Am I such a forgettable person?"

"Did I or did I not remember you?"

"Point taken."

"And nowadays my brain's a fog more often than not," he told her, slumping into his chair. He made a gesture for her to join him in the other rocker, and she did so. He flinched a squinty-eyed smile at his daughter, shrugging expansively. "I met Alice and her father Blackjack when I left home in the autumn of '53. They were the proprietors of Gallagher's Cove, a popular tavern in the riverfront district of Philadelphia, not far from dives and roughhouses."

Abbey raised an eyebrow. "A tough neighborhood."

"Served a tasty fish stew as a specialty. And hot apple cider," he said, nostalgia glinting in his eyes. "I ate and drank my fill, but not a bowl or a tankard since before the war. I worked in the abolitionist movement with Alice. We thought we were going to change the world, but no one could stall the terrible swift sword that came as punishment or atonement for the repulsive sins of slavery because *the judgments of the Lord are true and righteous altogether.*"

"We helped some folks, Deke."

"I suppose we did. Not enough though."

"You are too hard on yourself, Deacon," Abbey said, easily backpedaling. "Sounds like there's much recollecting and storytelling to do, so I will depart and leave you to it."

"No, please stay, Abbey."

Coburn nodded. "If Alice doesn't insist, I will."

Abbey held up a finger. "Give me two shakes." She smiled as she went inside, hastily returning with a chair from the kitchen. She held her skirt as she sat and crossed her legs. "You two do me a great kindness by inviting me. I am privileged to participate in this reunion, and I must tell you that my curiosity is entirely peaked. For starters, why Lucinda Enochelli?"

"Yes. Why that name, Alice?"

"It's not that big of a mystery, Deke."

"Perhaps not, but it's got me stumped."

"My mother was a spunky Italian lady named Lucinda," Alice replied, rolling her eyes wittily. "My father's slave name was Enoch, so I just combined the two with a flair and *voilà*, Lucinda Enochelli. I thought the inventive handle had a big city old world ring that fit."

"Alright, but *why* the name change?"

"My life never turned out as I expected, Deke."

"Nobody's ever does, Alice."

"I took a side-rail that was in no way pretty."

"As did I."

"Likely not as ugly as mine, Deke."

"It ain't a contest, is it?"

"I went to prison," Alice said plainly. "Our action-oriented band put no stock in yakking. In the early days of the war we set our goals on Southern sympathizer businessmen to destroy property and capital. We wanted to be all about disruption and choking off the cash flow."

Coburn rested his chin in the hollow of his right hand. The dampness of sorrow filled his eyes. "I killed hundreds of men. A sharpshooter squeezing the trigger at the behest of superior officers, genuinely convinced that I was involved in the noble cause of dismantling slavery. I was traumatized by the bloodletting at Fredericksburg, Chancellorsville and Gettysburg."

"Traumatized?"

"My mind was broken, Alice," he answered, slouching tiredly. "My daughter's mother, a beautiful woman inside and out, cared for me with an acceptance and tenderness that initiated the healing process. Without Angela's unconditional love, I might've been lost forever."

"So we've both been through the mill."

"By God's grace we survived and overcame."

"Mayhap you, Deke. Me not so much."

"You're alive and breathing."

"I'm a rotten person. I've done terrible things."

"Welcome to the human race, Alice."

"Ha-ha. Very funny."

"No humor intended," Deacon said strongly. "Ain't anyone righteous or clean. We've all been marked by the stain of sin and deceived into wrong-headed thinking. We've all done terrible deeds, which we want to remain hidden in the darkness, but God never quits on us. Ain't no one who doesn't stand in constant need of the grace and mercy of Almighty God."

Wetness welled up in her eyes. "None of that is available to me."

"You're mistaken, Alice. Time and truth will prove that out."

"I doubt there's any hope of that for me."

Coburn smiled, soft-eyed and gentle. "What are you doing here?"

Alice Gallagher a.k.a. Lucinda Enochelli moistened her lips as she opened the handbag. She reached inside and came out with an envelope. "I found this letter amongst my father's important papers at a time when I was searching . . . " A frigid lump slid icily into place and frosted her voice box. She gulped and swallowed hard. "Searching for myself, I guess."

He took hold of the correspondence. The paper was coarse and fibrous. His fingers trembled and his eyes popped wide when he discerned the name and return address written in the upper left corner. His saliva dried up—his mouth became parched and cottony; stinging, even. He exhaled loudly, and then, Deacon Coburn clenched his teeth in a befuddled grimace.

"Aren't you going to open it, Deke?"

At that moment, a passenger train blew its steam-whistle shrillness as the locomotive chugged into Willow Creek Canyon. Delores Solrizo, feeling grungy and fatigued, awakened. She rubbed her eyes, then from her window seat, studied the small wedge of Creede that could be seen, which amounted to the platform of the depot and a sheer rock wall of a mountain.

The trip had been strenuous and acutely frustrating because of being prolonged by an unforeseen series of peculiar and quirky circumstances. She was wearied and perturbed by the numerous delays. It seemed to her that stormy weather and mechanical problems had developed a dovetail conspiracy that taxed her patience and optimism to their limits.

When the train stopped, she stood and picked up her luggage, which consisted of a leather satchel and a jumbo-sized purse. She waited for others to move along the aisle, but since there were only a few passengers sharing her car the departure occurred without any hindrances. She took the narrow steps carefully, smiling as a warm breeze caressed her face. Immediately upon exiting, she heard a voice call her by the name that mattered to her the most.

"Mom! Mom!"

Delores looked and saw her daughter. She was holding hands with a dark-eyed girl whose satiny black hair was in pigtails hanging halfway to her waist. She hurried to them, slipping past those who lingered or were moving too slowly. She plopped the baggage down, and after giving and receiving a mammoth hug from her cowgirl offspring, she knelt in front of the youngster.

"Hiya, Miss Delores."

"My word, Bethsuelo, how long's it been?"

"Three years."

"Was that when I last visited?"

"Yes, Miss Delores. It was summertime."

Delores gave her button-nose a tweak. "You look so grown up."

"I'll be ten in September," Bethsuelo said, grinning proudly. "Just like LC and Yaz." She peeked upward. "Aunt Avis says that sometimes the three of us are too big for our britches."

"I expect Aunt Avis is exactly right," Delores replied as the laugh-lines around her eyes crimped. She touched the child's cheek, then pushed to her full height. "How's Deacon?"

"Not at all good, Mom. Weak and getting weaker," Avis reported pithily. "The past few days I've met the so-called noontime special, regardless of what time it actually gets in."

"Glad to finally be here," Delores said, nodding agreeably. "I need to bathe and get into fresh clothes all the way down to my skin. Is there a bathhouse or a hotel with proper facilities?"

"A bathhouse, yes," Avis answered, hands held out and head tilted in an expression that conveyed skepticism. "The hotel may or may not have a room available. Creede is always jam packed with an assortment of comers and goers. The parade and turnover has no end."

"Let's try the hotel first."

Just then, a massive explosion tore a chunk of the earth apart a few hundred yards northeast of the depot. The roar of dynamite was deafening and the shock quaked the platform. The new arrival glowered, mightily dismayed by the dirt and grime floating in the air, but her daughter didn't even react. Avis Lahay simply picked up the luggage and led the way, while Bethsuelo Twosongs Weitzel clutched onto Delores Solrizo by the hand and followed.

～～～

"Aren't you going to open it, Deacon?"

He glanced up at his daughter, blank-eyed with uncertainty. His mouth started to form words, but not a peep emerged. He licked his lips and lowered his eyes once more to examine the envelope. His name was scrolled in bold black ink and it had been sent in care of Gallagher's Cove, but it was who it was from that tipped him over into a flummoxed state of disarray.

Pain, akin to a darning needle weaving a pattern of sutures between his ears, jabbed incessantly. His eyes were raw and watery. He ripped the casing apart, shook the pages out and unfolded them. He took note that it was dated the week after the Confederates fired on Fort Sumter. Then, with Abbey Langton and Alice Gallagher watching, he silently read the letter.

April 19, 1861

Conoy Creek, Pennsylvania

Dear Deacon: Greetings. Yes, it is I, Josiah. You have been heavy on my heart since news of the events in Charleston, South Carolina reached us. Whatever your response to the cataclysmic happenings, and wherever you may be, I pray that you are experiencing the mercy and protection of God. May troops of guardian angels encamp all around you—may you also know that no matter what the days and chances bring, you will always be my big brother.

I disagreed with your decision to be involved in the abolitionist movement, and made no secret about it. However, my respect for you intensified as I observed how you wrestled through the process of coming to terms with troublesome choices. Whether I understood all that was in your heart and mind mattered not because I learned about integrity from your rigid adherence to honesty. One of the curses of a fallen world is that breaking through to fully comprehend the exactness of God's will in problematic circumstances is the polar opposite of easy.

Mother and I have deliberated on this topic on many occasions. Most recently yesterday when I spent much of the afternoon with her. Her faith is rock solid. I am often humbled by the confidence she constantly expresses. We spoke of you, and had an extended time of intercession and in boldness, approached the throne of grace on your behalf. Be encouraged that you are surrounded by heartfelt prayers. I will not be found wanting or slack in that area.

We had a good time together. I told Mother of my intention to write this, which gave us an opportunity to talk over her feelings. Her abiding conviction regarding the sovereignty of God came through loud and clear as she reflected on your life. She told me to remind you that you are dearly loved and to always strive to be centered. She thinks of you and prays for you on a daily basis. Her only concern is that you be true to the light shining within you.

She also asked that I share these verses from Psalm 139: "For thou hast possessed my reins: thou hast covered me in my mother's womb. I will praise thee; for I am fearfully and wonderfully made: marvelous are thy works; and that my soul knoweth right well. My substance was not hid from thee, when I was made in secret, and curiously wrought in the lowest parts of the earth. Thine eyes did see my substance, yet being imperfect; and in thy book all my members were written, which in continuance were fashioned, when as yet there was none of them. How precious also are thy thoughts unto me, O God! how great is the sum of them!"

Your times are in God's hands, Deacon. That is a sentiment directly from Mother; one which I wholeheartedly agree with because it is absolutely a Scriptural principle. I could not tell her what is coming next because, after weighing it out, I determined that it would be a violation of trust. It is about Father. I have spent many meditative hours attempting to sort through it and came to the conclusion that I am on safe and secure ethical grounds to proceed.

Three days ago, Father showed up at the mill over the noon hour. I was busy, but the moment I finished the order, he insisted that I take a break because he had an issue requiring my attention. We strolled down to the creek and sat on those benches you and I designed and crafted ten years ago, which by the way, are weather-beaten, but still strong and sturdy. The day was warm and windy. It became increasingly evident that Father struggled with an inner turmoil.

He repeated a contradictory line of reasoning, which in and of itself, ought to tell you something about the complexity of the dilemma in his mind. He asserted that our dialog was to be private and confidential, but then without any indication that he recognized the inconsistency, he intimated that he wanted me to communicate the gist of our conversation to you.

You know Father. Self-possessed and exceedingly restrained with his emotions. He took a roundabout route to peel the onion of his feelings, and when he finally did, there were tears and sniffling. Of course he tried to downplay and dismiss all of that by claiming that the wind was stirring up excessive amounts of springtime pollen, but of his real sorrowfulness, I never had any doubts. He kept returning to your last meeting with him. How there was friction and annoyance, which he should've defused, but did not because his pride and hackles were raised.

He made no excuses. Neither did he put any blame on you for the fissure in the relationship. He told me that he had been willfully disobedient when he refused your farewell handshake. His grief for withholding the right hand of fellowship from you haunts him. He asked over and over how he could possibly fix the wrongness of his actions. Listen to me and hear the underneath: He actually wished for a way to go back to say and do differently.

The paramount premise, which he reiterated repetitiously, was that there was tremendous repentance in him and he regretted his hardline behavior in every possible way, but he is Father. He is being stoic and putting up defenses and shutting others out, which will produce a bumper crop of detrimental fruit in his heart and soul, so I am greatly concerned for him.

Before he put an end to our time at the water's edge, Father declared to me that he prays for your safety and deliverance through the thorns and brambles, the troubles and trials of your journey. He sincerely cares for you Deacon, but because of a combination of his principles and the fact that he gives too much credibility to the views and opinions of the community, he will grapple to maintain appearances while the conflict within beats him down.

In closing, I'm not sure if this information will be at all helpful, but I sensed a prompting to write. I miss talking things over with you like we used to do. We are on divergent sojourns, but we are brothers shaped by our past closeness and camaraderie. I pray that this finds you well and in good balance. Be at peace and stay centered on the treasures of eternity.

With much affection and respect,

Josiah

By the time he came to the end, the words were blurred and jumpy on the page, but not because of the effects of the tumor inside his head—Deacon Coburn was weeping unashamedly. The deluge obscured his vision. He tried to stifle the crying, and in doing so, his chest heaved as he gasped. He hung his head. His shoulders shuddered with the fumbling release of emotions.

"Here, Deacon," Abbey said, compassion digging channels across her brow. She offered him a checkered handkerchief. Moments ago it had been the bandana holding her hair in place.

He took it and covered his eyes. A groaning emanated from some cavernous chamber of his heart to come retching out of him in huge wet wheezes that sounded painful. His breathing eventually settled, and as it achieved a calm pattern, he leaned over and carefully put the letter on the floor beside him. He blew his nose and sat back in the rocker, then with the soiled hankie crunched in a fist, he stared sober-eyed at the woman who'd carried the message to him.

"Are you alright, Deke?"

"Far better than alright," he replied, voice trembling. "You arrived in the nick of time, for which I will be eternally grateful. I am the beneficiary of your perseverance. You cannot know how desperately I needed to receive that olive branch and be assured of reconciliation."

"What was in the letter, Deke? I don't understand."

"You are an angel sent by God to grant me peace."

"I ain't no angel, Deke."

"God used you," he said gruffly. "All the protests you can muster will not change that fact, Alice. Thank you for being available to him." He reached for her. She grabbed his hand and started simpering. She huffed it in, but then, Alice Gallagher broke down in wrenching sobs. He took a knee in front of her. She buried her face against the side of his neck, and there, in the purity of mutual tears, a friendship from a long ago place and time was renewed by grace.

Bathed in the colors of twilight, Caleb Weitzel and Sally Twosongs were riding side by side toward Creede. He sat astride a broad-chested zebra dun stallion, while she was saddled on a black and white pinto mare. Bobo had the lead, loping lazily ahead of them. The lean redbone hound would periodically stop and wait, then scamper off on its own adventure.

Sally Twosongs made a gesture skyward, where a red-tailed hawk was circling. A smile lit up her dark eyes. "Despite our reason for traveling, it's a good day. Life and death, time and eternity. The line of separation can be papery thin, but the Creator is kind enough to provide a glimpse of hope for those who have eyes to see and hearts attuned to the truth of nature."

"And no one has eyes and a heart like *lucero*, my little bright star."

"Naomi is hurting," she said offhandedly. "She is keeping busy to avoid dealing with her feelings, but in spending the morning with her going over details, I sensed somber heaviness."

"That's to be expected. Her brother's dying," he replied, watching the hawk. "She'll have plenty of work to submerge herself in now that the Axlers will be holding down the ranch for a spell. She and Pete won't have a spare minute dark to dark. Neither will Amanda. I'm not sure what bug has gotten into her, but she has really stepped it up the last number of weeks."

"She's an old soul finding her way, Caleb."

"Not sure what that means, but trust your judgment, *lucero*."

"Deacon Coburn is an old soul, born with ancient wisdom that rises to the surface in the winnowing fires of troubles and hardships," she said, shifting to glance behind her. "He was in the midst of his journey when he found me. Our lives have been intersected ever since."

"Thankfully. Deacon is a rock."

Sally Twosongs, reflective and wistful, had a thousand-mile stare fixed on the red-tailed raptor. "I was bruised and battered when he rescued me. Silent and scared. Angry and frightened. And filthier than sin. He was my champion from the moment I saw him. I never took my eyes off him. He shot the monster-man, then buried him and said Scripture over the grave."

"That's Deacon through and through."

A sparkle of memories danced in her eyes. "I thought of him as Mr. Deke, and when I finally spoke that's what I called him. Sometimes that name still comes to mind. I wore one of his shirts with the sleeves rolled up and belted around my waist with a strip of buckskin. He took care of me. I got tucked into his bedroll and he kept vigil by the fire to watch over me.

"In the morning, he cooked biscuits and bacon, and treated me like a china doll. I will *never* forget his melancholy kindness. There was so much sorrow in him. I felt it, and somehow understood that most of his pain was for me, because of my ordeal. He never expressed it or had many words to say, but I always knew the tenderness of his compassion."

"Slow to speak, quick to listen, is Deacon's way."

"To a fault." She shaded her eyes to concentrate on the hawk as it soared in the gathering shadows and disappeared behind a copse of ponderosa pines. "After breakfast Mr. Deke and I set off. Kadesh, his big appaloosa, was gentle and savvy. He put me in the saddle and told the horse to mind my guidance. The bad man had an ill-tempered chestnut that stomped and tried to bite Mr. Deke more than once. He had to be stern and unyielding with that brute.

"We rode the trail together and in a few days came to the farmstead of a friendly Mexican couple. Mr. Deke asked the lady if she could fix me suitable garments and she sewed up a storm. He traded the cantankerous chestnut for a jenny donkey, which I was riding when Mr. Deke took me to Daniel and Consuelo, and soon thereafter, I became Sally Twosongs."

"All the more reason for me to be grateful to Deacon Coburn," Caleb said, casting a wry smile at her. "When I first met him he didn't even have the strength to knock on death's door. Metaphorically speaking, he had his whole weight pressed against that entrance. Our buckboard was loaded with supplies and I was coming home from the outpost of a town.

"Rainy was ranging ahead. In the distance three buzzards were circling and dipping low. I was alert for trouble. Rainy got antsy and took off into a hollow, then let loose a bawling yawp that sent chills down my spine. I pushed the mules to the limit. We were on uneven ground so the wagon was rocking and lurching. Rainy kept bellowing, then suddenly began whining.

"When I got to the crest of the rise, I saw a man in rags sprawled on his back at the bottom of the slope. Rainy hovered over him, whimpering and licking his face. He was horribly cut up and dehydrated. I checked him over, and wasn't sure if he was living or dead. I made a place for him beside the barrels and boxes, then hoisted him onto the wagon's bed. Rainy lay down beside him, then those mules raced home faster and harder than ever.

"Whether he would live or die was iffy for a long while, but Ma doggedly nursed him round the clock." He gave the reins a slight tug and the stallion halted. "Kind of strange how life works. I never could've figured all the connections that came from our relationship with Deacon Coburn, or that all these years later, we'd be linked together as a large extended family."

Sally Twosongs sidled the pinto mare closer to him. "The Creator's plans and purposes are beyond our ability to reason or comprehend. As it has always been and always shall be."

"I'd not argue."

"How could anyone?"

"There are those who do."

"They'd be wrong," she said, squelching a giggle.

Weitzel leaned back to study the sky, then gave a low-pitched whistle and listened. In a few moments, Bobo howled and yapped in response, and came scampering out of the woods. He grinned and pushed his hat up his forehead. "Bethsuelo will be happy her dog tagged along."

"Most certainly."

"We best get a move on it, Sally Twosongs." he suggested, giving her a prodding sideways glance. "Elsewise it'll be full dark when we set up camp on the outskirts of Creede."

"I'm in no hurry." A school-girlish gleam illuminated her eyes. "Is it not a sweet evening for a hand-holding ride?" She held out her left hand to him. His compliance was automatic. His face wrinkled expressively as whispers passed between them. Then, while the pinkish-orange shades of dusk spread into lengthening grays, husband and wife rode along hand in hand.

≈≈≈

Meanwhile, Eliezer Smith was on his porch chomping on a succulent apple as he appreciated the multicolored hues cast across the sky by the setting sun. His cheeks were flushed and his brow glowed rosy-red. Rumbling snickers burbled in his craw as he slurped each bite and smacked his lips to be sure to capture all the yummy juices. He was giddy with delight.

He cocked his head. He had the core munched down to the seeds so he tossed it aside as he jumped off his log bench. The happiness sketched on his face increased because chums were coming for a visit. "What're you boyos doing now? Who do you got there with you?"

LC Beadle waved both hands over his head as the threesome passed the split-rail fence and started to scuttle up the hillside. "Me and Yaz thought you'd like to meet Bethsuelo."

"Yeah-huh."

"Bethsuelo?" Eliezer queried, a cheery lilt in his voice. He clapped gleefully and did a quick two-step as though unseen fiddlers were playing a reel. He kept strutting in a heel to toe romp, then abruptly ended with a yee-haw. "Is she the lady who holds both your hearts?"

"Bethsuelo's our sister."

"Yeah-huh."

"Not really though," Eliezer said glibly.

LC frowned, mystified. "Yes, really."

"Yeah-huh."

"Is that so?" Eliezer asked as the trio stopped at the edge of the overhang. He loomed over them like a lofty giant. He lowered his butt onto the bench and bent forward, elbows resting on knees as he eyed the girl. "Step up here Miss Bethsuelo so as I can have a look at you."

She did so. "Hiya, Mr. Smith."

"These scamps told you my name, did they?"

"Yes, sir."

"I ain't no sir, Miss Bethsuelo. I ain't even a mister."

"Yes, you are, Mr. Smith."

He growled a bellyful of laughter and shook a finger at the brothers. "I see why you two get all weak-kneed and crooked-eyed when this lady's name comes up. She's a special one."

"Yeah-huh."

Smith studied her. "How do you make your hair look like hunks of rope?"

"Those are called braids," she answered politely. "I can do it myself, but mostly Mom or Grandmom or Aunt Avis fixes it for me. When I was littler I never liked it, but now I do."

"Ain't that dandy? It's pretty-pretty."

"Thank you, Mr. Smith." Her dark eyes got glassy and unfocused.

He shrank back, arms crossing over his chest. "What's wrong, girly?"

Bethsuelo sidled close enough to place a hand on his shoulder. She shivered and when she spoke her voice hummed vibrations like a tuning fork. "Your goodness will win because the hurt from the bombs is getting better. The thorn in your flesh will never be removed, but you will be used by the Creator. You will be a mighty helper and servant to those who are in pain."

"What?" Eliezer gasped, cringing.

"You will be a mighty helper and servant to those who are in pain."

"How? What?"

"The Creator will make it so."

Smith gawked at her, fear or wonder printed on his face. "What are you saying? How can you tell me such crazy things, Miss Bethsuelo? Are you pulling an old geezer's leg for a joke?"

The trance passed. Her eyes were normal. "Funning you? No."

"She knows and feels things," LC said matter-of-factly.

"Yeah-huh."

"What's that mean?" Eliezer asked in a croaky tone.

Yaz shrugged as a scowl crept over his brow. He did a quick hippity-hop onto the porch to stand shoulder to shoulder with her. "She knows what she knows. She feels what she feels."

Smith gawped at the mystical girl as though her pigtails were writhing like snakes. He flinched and cowered, eyes becoming bulgy and frightened. He gazed at the darkening sky and distress gripped him. "You best be scooting home or else the night terrors will get you."

"Night terrors?" Bethsuelo echoed, puzzled.

"The dark."

LC tented an eyebrow. "What about the dark, Mr. Smith?"

"Ain't you half-pints scared of the dark?"

They glanced at each other, then Yaz answered, "Nope."

Smith swallowed audibly. "What about the boogerman?"

"There ain't no such thing as a boogerman," LC stated, eyebrows drooping.

"Ain't no boogerman? Ain't no boogerman?" Eliezer quizzed, bug-eyed and agitated. "Don't be fooled! There's always a boogerman lurking in the darkness. When I was a boy in the hills and hollows, a boogerman terrorized us. He killed chickens and tipped over outhouses. And if any anklebiters were naughty, the boogerman would grab them up and steal them away."

"Jesus is good medicine," Bethsuelo said calmly.

"Even against the boogerman?" Eliezer asked, disbelieving.

"Jesus is good medicine against all manner of bad medicine," Bethsue-lo replied as she gave Yaz a subtle nudge. "We should be going just because we ought to be getting home."

"Yeah-huh."

"See you tomorrow, Mr. Smith." LC gave him a half-wave as he backed up.

Before he could answer, the triplets dashed off as one. When they were encompassed by the shadows, he hobbled inside. He crawled onto his rope-bed atop a dusty quilt that served as a mattress, and it was then that Eliezer Smith realized he was trembling. There was fear swirling in him, but beneath that tumult was hope—vibrant and living hope in the words of a child: *You will be used by the Creator. You will be a mighty helper and servant to those who are in pain.*

The heat was oppressive—suffocating, even. In recent days, clouds had accumulated on occasion and threatened refreshing rain, only to pass on and disperse without ever delivering even a drop of moisture. The scorching sun was at high noon above the prairie grasslands. Daniel Twosongs, riding bareback out of Abilene on a brindle mare, figured he and his companion would arrive at where his saddle and rig were cached by nightfall, and he said so.

Deacon Coburn, on a rental sorrel from the Twin Livery, gave an amiable nod. "Seeing an old friend get on his way is a blessing even while breathing air saturated with water."

"The humidity is a killer."

"That it is, but the weather is the weather," Deacon said, muffling a brief chuckle. "We ain't gonna change its quirks and whimsies by wasting words grousing about it."

"It's ironic, isn't it?"

"What's that, Daniel?"

"Life itself."

"In what way?"

"Changes, preacher. Surprises," Daniel replied subtly. "Nothing is ever as consistent as changes and surprises. Look at us, a pair of happy wanderers. When we met in that tent-town in Nebraska, neither of us had any inkling of the changes and surprises God had in store for us. Now we are the fathers of grownup daughters and tremendous responsibility beckons."

"God gives us gifts according to our ability."

"Agreed, but it's not going to be easy."

"Since when is anything worth doing ever easy, Daniel?"

"Agreed again, but my question has to do with the how of it."

"We adapt. We adjust. We be true to our instincts."

Twosongs removed his flat-brimmed hat and fanned his face. "I'd not argue against any of that, but how do we hold them close and let them go to be who God created them to be?"

"A difficult proposition, but not impossible."

"There is awesome light and goodness in Sally Twosongs," Daniel said, tucking his hair under his headgear. "Her prayers narrow the gap between heaven and earth in ways that are far beyond my experience. How do I encourage and exhort her to respect and develop that gift?"

"You think too hard," Deacon answered, flashing a flinty stare at his friend. "What part of *God gives us gifts according to our ability* do you not understand? We're talking about step by step trust and faith, nothing more and nothing less. You put spiritual sweat into steadily living out what you say you believe. Sally Twosongs will see and learn from your example."

"Is it really that simple?"

"Precept by precept faith, yes," Deacon replied, laying it on the line. "Straightforward action. Easy? Never. If it were easy peasy you and I would be perfect, which we ain't. I've got no other advice because, like you, I'm attempting to sort through this new arrangement."

"You're knee-deep in it, preacher."

Coburn chuckled grimly. "More like up to my neck. Abbey Langton came out of the past and shocked me into a swoon. A beautiful woman created in the image of her mother. Eighteen years old and going on thirty with a feisty stubborn streak that requires tempering to serve her well." He stared off into the middle distance of the flatlands. "Ramblers like us must find a balance between drifting and buckling down to provide encouragement and support."

"Wisdom is what we need."

"Lots of it, Daniel."

"So why not follow the counsel of James?"

"That's more than a fair question," Deacon said, adjusting in the saddle to give his tried and true cohort an unbending look. "*If any of you lack wisdom, let him ask of God, that giveth to all men liberally, and upbraideth not; and it shall be given him. But let him ask in faith, nothing wavering. For he that wavereth is like a wave of the sea driven with the wind and tossed.*"

It was then that Daniel Twosongs swayed jerkily and came awake, with the Scripture and voice ringing in his ears, along with the sharp squeal of steel on steel. His bearings were skewed in the darkness—it was 1892, not 1872. He shifted around as he oriented to his environs, which were rocking and scraping back and forth. The stench of manure puckered his nostrils. He was in the livestock boxcar of a train, slumped against the gate to the stall housing his horse.

"*If any of you lack wisdom, let him ask of God,*" he murmured pleasantly. There were still a host of miles to put behind him to get to *WT Ranch*, but moonlighting a ride was a godsend. He had made arrangements with a railroad employee, and boarded during a midnight watering stop at Walsenburg. He relaxed and palmed a sheen of perspiration off his forehead as he settled in to go back to sleep. Unbeknownst to him, a pair of friends were snoozing in a passenger car.

The next morning, when the sun was poking above the mountain, Delores Solrizo was in a rocker on the porch across from her longtime friend. Coburn had been outside squinting at his Bible when she surprised him. Their hug lasted close to five minutes and was accompanied by a plethora of tears. Now, while the boys were out and about on some errand with Bethsuelo and Aunt Avis, the never-to-be couple were browsing through emotional territory.

"How long have you known?" she asked, intent and fidgety.

"A fair spell."

"In unambiguous terms, please."

He inhaled hugely and flexed a down-to-earth shrug of a grin at her. "A whippersnapper sawbones in East Texas diagnosed me when I was there to say my goodbyes to Big Bull."

"Is that so?"

"Ah-huh."

"Was that before you visited me?"

"You know it was, Delores. We talked about Big Bull's death."

"You don't get my point, do you, Deacon?"

"My head ain't working right, you know."

"Allow me to be blunt so you understand," she said snappishly. "It would've been conscientious of you to give me a head's up before you left Santa Fe last September."

"There was nothing anyone could do or say."

"Specific prayers are something, Deacon."

"Alright, gotcha."

"Better late than never," she replied, giving his foot a tiny kick. "You and I have known each other for a quarter of a century. We've prayed and wept together, but despite all of that you mostly remain a boxed up riddle of emotions to me. You're always available and ready to listen and help anyone who is in need, but no one can slip inside your tight-lipped defenses."

"Ain't sure I get what you're saying."

"You keep your true feelings gagged."

"I am what I am by the grace of God."

"Blaming God for your shortcomings isn't like you, Deacon."

He stiffened. "I ain't doing no such thing."

"Likely not, but I got your attention, didn't I?"

"For what reason, Delores?"

"To complain."

"Ain't ever known you to be a complainer."

"Your secretive ways are worthy of a complaint," she said candidly. "You may not recognize you do this and it might even surprise you, but your habitual pattern of bottling up your hurts and sentiments can be exasperating to those who harbor tenderness for you."

"It's a mite late for me to change, ain't it?" he asked, scratching his moustache. "After all, my rendezvous with the grim reaper is set and there ain't no skipping that appointment."

"Are you being flippant?"

"Not at all, Delores. No use denying reality."

She began rocking the chair, lips pursed and eyes saddened. "Some of us need to piece together emotions to come to terms with your illness, Deacon. We're not all as stoic as you."

"I ain't stoic. Just accepting the facts."

"I see no sense in debating the meaning of words."

He smiled jokingly. "I ain't debating nothing."

"I suppose you *ain't*," she said, mimicking his tone.

His expression broadened. "There's the lady I know and love."

She shuddered a breath. "You are a complex package of a man."

"That I be, by the grace of God."

"I'm proud and grateful to have you as a big brother."

"Ain't you going to grouse about me needing a haircut?"

"No, I *ain't*, Deacon."

"That's a pleasure I'll miss."

"Glad to hear it."

"That's 'cause it's true."

Her posture became rigid. "Is the pain constant?"

"It is what it is, Delores," he answered dismissively. "Headaches come and go at will, my eyesight does the same. My digestive tract is unpredictable, which ain't appropriate parlor or even front porch discourse, but I tell you because I'll be needing to go for a walk soon."

"I'm sorry this sickness . . . "

"Don't be," he interrupted, raising a finger to her. "Shed a necessary tear or two, but mostly remember me with joy and laughter. Taken as a whole, I've enjoyed much fair weather and many smooth trails. In the context of eternity what do my troubles matter, Delores?"

"Your faith has been an inspiration to me."

"Good to know. To God be the glory."

"Amen." She shifted to gently kick his foot again. "Have you ever considered what sort of relationship we could've had if we'd met at a church social instead of in a whorehouse?"

"We've had that conversation," Deacon replied solemnly. "The fact that I'm ready to go home to glory ain't gonna change the particulars. Besides I ain't one to do hypotheticals." He gripped his Bible and stood. "You must excuse me, or else." He hurried off in the direction of the privy. She watched until he turned a corner, then Delores Solrizo wiped trickles of moisture off her cheeks and went inside to assist Abbey Langton in whatever way needed.

Bobo was running circles around Gilgal and Cookie, but both horses ignored the dog's antics. The spacious meadow alongside the Rio Grande was lush pastureland, which was being fully appreciated. Avis Lahay had spread a blanket near the riverbank and was positioned so as to have a view of the rippling flow and the grassy waves.

The trio of youngsters were sitting cross-legged around her listening raptly as she told them about her first time on the trail, riding a strawberry roan named Pumpkin while her partner Deacon Coburn was mounted on the silver-dappled buckskin. "It was springtime ten years ago. We rode from Santa Fe to Dodge City. He was patient and kind, and taught me much."

"Santa Fe to Dodge City? That's far, isn't it?"

"Close to five hundred miles was my estimate, LC," she replied quickly. "I charted every day in my diary at the time." She removed her skimmer and flipped it aside. "I recently took that journal off the shelf and carefully read those installments. It was twenty-five blissful days of learning and being schooled on an easy riding adventure that put a good mark on me."

"Would you take us on a journey like that, Aunt Avis?"

"Yeah-huh."

"Are you also in on that request, LC?"

"Absolutely, Aunt Avis!"

"It won't be from Santa Fe to Dodge City, but let's say in two or three years we plan a summertime trip to Gunnison?" she asked, expressive and bright-eyed. "We'll get Stace to join us. North to Lake City, then on to Gunnison. On our return we'll loop down to South Fork and when we get back to *WT Ranch* we'll have taken a circular route through the mountains."

"Yeah-huh."

"Where is Stace? I'm missing him," LC said, toying with Gilgal's bridle.

"He's doing business with Grandpa Weitzel."

"When will they be done?" Yaz asked keenly.

"Soon I pray," Avis answered, eyes straying to the gelding and mare. Her cheeks got rosy as a faraway smile crested on her lips. "The summer and fall of 1882 set my life on a course that impacts the present and future, or at least, the future for the short distance I can envision it."

LC tilted his head at her. "Whatcha mean?"

"Yeah-huh?"

"It was special and exciting," Avis replied, nodding. "Dodge City was thriving and wild. Never a dull moment. A cowboy or two set their sights on me, but I ignored them. I was treated like a princess because of my connection to Deacon Coburn. I got a job at the livery shoveling manure and caring for horses, which helped me comprehend the character inside me."

Bethsuelo crinkled her nose. "What's that mean, Aunt Avis?"

"God puts something special in each of us," she said spontaneously. "A spark, a gift, a talent, an inclination—something that is unique to that person. There are some folks who never make the discovery, so they can't ever tap into it, and that is truly tragic." She glanced at the blue sky. "I was born to handle horses and build relationships with family. Those are the things that push my happy buttons because that's the seeds and stuff God planted in my heart."

She made eye contact with the youngsters, then continued, "There's no perfect formula or hasty remedy, but each of you must seek and be open to become the person God created you to be. A long string of tomorrows isn't promised to anyone, but my prayer, hope and intention is to be around to help you all find your path, just like Deacon, Whitey, Abbey and Sam did for me.

"That summer came to an end in hurly-burly events." Sadness crept into her voice. "I was riding fast, exercising Pumpkin on the outskirts of town. We had an accident and I took a crazy soaring plunge and crash-landed. I was knocked out cold and dislocated my shoulder. Liam Greer rescued me and carried me to safety. It happened on the day you were born, LC."

"Me, too," Bethsuelo chirped, flipping her pigtails.

"Yeah-huh. Me, too."

Avis was bemused. "What?"

"It's really true," LC said, darkness edging his brow. "Mom and Standing Wolf were talking and comparing, asking questions and such. They concluded that to the best of their figuring Yaz has the same birthday as me and Bethsuelo, which we think is special."

"Yeah-huh."

"Aunt Avis."

"Yes, LC."

"That Greer man was an outlaw. He shot my father in cold blood."

"Yes, he did, LC," Avis said, somewhat rigidly. "Life is hard and brittle. Only batty nuts and crackpots would try to tell you otherwise. Liam Greer made bad choices that put him on a pathway of destruction. He was lost and sick in the head. The lesson for us is to determine that by God's grace and guidance we will choose not to be led astray into those same pitfalls."

Bethsuelo suddenly stood. Her dark eyes momentarily had a glazed glint. "We should go. Mr. Deacon is not well. His time is short." Her hands were fumbling with Cookie's bridle. She turned and whistled, then called, "Bobo! Come!" The redbone hound immediately stopped what it was doing and trotted toward her. The horses briefly waited before following the dog.

LC stepped close to her. "We'll walk back to town fast."

Yaz slipped between them. "Yeah-huh."

Aunt Avis flattened a smile. The bond linking the three had such deep roots that there were instances when they seemed to function as one. Her eyes inclined upward as she folded the blanket. Tightness filled her throat. A chill was in the air. Avis Lahay frowned. The morning had dawned cloudless, but now, big gray tumblers were forming along the northern horizon.

Deacon Coburn sat stewing and frustrated in the outhouse. His bowels alternated between constipation and a watery mess—just now it was the former state giving him fits. He was leaning forward with his closed Bible in his hands. There were slivers of sunshine slanting through holes and chinks in the backside wall, but it was too dark for him to even attempt to read.

Scripture wasn't particularly on his mind. It was the two letters within the Good Book that he was contemplating—the precious one that had been hand delivered in 1872 at the center and the one inside the front cover which had arrived yesterday via an old friend. The past was bittersweet flames burning through his veins, squeezing his heart and watering his eyes.

Choices. Decisions. Roads traveled, roads not taken. Forgotten faces. The petals of flowers being choked by vines of weeds. Beauty. Wonder. Conoy Creek. Philadelphia. A slave couple, Saul and Maggie—and their baby. Nightmares. Hardships. Gettysburg. Blood. Death. A farmhouse in southern Ohio. Angela. Love. Respect. A spitfire named Abbey. Lost. Forlorn. East Texas. Big Bull Wallace. *Double B Ranch*. Hard work. Friendship. Confidence. Healing.

He jerked as the mosaic of reminiscences jittering in the shadowy recesses of his skull became a singularly powerful memory that was so vividly real it was as though, sitting riveted on a seat in a privy, he could see and relive a pivotal turning point. There was no pain or fogginess in him as he witnessed a younger version of himself wanting to take hold of the future.

As lead hand on the *Double B* there was no rationale for him to be riding the nightshift, but there he was, seasoned and satisfied on a sturdy appaloosa gelding listening to silence and solitude. Tall and rawboned, with tree-branch shoulders, he cast a distinct silhouette. He was relaxed yet sat straight up, his backbone as stiff as a wrought-iron ramrod.

He stared vacantly at the full moon. It was bright white and tinged by a shimmer of yellow that seemed to glow. He found no comfort in it—curiosity perhaps at some deep level, but no comfort at all. He had killed men. Too many to even count; he simply knew he had been a coldhearted murderer. There were skeletons aplenty crawling around his head. He considered himself foul and abominable, beyond any promise of redemption. He was a Bible-reading man merely marking time until Judgment Day and the awful wrath of God.

The night was cool and crisp, the sky high and clear. He eased along a ridge overlooking the ranch, alone but never lonesome. To be on a fine horse in the wide open spaces was about the only place he ever felt any sense of peace or purpose. He'd been in the saddle for several hours, patrolling the perimeter and carrying on a whispered conversation with the animal.

It was his first time mounted on the mottled horse—he had selected it on an instinctive whim, liking its look and eager-to-please temperament. It was fifteen hands tall, thick-chested and muscular, and he soon discovered, as nimble and sure-footed as a mountain bred Indian pony. He appreciated how quickly an emotional connection had been made with it.

Off in the distance a coyote let loose a yapping howl. He listened to its song, passive and unperturbed. The neutered stallion had an equally docile reaction. Coburn patted its neck and spoke lowly. A breeze riffled a clump of brush off to his left. He lifted his hat and dragged a hand through his shaggy hair, untangling some of the knotted curls.

That simple action brought an unbidden flash from yesteryear. He could see Angela as clear as clear could be. Her lean cheekbones, her pale eyes; her charming top and bottom curves. The innocence of their nakedness was exquisite and compelling. She was fingering his hair, her breath sweet on his skin. Light flickered and danced from an arrangement of candles on the dresser, reflecting in the large mirror to make the room warm and pretty.

Her scent was in his nostrils. He shifted uncomfortably in the saddle. She was the only woman he had ever been with; the only woman to ever love him. She had given him hope; had offered him domestic tranquility, which he spurned with all the sneaky weasel traits of a fugitive. Coburn shook his head to be free of the imagery. He wasn't himself when he knew her, which was true enough, but he refused that knowledge, for it could do nothing to relieve the endless sorrow digging at him. Remorse and shame were jagged hooks sunk in his psyche.

He was far away from his birth place in Pennsylvania, but he never missed it much. East Texas had been good to him. It hadn't washed the blood from his hands or assuaged the guilt rattling around his soul, but he'd become proficient in all the skills necessary to fare well in the western lands. He had branded calves, cleared out water holes, mended fences, tracked and trapped wolves, and had run-ins with mossy-horned steers during spring round-up.

His cattle ranching days were over. It was time to take to the trail. He had to stay ahead of whatever was behind him because there were so many places to see before trouble caught up with him. His mind was set rock-hard on the matter. The walking mountain of a man who owned the *Double B* had talked him out of his resolve twice before, but no more.

At dawn he would return to the bunkhouse for a few hours of shut-eye then have a face to face showdown with Big Bull Wallace and this time he'd stick to his guns. Determination was a crackling fire in his belly and there'd be no backing down. By mid-afternoon he would be packed and headed northward to whatever danger or adventure awaited him.

The dying man in the outhouse gulped a breath. His eyelids shuttered as the stark and stirring remembrance was snatched away in a whirlwind to be replaced by a patchwork of mental photographs. Nebraska. Master Harvey. Daniel Twosongs. A cavern shelter, then a sweat lodge. Purgatory. A terrorized girl named Sally. A gunfight. Wanted: Dead or Alive. A posse. Renegade Utes. Smoky Crowe. Angel Peak badlands. Torture. Rebirth. Renewal. Twelve stones.

He blinked. The present predicament jettisoned the past. Tears were flowing down his cheeks. His eyes stung and his ears were ringing. His jaw was locked in a clench. He bore down on the task at hand, but despite his vigilant efforts, the likelihood of getting any relief from the tormenting cramps in his lower abdomen was the longest of long shots for Deacon Coburn.

"For crying out loud, Karl! This is ridiculous."

The door was slammed shut by her physician husband, who had his black leather doctor's satchel in hand and their son at his side. They had secured a room on the second floor of the Grande Rio Hotel, which was kitty-corner across the thoroughfare from the Denver & Rio Grande Railroad Depot. "Enough already. I've had it, Maxine. The argument is over."

"Over? You wish, Mr. Fralick."

"I suppose I do, Maxine."

"We're a short buggy ride from *WT Ranch*."

"Neither South Fork or *WT Ranch* are going to relocate overnight," he said in a restrained voice that palpitated with aggravated undertones. His face was flushed in discolored blotches and his blue eyes were as murky as muddy water. "After I examine you, then rest is prescribed."

"I'm fine, Doc."

"Rest is prescribed, Maxine. That's the verdict."

"Rest? For how long?"

Fralick exhaled a sigh as he pressed the heel of his right hand against his forehead. "If all is well with you and the baby, we'll rent a carriage and travel to *WT Ranch* tomorrow."

"Tomorrow!" Her eyes were fierce. "The delay is not acceptable."

"We got off the train a half-hour ago." He put his medical bag on the floor at the foot of the brass bed. He turned toward her and took an authoritative step. "You've been grouching and fussing the whole while, which is not at all healthy, so please, Maxine, heed my advice. You're enduring physical and emotional distress, and quite possibly are in the early stages of labor."

"I'm first-rate, Karl. I swear."

"If that is so, what's the problem?"

"Time, Karl! Time is being wasted by this detour."

"Your attitude is not helpful."

"I know my body, Doc. I am *fine*," she said, hot and adamant.

Cody Fralick had taken a seat on a hard-backed chair near a tall window facing the street. His cheeks were reddened and his brow wrinkly. "Being mad not nice. Scare me."

"We're not mad, son."

"Speak for yourself, Karl," Maxine muttered, plumping down on the mattress. She tapped her brow, teeth gritted as she eyed the child and slumped into submission. Mid-morning sunlight streamed through the glass to cast a brightness around him. She visibly softened. "Mommy is annoyed. Years ago, on horseback I would've made this trip faster than a jackrabbit. I'd never have to take a break, as we have almost every single day. We are nearly to our destination, but Daddy insists that I be a lazybones for twenty-four hours, which I think is ridiculous."

"It is in no way ridiculous."

"We disagree, Karl."

"Where does that leave us, Maxine?"

"At odds with each other."

"It doesn't have to be so," he replied, taking a knee in front of her. "This layover is a precaution. You do know that you're nine months pregnant, don't you? Walking here from the train station, how many times did we have to stop because you were wincing in pain?"

"It's false labor, Karl."

"Please remind me; where'd you study medicine?"

"Hardy har har," she scoffed, removing her sunhat. "I will surrender to your kindness and expertise, but don't expect me to be happy about it." She started to stand, and he shot up to help her. She took off her shoes and dress, then got situated on the middle of the bed in shapeless undergarments. She stuck her tongue out at him. "Is an examination in the offing, Doc?"

"Not just now," he answered, propping pillows behind and around her. He placed a palm on her swollen tummy and moved it around, gently pressing and prodding in spots. "If you can do so, I'd like you to first relax for a time. Will you please be a cooperative patient?"

"When am I not, Doc?"

He ignored the facetious question, head shaking. He chuckled, low and teasing. "I'll get our luggage from the lobby and have the clerk deliver a pitcher of cool water," he said, backing up. "Cody, you are in charge of this nice lady. Make sure she keeps her feet up."

He grinned, eyes shimmering. "Mommy feet up."

When the door closed behind Doc Fralick, she stretched her arms toward the boy. "Come snuggle me, Bear." He hop-skipped over and scooted in beside her, snickering. She put him in a tight embrace as he rested his head on her bosom. A contraction roiled through her midsection, and she nibbled on her bottom lip while trying her best to deny that the pain was real.

"Ain't this a timely *buenos dias*?"

Alice Gallagher snapped her head in the direction of the voice, smiling effervescently when she saw Deacon Coburn emerging from the privy. "We all have to do what we have to do whenever we have to do it, so I'd not be much embarrassed getting caught after the fact."

"I was sitting and thinking. My pipes ain't working."

"Being plugged up is nasty."

"True enough, but tell me, after thirty years we're actually gonna talk about happenings or lack thereof in an outhouse?" he asked, ambling alongside her. He moved slow and unsteady as he dealt with an obvious lag in his giddyup; his right leg was dragging. "Seems to me we ought to have no difficulty blundering upon a more significant theme to explore."

"An astute observation."

"Thirty years. Gone in a blink."

"Lots of upheaval in that blink."

"Just the earth revolving around the sun, Alice."

"But the world's gotten crazy."

"Changing of the guards, is all."

"Merely a generational shift?"

"New blood and new ideas, but still aligned in the grooves of history," he said, pushing sweaty tangles of hair off his forehead. "*The thing that hath been, it is that which shall be; and that which is done is that which shall be done: and there is no new thing under the sun.* Unless Solomon, the wisest of the wise, was a lunatic howling at the moon, which ain't likely."

"You're the one with Bible know-how."

"Soon it won't be through a glass darkly."

They began walking side by side. "What happened to you, Deke?"

"Life," he quipped in a rasp. "Age lassoed me."

"Likewise." She took hold of his hand to assist his balance. "I've been recalling the olden days. You were with Blackjack and me after Fort Sumter when the news came that the president issued a call for volunteers. The next morning you were gone. No so long, no adios, no farewell, no nothing. You vamoosed during the night and we never saw or heard from you again."

"I had places to go. Wrongs to right."

"Saying goodbye wasn't a priority?"

"I thought I'd be back in ninety days or so," he replied vehemently. "I swear, Alice. I presumed the South would buckle and be done with secession and slavery. I was naïve, perhaps even delusional. There was a pile of delusional ideas adrift in the North and South."

"Do you remember our late-night confabs?"

"I remember everything, Alice. All of it."

"Those pre-war times get sketchy for me."

"Not me. Every memory extracts its price."

"What happened to you, Deke?" she asked again, nudging him.

His grip on her hand tightened. He hesitated and in doing so, tilted and had to lean into a lopsided stutter-step. More and more his equilibrium was shaky and infiltrated by wobbles. He groaned wheezily and gathered his breath in tentative gulps. When he began to tell her his story, his voice lowered, but the narrative was strong and uncompromisingly honest.

She hung on each word. Activity was all around them, but for the friends on a tour of memory lane, it was as if they were alone. As far as they were concerned, the swirling noise and hubbub didn't seem to exist—children running or huddled in clusters; pedestrians rushing hither and yon, or loitering and bumming around; women hanging laundry on clotheslines that were strung in whatever spaces were available; a burly man in a tattered bib-apron splattered with grime and guts butchering a hog while mongrel dogs yapped for bits and pieces.

Her eyes became saucers and her mouth gaped open when Coburn spoke of his ordeal in the Angel Peak badlands. She tugged at him to stop. "Smoky Crowe? That's not possible."

"Why not? I ain't making it up."

She gawked at him. "I had no interest whatsoever in occurrences in the west, but when I was in prison I read newspaper accounts about Smoky Crowe and became fascinated. Over the years I gobbled up reports of his exploits which were sensationalized and scandalous."

He shrugged, stoop-shouldered. "Ain't no coincidence."

"What else could it be?" she inquired, dubious and unnerved; nonplussed, even. "Of all the news from west of the Mississippi that could have captured my imagination—massacres and atrocities and gold rushes and the like—why Smoky Crowe? How is *that* possible?"

"Currents."

"What?"

"Currents and eddies of connectedness," he answered, stumbling against her. He accepted her support and it took several moments for him to get stabilized. Though his eyes were dim and fuzzy, an unassuming twinkle briefly gleamed in the unclear pools. "I cannot explain it because it's one of the Almighty's mysteries that are too wonderful for me to ever comprehend, but I believe the ripples of our lives affect those we have touched or have sought to touch us."

Her eyes narrowed. Alice Gallagher was stumped. She had a pleading expression locked on him. Coburn started to say something, but then, his mouth twisted as his body convulsed. She used all her strength to prevent him from falling. The tremors passed and he clutched at her. She hitched a shoulder under his arm. They waddled along, with much exertion and fitfulness, until she finally got him into a rocking chair on the porch of his daughter's cabin.

Though it was midday, the swaying of the train had Daniel Twosongs snoozing in a coma of sleep. Exhausted from weeks of hard riding, it was as though the sandman had used a potent anesthesia to put him under. His body was as still as a corpse, but his head quivered as he snuffled so loudly that his black stallion in the stall snorted occasional complaints.

He heard music—it apprehended him and filled his soul with wondrous pleasure. The smooth and soft notes soared and dipped in spine-tingling fluidity. His eyes creaked open as he listened. There was soothing comfort and stimulating challenge in the melody. In the dream he got up and went in search of the song. He was outside amongst mountains, beneath the radiant canopy of a midnight sky that was a panoramic presentation of miraculous starlight.

The Navajo princess who was his daughter sat on the hillock doorstep of a cathedral of aspens, head bowed and eyes closed as her upper body subtly moved in response to the prayers arising from her flute. Her eyelids fluttered as the hymn-like composition struck chords that brought it to conclusion. She stared at the man from whom she had gleaned truths about the power of hope. "Father, I am glad you are here. My sincere concerns are heavy for you."

"I am saddened. My grief overpowers me."

"Mother's sudden death hurts me too, Father."

"It makes no sense. Why? Now? Why now?"

"The Creator does all things well and he makes no mistakes," Sally Twosongs answered, laying the cedar instrument aside. Her hands came together at the bottom of the swollen knoll of her belly. "Our Savior is our Lord. We are to be inspired by the assurance that Mother is at peace in the presence of Jesus, which is the mystery and majesty that awaits on the other side."

"That is difficult to grasp just now."

"You are being tested and tried, Father."

He squatted on his heels and stared at nothing in the middle distance, eyes bleak and aggrieved. "Defeat badgers me. I can find no motivation and meaning. I am bedeviled and helpless. There is discouragement in me that darkens and skews my perspective."

"Mother passed over to glory. The Creator called her home."

"I wasn't ready, Sally Twosongs."

"Neither was I," she countered strongly. "Which is neither here nor there, Father. Since when does the Creator require our advice or agreement in numbering a loved one's days? It is written again and again that life is a gift to be cherished day by day because the One who is from forever to forever is the author of life and death. Has God changed his way of thinking?"

"I am not inclined to offer an opinion."

"Does he now operate differently than in times past?"

"The parameters for this discussion do not exist, Sally Twosongs."

"Has the Creator's character been diminished or tarnished?" she asked, raising her arms with palms spread upward. "Behold the starry night, Father. Why Mother? Why now? The questions about life and death are worthy of contemplation only in the Creator's framework of eternity. We cannot ever forget that God makes everything beautiful in his perfect time."

"I have forgotten that and much more."

"Then you must find your way back to truth."

"Your womb has been blessed, but Consuelo will never cuddle her grandchild. Never change a diaper, sing a lullaby, tell a bedtime story or say prayers," he said, resentment in his voice as rows of ruts plowed across his forehead. "Those facts haunt and disturb me."

"All of that also bothers me, Father."

"Are you not angry at God?"

"Mother has been rewarded for her faithfulness."

His mouth clenched. "Are *you* not *angry* at God?"

"He is God, I am Sally Twosongs," she replied, urgent and succinct. "He is the sovereign king of glory. He does whatsoever pleases him. I am redeemed by the blood of the Lamb and so am invited to be involved in his story. If I trust him and am grateful when all is well, must I not exercise faith and thanksgiving when adversities and loss rip pieces off my heart?"

"God can be fickle and capricious."

Her dark eyes rested on him. "The truths I spoke of I learned from you."

"The light of my faith has been smothered."

"Then it must be resuscitated."

"Not possible, Sally Twosongs."

"Being on the trail will be healthy for you, Father."

"The horses to Fort Dodge? I shall not go now."

"The army contract has to be honored."

"Caleb can manage the stock without me."

"Please listen to me, Father," she said, stiffening her backbone. "You cannot be cooped up in ranch activities. I know you. You need to be on the trail to rediscover hope and renewal in the wonder of creation. Traversing the prairie on horseback will be good medicine."

"You make the decision for me, Sally Twosongs?"

"I politely request that you respect my counsel."

He mulled it over, moist-eyed. His hands fisted tautly. "I will do unto you as you have done unto me, Sally Twosongs. If there is any semblance of uprightness remaining in me, it demands that I heed your admonitions, so I will do so, engulfed in doubt and misgivings."

"I will assault heaven with songs for you, Father," she promised, reaching out to hold his hand. She squeezed it firmly. "May the Creator's peace and presence be made known to you."

"I feel the darkness," he said, dour and dead-eyed. There was a shriek of steel on steel, which awakened him in a heartbeat. The train was braking. A shiver gripped him. That encounter with Sally Twosongs was real and true—it had occurred less than a month after his vibrant wife crossed over to glory. He remembered the aftermath of his daughter's insistence.

The trip eastward ended at the Alhambra Saloon in Dodge City—he sat with Deacon Coburn, whose confrontational recap of theology instigated a journey of inner healing in which hope fixed him. Daniel Twosongs thought it now ironic that he was on a westward trek based on persistent words spoken by Consuelo in a dream: *"Go to Deacon. Now! He needs you."*

Late that afternoon in Creede, Sally Twosongs was on the cabin's porch face to face with Deacon Coburn. His grandsons and her daughter were in the alleyway engaged in an energetic kick-ball tournament with a ragtag gang of neighborhood waifs, which was organized and refereed by Avis Lahay. Laughter and high-spirited cheers pealed skyward.

None of that held any interest for Sally Twosongs. Her focus fluctuated between the broad-shouldered man and the swells of clouds gathering in the twilight. Her expression was lined by empathy. "Time is concluding for you, Deacon. You've run the race and are finishing the course. The Lord gave me a specific verse from Psalms for you: *Thou wilt shew me the path of life: in thy presence is fullness of joy; at thy right hand there are pleasures for evermore.*"

"God has been ever faithful to me. Even in my faithlessness."

"The Creator's character has no boundaries or limits."

"From everlasting to everlastings his mercies prevail, Sally Twosongs."

"I am grateful that our lives were entwined."

"Providential, it was," he said, stern and gritty-voiced. "God had his reasons to ordain it. I believe that with every vestige of strength I have left. You and I were destined to meet."

"I never thanked you for rescuing me from the monster-man."

"Sure you did, Sally Twosongs."

"I think not."

He drooped bonelessly. His fingers trembled on the arms of the rocker. "Your thanks is your life and your gifts, which you freely and liberally give to others in service and helps."

"Kind of you to say, but that view neglects reality," she told him, lips pursing into a winning smile. "My life would never have been if you hadn't killed the monster-man."

"He got what was coming to him, fair and square."

"You were the Creator's gavel of justice."

"I was just a man with a conscience and a gun."

"God used you to deliver me from evil, Deacon."

His jaw quivered. "I pray so, Sally Twosongs."

"That prayer was answered in the echo of your gunshot."

He cupped a hand around his chin. "I've been visiting with Charley."

"How is Charley?"

"Wise and at peace."

"He has not dwelt in my visions for years."

"I cannot interpret that, Sally Twosongs."

"The Creator has his purposes. That's all that matters."

"A lifetime of truth to be lived."

"Charley certainly did so."

"He has grown his hair out, Sally Twosongs."

"Really?"

"He is in heaven. Or someplace."

"Where do you meet him, Deacon?"

"In a longhouse."

"If it were not wrong, I would covet that dream. I truly would," she said, taking hold of the single thickly-plaited braid resting across her shoulder. She fretted with it. "I had a mystic linkage to Charley Jondreau. He walked through this world with integrity and dignity."

"The night I met him he had a pistol pointed at Pete Axler's belly."

She grinned a chuckle. "I heard that story."

"It's gospel true."

"Of that I have no doubt."

"Charley abided by his own code."

"Did that code ever conflict with you, Deacon?"

He put the chair in motion as he pondered the question. He glanced toward the latest kick-ball happenings, then in a shocking suddenness, he bolted upright and juddered so fiercely that the spasm threw him forward. He crumpled spread-eagled on the floor, twitching in frightful contractions. His eyes were bulging bubbles of whiteness. The seizure came equipped with a sick screech scratching from his lungs. He heard voices crying as he sank lower into a pit devoid of a smidgen of light, then the blackness descended over him and there was nothingness.

Abbey Langton got outside first, followed by Delores Solrizo and Alice Gallagher, who almost tripped over each other squeezing through the doorway onto the porch to assist Sally Twosongs and Avis Lahay. The women surrounded the stricken man. There were anguished tears as they carried him inside, and worked together to make him reasonably comfortable.

Deacon Coburn was immersed in living darkness. Throbbing cold slithered around him and spindly fingers grabbed at his flesh. His limbs were paralyzed and his chest was oppressed as he attempted to breathe air that was thick and soupy. Inflamed pain burned through him from the top of his head, down his spine and legs to the tips of his toes. He was flat on his back at the sandy bottom of an abyss, staring at the beastly blackness pressing down on him.

His brain functioned murkily. A wedge of light cracked the roof above him. Its faint and feeble glimmer was enough to spur him. He strained to reach toward it, but his arms were bound by bulkiness. There was the pressure of moist lips on his brow. Little by little the darkness became grayish, then the yellow of candlelight chased the gloom to shady corners.

He revived utterly disoriented. His eyesight was blurry. His daughter's face was close to his, and she was crying. He swallowed painfully. To the best of his ascertaining, he was on the bed in her room swaddled beneath a weight of covers. "How long?" he asked in a murmur.

"You've been unconscious for a couple hours."

"Angels."

"You see angels, Deke? Angels from heaven?"

He coughed. An impish grin lifted his overgrown horseshoe moustache and squished his face into wrinkles. "Five angels. Each one a beautiful jewel. Thank you, ladies. I have been a lucky man to have sojourned with such incredible women." He looked around. The array of candles on the dresser cast a flickering glow that shimmied in the air. "Where's Eliza?"

"She and Caleb are at the telegraph office hoping for a wire from Hans," Abbey said, a hand resting on his shoulder. "If none have been received, they'll send another one even though they're not sure if Hans and Stace are still in Denver or someplace between here and there."

Coburn nodded weakly. He coughed again—it was wet and garbled. He drew a wheezy breath that rattled in his chest. "It'd be good to see Hans and Stace, but if not on this side, we'll be together again where teardrops are no more." He licked his parched lips and tried to lift his head off the pillow. "Could I get a private audience with my grandsons and Bethsuelo?"

"Certainly," Abbey replied as she took a hesitant backward step. There was a rustle of movement as the women departed, then the trio were ushered in and the door got closed behind them. They stood shoulder to shoulder at the bedside, with Bethsuelo in the middle,

"I'm an awful sight, ain't I?"

"Yeah-huh."

Coburn grunted a hoarse laugh. "I want you to hear what I have to say before I go home. You three are siblings. Different parents, but tied together by unexplainable knots. A one-eyed blind man could see it. LC and Yaz, I have a charge for you to keep. You must watch out for your sister. She has a special light burning inside her. Protect her. Keep her safe."

LC fought back the tears. "Yes sir, Papa."

"Yeah-huh."

"Bethsuelo, don't let your brothers off the hook. Ever," Deacon said in a trembly voice. "They are made of nails and velvet that makes them know the rights and wrongs of this sweet old world, but there are forthright and direct roads intersected by broad and twisty roads. You know of what I speak. Help these gentlemen walk the line the Almighty has drawn for them."

She sniffled and beamed a smile. "I promise, Mr. Deacon."

"My main point I want to drill in is for the three of you to stick together." He expelled a gurgled tickle in his throat and struggled to gain enough strength to continue. The determination shone through the dull film coating

his eyes. "Model grace and forgiveness for each other. Never allow decep-
tion a foothold, for once it gets a place to cling, troubles of all kinds follow."

"Alright, Papa."

"Yeah-huh."

"Jacob deceived his father Isaac to steal Esau's blessing."

"That's a great illustration, Bethsuelo," Deacon rasped in a croak-rid-
den tone. "Esau foolishly traded away his rights as the firstborn for a bowl
of stew because he was hungry. Then, in the fullness of time, Jacob went
to extremes to hoodwink his father. The results were bitter and damaging.
Esau simmered with hatred and the brothers were estranged for decades."

LC was crying openly. "That won't happen to us, Papa. We promise."

"Yeah-huh," Yaz agreed, tight-lipped and dry-eyed.

"Stick together," Deacon restated as firmly as his condition allowed. He
gasped for oxygen and the clattering noise in his lungs was akin to pebbles
scraping through a sieve. He rallied to shakily deliver a prudent insight.
"Life is hard and beautiful, marvelous. Tend to the garden within and also,
the relational one intertwining itself around the three of you."

Bethsuelo tiptoed forward to lay hands on his chest. Her almond-
shaped eyes, dark and leaching an intensity that was profoundly tangible,
became glassy and narrowed into slits. The air turned warm around her. A
song hummed on her lips as her fingertips seemed to audibly vibrate. "Be at
peace, Mr. Deacon," she whispered, fragile and tinny. He produced a massive smile and breathed hugely, then Deacon Coburn exhaled wetness as he
sank into stillness.

"Mom! Come quick!" LC shouted, shrill and scared-eyed.

"Yeah-huh!"

~~~

June 1, 1892

*Dear Diary: I have two oil lamps situated on the railing on either
side of me, and could use another one even closer, but will make-
do. There is a pall hanging over this cabin. It is sad and tense, but
also prayerful. Everyone else is inside, so I am alone on the porch,
reflecting on my thoughts and feelings as I reconcile or pacify them
by putting words on paper.*

*The night is dark and dreary. Not a glimmer of light is view-
able in the heavens, and there is a brisk chill creeping and getting
colder by the minute, but my concerns outweigh the weather. Eliza
and Caleb returned from the telegraph office and had nothing to*

report. *No news is good news? I don't think so. Whoever came up with that adage was terribly mistaken.*

We've not had a telegram from Hans and Stace in several weeks. I'm afraid that they will not get back in time. In fact, given the rapid downhill slide in Deacon's condition I have resigned my-self to the fact that he will pass from time to eternity before Stace has an opportunity to speak to him one more time, which is an extra sadness sinking heaviness through me.

Midnight is still an hour or more away. I'm drained and ex-hausted, but not tired, which is weird. My mind is beleaguered by lightning bug ideas and remembrances flittering around so speedily that I cannot latch onto one long enough to examine it. Frustration has gotten a hold on me, so I am intentionally doing deep breathing exercises to gain perspective and balance.

Since Bethsuelo blessed Deacon he has not awakened. Neither are his lungs so stressed. His complexion remains white and pasty. There are some stirrings of hopefulness, even in me, but those are couched in false and selfish wishful thinking. We want to hold on and not let go, which I suppose, is entirely normal, but not at all fair or realistic. Deacon is ready to step through the door. He has lived with his eyes fixed on the great unseen destination.

I love and respect him so much. His steady hand and gritty demonstration of faith will always have an impact on me. I trea-sure every adventure and discovery we had on trails. His hand guided me through much, and I doubt he realized his influence as he modeled wisdom by wrapping it around the fundamental belief that the astonishing grace of God is for everyone, and is all about redemption and new beginnings. His attitude proclaimed that no one and no circumstance is ever unredeemable. I pray that I will embody that hope for others.

Brenda Hawkins just jumped to the forefront of my mind. Her life ended far too soon, but her legacy is alive and kicking in her son. Stace has her sense of responsibility and duty. His complex serious streak is sometimes difficult to decipher. His conscience is tender, but he is no pushover sissy because his mother had tough-ness which he inherited in spades. He stands his ground much like she had to do in order to seize a desperate chance at a fresh start.

More than once when she was on her deathbed we discussed the mysterious working of God as it related to second chances and new beginnings. Her faith was vital—it kept her on an even-keel and grew stronger as her illness progressed. She was wont to say that when death was camped upon the doorstep past choices and decisions could be seen with crystal clarity.

Brenda had courage and strength of character. Her story was inspiring. Her resolve to pack up a toddler and put her life in Las Vegas behind her had a touch of daring, but the Lord went before her and beside her. God had a purpose and plan because he knows the beginning and the end. He prepared a future that included a home and family for her and Stace. She rode with Mom on a stagecoach from Las Vegas to Dodge City, and they developed a friendship.

That led to a sisterly camaraderie between us that blossomed immediately. It was apparent from the beginning that we were kindred spirits. I shall never forget the train to Santa Fe in the autumn of '82. Brenda and I shared secrets and dreams and laughter while chattering like schoolgirls—I made a natural and easy connection with four year old Stace, mostly because my arm was in a sling and he was ever watchful to make sure I was not going to break.

Then when Brenda got sick and it became clear that the prognosis was fatal, I made a solemn promise that I would take care of Stace and do all that was possible to keep him on the straight and narrow. I vowed to raise him as my own, but would never let him forget her. I've done my best to be true to my words, and pray daily that I am accomplishing the task.

There are moments when I am confident in my role, but more often than I care to truly acknowledge, I do battle with that old bugaboo of self-doubt, which I suppose, is a prompt for me to be vigilant and faithful in my devotional life, and also, to lean solidly on the support network of family that is the richest of blessings from my heavenly Father. We definitely need each other, and in the next few days will be pulling together and tightening the ties that bind us.

And that's a fine sentiment on which to end this installment.

As was her longstanding habit, she began to peruse what she had written. A thought popped up, which caused her head to tilt inquisitively. She wondered if it would be wise to allow Stace to read the section about his mother. She made a mental note to self to give the idea over to prayer, but even as she did so, she had an inkling that the answer would be no. The daybook was and always had been a refuge for her to record and process her private ruminations.

She suddenly halted. A tiny smile pinched at her lips. She heard a familiar click-click and scurrying footfalls. She came out of the chair in such a hurry that the pen and journal dropped to the floor. She scooped them up and placed them on the vacant rocker, then stepped to the edge of the porch and saw Eliezer Smith and Whitey Fitzgerald emerging from the darkness.

Her heart leapt. Avis ran toward them and slammed into the cotton-topped barber so hard that he almost tipped over. He locked his arms around her. She clung to him, shivering sobs as all the turbulent emotions cascading through her were released. She squeezed her eyes shut as a measure of re-laxation struck an inner chord because of the security found in his embrace.

"I be here for you, sweetie."

"Mr. Weitzel."

"How many times do I have to tell you to call me Hans?"

"Have you met my Aunt Avis?" Stace asked, grinning as he turned away from his reflection in the window. Dim light from a few wall mounted lamps cast pale hues throughout the nearly vacant passenger car. The train was chugging at a stop and go pace, and had been doing so since nightfall. "You think there's any chance we're ever going to get home?"

"It's past midnight now, so we better be in South Fork before noon-time," Hans replied, weariness threaded through his voice. "And yes, I do know your Aunt Avis, so now, while we are both wide awake is as good a time as any to hash this issue out and be done with it."

"What issue?"

"The tension in our relationship."

"There's no tension between us, Mr. Weitzel."

"What did you just call me?"

"Aunt Avis says adults are to be addressed properly."

"Perhaps Aunt Avis needs to be corrected."

"I wouldn't be the one to broach that topic."

"The lady has a steel spine, doesn't she?"

"Yes, sir."

"Now what's that? Sir? I thought we were friends, Boss."

"We are, Mr. Weitzel. Great friends."

"So why not call me by name?"

"Aunt Avis taught me that it's about respect."

"Wouldn't it be respectful to honor my wishes?"

"You're putting me into a corner."

"Not my intention, Boss."

"Until I am a man myself, you are Mr. Weitzel."

"Let me be the one to break the news to you, Boss. You're more of a man now than many who are twice and three times your age," Hans said, arms folding over his chest. "The way you handled that pompous banker who was dragging his feet was masterful and courteous."

"All I did was repeat the salient facts."

"You did more than that, Boss."

"How so?"

"Spoke truth to power."

"Really? I don't think so."

"Put me in mind of Deacon Coburn."

"That's far-fetched, Mr. Weitzel."

"No hedging, no soft-soap baloney. Stern straight-talk delivered without animosity. An ability which has eluded me my entire life." Hans smiled slyly as he removed his tweed flat cap and jostled it in his hands. "The capacity to remain unruffled up against blarney and stupidity is an attribute to nurture. And I will be happy to convey all this information to Aunt Avis."

"Thank you, but you're exaggerating."

"Nope," Hans answered frankly. "I was about ready to pop a blood vessel, but you calmed the mood and got the joker's attention. Your poise even took the blowhard wind out of my sails, which as you know, can be a rare occurrence. The clearing of your throat started it. Then you leaned forward, tapped on the edge of his desk and increasingly held his gaze as you explained that there was no chance we would back down in any further negotiations."

"Water rights. I simply retold the strategy we had settled on before we left home," Stace said, shrugging. "Caleb was wise to purchase that land-locked acreage when he had the chance. Though it is severed from the main property of *WT Ranch*, we maintain the water rights so that was always our ace. The consortium's offer ignored the water rights. My suspicion is that the bank itself or the banker was in partnership or collusion with the prospective buyers."

Weitzel sat upright, eyes spreading wide. "Pardon?"

"The banker had ulterior motives."

"What clued you in?"

"I sensed it. I read people."

Weitzel's lips pursed to hiss a sharp whistle as he put the hat on. "I had no red-flags. No inkling that things weren't on the up and up, but shady double-dealing shines bright lights on the hold-ups." He raised his hand and shook a finger at the young man. "There was hornswoggling afoot and I missed it. I got bushwhacked. What kind of enfeebled old fool have I become?"

"No kind, sir. We settled the details exactly how we intended."

"Thanks to you, Boss," Hans said, methodically eyeing him. "I'll say it again with no qualms: You're more of a man now than many who are twice and three times your age."

"I will hide that commendation in my heart, Hans."

Weitzel chuckled. The amusement in his throat started low and restrained, but built into belly laughter. He twined his fingers together high on his chest. When his jocularity passed, the men exchanged expressions that communicated mutual admiration and much affection, then the evocative moment dissolved, but not before putting its stamp on both of them. The locomotive plodded through the night while Stace Hawkins and Hans Weitzel attempted to snooze.

Abbey Langton sat on a hard-backed chair, alone in the bedroom with her father, which was exactly how she wanted it. The door was closed. He had not regained consciousness. His breathing was so weak and shallow as to be imperceptible. Her hands were pressed together on her lap while a tide-pool of silent tears soaked into the bodice of her dress.

She had been in this situation in the past. Her heart was numb, her memory speeding to another bedroom in a far-off place, where her mother, haggard and shrunken, lay dying in awful agony. She glanced around. Two striking similarities skewered her—the collection of candles were pretty as the tiny flames flickered to stave off the darkness, and her impeccably dreadful sense of helplessness was the same now as it had been twenty-three years ago.

In her mind she could see and hear the woman who bore her; the strongminded woman of character who instilled in her truths about life and living that she was now urgently trying to pass along to her sons. She closed her eyes and it was like she was fifteen years old all over again, unable to do anything except wait for the inevitable. She felt scared and angry. The disquiet within was an agitation that provoked sour queasiness in the pit of her stomach.

There, sitting vigil at the deathbed of her father, words spoken by her mother came back precise and certain. "*I'm going to die, and you, dear daughter, are going to live. There's a great big wonderful world waiting for you to explore. Put my dying behind you. Walk away from my grave to go and do and see. Whatever days are ordained for you, cherish every moment. If you treasure the gift, your life will be colored by the brushstrokes of dreams.*"

A breathy sigh flittered off her lips. She had tried and kept trying to be faithful to that counsel, but as memories and confusion spiraled through her, doubt twirled in snide mockery, and she honestly wondered if her mother would be proud of her efforts and accomplishments. The taunts hurt. She ached with such deepness that her bones felt spongy.

Her eyes came open. A desire to escape the myriad emotions reared up, but instead of running away, she purposely calibrated her focus. She looked at the ragamuffin man and recalled being nine years old when she met him. He was clad in a tattered blue uniform and wandered onto the farmstead, where he compulsively made repairs and improvements. She remembered an incident that was truly indicative of the foundational beginnings of their relationship.

The day was a scorcher. She had an absorbed smile as she squatted on the top of a stump from a gnarled old tree he had felled, which he was now cutting and splitting to be stacked for firewood in anticipation of wintertime. He worked at an uninterrupted tempo that wasted no muscle or movement. She was being entertained by his quickness and efficiency.

"Hey, Mr. Lawrence, whatcha going to do next?"

"Finish this job first," he answered, while never breaking the axe's rhythm. "Always best to get one task done before having your attention taken by another project. No need to worry on the next chore because tomorrow always takes care of itself. Each day has its own jobs."

"Not tomorrow! Today! Whatcha going to do today?"

"Chopping wood will keep me at it until suppertime, Miss Abbey."

"Yuck. I wanted you to check the vegetable garden."

"That's your job, ain't it?"

"Mom said you might help me, Mr. Lawrence."

"Did she?"

"Yes. She told me to ask nice."

"I don't think you even asked, did you, Miss Abbey?"

She pouted, bottom lip protruding. "That ain't fair."

"Fair? Not sure you got a complaint, young lady," he said, abruptly stopping. He sank the axe-head into a log. "Tell you what." He pulled a handkerchief from a pocket and mopped his face. "You lug a bucket of fresh water and the dipper over here, then after I've drank my fill, if you get the basket, I will show you which tomatoes and peppers are ripe for the picking, but afterwards, you cannot distract me until the carcass of this tree is split and piled."

"Until Mom calls us for supper?"

"Those are the terms."

"You got a deal, Mr. Lawrence."

"Get to it, girl. I'm as parched as the Sahara Desert."

A frown started to knit itself across her brow, but was unraveled by a rosy-cheeked smile. She jumped high up off the stump and was running as fast as possible the instant her feet hit the ground. Behind her she heard the cadenced clacking of steel biting chunks out of wood; the sound encircled her and blended together with the giggles ringing in her ears.

The memory vanished. There was no sunshine for it was nighttime—there was no echo of an axe and no giggles. All was quiet except for the torturous gasping of irregular breathing. She tilted forward to study the man she had known as Mr. Lawrence, and for a spiraling instant, the present reality became an unreal pressure that seemed to want to crush her to smithereens.

Her heart pounded, wild and uncontrollably. "Dear God," she murmured as her hands unlocked. She stood in a teetering quaver and had to grab onto the back of the chair to gain a rickety balance. Teardrops spilled down her face as she cautiously adjusted Deacon Coburn's pillow. Bleak questions leapfrogged through her. She felt scared and yearned for answers, but then, Abbey Langton expressed only one uncertainty, and that in a faltering voice. "What am I going to do?"

chapter four

Endings & Beginnings

"I will pay my vows unto the Lord now in the presence of all his people. Precious in the sight of the Lord is the death of his saints. O Lord, truly I am thy servant; I am thy servant, and the son of thine handmaid: thou hast loosed my bonds."

~THE PSALMIST~

THE WOODS WERE DARK. Oppressive clouds cloaked the nightlights. Deacon Coburn was alone and unafraid. Silence, as absolute as the interior of a crypt, thudded against his eardrums. A moment ago, he had been in the grips of arctic cold, but now, the air oozed a warmth that seeped to his bones. He ambled at a decisive pace and never veered to the left or right.

He came to a meadow, and though visibility was less than three feet, he didn't slow or stagger. His arms swung at his sides as he proceeded across the field with an anticipatory bounce in his steps. Awareness of his location and circumstances surged excitedly through his veins. His gait and eagerness increased. The darkness faded to a dull and foggy bubble shining above a longhouse village, and his heart jumped. He hurried straightaway to a particular dwelling.

Upon entering, the vivid enthusiasm in his bloodstream intensified. His old comrade sat at a glittery campfire petting the back of a large red-tailed hawk perched at his side. His other hand was inevitably fidgeting with the stone. Coburn appreciated the sight as he crouched low and settled on his haunches near him. "I now know what I'm doing here, Charley."

"You finally get it, eh."

"I reckon I do."

"Your brother Josiah?"

"You know of the letter?"

Jondreau grinned. "I *see* things, preacher-man."

"Even here?"

"The gift is forever."

"It's a mystery, Charley."

"Eternity illuminates all mysteries."

"I will soon test that theory."

"The past caught up to you, eh?"

"Reconciliation tracked me down."

"The wound of a son is healed?"

"On the blood and bone side of glory, yes."

"And the balm of your forgiveness?"

"Applied and at work, Charley."

"Time does shorten, preacher-man."

"Is there nothing remaining for me to say or do?"

"A crown of righteousness awaits you, eh."

"Have I truly finished the race?"

Jondreau removed his hand from the bird of prey. It craned its neck to watch him. He cupped his hands together for a split second, then just as quickly snatched the stone up and rolled it between thumb and forefinger—it was unsurpassed in its iridescent whiteness. He smiled shrewdly at his visitor. "My feathered guardian will provide you expert guidance, eh."

"To where?"

"The city of Zion and life everlasting."

"My time of dying is now?"

"You have seen your last tomorrow, eh."

"No more battles, no more burdens?"

"The weaknesses of the flesh and the wiles of the ancient deceiver are defeated," Charley replied, radiant as he stared at the stone. "A death-song of my Cheyenne kinfolk understands truth and life, preacher-man: *Today is a good day to die; only the stones live forever.*"

"Tell me of the stone in *your* hand, Charley."

"You will receive yours in a twinkling of an eye, my preacher-man friend," the Iroquois warrior said heartily. "The Great Spirit commands it: *To him who overcometh I have given hidden manna and a white stone with a new name written on it that only he knoweth.*"

Everything instantaneously changed. The blackness of a tunnel fenced him in. He stood stockstill. Then, a thin sliver of phenomenal light appeared way off in the distance and beckoned to him. There was conflict deep within because he heard a tender voice and felt a kiss upon his forehead. Tension seized him. Coburn longed to reach for the brightness; to run faster than humanly possible toward it, but could not because a prickly resistance held him captive.

His eyelids pulsed open. He blinked rapidly. His daughter's face was inches from him. Tears poured down her cheeks which were creased by fragility and hope. He summoned a weak remnant of strength. His tongue touched his lips and he strained to speak. His voice, coarse and thickened, arose in a clear whisper. "*The lines are fallen unto me in pleasant places; yea, I have a goodly heritage.* Weep not, Miss Abbey. I'm going home where I'll be free from the bondage of sin and death."

He exhaled a blast of air and gasped his final breath. His eyes fluttered and he was absent from the body. Perfect healing washed over him. Every residue of pain was gone; heartaches and sorrows were so far behind him that all grieving had vanished and was forgotten. The prison of human skin had been shattered—corruptible flesh was incorruptible. The sting of death was a momentary glitch of time, which was replaced by the glorious spectacle of victory.

Coburn was standing on a mountaintop overlooking the celestial city of God. He was young and strong and clothed in shimmering beauty. Concealed in his fisted right hand was the treasured pure white stone. A magnificent aria surrounded him—the poignant music filled his soul. His arms were outstretched in wonderment and worship. He looked and saw the red-tailed raptor leading him homeward in the direction of the great company of a heavenly choir.

It was bitter cold and snowing on the morning Deacon Coburn, the River Brethren man from Conoy Creek, shed his earthen shell. The fleecy snow would be the last of the season. It fell to the accompaniment of blasts of dynamite. Particles of ash and grungy dust mingled with the flakes to create a grayish tapestry on the rooftops of Creede. Ashes to ashes, dust to dust.

Avis Lahay had the bead of the chinstrap on her skimmer tightened against her jawline as she rode hard and fast, with more gusto and conviction than she had ever ridden in her life. Every muscle in her body seemed to be twitching electrically, and she was in complete accord with the strawberry roan beneath her. She had her knees pulled up and was leaning forward.

The air was frigid. Her red-rimmed eyes, puffy from tears and lack of sleep, were narrowed into slits because of the snow; it had begun in sporadic spurts just before dawn and was now, an hour and half later, tumbling steadily from a concrete sky. Emotions were loose and racing violently through her. She had her cheek pressed against the animal's sweaty neck.

Cookie was galloping flat-out toward Wagon Wheel Gap and *WT Ranch*. Mud was turning the roadway into a sloppy and treacherous mess, but the limber and fleet-footed mare had enthusiasm and pleasure coursing through its veins. Chugs of steam spouted from its nostrils. The plop-plop of its hoofbeats was in rhythm with the pounding heartbeat of the woman.

She spoke its name and relaxed her thighs. The horse, apparently sensing her turmoil and urgency, ignored the understated prompt and kept running at full speed. She repeated the prod a bit more insistently and added a slight tug on the reins. The strawberry roan snorted and neighed in protest, but then began to gradually decelerate. She relaxed some and straightened in the saddle. Over the course of fifty yards or so, the mare slowed until it was walking.

Her thoughts were coalescing into a whirligig montage that whipped up her sense of responsibility. Deacon Coburn had died an hour ago. Her sharp-cornered feelings demanded to be vented. She was self-aware enough to understand that administering the complex jumble would be an ongoing procedure requiring unrepentant candor and authenticity.

Loss came equipped with barbs that cut to the core—sadness hurt. To claim otherwise was a disingenuous approach to heartaches. To maintain health and balance necessitated honesty, and though all her introspection would unquestionably find its way into her journal, she thought it best to make an attempt to begin governing the rawness whilst she was alone and mounted on a faithful friend, so as to be able to pilot the young ones through grief.

Her mind drifted to LC, Yaz and Bethsuelo—three unique personalities who often functioned singularly. LC had gut instincts and fiery emotions; Yaz was unflappable and driven by the practical application of hands on tactics in all matters; Bethsuelo possessed an extrasensory intuition augmented by spontaneous faith and spiritual vigor.

Avis suspected that their pattern of seeking her out as individuals to talk through issues and feelings would continue in this sensitive instance. After they had hashed things out amongst themselves, they would come together to share bits and pieces with her. She prayed for the fortitude and wisdom to provide effective counsel and a dependable guiding hand.

She removed her hat and tilted her head upward. The fluffy snowflakes were like large cotton balls melting into a soothing lotion that bathed her skin. With Creede two miles behind her the crystallized moisture was white and unblemished—immaculate and innocent. She opened her mouth to taste the pristine sweetness. A favorite fragment of Scripture dashed out of the swirling assortment of ideas, and her lips instantly spread wide in a toothy grin.

"*Though your sins be as scarlet, they shall be as white as snow,*" she quoted, ruffling the horse's mane as it plodded along through the snowy muck. "The Lord is my shepherd, my rock, my deliverer, my provider, and my strong tower. I am going to put one foot in front of the other and trust him moment by moment." She tucked her wavy hair under the skimmer, then Avis Lahay murmured affectionately, and the strawberry roan sped up into a loping canter.

"I told you so."

Her husband gazed over the rim of his coffee mug and gave her a lackadaisical shrug. "Yeah, you did, Naomi." He sipped a swallow, weary and tired-eyed. The first round of daily chores were done. He scratched at the grizzled gray stubble of a week's growth and smiled at the intermittent sunbeams playing hide and seek on the kitchen floor. "A premonition of sorts?"

"I woke up in the middle of the night and just knew."

"I recall," Pete grunted as he drank a mouthful. He adjusted his posture on the chair. "It wasn't even four o'clock and you had the oil lamps lit and were packing a suitcase."

"You had to get up soon," she said softly.

"Another hour would've done me fine."

"I apologize, Pete."

"No need to, dear. I understand."

She took a look out the window above the sink. It had stopped snowing and the slate-gray clouds were breaking apart to allow occasional splinters of sunshine to bless the countryside. Her brown eyes were soulful and damp. Acceptance and resolve were rising in her. She sighed and took a seat across from the father of her children. "Avis rode Cookie hard. Too hard."

"She had reason. Plus she knows horses. Especially her own."

"Her heart must be aching."

"As is yours, Naomi."

"Yes," she admitted, shoulders slumping. "I have cried myself dry and will likely do so again, but my sorrow is personal. I grieve because I will miss my brother, but make no mistakes, he has won the race. Saying our goodbyes should be a celebratory remembrance of his life. My heart will recuperate quickly if we emphasize that he has triumphed over death."

"He'd want it no other way."

She gazed at him thoughtfully. "Do you remember when you met Deacon?"

"Sure. Like it was yesterday."

"Please don't make me drag it out of you, Pete."

"The spring of '71," he said, finishing off his coffee. He stood and poured another cup. Then delivered a mug to her before returning to his chair. "My belly was empty and gnawing on my backbone so I needed a job. I hired on as an auxiliary lawman in Abilene. Every shipping season the town got lawless because of the rowdiness that came with the Texas cattle drives. Drinking and gambling led to fistfights and gunplay. Wild Bill Hickok was the marshal.

"On my first nighttime tour of duty Hickok introduced me to Deacon at the Alamo Saloon, and in doing so, made a cavalier wisecrack about your brother being an honorable tough guy who knew the Bible better than most preachers. The next afternoon Deacon sought me out. I was passing time thinking and whittling on a bench in front of Moon's Frontier Store.

"He sat down and right-off, we talked of life and ideas. Struck up a friendship from that day forward. I trusted him from the beginning, and have relied on his judgment more times than can be counted. He urged me to follow my heart into horse ranching and vouched for me with Caleb, so I am aware of my liability to him. A debt of gratitude I could never repay."

"He would slough it off."

"Again, he'd want it no other way."

Her lips parted in a wistful smile as a childhood memory formed into a full-blown picture that dominated her mind. It was crisp and bright, and surrounded by warmth, which filled up her senses. She took a swig of coffee. And another. Enjoyment flooded her eyes. She started to put the reminiscence into words, but was interrupted when the front door got slammed in a rush.

"Mom!"

"What is it, Amanda?" Naomi asked, putting the mug down as she jumped to her feet. She hurried into the hallway and almost crashed into her daughter who was coming just as rapidly from the other direction. "Are you hurt? Is something wrong?"

"No, Mom," Amanda answered, sympathetic and subdued. She wore baggy dungarees and a chamois work shirt—her reddened cheeks were streaked by smudges of dirt. "Aunt Avis is almost finished giving Cookie a rubdown. Then she'll hook up a mule for the buggy and be ready to take you to Creede." She took a backward step. "Before you leave, can we talk?"

"Certainly."

"In private." The fourteen-year-old curtly spun around and proceeded to her bedroom. She held the door for her mother, then closed it and stood with her backside against it. Her hands were flexing nervously and she had drawn her bottom lip in between her teeth. The room was spic and span, with a place for everything and each item occupying its precise spot.

"What is it, Amanda?"

"I want to say I'm sorry."

"Uncle Deacon's at peace."

"Yes, but that's not what I mean, Mom."

Naomi furled her brow in confusion. "What then?"

"In recent weeks Daddy and I have had a few go-arounds," she replied flatly. "It's kind of funny because he thinks he is being sly, but no matter how he approaches the topic it boils down to a variation of choices and consequences." She tried on a smile, but it slipped off. "And Aunt Avis was just telling me some important things that made my heart hurt in a good way."

"How can I help, Amanda?"

"Hear me out."

"I'm listening, honey."

"I don't know what I want to do or be. Or where I want to go" she said, rolling her eyes and flinching her lips. "I acted like a spoiled brat, making lots of noise about moving to Creede and complaining because I was stuck here, but now, I'm truly attempting to think different."

"I've seen the mindset change, Amanda."

"Really?"

"Of course."

"And?"

Naomi smiled—it was somewhat forced, but enthusiasm shone through the sadness in her eyes. "Pride is swollen up inside me. You are a remarkable young lady, Amanda Irene. We may butt heads again over something, but that's all part of you growing into the woman God created you to be and me letting go to allow it to happen. Not sure which of us has the harder job."

"Me neither," Amanda jested drolly. She edged closer to her. "It falls to Daddy and me to stay and handle the business here. Don't worry about

Daddy while you're gone. I will take care of him and make sure he gains at least a little sleep. We'll get all the essential work done."

"Of which I have no doubt."

Amanda moved with suddenness to wrap her arms tightly around her mother. Her voice heightened into a wavering falsetto as she said, "I love you, Mom. You know that, right?" The words caused an upsurge of emotions, culminating in weepy affirmations that did much to put salve on the breach of tension between them. It was a long while before the embrace ended.

The skies were no longer overcast—the leaden-hued clouds had broken into isolated islands that were being eroded by sweeping oceans of blue. A warm zephyr sang a refreshing song of newness through the aspens and did much to hasten the snowmelt. The mule's tail swished happily as the two-wheeled carriage sloshed along the mucky roadway.

Naomi Axler had the appearance of standoffish royalty being squired to some formal social occasion. She sat in the passenger seat, back straight and shoulders stiff. "I'm grateful, Avis. Whatever advice you gave Amanda were words that had a positive impact."

Avis was hunched forward, exhibiting trust in the animal by holding the reins loosely. "I was just being me." She gave her a crooked sideward grin. "I merely paraphrased some precepts from Ecclesiastes that I'd heard repeatedly from Deacon. When someone passes on, the living should remind ourselves that death awaits us at some unknown crossroads, then adjust our attitude and perspective based on the fact that no one is guaranteed another day."

"She said it made her heart hurt in a good way."

"I'm glad. Life is short and eternity is long."

"That's a reckoning straight from Deacon."

"It is indeed, for which I do not apologize," Avis said, eyes bright and vivacious. "He had an incredible influence on me and I intend to dust off lots of Deacon-isms. I was eighteen when I was first on the trail with him. Santa Fe to Dodge City. Every day we rode and sightsaw mostly in silence, but our evenings at the campfire rendezvous were spent talking Bible and nature, and all the intersections between them. I got a rigorous and pragmatic theological education."

"You obviously learned the lessons well."

Avis nodded pleasantly. "I hope so, but I got miles and miles to go. His faith expression was natural. There was never any pretense or phoniness. He accepted everyone where they were at without judgment or condemnation, and lifted others up because he genuinely lived grace."

"That was my brother."

"He will be missed, though he'd say no."

"True enough," Naomi agreed, chuckling. She shifted her weight and shaded her eyes against brightness and wished she'd worn a sunbonnet. "When I was little he was my hero. He had a gift. He could speak Bible truths in dynamic ways. The elders tapped him on the shoulder. He was to take on an apprenticeship amongst the River Brethren to be instructed as a preacher. Mother and Father were ecstatic. When he went his own way there were repercussions.

"I was a child, but I heard all the back-fence chatter. There was confusion and tension in our home because of pressures placed upon our family by the brethren. Deacon was shunned or disciplined, I don't remember the exact phrasing used, but I do recall that there were changes in our family life and also, our status and reputation within the community was different too."

"That was wrong. Deacon followed his conscience."

Naomi shook her head regretfully. "Not according to the River Brethren leadership. He was supposed to obey and be in submission to the dictates determined by the community." She folded her hands on her lap. "As I got older and learned some details about what he went off to do, right or wrong, I thought of him as a knight in shining armor doing battle against evil."

"Some fanciful imaginings?"

"That was surely part of it," Naomi replied pensively. "A memory struck me earlier. I was ten years old. It was the summer before Deacon left home. Late August or early September. I was filled with butterflies because of my first and only crush on a boy. Adam Engle. He was a teaser. I picked some flowers and tried giving them to him, but he got all huffy. He threw the bouquet at me, called me a sissy girl and told me to never talk to him again.

"I was devastated. So much so that I ran away from home. It was the end of the world. I didn't want to speak to anyone. The embarrassment made me so angry that I actually held my breath and stomped my feet. There's a great deal of humor in my histrionics now, but not then. I thought my life was over." She uttered a hiccup of a laugh. "I cried all afternoon, continually wiping my eyes on one sleeve of my dress and blowing my nose on the other.

"It was near sunset when Deacon found me hiding at a secluded nook of Conoy Creek. He was grim and serious when he knelt in front of me. His chin and cheeks were darkened by whiskery stubble. Why the dickens would I remember *that* detail?" she asked rhetorically. "He was so kind, so gentle. I can see him now; head tilted to the right, eyes crimpled and full of compassion that I could feel. He told me that I was the prettiest and smartest girl he knew.

"I giggled. He thumbed moisture off my face and gave me a hug that made me feel like I was the only person who mattered to him. Then he explained boys to me and provided a special insight about Adam Engle. He said that teenage boys could be dunces when it came to dealing with girls. According to Deacon's assessment, Adam was sweet on me but because I was so pretty and smart he didn't know what to do with his notions or how to act around me.

"Evidently my big brother was exactly right. Not too many years later Adam sought permission from Father to court me. I was enamored on our first outing together. Our wedding night was months before my eighteenth birthday. Sometime in the next number of days Adam brought up the incident with the flowers and expressed repentance for his braggadocio."

"Ah, that must have made you cry."

"Afterwards, yes."

"Afterwards?"

Naomi suppressed a smirk. "After enjoying my wifely duty."

"Naomi! I know nothing of such carryings-on."

"Maybe someday?"

"Nope. I'll not marry."

"How can you be so certain what the future holds?"

Avis gave her a gregarious shrug. "Just a sense and a growing understanding of who God created me to be. I have come to believe that I am called to ride herd on a flock of young people. Stace, Jesse, Amanda, LC, Bethsuelo, Yaz. They are and will be my priority and focus."

"Your heart is committed and determined, isn't it?"

"Are you asking me?"

"Not really, Avis. I hear gritty certitude in your voice."

"I'm at peace about it I can tell you that much."

"You have a noble and commendable mission."

"And ofttimes scary."

"Fear not, Avis. God will equip you for the task."

"I pray so."

The breeze gusted, which caused the mule to bray and twitch its ears. Avis made a minor modification on the reins to guide the animal through a snowbank lengthened across the road. A boom in the distance shot a column of dirt above the tree line. The temperature was on the rise at a rate comparable to the sun climbing toward its summit. Quietness crept between the ladies.

Naomi Axler had her mind fixed on the stuff of eternity.

It was past high noon when Stace Hawkins sprightly exited the train at South Fork. The already crowded platform of the Denver & Rio Grande Railroad Depot was becoming even more congested with disembarking passengers. He stretched and rotated his shoulders forward to release knotty muscle kinks. He breathed deeply and took a look around while he waited.

Activity at a boxcar in front of the caboose drew his attention. The side door was open and a workman had just finished sliding the ramp out. A squat man with a distinctive bearing led a black stallion down it. He stopped and conversed with the railroad man. Stace smiled a frown as he leaned and took a stride in that direction, but then there was a commotion behind him.

Hans Weitzel bulled his way through the doorway and onto the stairs barking orders to the baggage carrier in front of him who was weighted down with armloads of luggage. To say that Weitzel was in a foul mood would be an understatement of grand proportions. He was a walking earthquake and every resounding step caused another fault line to split apart.

The porter, a light-skinned Negro, did his job with thorough efficiency. When he was finished stacking the suitcases and satchels, he turned toward the grumpy man, and standing as erect as a soldier, he asked, "Will that be everything, sir? Or can I be of further service?"

Weitzel dug into a pocket and came out with his wallet. "Sorry for yammering at you," he said, forcing a sunny expression at the man. "I'm really not a bad sort, believe me." He retrieved a twenty dollar bill and handed it over. "You pocket this and don't you dare give a cut to any of your superiors. You're the only sonofagun in this outfit who knows what he's doing."

"Thank you kindly, sir."

"Tell the big shots to replace the boiler."

"It be a burping mechanical monstrosity."

"Don't I know it?" Hans asked in a growl. "Stop and go, stop and go. Two days of the nonsense. It'll take a week to recover from the shakes. If you point me to the president of the company I'd gladly punch him in the nose just to see how he likes getting jerked around."

"I'll pass along the remarks to the uppity-ups, but I be just a peon."

Weitzel dismissed the porter with an exaggerated wave. He watched the man shuffle onto the next task. "I swear, Boss," he griped, hands balling into fists to be jammed on his hips. "I've run out of steam. If I don't get a mattress under me soon I'm going to drop in my footsteps."

"We've got another delay, Mr. Weitzel. I mean Hans."

"Good Lord! What is it now?"

Hawkins spread his arms wide in a gesture toward the bow-legged man in a flat-brimmed hat loitering near the boxcar beside a black horse. "Looks like company has come calling."

Weitzel swiveled his head in that direction and his face became a beaming smile that seemed to immediately energize him. "Daniel Twosongs!" he shouted as he hurried toward him. "Where have you been? Haven't seen or heard from you in better than two years and here you pop in out of nowhere." The in-laws clasped forearms in a firm and vigorous handshake.

"How's our granddaughter?"

"She's your daughter's daughter and my son's precious jewel," Hans replied, cheeks flushing with pride. "Bethsuelo is growing up straight and fine. Smart as a whip. She ciphers numbers and angles in her head, but don't let her quick mind fool you. The girl is full of beans and vinegar. She's zinged me with her crafty sense of humor more times than I can count."

Hawkins had sidled in close to innocently eavesdrop, and now, made eye-contact with the new arrival as his lips squiggled into a grin. "This is a great surprise. Good to see you, sir."

"Sir? It's Daniel, Stace."

Weitzel chortled jovially. "Avis makes him mind his p's and q's."

"Avis is a smart and substantial lady," Daniel said, taking hold of the reins. His face contorted in an attempt to keep at bay a yawn that came and went attended by a gasping groan. "I am tired to the bone and my stomach is a bottomless pit of emptiness. I need a meal and a decent place to bed down, or else I may faint. Getting old is not for quitters or pansies."

"Weaklings need not apply," Hans intoned, glibly serious.

Hawkins spoke around a scarcely concealed snicker. "If you elderly gentlemen would permit me some latitude, I may have a plan to put into action that'll satisfy all concerns."

"What have you got, Boss?"

"Can you manhandle our luggage over to the Grande Rio Hotel?"

Weitzel scowled. "Old don't mean feeble."

Twosongs shrugged nonchalantly. "Some days it does."

"I suppose that's a fair assessment."

"You put on more years, Hans. I logged more miles."

"What have you got, Boss?" Hans asked again, gruff and blunt.

"Get checked in at the hotel," Stace answered directly. "Have some grub in the dining room and hit the sack. While that's a go, I'll take Daniel's horse to the livery and see to its care, then settle his bill and ours, and also arrange to have the three mounts ready in the morning. After that I'll deliver the packet of documents to the lawyer and have them notarized."

"Do you have enough cash for the livery?"

"I expect I do, Hans."

"Get a receipt, Boss."

"You don't need to tell me the obvious, sir."

Weitzel puckered a grin. "Of that fact you are correct." He stepped close and impulsively wagged a finger at him. "Don't accept any hemming and hawing guff from the lawyer."

"I'll take care of business."

"You got the legal paperwork?"

"You entrusted it to me, did you not?"

"I did indeed, Boss."

"It's safe and secure," Stace said soberly. He opened his waist-length jacket and patted the bulge sticking out from the top of the inside breast pocket. "Put all misgivings to rest. I've got everything under control." With that bold assurance, he took hold of the black stallion's reins and strode away. The animal neighed and high-stepped eagerly alongside him.

"Many thanks, Stace," Daniel called, touching the brim of his hat.

Hawkins acknowledged the gratitude by tilting him a sideward nod. Despite a rigid posture, his amble had a deceptive carefree manner, but to regard the driven young man as easygoing would be a mistake. Five months before his fourteenth birthday, Stace Hawkins already possessed a purposeful disposition that produced an authoritative demeanor.

The ladies at the table were red-eyed and sniffling. It was a place of bittersweet memories of the man who had been the glue that held them and so many others together. Everyone else was off running errands or making preparations, so Abbey Langton, Avis Lahay and Naomi Axler had privacy in the kitchen. The afternoon was being shortened by elongated shadows.

Abbey had a cream-colored pen in hand as she studied a to-do list. "We can have no lapses or slip-ups in planning the funeral service." She fingered the open notebook. "It has to be appropriate and consistent to his character. He'd not want a fuss made over him, but giving others an opportunity to process and say their goodbyes would be important to him."

"Deacon deserves nothing less than the best we can do."

"Yes." Naomi was sipping steaming black coffee. "We three are of the same mind, I'm sure. An emphasis on him finishing the race strong to receive his reward must be a priority."

"Blessed Assurance."

"Yes, Avis!" Abbey exclaimed gladly. "That's *the* perfect hymn."

Naomi set the stoneware mug down. "It expresses so much."

"I well remember singing it at the Union Church in Dodge City when Deacon took the congregation on a journey through the book of Hosea," Avis said, thumbing aside a tear. "The message resonated with me. I wrote one conclusion he spoke in the margin of my Bible and later memorized it. *God is continually in the business of redemption and no one is ever too immersed in evil to be unredeemable—all are within the reach of God's merciful kindness.*"

"That was my brother's dominant article of faith," Naomi stated positively. "I doubt he ever stopped being amazed by the mysterious wonder of grace and the extreme lengths to which God goes because it is the Lord's nature to be benevolent. Deacon's belief in the power of hope and redemption became stronger and stronger the longer he lived and the more he saw."

Avis nodded vehemently. "Deacon most definitely embodied Peter's pronouncement: *The Lord is not slack concerning his promise, as some men count slackness; but is longsuffering to us-ward, not willing that any should perish, but that all should come to repentance.*"

"God is not willing that any should perish," Naomi said, eyebrows rising in a slight arc. "I'm not sure I ever heard Deacon quote that passage, but it could've been his motto."

Abbey laughed lightly. "I saw many examples of him living it."

"Stories. We need to tell stories."

"Lots of stories, Avis," Abbey said, sitting up straight as she put a check beside an item on her list. "I think that it's in our shared stories that we honor and pay homage to his influence. I want to have a family meeting this evening and involve all who have a connection to Deacon. He would want no one to be excluded. I imagine the cabin will be packed to overflowing."

"We will manage just fine, Abbey."

"What needs doing now?" Naomi asked, slipping a hand around the mug.

Abbey glanced at her notes, lips pinching. "We're doing it. Whitey is making arrangements for the casket, which we concurred would be an unpretentious pine-box."

Avis bobbed her head agreeably. "Of course."

"Eliza, Delores, Alice . . . "

"Oh, my," Naomi interrupted with a contrite snicker. "Avis filled me in on Lucinda Enochelli's true identity. Quite a tale. Reveals another layer in the mysterious workings of God. Not sure why she was compelled to be secretive, but I feel bad for the way I dismissed her."

"What's done is done."

"I do want to make amends, Abbey."

"Alice will appreciate the effort," Avis said, smiling confidently. "I had a nice visit with her. She has softened some since she came to *WT Ranch* looking for Deacon. Her personality is still presumptuous and brassy, but tenderness is coming to light underneath the audacity."

"Back to my thoughts," Abbey interjected, brusque and on task. "Eliza, Delores, Alice and I talked matters over this morning, and we decided that the undertaker's services would not be required because we can do it all, and do so with loving care. We'll finalize plans tonight."

"At sunup I intend to pick enough flowers for a least a half-dozen bouquets." Avis folded her hands together on the tabletop. "I anticipate having three young allies join the project."

"Thank you, Avis. Keep them busy and involved."

"What's in the works to be done just now, Abbey?"

"Shall we get supper started, Aunt Naomi?"

In the meantime, Alice Gallagher was sitting on the top step of the boarding house's stoop, thinking about her motley past as she waited for her escorts. After being on vigil all night, she had washed and gotten a few hours of restless sleep, and now, in a fresh change of clothes, she pondered ways she could intentionally put Lucinda Enochelli behind her. To that end, she was prudently evaluating the full particulars of more than one difficult conversation.

She reached for her purse, but then, decided that she could do without a tobacco fix, so the handbag remained at her side. There was movement at the juncture of the main thoroughfare and the backstreet. She looked and saw three companions scampering toward her. The trio skidded to a stop in front of her. "I was beginning to think you had forgotten me."

"No, ma'am, Miss Alice."

"Happy for it, LC."

"We went to the store for Mr. Smith," Bethsuelo reported breathlessly.

"Yeah-huh."

Alice leaned forward. "I have to talk to that dear man, but here and now, there are words I must say, so stand still and listen." A scowl overshadowed her brow. "LC and Yaz, it was wrong to deceive and use you nippers the way I did. You were duped for reasons that have no possible explanation. I got you all spun up and have no excuse for my unacceptable behavior."

"Everyone makes mistakes, Miss Alice."

"Yeah-huh."

"I humbly beg your forgiveness, boys."

"Alright. We're trying hard to live the Golden Rule."

"Yeah-huh."

"Miss Alice," Bethsuelo piped up, squeezing between her brothers. "LC and Yaz enjoy mischief, so it doesn't take much to get them off track." She flicked her pigtails as she inched closer to her. "Aunt Avis told us why you came to Creede and we're all glad you did."

"Thank you," Alice said, wet-eyed. "Your kindness is precious, though considering your relationship to Deacon Coburn I ought not to be surprised." She dabbed a forefinger against her cheek to remove a teardrop. "I knew him when he was a young man. He was kind and thoughtful then, and unmistakably those traits did not diminish, but rather, increased over the years.

"I called him Deke. He always extended himself on behalf of anyone who needed assistance. He was intelligent, but somewhat naïve. That greenness disappeared in an almighty hurry as he boldly confronted the evils of slavery. There was no job too small or no engagement too trivial for him. He became a conductor on the underground railroad, and while rescuing men, women and children from injustice, he risked his life more times than I can ever know."

Yaz scrunched his lips. "He never talked about those days."

"He was legendarily closemouthed."

LC grinned unevenly. "Always was according to Mom."

"I can tell you this much," Alice said, standing. "I made monumental bad choices and my life got redirected, but Deacon Coburn never stopped caring for or helping others. He was a one of a kind man." She eased down the stairs. "Let's go get groceries to stock Abbey's pantry."

Bethsuelo twittered a giggle. "Let's do."

"Yeah-huh."

Alice looped the handle of her purse over a forearm, then led the way. Within ten yards the boys were skip-hopping back and forth ahead, while Bethsuelo stayed close. In a moment, the girl switched sides to take hold of the dark-complexioned woman's free hand. It was then that Alice Gallagher experienced a spasm of blinking against an outpouring of waterworks.

"This morning? He died this morning?"

Pete Axler, leaning on a pitchfork, stood in the doorway of the barn beside his daughter, who had her hands on her hips and was worn-out, but kept trying to project a smile. He slouched his shoulders regretfully and cast a disheartened expression. "That's the way of it."

"Damnit." She spat the cuss out as though it was a hot coal. She tried to stop her bottom lip from quivering by clamping her top teeth over it, but that did nothing to prevent the trembles. The weakness irritated her, but there wasn't much Maxine Fralick could do about her off-kilter emotions. "The timing galls me. I swear, Karl, I've got no luck at all in these matters."

"I'm sorry, Maxine."

"All the sorrys in the world won't change a damn thing, will it, Doc?" she queried, sour and insolent. He was beside her, compassion and empathy coercing the strained lines around his eyes. She sat inflexibly on the seat of the carriage and glared upward at the large *WT* burned into the wood above the main door. A drip-drip-drip of tears dribbled down her flushed cheeks.

"Mommy crying again."

"We have to take care of Mommy, son."

"You should've listened to me yesterday, Karl," Maxine scolded, gulping a weepy breath. "If we would've come immediately after the train arrived in South Fork, I'm certain I might've been able to talk to Deacon one more time. You were wrong and this just isn't fair."

"Fair has got nothing to do with life and death, dear."

"You dare to spout philosophy?"

"Stating facts, I'd surmise."

"You don't understand, Karl. That's the be all and end all of it."

"I'm sorry, Maxine."

"Say it again, Doc. That'll help."

Axler had a gander at the graying skies streaked by reddish strands of dusk. "Amanda, I'll finish here while you accompany our guests to the house. When they're settled bring the buggy back and we'll see to the needs of the horse, then go to the kitchen and rustle up some grub."

"Sure thing, Daddy."

"Thank you, no. We'll go on to Creede," Maxine said sassily.

"Thank you, yes," Karl countered, shifting sideward to take hold of her hands. "I will tolerate no deal cutting or arguments, Maxine. Logical or otherwise. It's obvious that you are in distress. You need to rest and get your feet up. I am concerned for your health and our baby."

"Damnit, Doc!"

"A potty mouth is not acceptable either, Mrs. Fralick."

Her face, swollen and puffy, was discolored by blood-red blotches. She winced and bit down even harder on her bottom lip. "You are the most infuriating man, Doc Fralick."

"Maybe so, but the decision is final."

"Tomorrow's another day," Pete offered, low and earnest.

"I feel so helpless," Maxine muttered, eyes bulgy. Her hands began shaking in a frenzy. She promptly gripped them together. "I wanted to see Deacon one more time to explain that his telling and application of the story of the stones changed my perspective and life."

"He saw the frame of our wedding picture, Maxine. He knew."

"Did he? Did he really know?"

"I'm certain of it, Maxine."

Axler weighed in. "Deacon never missed much."

"An accurate observation, Pete," Karl said, palpably appreciative.

"Oh, Karl," she whimpered, slumping against him. The drip-drip-drip of teardrops became the downpour of a cloudburst. Her upper body quaked as the gagged sobs of annoyance and frustration shuddered from her lungs. She grimaced and cradled her extended belly as her husband embraced her, while her son squeezed into the hug to snuggle against her.

Two hours later, the Axler living room was softly lit by oil lamps, and the fireplace had pine logs crackling and hissing in sporadic, spurting flames. Maxine Fralick was as comfortable as possible given the girth of her maternity. She sat in an overstuffed chair with her swollen feet resting on a matching ottoman. Her husband was in a sturdy rocking chair beside her.

Pete was perched on the edge of a bench, elbows propped on knees and hands fidgeting as though he was shaving curls off a piece of wood. He was enjoying the entertainment provided by the antics of his daughter with the little one. Amanda was engaged in a catch-me-if-you-can game, feinting and weaving to keep just out of the lad's overly enthusiastic reach.

"Manda! Manda!" Cody exclaimed, gurgling laughter.

"Amanda, son," Maxine corrected halfheartedly.

"Manda sounds mighty sweet squealing off his tongue," Amanda said, dodging away from him on her hands and knees. "It's perfectly fine and no problem with me."

"So be it," Maxine said, hands absently rubbing her belly.

Amanda suddenly stopped and he slammed into her giggling happily. She wrestled him into submission, then leaned back against the ottoman and held him on her lap. "Let's sit quiet and watch the fire, Cody. See how long it takes for that big log on top to crash down."

"Good enough, Manda."

"Good enough?" Karl echoed, frowning at his wife. "That's new."

"First time I heard it."

Fralick studied her face. "Your color is much better now, Maxine," he remarked, laying a hand on her forearm. "Do you have anything to report regarding pressure or cramps?"

"No, I do not, Doc. Not here, not now."

"Will you please keep me informed?"

"After me, you'll be the first to know, Doc."

Axler scratched at his whiskery chin. "Seems to me that nature takes its course and seldom needs much help. The apple will fall off the tree when it's ripe and ready."

Maxine snickered giddily. "Thank you, Pete."

"Indeed, Pete. Thanks for that pithy nugget," Karl said, hot and agitated.

"Easy, Doc," Maxine counseled, brow crunching into deep furrows. "I've heard you voice those same sentiments on countless occasions to patients who were apprehensive."

"All of which may be true as far as it goes, but I assure you there are vast differences between apples dropping off a branch and babies being born," Karl replied testily. "Apples do not travel down a birth canal. Apples do not breathe air or have a heartbeat. Neither do apples remain attached to the lifeblood of the tree via the placenta and umbilical cord. Nor is there the outside chance of hemorrhaging involved in nature depositing an apple onto the ground."

"My mistake, Karl." Pete produced a down-to-earth smile and altered his posture to make eye-contact with him. "A lame attempt at being folksy. You are the doctor in the house."

"Yes, he is," Maxine said succinctly. "I apologize, Karl. Honestly. Your forbearance in putting up with my belligerent ways makes you a candidate for sainthood." She took hold of his hand and gave it a tender squeeze. "I should be a far better patient than I am, but sometimes the Texas wildness in my bloodstream gets the upper hand on me. Especially in this instance when the timing galls me to my core. I swear, I've got no luck at all in these matters."

Amanda peeked at her. "You said that earlier and it made me wonder."

Maxine pursed her lips into the pucker of a beached fish and exhaled a sound that was halfway between a whistle and a sigh. "I'm not sure I want to travel that road, Amanda."

"It might be beneficial to tell your story, Maxine."

"You think so, Doc?"

"I do, dear."

Axler agreed with a grin. "I'd like to hear it."

"As would I," Amanda said cheerily. "Very much so." She held Cody, who was mesmerized by the tongues of fire, in an embrace that had his head resting on her bosom.

"With such a captive audience, how can I resist?" Maxine asked pertly. She struggled to adjust the placement of her bottom whilst gathering her thoughts. The strain in the lines of her face increased, then as she got settled, her expression incrementally relaxed. "In the winter of '78 I was tracking my father out of San Antonio," she began dryly. "He had quite a jump on me, but we were both ultimately chasing Smoky Crowe, who had terrorized and slaughtered my mother. That Ute butcher and my Daddy had history going back to when I was a little girl.

"South of Santa Fe I got waylaid by an epic snowstorm. I found my way to the Suncurl Café. Not long afterwards Deacon Coburn arrived with a ne'er-do-well vagabond in tow. He had rescued the injured rogue from misadventures suffered in the blizzard. Deacon and I had a good connection and conversations that resulted in him insisting on us being partners for a spell.

"When the weather broke, we rode together to *Freiheit*, the Weitzel homestead not far from the Angel Peak badlands. Unknown to me, Daddy had tangled with Smoky Crowe along the way, and the one-eyed witch put a poison arrow in my father's shoulder. Disoriented and near death, he collapsed in front of a sizeable charred cross at *Freiheit*."

Maxine shook her head. Her mouth twisted irritably. Sorrowful moisture overflowed her eyes. "Eliza and Hans did all things possible to nurse him back to health, but the toxin was lethal. My Daddy died mere minutes before Deacon and I arrived. I never got to see him or say thank you for raising me the way he did, or to even say goodbye. It was a helluva end."

"And now you missed seeing Uncle Deacon."

"Yes, Amanda," Maxine answered, palming teardrops off her cheeks. "My heart aches something fierce. There's more discomfort in my chest than anywhere down below."

Pete coughed and pressed his hands toward her. "That's plenty enough information." He got to his feet and stretched. "Time for me to check on the stars and get some fresh night air."

"I'll join you," Karl said, rising from the rocker.

"You're going to trust me to be alone, Doc?"

"Amanda and Cody can keep you reined in for a bit."

"You'll be a shout away, correct?"

"And I'll come running, Maxine."

The men departed. Coolness entered from outside, then the front door closed. Amanda bolstered the child in a firm clinch and stood, balancing his bottom on her hip. "If it's alright with you I'd be happy to care for Cody tomorrow when you go to Creede. He can stay with me for as long as necessary. He'll get to run in the barn and have fun while I'm doing chores."

"That'd be a great blessing, Amanda."

"Then it's done and done."

"You are blossoming into a beautiful young lady, inside and out."

Amanda blushed demurely. "So I've been told."

"What are your plans for the future?"

"That's a fair question, Maxine," she replied, eyebrows arched quizzically. "My brain has been doing some heavy lifting of late, but I haven't hit upon any definitive options."

"You got time, Amanda."

"Maybe travel some. Or go to college."

"Choices and possibilities are always exciting."

"Or fall madly in love and get swept off my feet."

"Any prospective candidates, Amanda?"

"Not really," she answered, pouty-faced. "Seemingly I'm invisible."

A knot in a log exploded with a snapping pop that was surprisingly loud. The box-fire foundation collapsed in a rush of swirling sparks and embers, but the two-year-old who had been enthralled was oblivious to it because sleep had captured him. Pleasantness passed between the ladies. Maxine Fralick beamed contentment as the baby vigorously stirred in her womb.

That evening in Creede, it was standing room only at Abbey Langton's log cabin. News of the meeting had gone out on the town's grapevine, and the response was overwhelming. Every chair was occupied and a dozen were on their feet or squatting on their haunches. Windows were open to prevent stagnation by providing a flow of air. The triplets were on the porch scrunched halfway through the doorway, with the redbone hound almost on top of them.

Abbey facilitated the gathering, with friends and family participating: Whitey Fitzgerald, Avis Lahay, Caleb Weitzel, Sally Twosongs, Eliza Weitzel, Naomi Axler, Delores Solrizo, Alice Gallagher and Eliezer Smith. Plus there were neighbors and several strangers off the street whose paths had crossed Deacon Coburn's in Abilene, Dodge City or somewhere on the trail.

Fitzgerald had the floor and he was cranked into an excitable click-click storm. "Deacon he come back and haunt the bunch of us if we be extravagant and showboat this here deal."

"Word's out, Whitey. Ain't no stuffing it down," a droop-eyed cowboy turned miner said, tapping tobacco into paper to tailor a cigarette. "Coburn's reputation precedes him. He kept a low profile, but a man of his fairness and integrity garnered respect from all quarters."

"That's truer than true," another miner concurred in an abrasive sandpaper voice. "Coburn had a kindness that won't soon be forgotten. He crossed lines without hesitation and treated everyone fair and square. Gamblers, drunkards, whores, firebrands, preachers, bankers, businessmen. He never saw no difference. No bigwig dignitaries and no jailbird loafers. People was people to him and he always had a helping hand extended. You can bet big money that this here service being planned will be well attended. Half the town or more will turn out."

"Thank you, gentlemen," Abbey said, twirling a pen around as though it was a miniature baton. "I appreciate your insights and expect that you are correct in your assessment."

Smith slapped a knee and exclaimed, "They be right. Absolutely right."

"Where shall we hold the service?" Abbey asked, shoulders hunched.

"The Orleans Club or one of the tent saloons would work."

"And be entirely fitting, Whitey," Delores said heartily. A smile shot up her cheekbones and ignited a blaze of remembrance in her emerald eyes. "Deacon spent hours camped out at a table in such places wherever he traveled. In Abilene he almost lived at the Alamo Saloon."

"Just one problem," Alice advised, cautious and soft-spoken. "Soapy would most definitely figure a way to make a profit and stuff chunks of change into his pockets."

Fitzgerald clicked-clicked a chuckle. "That be a given."

Delores shook her head. "Unacceptable and inappropriate."

"I had an idea, Mom." Avis said, chirpy and forceful. "There's a sprawling meadow beside the Rio Grande where Deacon took his last horseback ride on Gilgal."

"An open-air affair?"

"Why not?" Naomi asked bluntly.

"Or we could erect a tent."

"Where'd we get one big enough?"

Fitzgerald click-clicked another chuckle. "Soapy Smith."

"He's a criminal," Caleb said, level and nonjudgmental.

Fitzgerald clapped his hands. "That he be."

"What kind of scam might he run?" Caleb queried candidly.

Delores nodded. "That'd be my concern."

"We can have a conversation with the man," Whitey answered, head bobbing. "Mr. William Jefferson Smith is as crooked as a dog's hind leg and quite devious when it comes to fixing odds in his favor, but he gots a tender heart and an active community spirit. He also gots some respect in him. Nots to mention that me and him are quite tight. He'll light a fire under a crew of laborers for us to be sure. He can also arrange for a supply of folding chairs."

"I'll want to participate in those discussions, Whitey."

"That be good, Caleb. I need you at my side."

"*WT Ranch* will cover whatever expenses are incurred."

"That's not necessary, Caleb."

"Yes it is, Abbey," Sally Twosongs declared, smiling affectionately.

Abbey began to protest, but Eliza cleared her throat and spoke in a stern tone that had a shiver of emotion thickening it. "Hans would refuse to take no for an answer. As do I."

"Pete would be adamant. As am I," Naomi said formidably.

"I humbly acquiesce with much gratitude." Abbey absentmindedly toyed with the pen. "I insist that any and all provisions made with Soapy Smith be on the up and up. What do others think?" she asked, eyes straying from face to face. "If Whitey and Caleb become satisfied that there will be no sleight of hand shenanigans, do we go forward? Is there consensus?"

"As far as I am concerned there should be," Delores replied, cheerfully direct. "I suspect these arrangements would get a squinty-eyed smile stamp of approval from Deacon."

Alice folded her hands on the tabletop. "I am in complete agreement."

"Any naysayers?" Whitey inquired, grinning.

Abbey hesitated a moment, then suggested, "Over noontime tomorrow?"

"Or a bit later," Whitey answered quickly. "Caleb and I will be sure to have everything set up for noon, but then give folks an hour or so for the viewing and to pay their respects."

"Who will officiate?" Eliza asked, glancing around the room.

Abbey shrugged automatically. "Us."

"Yes." Sally Twosongs had no uncertainty. Enthusiasm showed in her dark eyes. "Those of us who loved and were loved by him should all have an opportunity to say a piece."

"That be right," Whitey said, eager and animated. "We'll bury him in the graveyard up on the hillside overlooking town. He'd be tickled. I ain't going to say nothing in the service, but at the graveside I wants to pray and sends him off proper. No highfalutin religious phrases. I'll be sniffling and sobbing and snot will be running out of me like water, but I gots to tell the Good Lord what's in my heart. I canst be trusting no one with the interment prayer."

Smith, who had been sitting on his heels, stood and clasped his hands together at his beltline. "Before Whitey prays, I'd like to quote some Scripture and say some words."

Avis flashed him a kindhearted look. "That'd be fitting, Eliezer."

"Pallbearers?"

"That need slipped my mind, Abbey."

"Any ideas?"

Eliza tapped her chin as her eyebrows dipped low. "Off the top of my head: Hans, Stace, Daniel, Caleb, Whitey, Avis. However, chances are that Hans and Stace will not make it in time, and as for Daniel, who knows? He's been off on wayfaring excursions for a couple years."

"Then we must be flexible."

"What do you have in mind, Abbey?"

"If they don't arrive, my recommendation has to do with Alice and the two gentlemen who spoke earlier," she replied crisply. "Those three should join Caleb, Whitey and Avis."

Alice balked, eyes lowering. "I'm not worthy of that privilege."

"I disagree . . . "

"We all disagrees, Miss Abbey," the white-haired barber cut in smartly. "Let me tell you something, Miss Alice. You knowed Deacon from before the war that set me and my kind free by tearing lives apart. I wished I'd met him way back when, but that was not to be. I don't knows and I doesn't needs to know what was in that letter you faithfully delivered to him, but you be family and that be a surefire truth." He click-clicked and emphatically twitched an index finger in the air. "One more thing. LC, Yaz and Bethsuelo ought to be honorary pallbearers."

Abbey snuffled softly. "That'd please Deacon."

It was then that the trio of youngsters crept away from the doorway and off the porch, with Bobo sticking close to their heels. They moved through the deepening gloom of darkness as one—single-minded in a determined purpose. When they raced a hundred yards or so, they ducked into a crevice of an alley where they faced each other in a tightknit huddle.

"We have to do something special," LC said in a hushed voice.

"Yeah-huh. For Papa. Tonight."

"Whatcha got in mind?"

"Not sure, Bethsuelo. Any ideas?"

"Not yet, LC. I'm thinking."

"Yeah-huh."

"I know something for sure," Bethsuelo whispered, taking a knee. The boys immediately joined her as the hound dropped onto its buttocks. She moistened her lips and began twining her pigtails together. "Pap Whitey is hurting awful bad. I can feel his tears crying inside him."

"Yeah-huh. His heart is broken."

LC kinked an eyebrow. "We need to look out for him."

"How so?" Bethsuelo asked thinly.

"We stick close to him at the funeral."

"Yeah-huh."

"No matter what happens."

"Yeah-huh."

"At least one of us stays beside Pap Whitey."

Bethsuelo touched their shoulders. "It's a pact between us."

"Yeah-huh."

"Alright."

Yaz suddenly cackled a laugh as his face cracked open in a whopper-sized grin. "I got an idea about what we must do for Papa. We have to be sneaky quiet and speedy about it."

"What's the plan?"

"Tell us, Yaz," Bethsuelo urged, poking him.

Yaz Lightfoot proceeded to explain what had bloomed in his thinker. His voice was low, his tone and cadence measured and without emotion. His brother and sister listened intently, eyes widening and heads nodding in unison as the significance of the objective were grasped. When the scar-faced Lakota boy finished, the three bumped their right fists together.

"It's good, no?"

"It's good, Bethsuelo. Real good."

"Yeah-huh. What's the holdup?"

"No holdup," LC answered sharply. "Let's go."

~~~

The sunrise on the morning of Deacon Coburn's funeral was a stunningly brilliant display of purples and golds and reds. Abbey Langton was up bright and early, in a rocking chair on the porch silently praying. Her Bible was closed on her lap. She had read Psalm 90 numerous times and was meditating on the final verse. *And let the beauty of the Lord our God be upon us: and establish thou the work of our hands upon us; yea, the work of our hands establish thou it.*

She spoke it aloud in a voice so fragile that the words were whispery fragments. Deep grooves darkened her brow as she told herself that she had to be strong and true on this particular day—no weakness or public display of tears were allowed. The door cracked open and one of her sons slipped outside. He pushed back his rumpled hair as he sat in the other rocker.

"Have you been awake all night?"

"No, son. I slept several hours."

"I didn't hear you get up."

"For some reason the floor didn't creak."

"Are you alright, Mom?"

"Are you, Langton?"

"I think maybe so."

"You looked weighed down."

"Thinking, is all."

"I can imagine those thoughts, son."

"My brain is kind of jumpy."

"That's natural and to be expected."

"Me and Yaz haven't talked much."

"What about Bethsuelo?"

"She told us some worthy words."

"Where'd you three disappear to last night?"

He hedged for an instant—it was brief but not at all unnoticeable. He pulled his knees up and wrapped his arms around his shins. His eyes narrowed. "The livery to talk to Gilgal."

"An interesting conversation?"

"I guess. Why do people we love have to die?"

"There's a question for the ages, LC."

"There's really no answer, is there, Mom?"

"Lots of different points of view and ideas."

"Any that make sense?"

"That depends, son."

"On what?"

"Our choices."

A scowl pinched his forehead. "Not sure I understand."

"How do we choose to respond to the inevitable end of life? Anger, or acceptance and grace?" she asked, smiling bravely. "Death is the portal to eternity. Nothing but a doorway. I'm sure some poet or philosopher somewhere along the course of history made the analogy that heaven is a bed of roses and death are the thorns. One cannot have roses without thorns."

"Death is so arbitrary."

"Arbitrary?"

"An unrestricted or unsupported decision."

"You've been reading the dictionary again."

He grinned easily. "Words are fascinating."

"Good for you, son. You'll soon be a walking resource book."

"All the words in the world won't change the mixed up feelings," he said, rolling his eyes. "My head is full of questions that sentences cannot straighten or make right."

"Faith and grace and truth and time, LC."

"Pardon?"

"A faith response to the death of a loved one is the only positive choice," she replied pointedly. "Faith and grace and truth and time produces wisdom and understanding. A simple equation that works itself out as we put it into practice: When we exercise faith in the God of all grace and truth, time percolates it together to provide wisdom for dreaming big dreams."

"Sounds easy, but I betcha it's not."

"Nothing worth doing ought to ever be easy. Eternity, son. Eternity," she said, riveted on him. "From our earthbound perspective, death often has all the appearances of being arbitrary or capricious, but the view from heaven's shores is different. Through the eyes of our Maker and Lord, life and death has a why and wherefore—each life, each death. Mostly the purposes are beyond the realm of our ability to comprehend. The ways of God no one can fathom."

"God is mysterious. I get that, I think."

"Not quite, LC. It's a lifelong revelation."

"Why'd my father have to die before I was even born?"

"Unanswerable on this side of eternity."

"The question tasks me."

"As it does me more often than I likely realize, LC."

"Really?"

"My father was buried in the morning and I was born that afternoon. You know my story," she told him, ruffling his hair. "Some queries remain in tension and unresolved."

"Unfair. It's so awfully unfair."

"As is much of life, son. We make fairness wherever we can."

"I know, Mom."

"Knowing and working for fairness is a continuous enterprise," she said solemnly. "Sam Beadle, the jack-of-all-trades newspaperman who sired you, would be proud of the man you are becoming. Your righting wrongs, your adventurous curiosity, your acceptance of discipline, your taking charge and being responsible." She leaned closer to brush aside a strand of unruly hair, then sat back and gave him a wide-eyed smile. "Your love of language would thrill him."

"I see words in my head."

"That's a special gift, LC."

"I wondered about that, Mom."

The upward curve of her lips expanded. "My experience is not the same. I am passionate about writing, but I'm more of a technician. The words don't come alive in my mind's eye."

"What will I write about?"

"I cannot say or suggest," she answered, folding her right palm over the locket on the spindly chain around her neck. "I can tell you this: Treasure the gift, develop the gift. Learn all you can about the craft of writing and believe me, the tales and stories will find you."

"Are you sure?"

"No doubts whatsoever, LC."

"Why not?"

"A mother's intuition," she replied convincingly. "You're probably destined to travel to all corners of the world because I know the prayers I pray for you and have some comprehension of the kernels germinating in your heart. Your Lakota Sioux name: *Hé Tuwá Oyúmni.* When the time of your leaving comes I will give this precious necklace to you as a special keepsake so wherever you go and whatever you do, you'll carry a piece of your father and me."

"It will bring me home to wherever you may be, Mom. Always."

Whitey Fitzgerald entered the bedroom as inflexibly as a wooden marionette. He stood rigid still, eyes flitting about while his backside remained pressed against the closed door. His barber kit was under an arm for he had a job to do. Deacon Coburn lay flat on his back, arms at his side and bare-chested with a sheet pulled up and folded across his belly button.

Alone with the corpse of his friend, Fitzgerald was click-clicking spasmodically. He stepped to it and began talking. "I gots some things to say to you, Deacon. And this be one time when you ain't gonna be disagreeable and argumentative or the like. I'll keep my voice soft and quiet so folks in the other room don't think I'm goofy-nuts, but I's spilling my guts."

He spread out his barbering rig on a nightstand, then spent a fastidious moment selecting particular scissors and a comb. He got busy with the tools. "Miss Delores told me I had to do something to fix your sheepdog look and Miss Abbey agreed, so I's got to make you pretty. I tried to tell 'em that it made no nevermind to the Lord Almighty, but they be iron-willed ladies and a nigger-man likes me learned long ago there ain't no changing feisty minds.

"So you is gonna listen and if'in you gots a problem with what I says, you can be cantankerous with me in the hereafter whenever the Good Lord calls me way over yonder. Are we clear?" he asked, combing out the beard and making the scissors sing. "We had us a time and I be grateful for much. You be a real peach of a companion, but there be time to time situations when you 'xasperate me 'cause you done left me high and dry. I gonna give you examples.

"I had me a fine set-up in Abilene. My own barbering and dentistry shop, and plenty of customers to keep me fed and sassy. You comes along and we strikes up a friendship. We had us a connection and between laughs worked in some fair to middling philosophizing. There we was sitting on the stoop jawboning one summer afternoon after the wind whipped up a godawful tornado. We babbled and made plans to relocate to Dodge City come springtime.

"Off we went. I got dug in doing my clipping and extracting at the Tonsorial Parlor, but then my loins deceived me and I was charmed by that Eloise gal who was in cahoots with Huey Butters. I had me a loopy downfall and my life was in a whiskey crapper. Did you come and give me the swift kick I deserved? No sirree. You coulda died riding to Santa Fe through a monster blizzard to tell me face to face that there was no shame or condemnation.

"You stuck at my side. We had us a fine spell on the trail returning to Dodge City. I shot me a pronghorn and we made us a batch of tasty jerky. Ain't never had any better. I done me some healing whilst you schooled me in grace and theology. I gots back into barbering and gossiping, but had me another nasty slide when Big Bull came along and pulled some slick moves on the conman I knowed as Huey Butters. You done yanked me from the brink.

"Lord, have mercy. I be getting to the 'xasperating part now. Remember that day I was giving Hamilton Bell a shave and you poked your nose in and sez, let's go for a ride just to go for a ride? That adventure brought us all the way to *WT Ranch*, but after a six month stretch you got restless and done abandoned me so as you could wander God knows where and I got stranded. The Weitzels, Axlers, Miss Avis and Stace were nearby, but I ain't no ranch man.

"Whew doggies, I canst keeps up. My brain be spinning inside my head." His hands were busy as he focused on cropping hair off his shoulders. "We was never a pair for jabbering about nothing. When we gibbered up a storm we stripped them brass tacks bare on the essentials. The happenings and intrigues of the Good Book got merged into almost every conversating time we ever had, so it's no wonder the stuffing between my ears is overtaxed just now.

"What I be trying to tell you is that meeting you changed my life. When I skedaddled from Alabama after the emancipation war I was in the company of a herd of Exodusters. I got to Abilene and I made me a good life, God helping me at every turn of the way. Then you comes along with your itchy feet and rambling ways, and infected me with that bug.

"I was born a slave in Alabama, but I spent many a miles on a mule riding alongside you as a free man equal to anyone and not better than no man. I knows what real freedom is 'cause of you. Now that you done shuffled off to glory, when the Lord comes a looking to call me home for suppertime, he gonna find me amongst these mountains in Colorado. Likely right here in Creede since I ain't sitting in no saddle no more. My bones got the arthritis terrible bad.

"Lord, have mercy!" He bit off the exclamation and drew into an intense silence for several minutes while he cut and combed—combed and cut. The click-click between his cheek and gum was in almost perfect rhythm with the blades of the scissors. He concentrated on the finishing touches with a meticulous determination to strike perfection. When he was finally satisfied as to the haircut and beard trim, he drew a hefty lungful and knelt at the bedside.

"Lord, have mercy," he said once more, choked and wavering. "I wants you to know that I loves you, Deacon." He gulped as emotion poured out of his eyes and obstructed his throat. His shallow chest heaved mightily. "You be the onliest brother I ever had. I's gonna miss you. I ain't ever gonna forget you, nor as long as I gots breath in my body, let anyone else forget you."

He pushed to his feet and teetered unsteadily. It took several intentional moments for his lungs to settle into a normal rhythm. "I is gonna brush you off some, then the ladies will come to get you decked out in fancy duds. Afterwards Caleb and Eliezer will put you in the box." He got a hanky out and blew his nose. He backed up and nearly lost his balance. His hands shimmied as he completed his responsibilities, then Whitey Fitzgerald shuffle-stepped into the kitchen.

"I knew this would be difficult . . . "

When her niece's voice broke, Naomi Axler eased close enough to surround her in a warm embrace. "This is the sum and substance of our final act of affection for Deacon."

"Yes, Aunt Naomi," Abbey murmured, returning the hug. "I had no illusions regarding the difficulty of this chore, but never anticipated that I would be crying the whole while."

"We'll get through it together, Abbey," she said sincerely. "Is it not tender to think that as we cleanse this goodhearted man's body, our tears will be mixed in with the wash water?"

Abbey sniffled. "Exceedingly tender."

Naomi held her at arm's length. "Mother suggested such a thing to me when I helped her prepare Father for burial. The idea provided some peace and comfort then, as it does now."

Abbey took faltering steps to the nightstand. "I chose to see to my mother's needs all by myself." She wrung out a washcloth in a basin of soapy water, which was tepid. "There were others from our church and community who offered to wash and dress her, or to assist me, but I stubbornly refused. I was fifteen and overawed by a commanding sense of obligation."

"You were crushed. Emotionally crippled."

"I'm not sure what I was, Aunt Naomi," she replied, subtly reflective. "Looking back on that time, I am cognizant of the fact that the initial stages of healing and closure were embedded in my heart and soul in those precious moments of tending to and caring for Mom."

Naomi was slowly washing his feet. "You possess an extraordinary resolve and strength that is admirable. It was no doubt shaped by your mother's guiding hand, then tempered and turned into steel by how you chose to react and respond to her sickness and death."

"I miss her, Aunt Naomi. To this day I miss her."

"Which is testimony to the influence of her character on you."

"She was tough, but fair," Abbey said frankly. "Always hopeful. Even as the sickness increasingly took control and withered her from the inside out, she never uttered a hurtful word or took issue with God. To the end she expressed faith in the mysterious workings of God's sovereign purposes. She instructed and inspired me to go and live an abundant adventure."

"You certainly followed that counsel."

Abbey dabbed the cloth against his forehead and cheeks. "I pray I will continue to do so, and also, instruct and inspire my sons to do the same. There is still wisdom from my mother to pass along to them, plus mountains of insights and perspective from this kind man who treated a smart-alecky nine-year-old with the firmness and unconditional love of a father." She struggled to control her emotions. "My one regret is that across the years I never once called him Dad. A mistake that I will publicly rectify in my remarks at the service this afternoon."

Naomi was silently weeping. "Whitey did fine, did he not?"

"I was thinking the same." Abbey answered, dragging the back of her hand under her nose. She hitched in a hugely audible breath. "I've been considering those scars. The crisscross pattern on his chest and back. I never saw them until we took his shirts off yesterday."

"Me, neither."

"Wretched. It was a miracle he survived Smoky Crowe's torture."

"I never heard about any of it from Deacon."

"He guarded his story, Aunt Naomi."

"Not Angel Peak, not Smoky Crowe. Not a solitary word."

Abbey nodded knowingly. "I pried fragments from him here and there. He was mostly mum about so much. It was his life, for which he was not going to make excuses or apologize. Little by little I pieced it all together." She twisted excess water from the washcloth, folded it and laid it across the rim of the basin. "He viewed his troubles with Smoky Crowe at Angel Peak as something that just happened. The nexus where he found rebirth and renewal."

"Carrying the evidence to the grave," Naomi said, grimly pensive. "Makes me speculate on whether what is true in the physical is true in the spiritual; if so, then along with this ugly scar tissue imagine the depth of the pockmarks on his heart and soul from the slaughter and butchery of the war. Yet, he never flagged, but instead, always soldiered on to be there for others."

"Now we must carry his legacy forward."

≈≈≈

"There's something different about you."

Amanda Axler ignored him and finished saddling the third horse, a white-socked gray mare with a silvery swatch on its snout. She did a walk-around to double-check the cinches, then stepped into the saddle. "Are you about ready or what? There's a little one occupied on our front porch who will be needing my attention. We're in a hurry, don'tcha know?"

Stace Hawkins gave her a gape-mouthed frown that transformed his eyes into mere slits. "What's up with you? When did you become such a demanding taskmaster? Mr. Weitzel and Mr. Twosongs could use a short respite. We rode hard to get here, hence the need for fresh horses." He mounted a bay gelding and grabbed the reins of a stippled-chestnut stallion.

"You should've gotten here quicker."

"The last telegram we saw informed us that Deacon was sick," he fired back, glaring at her. "The fatal nature of the illness was not conveyed. Any urgent wires sent never reached us, which will certainly have Mr. Weitzel fuming for a number of days. You can bet that there will be a rant or two about the so-called conveniences of modern times being utterly useless."

She tweeted a happy-go-lucky giggle. "Mr. Weitzel can be so comical without even knowing it." She nudged the gray with her heels and it started walking. She glanced across the barnyard at him. "Let's get these steeds to the house. Leave the barn door open. After you three leave, I'll bring Cody back and care for your horses, then set them loose in the corral."

"Thank you, Amanda."

"You're welcome, Stace."

"What's different about you?"

"Nothing that concerns you, Mr. Stace Hawkins."

"What's up with you?"

"None of your beeswax," she said, flip and smart-mouthed. "I don't care how often Mr. Weitzel refers to you as Boss, you can be dang sure I'll never call you that, Mr. Hawkins." Her lips parted in a sparkly-eyed smile as she tossed her hair back. Her cheeks were flushed and ruddy—smudges of sweat streaked dirt dappled her forehead, but the sheer prettiness of her feminine beauty shone through. "By the way, there's nothing different about me."

"Yes, there is, Amanda. I just can't put my finger on it."

She sidled the horse near enough to him that their legs almost bumped. She swiveled to stare straight at him. "I'm just starting to see things through grownup eyes. Perhaps 'tis time for you to do the same." Her head tilted as her face crinkled into a mask of bemused teasing.

Hawkins was tongue-tied. An unreasonable agitation in his chest erupted upward to convert the saliva in his mouth into a gluey sludge. "I've no time for your silliness."

"Excuse me. Sorry to bother you."

"I got a funeral to attend," he said, thick and brooding. He cast a look at the sun, which was an hour or so east of its zenith. He gave the horse a slight kick and it broke into a trot ahead of her, along with the tagalong stippled-chestnut. His stomach muscles clenched into a cluster of knots when his ears were struck by a breezy burst of exuberant laughter. His cheeks grew hot, and Stace Hawkins stiffened his grip on the reins because he felt queasy and weak inside.

At noon, a large red-tailed hawk completed the finicky undertaking of cleaning itself, then leapt from its perch on a lofty pine tree and dipped low. The bird of prey coasted close to the ground for fifty yards before releasing a shriek as it flapped languidly to ascend the pristine blue sky so as to purposefully investigate the human activity a mile or so away.

It had lazed much of the morning away watching the bustling ruckus—an enormous white structure was erected in an empty meadow beside the peaceful currents of the river. Wagons came and went while workmen scurried to and fro like an over-sized colony of ants. Now, the hawk dropped in a descending spiral that repeatedly circled the canvas shelter.

Bobo reacted to the raptor first. The hound bayed twice as its front paws dug up chunks of grass. LC Beadle saw what had excited the redbone and ordered the dog to dummy-up, then pointed with an aggressive urgency. His brother and sister followed the gesture, immediately nodding. The threesome stood and watched in fascination as the feathered interloper waggled and fluttered its wings until it roosted on the top of the middle pole of the tent.

"What's it mean?" LC asked, pushing up on his tiptoes as if to get closer to it. He had his left hand cupped around a bulge under his shirt. "That's the biggest hawk I've ever seen."

"Majestic."

"Yeah-huh."

"What's it mean?" LC repeated curtly.

Bethsuelo scowled at him. "A messenger from heaven."

"Yeah-huh."

LC scrunched an eyebrow. "What's the message?"

"Your heart knows."

"Really, Bethsuelo?"

"Yes, LC."

"I was worrying on Pap Whitey."

"Yeah-huh."

"Me, too. So there's the meaning of the red-tail's arrival or at least part of it," Bethsuelo said, eyes widening. "Our concern and prayers for Pap Whitey have been heard and are being answered, but there's a bigger swell bursting in my heart. What do we want just now?"

"To honor Papa."

"Yeah-huh."

"Do you two get it?" she queried, almost whimsically.

"Get what?"

"The bigger message, LC."

"My heart is full of hope, Bethsuelo."

"Yeah-huh. The hawk encourages me."

"That is its purpose, my brothers," she said, playfully slapping them. "The presence of the red-tail is assurance that our plan to do something special is blessed from on high,"

Yaz grinned lopsidedly. "A good omen from the Creator."

"We must be humble and grateful."

"As we are, Bethsuelo."

"Yeah-huh."

LC grunted a laugh, eyes gleaming. "Lots of people coming."

"Yeah-huh. Papa knew everybody."

"We ought to get to it." Bethsuelo gave them an exhorting nudge, but then abruptly knelt and put her arms around the redbone hound's neck. The boys crouched on either side of her, both consumed by frowns. Bobo yawned and whined. In an undiscussed decision, the trio chose to linger near the water's edge some distance from those coming to pay their respects.

They hunkered closer together. The dog fussed another whine, and was ignored again. A carriage entered the meadow at an angle that brought it directly past them. The driver, a lean redhead, had discernible tension in his posture and stamped all over his face. He steered close to the wide open entranceway, then jumped off the seat and hustled to the passenger side.

The woman, heavily pregnant and appearing awkward, stood and accepted his assistance by holding onto his forearm as she got out of the buggy. He started to escort her inside, but she unexpectedly stopped and made a sweeping motion toward the red-tailed hawk alighted on the roof of the makeshift chapel. Her excitement was explicit—her voice elevated in joyful tones, but the triplets couldn't hear her words. She waddled as he guided her into the tent.

"Who is that?"

"Not sure, Yaz." Bethsuelo replied dully. "She kind of looks familiar."

"What was with her?"

"Who knows, LC?"

"Yeah-huh."

Bethsuelo hastily rose. "Are we ready to get to it?"

"Yeah-huh."

LC reached inside his shirt and retrieved what had been concealed—Gilgal's bridle with the twelve stones in it. He held it forward and each one prayerfully placed a hand on it as if in a threefold oath and benediction. All eyes seeped tears as three pairs of lips quivered. They each muzzled a sob, then LC Beadle forcefully spoke the words that put them into action.

"Let's go."

Against the back wall of the tent, Maxine Fralick was mustering every ounce of resilience she could summon. She used the extreme physical and emotional discomfort as motivation to get through the stress that was draining her. The bloated heaviness of her body was wearisome, but the interior wrenching was worse—it felt as though her heart was pumping shards of glass.

Karl held her hand, which was damp and trembly. She stared and studied the crowd, eyes inquisitive and prying. She took note of those she could identify, but amongst the mourners there were an uncountable number unrecognizable or unknown to her. Her attention wandered to the roughhewn podium center-front of the tarpaulin sanctuary, then her gaze drifted to the grievers gathered in loose-knit clusters on either side of the pine-box atop a pair of sawhorses.

A threesome of youngsters boldly entered as one—two stern-faced boys with a pigtailed girl between them holding their hands. Maxine supposed that she should be familiar with them, or at the very least know of them, but her mind was such a muddle of thoughts and memories that she could not make the connections. They were in a strikingly distinct hurry because they didn't slow or even break stride; neither did their focus veer to the left or right.

As they swept past, her stomach lurched into a slow roll due to what they had in their possession. She gasped and disengaged from her husband's grip to clumsily follow them. Doc started after her, but stopped in his foot-steps to stay put. The trio sped hand in hand down an aisle and pressed past the assembled adults, halting in front of the coffin.

Maxine was close behind them—near enough that her protruding midsection almost bumped against the girl's shoulders. Heads all over the room turned toward them. The hum of conversations that had been ongo-ing in the tent was now an anticipatory silence; it was as if everyone present was holding their breath to watch the surprising exhibition unfold.

The woman, who in an era of wildness was known as Max and carried the nickname Badger as an accurate description of her personality, dug deep within to deflect and overpower the labor pains that were beginning to put pressure on her privates. Her lungs hurt so much that she thought her rib-cage had become a vise squeezing with ever increasing compressions—the crazy idea chased through her head, which gave rise to a snugly tweaked smile.

Maxine inched even closer to the children. She felt the cotton fabric of her formless dress graze the girl's backside; she could hear their emotionally charged breathing patterns. She wanted to kneel beside them, but instantly realized that was a physical impossibility. Her ears perked up when one of the lads produced a scratchy cough and inhaled croakily.

"Papa, me and Yaz and Bethsuelo are here," he whispered, leaning forward. "We know the story about Joshua leading the Israelites across the Jordan River. How he told them to pick out twelves stones and make a marker at that place to remember what the Lord had done to deliver them. We wanted to do something that would be meaningful to us and to you."

"Yeah-huh, Papa."

"It was Yaz's idea, Mr. Deacon."

"That's true, Papa."

"Me and LC agreed."

"Yeah-huh."

"We know these twelve stones in this bridle were important to you," LC said, low and intense. "We aren't aware of all the ins and outs of the story, but figured it'd be good for us to do this for you." He hiked in a rasp of air. He glanced at his siblings. His shivers had him on the verge of blubbering like a baby, which was mirrored in them. With three sets of hands trembling as one, the bridle got carefully positioned alongside the body of Deacon Coburn.

"We love you, Mr. Deacon," she said, sobbing. She draped her arms around her brother's necks and backed into the pregnant lady. The triplets muttered words in unison that served as an excuse us, then as they sidled jerkily, a bustle of tearful adults surrounded them.

Maxine grasped the edge of the pine-box for a moment to steady her balance. Her cheeks were soaked. "It's a helluva end," she murmured, touching his folded hands. She examined the windblown wrinkles on his face, remembering his instinctive grit and grace. "Those stones and their depth of meaning to you had a consequential impact on me, Deacon. I wanted to tell you such that evening we spent together in March, but for some reason never got around to it."

"Max?"

Maxine recoiled and had a knee-jerk intention to correct the person, but instead, simply continued gawking at the man ensconced in the coffin. She felt an incessant tap on her upper arm, and turned to see a wet-eyed woman who resembled a girl from her past. The hodgepodge swirl inside her head spun her backwards in time to shooting pool at the Suncurl Café. Her jaw dropped and her complexion brightened to crimson as she shook her head in disbelief.

"Max, is it really you?"

"Avis?" she answered, skeptical and questioning. A tender look of remembrance passed between them, then the two collapsed against each other, clingy and desperately demonstrative. They wept uncontrollably. The embrace extended for several minutes, and in the midst of it, Maxine Fralick endured pangs in her lower regions that made her rubbery-legged.

Ten minutes later, Delores Solrizo was holding court and reminiscing in a side section of the arranged folding chairs. Her audience was captivated: LC Beadle, Yaz Lightfoot, Bethsuelo Weitzel, Whitey Fitzgerald, Eliza Weitzel, Abbey Langton, Naomi Axler, Alice Gallagher and Avis Lahay, who was situated between Maxine and Karl Fralick. Also present were dozens of locals who had heard of or encountered the deceased at some juncture on the trail.

"Oh, of course," Delores said in response to a query from a skinny woman of easy virtue who was one of Soapy Smith's employees imported from Denver. "I knew there was something unique about Deacon Coburn a minute after we first met. I spent that much time flirting with him in an establishment where that sort of behavior was expected, but he diverted me with strong-minded expertise that made clear he had no interest in such doings.

"He did the same the next few times I tempted him. He visited that house of business for the sole purpose of retrieving his rancher boss. That was Texas in '65 and '66. We went our separate ways, but reconnected in

Abilene in the summer of '70. I was making an effort to reform and put boots to the past. I learned that he was a spiritual man who shouldered his own yoke while caring for those who were hurting. We struck up an abiding friendship.

"He had a sweet spot in his heart for down and outers. No one, and I do mean no one, was ever turned away by him. Those who were burdened or those who merely required a listening ear were welcomed by him. Everyone came to know that to receive compassion and help all they had to do was look up Deacon Coburn at his back corner table in the Alamo Saloon."

"I can attest to that as a veracity, Miss Delores," a man butt in, grinning happily—it was the droop-eyed miner who had spoken up at the log cabin meeting. "They call me Johnny Shade because when the workday is done it ain't ever difficult for me to find a resting spot out of the sun. In the spring of '71 I went on my first cattle drive. Hundreds of longhorns from Texas to the Kansas railhead in Abilene. I was sixteen years old, a novice tenderfoot and dumbstruck.

"At the end of the line I got paid more money than I'd ever seen. I thought I was a rich tycoon or big city banker. I went bananas wild; drinking, gambling, messing with all the pretty ladies. I was dead broke inside of three days, and over my head in sinking sand debt at the Bull's Head Saloon. Phil Coe, didn't take kindly to getting stiffed, so I was made an example of and the arrears got taken out of my hide. The bloody pulp beating blackened my eyes.

"I begged in the street for work or a bite to eat. I was ashamed and downcast. The town was overrun with cowboys, but guilt put me in a place of loneliness. My belly was puckered up and twisted like a dishrag. Someone pointed me in the direction of the Alamo Saloon and told me to have a talk with the resident Bible-reader. I smothered my shame and got my courage up.

"I was a ragged rubby-dub, but when I introduced myself, Deacon greeted me like an old friend. He listened to my woe-is-me sniveling and offered not a word of judgment. He gave me stern advice and in no uncertain terms told me about the ways of the world and the facts of life. Out of his own pocket he handed me two days wages and instructed me to use it only for grub. He sent me to Ed Gaylord's Twin Livery and said I was to tell them that he'd vouch for me.

"I got a job shoveling horseshit and such." He locked his arms over his chest. "The first payday I took my earnings to the Alamo Saloon to discharge the liability, but Deacon Coburn refused to accept payment. Acted offended. Said it wasn't a loan, but an investment. I was to set that money aside and somewhere down the line pass it along to someone in dire straits as freely as I had received it from him. That attitude and kindness changed my way of thinking."

"Excuse me," LC blurted, big-eyed with curiosity. His lips tensed and an eyebrow arced downward. "Did you ever have a chance to handout that money to anyone, Mr. Shade?"

"Over the years more than once, sonny," he replied, nodding. "I carry twenty dollars in a hidden slot of my billfold just to be used for benevolence. When it gets paid out, I replace it as soon as possible to be ready for the next time. After that summer in Abilene I never saw Deacon Coburn again until a few weeks ago when he sprinted to the Prophet Eliezer's rescue."

"Oh, my," Delores exclaimed cheerily. "Thank you, Johnny Shade. That took me to the streets of Abilene and defined the Deacon I knew and loved. Remember way back then, Whitey? All the happenings that summer and autumn? The troubles that Wild Bill stepped in?"

"You tells it, Miss Delores. I likes listening to you," Whitey said, click-clicking. "I ain't ever had a fussier customer than Wild Bill Hickok. He had a just-so way for me to trim his facial hair because of his tendencies to be a dandy, but he was a fair and honorable man."

"Wild Bill was Marshall in Abilene for most of '71," Delores began, swishing her skirt to cross her legs. "He and Deacon had a passing acquaintance and a few encounters. One horribly noteworthy experience to which I was a looker-on. To be honest, I enjoyed warm feelings for both men. They were similar, but had significant differences. The war put a tattoo of ugliness on and in them, but neither ever referred to the death and destruction that haunted them.

"The aforementioned Phil Coe and a fellow gambler and gunman named Ben Thompson were the proprietors of the Bull's Head Saloon. It featured an offensive painting of a longhorn exposing its masculinity that left nothing to the imagination. Wild Bill preferred the Alamo, which led to an antagonistic conflict. Bad blood developed between them."

"How come?" LC asked in a puzzled tone.

"Yeah-huh."

"Men will be men. It's that simple, boys," Delores replied pithily. "No explaining egos and rivalries, or where people decide to draw their lines. What I do know is that on an October night it all came to a boil when Coe and a gang of hooligans went on a shooting spree. There was a showdown confrontation between Phil Coe and Wild Bill in an alley behind the Alamo. Threats were uttered that resulted in gunplay. Coe was gut-shot. He died two days later.

"Mike Williams, a deputy and Wild Bill's friend, came running to aid him. The gunsmoke was thick as well as the darkness. In the melee, Wild

Bill mistook Williams as a menace to him and pulled the trigger once more. Williams was killed. Wild Bill, supposedly a stone-cold killer, was mortified and wept shamelessly." She touched the tip of her tongue to her lips. "Pete Axler was also a deputy then. I knew him from Fort Smith," she added in an aside.

LC squirmed and shifted onto the edge of the wooden folding chair. "I didn't know Mr. Axler had been a lawman in Abilene. That must've been exciting. Was he a quick-draw?"

"He was a whittler and calming influence."

Naomi chuckled jauntily. "Still is, Delores."

"I would've never guessed otherwise."

Fitzgerald click-clicked, terse and glum. "That 'twas a ghastly gunfight."

"Sam Beadle wrote the definitive account of the shootout," Delores said, casting warm eyes on his widow before allowing her gaze to settle on his son. "It was picked up in the eastern papers and made quite an impression as I understand it. What Sam didn't write about, at least as far as I know, was the aftermath. He was with me in the Alamo Saloon until past dawn. There were a few other comers and goers, but we remained to mostly observe and sit vigil.

"James Butler Hickok known to history as Wild Bill was despondent. His mood had a bleakness that was oppressive. It hung on him like chainmail weight, stooping his shoulders and sagging his posture. He sat slumped in that near deserted barroom pouring out his anger and grief to Deacon Coburn. His eyes were raw, his defeat complete. He had accidently killed a friend."

"What did Papa say to him?" LC cut in again, forcibly direct.

"Not much. He mostly listened, attentive and empathetic," Delores answered, getting to her feet. "That conversation happened in fits and starts with lots of dead air and phrases trailing off into nothingness. Deacon never once opened his Bible, but when he spoke, it was hope and redemption purloined from the pages of the Good Book. Despite that solace and inspiration, Wild Bill was never the same after that heartbreaking tragedy. Neither was Abilene."

"Thank you, Delores. I savor stories about my father," Abbey said, standing. "It'd be good to get with you before you return to Santa Fe so I could pick your memory while I have pen and paper in hand because writing these tales down will be emotionally fulfilling for me."

"Saying them aloud soothes my heart, Abbey," Delores replied, "so it will be my sincere pleasure to spend an afternoon or two visiting and remembering. Just now, I think we should all circulate some before the service starts. Appears as if it'll be an elbow-to-elbow crowd." She clasped her hands together at her waistline and strolled to the nearest group of funeral-goers. In a moment, gracious and charming, Dolores Solrizo was cordially inter-acting with strangers.

"What made Uncle Deacon so special?"

Pete Axler plunked his hoe down, then peeled off a pair of calfskin gloves. He rubbed his whiskery cheeks as he gazed skyward. "I'm plum done-in and daylight's hardly half gone."

"The garden is my responsibility, Daddy."

He moseyed over to the woodpile and sorted through the billets ripe to be split. He found a stool-worthy log, placed it on a level spot and sat down. He shook his head in slow motion as he inevitably bent forward to rest fore-arms on knees. "We're on a break, Amanda. I need a rest, and that question ain't easy. It'll necessitate some formulating my thoughts to do it justice."

"Resting won't upset me none," she said, finding her own stump of timber to put to use as a seat. "Not sure why you're even here. I told you I can handle the weeding. For now Cody and I have it covered. Look at him. When he's not chasing butterflies he's a big help."

The boy was twenty yards away, squatting on a patch of grass as if he was lying in wait for a butterfly that was hovering just out of his reach. Axler watched the drama for a minute or more while his brain processed bits and pieces of days gone by. "First off, you've got more than enough responsibility without me being a slacker. We're in this together, peanut. That means we work side by side and relax side by side. What absolutely must get done will get done."

"I'm not arguing, Daddy. You work too hard, is all I'm saying."

"So do you," he answered, squinting a grin. "Secondly, your Uncle Dea-con had many admirable qualities. His calling cards were kindness, patience and respect. He met folks on equal terms. He always had a listening ear and a willingness to talk through the hard stuff of life. His beliefs were alive and real, and he never stopped being true to what was inside him."

"Whenever he was around, I so enjoyed his Bible stories."

"Yep. He could tell them like no one else I ever heard."

"Have you a favorite memory of Uncle Deacon?"

"I've been deliberating on just that, peanut," he replied, scratching at his chin. "It's been heavy on my mind lots today." His eyes flinched and he shifted to resettle his hands in their customary position between his knees. "He never shied away from trouble or conflict. He readily put himself in harm's way on more occasion's than I can know. The time he did so on my behalf defused a situation that could've ended with me bleeding out on a barroom floor."

"That's a story I want to hear!"

"The scariest minute or so in my life, though it felt like an hour of me twisting in the wind," he said, glancing in the direction of the two-year-old. Cody was still fascinated by the butterfly and remained in his ready to pounce stance. Axler tightened his hands. "It was June '72, twenty years ago. Drier than dry with a blistery heat that had no end and about done me in. I served as an auxiliary deputy in Abilene, which was in its last days as a cowtown.

"Nonetheless, cowboys and cattle were plentiful on the streets, which meant rowdiness and carousing. I was on a routine night patrol when I discovered a body hidden at the livery. My investigation led me to the owner of a piebald pinto that was stabled in the stall next to the dead man. I found Charley Jondreau at a table in the Alamo Saloon sipping whiskey."

"Charley Jondreau?" she sliced in, a confused expression squishing her eyes. "The kin of Sally Twosongs? Mom told me he prayed a blessing over me not long after I was born."

"That's the truth," he answered, rolling his shoulders frontward. "The night I met him he was a mysterious newcomer who I figured had something to do with the killing and stashing of the body. Or at least knowledge of the murder. All I wanted to do was have a conversation, but he wanted nothing to do with the law. He stuck his horns out and I almost got gored.

"Abilene was in the midst of a crackdown on the excesses of revelry and drunken behavior, so there was an ordinance against firearms inside city limits. Charley had a handgun holstered on his hip. The tension in the air was thicker than a wet sponge. We bantered back and forth about him coming to the jailhouse for a private sitdown talk, then he casually threatened me. It was none too sly a warning that I'd be taking a dirt bath if I forced the issue.

"I presumed I had him. Both hands were on the tabletop and he was tapping out a drumbeat with his fingers. I reached for my pistol, and a sliver of a second later, his revolver was above the table and had me covered. I have no clue as to how he could be so fast. My gun never even cleared leather. I gulped down my heart and held my hands up high and open."

"Oh, my gosh, Daddy!"

"It was touch-and-go, Amanda. He never lowered his weapon. He was in total control. Cool and calm, which put me betwixt and between nowhere to hide. We prattled some more, but it amounted to nothing but a refusal to cooperate from him along with a recommendation that I say my prayers and I was ready to, but then Deacon inserted himself into the middle of it.

"Your uncle proceeded to have a discussion with the man about bloodshed and carnage on the battlefields of the war. The two parlayed, and Deacon negotiated with him. All the while I'm staring down the barrel of this stranger's pistol aimed at my belly. If his trigger finger twitches, I take the bullet above my beltline and it's a forever goodnight for me.

"Something freaky happened with Jondreau's eyes, then in lickety-split fashion, he spun the gun over in his hand and offered the butt to me. I took it and almost swooned in relief. Air gushed out of my lungs. As Deacon and I shepherded Charley to the lockup, I was sick and woozy. It was an hour before the bile in my stomach stopped squirting up my throat."

"Did you and Uncle Deacon talk about that night?"

"Nope. Not really. We never did." He looked up. His eyes had been fixated on his hands. He saw that the toddler had climbed onto his daughter's knee. He yawned and twined his fingers together behind his head. "What say we call it quits and go to the house? All this recollecting has depleted me. I'm pooped and hungry. It's past lunchtime, so a nap is on the horizon for Cody."

"He'll conk out after we eat."

"I may just join him."

"I'll finish the garden in the cool of the evening."

"You mean we will."

"Sure thing, Daddy. Thanks for telling me that story."

"It ain't no big thing. Just a happening."

"Can I change the topic?"

"I don't see why not, peanut."

"Well," she said, rising to her feet with the child braced on her hip. She took a sideward step. Her eyes darted to the ground then focused on some unseen point in the outlying reaches of the valley. She moistened her lips and it was clearly perceptible that a thoughtful delay had gripped her. Her voice was whispery thin when she asked, "What do you think of Stace?"

"Not sure I like the tone of that question, Amanda Irene."

"Oh, Daddy!"

Even from a far-off distance and above the pounding hoofbeats, the strains of singing reached their ears and wafted past them. Hans Weitzel had the stippled-chestnut stallion trotting slothfully at the rear of Daniel Twosongs, who was saddled on the white-socked gray. Stace Hawkins had a commanding lead, not so much because the bay gelding was faster and stronger than the other horses, but rather, due to the rider's youthful energy and exuberance.

Weitzel shouted loudly. No word was actually pronounced—the noise roaring from his throat was nothing more than an overwrought grunt. Twosongs slowed the mare to a walk and turned to see that his in-law had done the same. Hawkins wheeled the bay around. A smile crested on his lips as he cantered back to them, his horse high-stepping eagerly.

"We're here," Hans said, removing his tweed cap. He backhanded sweat off his forehead. "No reason to gallop in and disturb the service." He surveyed the meadow. Fifty-odd yards away, horses, buggies and various other carriages and wagons were parked helter-skelter around a huge circuslike big-top tent. His eyes glinted approval. "Let's dismount. Stretch our legs from here."

"And listen to the hymn."

"Sure, Boss. Sounds grand."

Twosongs nodded. "Sentiments laced together by hope."

Weitzel bowed his head. "Yes, Daniel. Hope."

The three led their horses side by side, with Hawkins between his elders. To a man, their expressions were solemn and sober-eyed, their gait melancholy. The poetic phrases written by Fanny Crosby were being sung off-key by a ragtag congregation led by three females whose alto voices struck each note perfectly and harmonized above all other singers. Weitzel felt a gnarly lump in his throat because he recognized the *WT Ranch* ladies—Eliza, Naomi, Avis.

> "*Perfect submission, perfect delight,*
> *Visions of rapture now burst on my sight;*
> *Angels, descending, bring from above*
> *Echoes of mercy, whispers of love.*
> *This is my story, this is my song,*
> *Praising my Savior all the day long;*
> *This is my story, this is my song,*
> *Praising my Savior all the day long.*"

As the chorus began the men were hastening to find a clear patch of grass to picket the horses on short lines. That done, they moved toward the wide-open entrance. The flaps were bunched up and tied to resemble dull-colored, but functional bunting. There was hesitancy in their steps. Daniel Twosongs looked up and saw the red-tailed hawk poised on the principal pole of the canvas cathedral, plainly unperturbed by the somewhat boisterous vocalizing.

Twosongs had a subtle smile plastered on his lips as he took off the flat-brimmed hat and followed his companions into the overcrowded chapel. Weitzel led the way, cap in hand and eyes lowered. Hawkins sidled alongside him as he located a spot against the back wall to stand. The men were granite-faced, but despite all efforts to curtail tears, wetness glistened in their eyes.

Abbey Langton had taken her place in the front row before the singing began. When the congregation stood for the anthem-like proclamation of assurance, she opted to remain seated and silent. She altered her posture and stiffened her backbone. Her sons were on either side of her. She nudged them to rise and join in, which they did with palpable reluctance.

Fuzzy needles prickled her tongue and crawled across the roof of her mouth. She tried to swallow to lessen the uneasiness, but there was no relief. Her heart was thumping so fast that she could feel it. She closed her eyes and consciously attempted to breathe in a slow and deliberate manner, but that exercise did not quell the pulsating beat speeding inside her chest.

The words and notes enveloped her—she pressed her hands against the leather book on her lap and distractedly caressed its smoothness. Her eyelids flickered and she flashed back to days of yore. The vividness of the never to be forgotten images were as heart-wrenching as when she was fifteen years old. In her mind's eye she was in Xenia reliving her mother's funeral.

It was in the whitewashed church of her childhood. A clapboard structure with a stubby steeple. She stood beside the casket, as numb as numb could be—many pious and tenderhearted congregants were providing well-intentioned counsel, but it all seemed so inane and insensitive to her: "I know just how you feel." "You're old enough to have known her, but young enough to get over her passing." "She's in a better place." "You should be happy for her."

Her mother had only reached the age of thirty-five, which she deemed to be unjust and unfair. The pain and anger of that teenage bewilderment came back in a rush of vitriol; she could taste its bitterness bite at the back of her throat. Her jaw clenched. The scene immediately changed. She was in the Union Church in Dodge City at her husband's funeral, weak and distraught, shaking and sobbing as she clutched her two-day old son in her arms.

A raging anguish, possessing not an ounce of mercy, clawed at the foundation of her faith. The horror of Sam Beadle's coldblooded murder relentlessly surged through her in barbed waves. Deacon Coburn sat sideways on the pew next to her, an arm draped around her shoulders and a hand resting on her knee. She leaned into him for support. Whitey Fitzgerald was on her other side, weeping soundlessly—even his habitual click-click had been silenced.

The box containing Sam Beadle was positioned on a platform in front of the lectern with its lid nailed shut. There had been no public viewing because his head was grossly disfigured by a bullet from a vengeful desperado. She was at his side when the fateful lead slug splattered bloody bone and brains over her; bits of gore and ooze got embedded in her hair.

The church-house was wall to wall people. She stared blankly at the Reverend Ormond Wright as he endeavored to speak eloquence and redemption into an impossible circumstance. Ancient words of comfort from the Psalmist spilled over her as meaningless banalities that poked and aggravated the raging anguish within her soul. The hinges of her jaw were throbbing.

Then, as quickly as the cheerless memories had seized her senses, she returned from the mourning of former times to hear the vibrancy of fervent voices professing Blessed Assurance. She gulped a whimper and realized her lips were quivering. All the broken pieces of penetrating grief that had tumbled through her head had done so in a brief onslaught of seconds.

She reacquainted herself with the present reality, which required at least a dozen intentionally measured breaths. A flurry of blinking afflicted her. When it passed, fragile bits of determination from an inner wellspring fortified her. She steadfastly patted her father's Bible on her lap. She opened it—in the center was a well-worn tri-folded paper. She inhaled powerfully, then for the first time, read words written in her mother's hand as she was dying.

June, 1869

Xenia, Ohio

Dear Deacon: I'm glad to finally know your given name, but you will always be remembered as Lawrence to me. Thank you for your letter. I received it with a mixture of joy and remorse. Joy to learn that you are safe and well—remorse for the life we could have enjoyed.

You seek my forbearance and forgiveness. I freely grant all that you request. I do not regret the night we shared together. I treasure it, wishing there had been many more. Neither do I have any shame for the love I've nurtured in my heart for you. Know that my deep, abiding affection has never wavered.

I'm certain that sooner rather than later Abbey will make her way west. She is headstrong and full of dreams. If your paths ever cross in those western lands, please care for her as you would your own daughter. She harbors tender feelings for you.

Life has given me a bit of a kick. I'm not long for this world. Your sweetness has stayed with me all these years and sustains me in these difficult moments. If at all possible, I will wait for you just inside the Eastern Gate.

All My Love,

Angela

Her eyes were red. She visibly hardened her spine and posture once again. Her lips pursed into a bloodless line. She shakily returned the letter to its treasured spot. The hymn had concluded. She felt all eyes fastened on her—it was the scheduled time for her to commence sharing. Her chest swelled with oxygen as she rose and walked directly to the open casket.

She laid a palm on his cheek and allowed a thumb to push moustache whiskers aside. She murmured words of love and admiration, then painstakingly placed the Bible in its owners folded hands. In doing so, she truly adhered to his bidding specified in the Alamo Saloon twenty years earlier. Her vision was blurred by a film of tears. She kissed his forehead for an affectionate moment. "Thank you for being my Dad," she whispered in a tone saturated by emotion.

Amazingly, her heart had quieted. She stepped to the podium and scanned the collection of folks who had come to say their earthly farewells. Her gaze lingered on each of her sons. She tipped a wink to Whitey Fitzgerald who had taken the seat she'd vacated. She smiled warmly at Aunt Naomi before her eyes connected with her sister Avis. Intensity and encouragement passed between them, and then, Abbey Langton assertively addressed family and friends.

Afterwards, when the afternoon was growing long and leaning toward twilight, the tent chapel had become a gathering place for those who desired to hear or say more. Chairs were formed into a circle and a pair of torches had been lit and staked in the ground at strategic spots. The welcoming shadows enhanced the tranquil spirit of companionship.

Whitey Fitzgerald served as the host. He alternated between sitting close to the triplets and strolling around. Just now he was on his feet, smiling and click-clicking. "Deacon be in the land of jubilee. He beat us to that glory shore. We still has to muck through the sludge, but there canst be no more sadness. This be a celebrating get-together honoring a man. A real man."

Hans Weitzel abruptly stood and held a hand up. "A real man. Deacon Coburn was that and more." He took his cap off and apprehensively fiddled with it. "I had a wariness and mistrust when it came to God and Bible matters. I think I always believed, but there was much doubt and a thinly-veiled antagonism that colored my perspective. Faith was for priests, who collected money and uttered clichés. Prayers were for those who found some comfort in them.

"For the most part I avoided religious types. My experience was that black-coated sermonizers employed Bible words like a club to beat others down and keep them under their thumbs. Until Deacon. There was something different about Coburn. His faith had vitality. When he used phrases out of the Bible he made them real and meaningful. Even so, at the beginning of our relationship I kept my guard up whenever talk took a turn toward the spiritual.

"His honesty wore me down. I remember once when we were digging a grave." He glanced around until he saw the strawberry-blonde sitting beside her physician husband. "We were digging a grave for your father, Maxine." He nodded and smiled tersely. "The ground was a frozen challenge that strained us, which served to put Deacon in mind of an irresistible truth. He spoke about making our choice for or against the hope of the resurrection.

"His telling of the first Easter morning had an impact on me. Subsequently, after some fruitless wrestling and resisting, I finally made my peace with God." His brow wrinkled and his butcher-block body shuddered. "I'm no saint and don't pretend to be, but I stand here now to tell you that between Eliza's faithfulness and Deacon's integrity, I got hold of saving grace."

Teary-eyed, Eliza grabbed his hand. "That's a fine testimony."

Weitzel was only halfway onto his seat beside his wife when, across the circle from them, Alice Gallagher shot to her feet. "I know I don't belong here, but could I say something please?"

Fitzgerald hastily click-clicked. "You certainly belong here, Miss Alice."

"As much or more than any of us," Delores said, beaming a smile at her.

"Thank you," she replied as others articulated approval. Her right hand rested on her hip, her left had a bunched fistful of her skirt. "I ruined my life. I was misguided and stubborn in my self-righteousness. I believed I was doing justice and that belief fueled many destructive choices and actions. I participated in a bombing in which my partner burned alive. I went to prison.

"My guilt ate at me. I dreamed of a do-over. I was released in the autumn of '68, and straightway became Lucinda Enochelli, and remained that person until a few days ago. In '86 I discovered an envelope addressed to Deacon in a safe-deposit box stashed amongst my father's important papers. I was enthused and duty-bound to find him for reasons I cannot explain.

"There was urgency in me. I had and still do not have a clue what message the letter contained, and that is not important, because I did the right thing. For the first time in my life I did the right thing. You all need to know that the reception I received here has kindled passion and an aching hunger in my heart and soul. I haven't attended church since my mother died in the late forties, but I'll be darkening that doorway again. I'm going to buy a Bible, too."

Abbey was up and moving to her. Others promptly joined in, and it became a rush that naturally resulted in Abbey, Delores, Naomi, Avis and the trio of youngsters surrounding Alice in an earnest and entangled huddle. "You're family, Alice. Always will be," Abbey said in an expressive murmur. "I am grateful that you brought my father a measure of peace."

There were various supportive utterances and tearful exclamations. Many of those who remained seated were sniffing or wiping moisture away from their eyes. When the torrent of raw emotions were spent, the knotted hug unraveled on its own, and Eliezer Smith stood, Bible in hand. "I want to read again the passage I shared at the graveside, then reflect on it.

"From Isaiah: *And if thou draw out thy soul to the hungry, and satisfy the afflicted soul; then shall thy light rise in obscurity, and thy darkness be as the noon day: And the Lord shall guide thee continually, and satisfy thy soul in drought, and make fat thy bones: and thou shalt be like a watered garden, and like a spring of water, whose waters fail not. And they that shall be of thee shall build the old waste places: thou shalt raise up the foundations of many generations; and thou shalt be called, the repairer of the breach, the restorer of paths to dwell in.*"

His voice crackled near the end of the passage. "Amen and amen. Deacon Coburn met me in my most desperate hour. He nursed me and bound up my inner wounds. He was a spring of sweet and refreshing water to me. He raised up the old waste places and rebuilt my foundation. He walked me out of darkness and into light. Indeed for me, and I suspect for a host of others over the years, he served as the repairer of breaches and the restorer of paths."

"He was that to me," Sally Twosongs said, cheery and sincere.

Hawkins rose and coughed faintly. "He instilled courage in me. When my mother died Uncle Deacon gave me room to grieve and be sorrowful, but when he detected an opening, he talked me through all my yucky feelings." He hesitated, then sat on the edge the chair.

"God's glory and purpose was in Coburn," Eliezer opined, head bobbing.

Sally Twosongs grinned. "Methinks we had a glimpse and affirmation of that fact. Did you all see the visitation from heaven? A mature red-tailed hawk was present at the service and followed us to the cemetery for the interment. It watched over all of today's proceedings."

"A blessing," Maxine said staunchly. "My supposed guess, or perhaps the longing in me, is that we witnessed a special message from Charley Jondreau. He is at peace, as is Deacon."

"My heart tells me you are correct, Maxine."

"That provides great consolation, Sally Twosongs." She went to adjust her girth, but then, a gasp tore from her throat and there was a gushing splash—Maxine Fralick's water broke and in an instant she was in the throes of extreme labor. Her face twisted into an eye-bulging grimace. "Oh, Lord Jesus," she shrilled, clutching air with one hand and her husband with the other.

Hans Weitzel and Daniel Twosongs wasted not a moment. They worked at hustling and shooing all the males outside. The scuffling scramble went unnoticed by Doc Fralick. He was encompassed by a bevy of ladies as he knelt and removed his wife's bulky bloomers, then positioned her to deliver their child. Maxine bore down, tenacious and uninhibited.

There was joyful laughter when the newborn, scrunchy-faced and squawking, came writhing into the world. In the shadow of death, there was life, but that was of no consequence to Deacon Coburn. His soul had been cast upon the altars of tomorrow just inside the Eastern Gate, where he was reunited with Angela Langton, the only woman he had ever loved.

June 4, 1892

Dear Diary: The morning dawned with a sunrise that was breath-takingly beautiful. I woke with such enormous emotions to process that I decided to get away from family and friends, so I snuck off. I've spread a blanket on a cushion of grass in the meadow beside the Rio Grande. Gilgal is grazing nearby as I think and pray while writing, and in between, vaguely watch the workmen load chairs onto wagons and loosen ropes on the tent pegs.

Yesterday ran the full gamut of emotions. Sorrow and a sense of loss mixed in with triumph and celebration. LC, Yaz and Bethsuelo caused an emotional volcano to erupt. Those of us who saw them place Gilgal's bridle in the coffin were completely undone. It would've been nice of those stinkers to give us fair warning. For me, I was reeling from their sentimental and entirely appropriate act of remembrance, when another surprise knocked me for a loop.

Max Dawson's presence startled me. When I met her I was fourteen years old and trying to find my way through woes and difficulties leftover from my upbringing. She was a hardnosed straight-shooter who took a backseat to no one. I almost didn't recognize her, partly because of her attire and swollen condition, but mostly from the shock of her arrival, seemingly out of the blue. My head was spinning so fast I actually thought I might be imagining her.

From time to time I'd heard scuttlebutt about her from the family network, but I have not seen or heard from her since the winter of '78. We spent a mere week or so together, but we got along fine. She inspired and set a pattern for me. I had an inclination toward horses and ranch type work, along with the tendencies of a tomboy. Her attitude and cowgirl ways gave me much encouragement to be true to what was inside me. I've taken rigmarole blather from blowhards now and again, but never waned or wilted because I'd recall how Max carried herself.

Now, lo and behold, Max is Maxine Fralick. She's married to a doctor and the mother of two. Who could've possibly surmised that as a probable destiny for her way back then? I'll meet her son Cody upon returning to WT Ranch this afternoon. I wonder how that fella is going to respond to Charlene Jane, a hale and hearty little sister. Her birth was a marvelous event to observe and occurred with no problems. Doc Fralick had all issues under control.

I am grateful to God for answered prayers. I had worked myself up over the absence of Hans and Stace. Then, as so often happens, the Lord amazed me. I did not know that they had gotten there until it was my turn to share. I started to say my tribute when I saw them standing at the back. My voice went into a high-pitched falsetto and I could feel myself losing control. I held onto the podium for dear life. I was actually afraid my legs were going to fail me.

Stace perceived my disquieting predicament, and regardless of protocol or what others might think, he bolted forward to give

me a strong-armed squeeze. We held onto each other for an ex-
tended while, then he stood tall at my side with an arm around
my shoulders to hold me steady as I spoke. I emptied my heart
without any further emotional breakdowns.

He is becoming, or maybe already has become, a man of char-
acter and responsibility. When I consider the years we have had
together, and the tension within me to fulfill the promise I made to
his mother when she was on her deathbed, I cannot help but be in
awe of God's tender mercies. I have more than likely made many
mistakes, but the Lord has taken my intent and blended in doses of
grace so that raising him as my son has been rewarding.

It was also so satisfying and worthwhile to be with Daniel
Twosongs again. He and I spent several hours together last night
talking and laughing and musing over life and death. He told me
that he knew Deacon was in some sort of distress because it was
revealed to him in a dream. Another example of the marvelous
mystery of how our creator works his ways.

Now, as I reflect on the journey I was blessed to have with
Deacon, I am disposed to wonder about tomorrow and however
many tomorrows will be allotted to me. Gratitude for the life God
has provided is profound, so pondering too long on the future
pushes me to try harder to daily apply these words of Jesus: "But
seek ye first the kingdom of God, and his righteousness; and all
these things shall be added unto you. Take therefore no thought
for the morrow: for the morrow shall take thought for the things of
itself. Sufficient unto the day is the evil thereof."

What does tomorrow hold for Stace? For me? I keep learning
that God's will is really not the pathway we travel, but much more
so, it's about how we respond to the ups and downs that are part
and parcel of every footpath we traverse. Our paths are full of ruts
and pain, adversity and detours, BUT God's will is not an occur-
rence on the trail we walk—rather, we find God's will in how we
choose to deal with those pothole happenings on the road of life.

We endeavor to seek first the kingdom of God, and when
hardships or setbacks come, our response is to put faith into action
and strive to live what we say we believe. With God being my rock
and helper in all things, that is the deepest desire of my heart. I
sincerely pray for the wisdom to press on and go forward trusting
the Lord's provision one step at a time.

Here endeth my contemplations on this day. That is all.

She took the time to thoroughly read the entry, smiling pleasantly. Her
heart was full, her emotions alive and unruffled. She closed the reddish daybook and slipped the silver fountain pen in its spine. Her index finger traced

the outline of the butterfly engraved on its front cover, and then, Avis Lahay sat and wept blissful tears as she watched the big-top tent being collapsed.

Meanwhile, Abbey Langton and LC Beadle had the log cabin to themselves. Everyone was off doing one thing or another. The rooms were filled with empty spaces. She moved about cleaning and straightening while gently humming the tune of Blessed Assurance. He sat at the dinner table studying the note written in the Bible his Papa had given him. His expression was introspective, as though he was puzzling over and probing the depth of the message.

"A penny for your thoughts, son."

"Not sure I can explain my thinking."

"Venture a try for me."

"Alright." He closed the Bible and rested his hands on it. "I'm trying to figure ways I can guard the wellspring of my heart, but I'm not sure how to go about doing it. I guess I should've asked Papa what steps to take. Maybe he might've given me examples to follow."

"He surely could've, which would've been helpful, but we each have to find our own way in caring for our heart," she said, standing beside him. "There are principles in a verse from the Psalms that assist me in my attempts to remain vigilant: *Lord, my heart is not haughty, nor mine eyes lofty: neither do I exercise myself in great matters, or in things too high for me.*"

"Thanks, Mom." He glanced up at her. There was dreamy preoccupation evident in his face as one eyebrow dipped and the other lifted. "Me and Yaz were talking. Bethsuelo, too."

"About what?"

"All those stories."

"Which stories, LC?"

"About Papa."

"It was good to hear them."

"They should be written down, Mom."

"You three think so, huh?"

"We do."

"Where are Yaz and Bethsuelo?"

"Running an errand for Mr. Smith."

"Why aren't you with them?"

"Bethsuelo thought it best that you not be alone."

"Is that so? I appreciate the kindness."

"You should write Papa's story, Mom."

"I've been jotting odds and ends down, LC."

"I mean the whole story. To be published."

"That's a huge mission, son."

"So?" he queried insistently. "What about the Robert Browning poem that said *a man's reach should exceed his grasp*? You told me and Yaz that we ought not to retreat from big jobs, but instead, we are to live courageously and always be ready to tackle great challenges."

"Aren't you the sly motivator?" She left the kitchen in a rush and returned just as quickly, carrying a pen and tablet. She took a seat across from him. His elbows were on the table, hands tightly fisted against his cheekbones. She thought for several moments, then Abbey Langton nodded enthusiastically as she wrote the opening sentence of her father's story.

When the man walked out of the badlands he was an emaciated wreck.

~The End~

HISTORICAL POSTSCRIPT: ON JUNE 5, 1892, *the day after Altars of Tomorrow ends, a firestorm raged through the business district of Creede and destroyed most of the buildings. Three days later, on June 8th, Robert Ford (the killer of Jesse James) was shot to death in his temporary tent-saloon by Ed O'Kelley. Those events signaled the beginning of the end of Creede's boom. Shortly thereafter, Soapy Smith and other shady business-men returned to Denver and reestablished their criminal operations in that city. Then in 1893 the Silver Panic struck and the price of silver plummeted. Most of the silver mines closed. Creede's population dwindled.*

www.ingramcontent.com/pod-product-compliance
Lightning Source LLC
Chambersburg PA
CBHW070837030726
47504CB00005B/1135